CONCEALED IN DEATH

CONCEALED IN DEATH

J. D. ROBB

G. P. Putnam's Sons

A MEMBER OF PENGUIN GROUP (USA)

NEW YORK

PUTNAM

G. P. PUTNAM'S SONS
Publishers Since 1838
Published by the Penguin Group
Penguin Group (USA) LLC
375 Hudson Street
New York, New York 10014

USA · Canada · UK · Ireland · Australia
New Zealand · India · South Africa · China

penguin.com
A Penguin Random House Company

Library of Congress Cataloging-in-Publication Data

Robb, J. D., date.
Concealed in death / J. D. Robb.
p.   cm.—(In death)
ISBN 978-0-399-16443-9
1. Dallas, Eve (Fictitious character)—Fiction.   2. Policewomen—New York (State)—
New York—Fiction.   I. Title.
PS3568.O243C655   2014   2013025094
813'.54—dc23

Printed in the United States of America
10 9 8 7 6 5 4 3 2 1

BOOK DESIGN BY MEIGHAN CAVANAUGH

Thou art my hiding place; thou shalt
preserve me from trouble; thou shalt
compass me about with songs of deliverance.

—PSALMS 32:7

A simple child,
That lightly draws its breath,
And feels its life in every limb,
What should it know of death?

—WORDSWORTH

CONCEALED IN DEATH

**I** NEGLECT COULD KILL A BUILDING BRICK BY brick. It was, to his mind, more insidious than hurricane or earthquake as it murdered slowly, quietly, not in rage or passion, but with utter contempt.

Or perhaps he was being a bit lyrical about a structure that had served no purpose other than housing rats and junkies for more than a dozen years.

But with vision, and considerable money, the old building, sagging its shoulders in what had once been Hell's Kitchen, would stand strong again, and with purpose.

Roarke had vision, and considerable money, and enjoyed using both as he pleased.

He'd had his eye on the property for more than a year, waiting like a cat at a mousehole for the shaky conglomerate that owned it to crumble a little more. He'd had his ear to that mousehole as well, and had listened to the rumors of rehab or razing, of additional funding and complete bankruptcy.

As he'd anticipated, the reality fell between, and the property popped on the market. Still he'd waited, biding his time, until the fanciful—to his mind—asking price slid down to a more reasonable level.

And he'd waited a bit more yet, knowing the troubles of the group that owned it would surely make them more amenable to an offer well below even that level—with some additional sweating time.

The buying and selling of property—or anything else for that matter—was a business, of course. But it was also a game, and one he relished playing, one he relished winning. He considered the game of business nearly as satisfying and entertaining as stealing.

Once he'd stolen to survive, and then he'd continued when it had become another kind of game because, hell, he was damn good at it.

But his thieving days lay behind him, and he rarely regretted stepping out of the shadows. He might have built the foundations of his fortune in those shadows, but he added to them, wielded the power of them now in full light.

When he considered what he'd given up, and what he'd gained by doing so, he knew it to be the best deal of his life.

Now he stood in the rubble of his newest acquisition, a tall man with a lean and disciplined body. He wore a perfectly tailored suit of charcoal gray and a crisp shirt the color of peat smoke. He stood beside the spark plug of Pete Staski, the job boss, and the curvaceous Nina Whitt, his head architect. Workers buzzed around, hauling in tools, shouting out to each other over the grinding music already playing, as Roarke had heard it grind on countless other construction sites on and off planet.

"She's got good bones," Pete said around a wad of blackberry gum. "And I ain't going to argue about the work, but I gotta say, one last time, it'd be cheaper to tear her down, start from scratch."

"Maybe so," Roarke agreed, and the Irish wove through the words. "But she deserves better than the wrecking ball. So we'll take her down to those bones, and give her what Nina here has designed."

"You're the boss."

"I am indeed."

"It's going to be worth it," Nina assured him. "I always think this is the most exciting part. The tearing down what's outlived its time so you can begin to build up again."

"And you never know what you're going to find during demo. Pete hefted a sledgehammer. "Found a whole staircase once, boxed in with particle board. Stack of magazines left on the steps, too, back from 2015."

With a shake of his head, he held the sledgehammer out to Roarke. "You should take the first couple whacks. It's good luck when the owner does it."

"Well now, I'm all about the luck." Amused, Roarke took off his suit jacket, handed it to Nina. He glanced at the scarred, dingy wall, smiled at the poorly spelled graffiti scrawled over it.

Fuk the mutherfuking world!

"We'll start right there, why don't we?" He took the sledgehammer, tested its weight, swung it back and into the gyp board with enough muscle to have Pete grunt in approval.

The cheap material broke open, spewing out gray dust, vomiting out gray chunks.

"That wasn't up to code," Pete commented. "Lucky board that flimsy didn't fall down on its own." He shook his head in disgust. "You want, you can give it a couple more, and she'll go."

Roarke supposed it was a human thing to get such a foolish charge out of destruction. He plowed the hammer into the wall again, shooting out small sprays of gypsum, then a third time. As predicted, the bulk of the wall crumbled. Beyond it lay a narrow space with spindly studs—against code as well—and another wall.

"What's this shit?" Pete shifted over, started to poke his head through.

"Wait." Setting the hammer aside, Roarke took Pete's arm, moved in himself.

Between the wall he'd opened and the one several feet behind it lay two bundles wrapped in thick plastic.

But he could see, clearly enough, what they were.

"Ah well, fuck the motherfucking world indeed."

"Is that . . . Holy shit."

"What is it?" Nina, still holding Roarke's jacket, pushed against Pete's other side, nosed in. "Oh! Oh my God! Those are—those are—"

"Bodies," Roarke finished. "What's left of them. You'll have to hold the crew off, Pete. It appears I have to tag up my wife."

Roarke took his jacket from Nina's limp fingers, drew his 'link out of the pocket. "Eve," he said when her face came on screen. "It seems I'm in need of a cop."

Lieutenant Eve Dallas stood in front of the soot-stained, graffiti-laced brick of the three-story building with its boarded windows and rusting security bars, and wondered what the hell Roarke was thinking.

Still, if he'd bought the dump, it must have some redeeming or financial value. Somewhere.

But at the moment that wasn't the issue.

"Maybe it isn't bodies."

Eve glanced over at Detective Peabody, her partner, wrapped up like a freaking Eskimo—if Eskimos wore puffy purple coats—against the iced-tipped December wind.

At this rate, 2060 was going out on frostbitten feet.

"If he said there were bodies, there're bodies."

"Yeah, probably. Homicide: Our day starts when yours ends. Permanently."

"You should sew that on a pillow."

"I'm thinking a T-shirt."

Eve walked up the two cracked concrete steps to the iron double doors. The job, she thought, meant there was never a lack of starts to the day.

She was tall and lanky in sturdy boots and a long leather coat. Her hair, short and choppy, echoed the whiskey shade of her eyes as it fluttered in the brisk wind. The door screeched like a grieving woman with laryngitis when she yanked it open.

Lean like her body, her face, with a shallow dent in the chin, briefly reflected her wonder when she took her first look at the dirt, the rubble, the sheer disaster of the main-floor interior.

Then it went cool, her eyes flat and all cop.

Behind her Peabody said, quietly, "Ick."

Though she privately agreed, Eve said nothing and strode toward the huddle by a broken wall.

Roarke came toward her.

He should've looked out of place in this dung heap, she thought, dressed in his pricy emperor-of-the-business-world suit, that mane of black silk hair spilling nearly to his shoulders around a face that spoke of the generosity of the gods.

Yet he looked in touch, in place, in control—as he did mostly anywhere.

"Lieutenant." Those wild blue eyes held on her face a moment. "Peabody. Sorry for any inconvenience."

"You got bodies?"

"It appears we do."

"Then it's not an inconvenience, it's the job. Over there, behind the wall?"

"They are, yes. Two from what I could tell. And no, I didn't touch anything after smashing through the wall and finding them, nor allow anyone else to. I know the drill well enough by now."

He did, she thought, just as she knew him. In charge, in control, but under it a sparking anger.

His property, he'd think, and it had been used for murder.

So she spoke in the same brisk tone. "We don't know what we've got until we know."

"You'll know." His hand brushed her arm, just the lightest touch. "You've only to see. Eve, I think—"

"Don't tell me what you think yet. It's better if I go in without any preformed ideas."

"You're right, of course." He walked her over. "Lieutenant Dallas, Detective Peabody, Pete Staski. He runs the crew."

"Meetcha," said Pete, and tapped his finger to the bill of his grimy Mets ball cap. "You expect all kinds of crap in demo, but you don't expect this."

"You never know. Who's the other suit?" Eve asked Roarke, glancing toward the woman sitting on some sort of big overturned bucket with her head in her hands.

"Nina Whitt, the architect. She's a bit shaken still."

"Okay. I need you to move back."

After sealing her hands, her boots, Eve stepped to the hole. It was jagged, uneven, but a good two feet wide at its widest point, and ran nearly from floor to ceiling.

She saw, as Roarke had, the two forms, one stacked on the other. And saw he hadn't been wrong.

She took her flashlight out of her field kit, switched it on, and stepped through.

"Watch your step, lady—Lieutenant, that is," Pete corrected. "This wall here, the studs, they're flimsy. I oughta get you a hard hat."

"That's okay." She crouched, played her light over the bags.

Down to bones, she thought. No sign of clothing, no scraps of cloth she could see. But she could see where rats—she imagined—had gnawed through the plastic here and there to get to their meal.

"Do we know when the wall went up?"

"Not for certain, no," Roarke told her. "I did some looking while we waited for you to see if there's been a permit pulled for this sort of interior construction, and there's nothing. I contacted the previous owner—their rep, I should say. According to her, this wall was here at the time they bought the property, some four years ago. I'm waiting to hear back from the owner prior to that."

She could have told him to leave that to her, but why waste the time and the breath?

"Peabody, send for the sweepers, and put a request in for a forensic anthropologist. Tell the sweepers we need a cadaver scan, walls and floors."

"On it."

"You think there might be more," Roarke said quietly.

"We have to check."

She stepped out again, looked at him. "I'm going to have to shut you down, until further notice."

"So I assumed."

"Peabody will take your statements and your contact information, then you'll be free to leave."

"And you?" Roarke asked.

She shrugged out of her coat. "I'm going to get to work."

Back between the walls, Eve carefully recorded the wrapped bodies from all angles.

"The skeletal remains of two victims, both individually wrapped in what appears to be heavy-grade plastic. We've got holes in the plastic. Looks like vermin chewed through. Increased the air—heat and cold to the bodies," she said half to herself. "And that probably accelerated decomp. No data, at this time, on when this secondary wall was constructed. It's impossible, from an on-site eval, to determine TOD."

Leaving the plastic in place for now, she ran a scan to determine height. "Centimeters, crap." She scowled at the readout. "Convert that to American—to feet." Her frown stayed in place as she studied the new readouts.

"Victim Two—top—is judged to be approximately five feet in height. Victim One—bottom—four feet, eleven inches."

"Children," Roarke said from behind her. "They were children."

He hadn't stepped through the opening, but stood just in it.

"I'll need the forensic expert to determine age." Then she shook her head. He wasn't just a witness, wasn't even just her husband. He'd worked with her, side by side, on too many cases to count. "Yeah, probably. But I can't confirm that. Go ahead and give Peabody your statement."

"She's taking Nina's." He glanced back to where the stalwart and sympathetic Peabody dealt with the shaken architect. "It'll be a bit longer. I could help you."

"Not a good idea, not just yet." Carefully, she began to peel back the plastic on Victim Two. "I don't see any holes in the skull—so no obvious evidence of head trauma. No visible damage to the neck, or nicks, breaks in the torso area." She fit on microgoggles. "There's a crack in the left arm, above the elbow. Maybe from an injury. This finger bone looks crooked, but what do I know. Looks crooked though. I can't see any damage or injury to determine COD, at this time. Identification from skeletal remains must be attempted by ME and forensics. No clothing, no shoes, no jewelry or personal effects."

Sitting back on her heels, she glanced up at Roarke again. "I only know the bare bones, but generally the jawline in a male is more square—and this looks more rounded to my eye. Plus the pelvis area is usually larger in males. It's just a guess—and needs verification—but these look to be female remains to me."

"Girls."

"Just a guess, and I don't even have that on TOD or COD. We may be able to estimate when this wall was built, because the probability's high it was put up to conceal the bodies. Between that and the forensics, we'll get approximate TOD."

She pushed up. "I'll need forensics to help determine IDs. Once we know who they are, we can start working on how they got here."

With little more she could do, she stepped out beside him.

"They're close to the same height," he pointed out.

"Yeah. Possible: Same type of female vic—close in age, maybe, in size, maybe race. Maybe they were killed together, maybe they weren't. I can't see any signs of trauma, but further testing may pull that out. Hold on."

She walked over to where Peabody finished up with Nina.

"I'm sorry I'm not more help. This is so upsetting. I've never seen . . ." Nina glanced over to the open wall, away again. "I didn't even see clearly really, but . . ."

"Did you examine the walls, the floors," Eve began, "when you got the job?"

"We did several walk-throughs, of course. Measurements. Roarke's directive was to gut the building, and to design spaces within the shell. We have all the blueprints and specs—architectural, engineering, mechanical. The bones—" She broke off, paled. "That is to say the shell, the structure is very sound, but the interior isn't. It contains a lot of cheap material, a lot of poor design, quick fixes that were done over several decades, all leading to a number of years of neglect."

"How many years of neglect?"

"Our research indicates the building hasn't been used, officially, for about fifteen years. I did research some of its history, just to give me some background for the new design."

"Send me what you've got. You're free to go now. Do you have transportation?"

"I can get a cab. I'm fine. I'm not usually so . . . delicate. Can I speak with Roarke a moment before I leave?"

"Sure." Eve shifted her attention to Peabody. "I think they're kids."

"Aw, shit, Dallas."

"Not a hundred percent, but that's my initial take. I need you to take Roarke's statement, it's just less sticky that way. I'll take the job boss." She looked over as the first of the sweepers came in the big iron door. "In a minute."

With little more to do than direct, Eve set the sweepers to work, took Pete's brief but colorful statement, then moved back to Roarke.

"The best thing you can do is find out everything you can about who and what and where and when regarding this building in the past fifteen years."

"You think that's when they were put there."

"If the place hasn't been used, or rarely, in that time, my best guess is, yeah, it's going to be sometime between then and now. Now, allowing time for the decomp. If you can get me data on that, and another ream of data detailing, say, the five years before that, we may have something to play on."

"Then you'll have it."

"What's that over there? Where that portion of the wall's removed."

"That would be the previous owners, taking a look at the old wiring. There's a similar break on the second level where they poked at the plumbing."

"Too bad they didn't hit this spot. We'd have found the remains sooner and you'd have got it cheaper."

"It was cheap enough. Getting an actual inspection of the wiring and plumbing's what put them in a mad scramble for more financing, or some backers. Neither of which they managed."

"And you came along, swooped it up."

"More or less. It and everything in it."

She understood how he felt. "I can pretty much guarantee you didn't own this place when they were put there. You found them, and they needed to be found. You can't do anything here, Roarke. You should go, deal with the ten thousand meetings you've probably got on your schedule for the day."

"Only a couple thousand today, so I think I'll stay a bit longer." He watched two of the sweepers in their white suits and booties run scanners over another wall.

"Okay, but I've got—" Eve broke off when the door screamed open again.

The woman who walked in might have been stepping onto a vid set. She wore a long sweep of coat in popping red, a flowing scarf that bled that red into silvery grays. A sassy red beret topped a short, sleek wedge of black hair. Gray boots with high skinny heels ran up under the hem of the coat.

She pulled off a pair of red-framed sunshades and revealed iced blue eyes that made an exotic contrast with smooth caramel skin. She tucked the shades into a gray bag the size of Pluto, took out a 'link with an ornate protective cover, and began to record the scene.

"Who the hell is that?" In quick strides, Eve crossed the dusty space. Some reporter, she thought, trying for a scoop. "This is a crime scene," she began.

"Right, yes. I find it helpful to have a clear record of the environment. Dr. Garnet DeWinter." She stuck out a hand, gripped Eve's, gave it two firm shakes. "Forensic anthropologist."

"I don't know you. Where's Frank Beesum?"

"Frank retired last month, moved to Boca. I took over his position." She gave Eve a long, steady study. "I don't know you either."

"Lieutenant Dallas." Eve tapped the badge she'd hooked to her belt. "I need to see your ID, Dr. DeWinter."

"All right." She reached into the bag Eve speculated could hold a small pony, drew out her credentials. "I was told you have skeletal remains. Two."

"That's right." Eve handed the credentials back. "Wrapped in plastic, which was compromised, I believe, by vermin. They were discovered as demolition began, with that wall."

She gestured, then led DeWinter over.

"Now, you I know." DeWinter's vid star face lit on Roarke's. "Do you remember me?"

"Garnet DeWinter." To Eve's surprise, he leaned down, kissed both her cheeks. "It's been five years, six?"

"Yes, six, I think. I read you'd married." DeWinter spread her smile over him, and Eve. "Congratulations to both of you. I certainly didn't expect to see you here, Roarke."

"He owns the building," Eve told her.

"Ah, bad luck." She looked up, around, down. "It's kind of a wreck, isn't it? But you're a genius at transformations."

"As you are on bones. We're fortunate to have her, Eve. Garnet is one of the top forensic anthropologists in the country."

"'One of'?" DeWinter said, and laughed. "I found myself unsatisfied in the lab in The Foundry in East Washington, so I jumped at the chance to take the position here, have a more hands-on opportunity. And I thought it would be a good change for Miranda—my daughter," she said to Eve.

"Great, good. Maybe we can all catch up later over drinks and beer nuts, and I don't know, maybe you'd like to take a look at the remains. Just for something to do."

"Sarcasm. Ouch." Undaunted, DeWinter swept off her coat. "Would you mind?" she asked, handing it to Roarke. "Through there?" At Eve's nod, she moved to the opening, once again used her 'link to record.

"I have a record," Eve began.

"I like my own. You opened the plastic wrapping on the top remains."

"After a full record."

"Still."

"You're not sealed," Eve said when DeWinter started to step through.

"You're right, of course. I'm still getting used to the protocols." Out of the bag she pulled a white sweepers suit. She unzipped her boots, slid them off, then pulled the suit over her trim black dress. Then she took out a can of Seal-It, coated her hands.

She took the bag with her through the hole.

"Friend of yours?" Eve murmured to Roarke.

"Acquaintance, but she makes an impression."

"You got that right," Eve said and went through the hole.

"The remains on top—"

"Victim Two."

"All right, Victim Two appears to be approximately 1.5 meters in length."

"Just barely over, I did the measurement. Victim One is nearly the same, just under that."

"Don't take offense, but I'll just remeasure, for my own record." Once she had, DeWinter nodded. "From on-site visuals of the skull shape, the pubic area, Victim Two is female, between twelve and fifteen years. Most probably Caucasian. I see no outward sign of trauma. The crack in the right humerus, just above the elbow, indicates a break. Most likely between the ages of two and three. It didn't heal well. There's also a fracture of the right index finger."

"Looks like more a twist than a break."

"Agreed. Good eye. As if someone grabbed the finger, twisted it until it snapped."

DeWinter drew out microgoggles, slipped them on, tapped them, and a light focused down. "She had a few cavities, and her twelve-year molars were through. A tooth missing. I also see some damage to the eye socket, left. An old injury."

Slowly, systematically, DeWinter worked her way down the body. "A rotator cuff injury. Again it looks like a wrenching injury—someone grabbing the arm, twisting forcibly. Another fracture here, looks like a hairline in the left ankle."

"Abuse. That's a pattern of physical abuse."

"Agreed, but I'll want to study these injuries in my lab."

She glanced up at Eve, her eyes huge behind the goggles. "I'll be able to tell you more once I have her there. I need to move her to examine Victim One's remains."

"Peabody!"

Peabody popped into the doorway. "Sir!"

"Help me lift these remains."

"Carefully," DeWinter warned. "If you could take them out, and have Dawson secure them for transport. Do you know Dawson?"

"Yeah. Let's get her up and out, Peabody."

"Poor kid," Peabody murmured, then gripped the plastic, lifted it with Eve like a hammock. "Who's the fashion plate?" Peabody asked under her breath when they'd moved the remains into the main room.

"New forensic anthro. Dawson!"

When the head sweeper glanced her way, she signaled him. "Tell him to secure and arrange for transport," Eve ordered Peabody, and went back through to rejoin DeWinter.

"In the same age range as the other. With the skull characteristics, I believe mixed race. Most likely Asian and black. Two strains of my heritage as well. Again no outward sign of trauma. A clean break in the tibia, healed well."

DeWinter moved slowly, carefully along the remains. "I see no other breaks or injuries. All of the injuries, on One and Two, show they'd healed, and none were COD or incurred near TOD."

As DeWinter's light shone, Eve caught a quick sparkle.

"Wait." She crouched, peered down through the eye socket of the skull. "There's something here." Grabbing a tool out of her kit, she reached through, clamped the tiny glitter.

"Excellent eye, indeed," DeWinter said. "I missed it."

"An earring."

"I think a nose ring, possible brow ring. It's a very small stud, so I'd lean toward the nose. It simply dropped off and down during decomp."

Eve slid it into an evidence bag, sealed it.

"We'll begin drawing out DNA, starting facial reconstruction. I assume you want ID as soon as we can possibly determine."

"You assume right."

"Cause and time of death may take longer. I could use a detailed history of the building, when the outer wall was constructed, what its purposes were."

"Already being accumulated."

"Excellent. Dawson can secure these remains as well. I'll start on them immediately, and contact you as soon as I have anything useful. I look forward to working with you, Lieutenant."

Eve took the offered hand again, then let it go when she heard the shout.

"We've got another one!"

She met DeWinter's eyes. "Looks like you're not done here yet."

"Nor you."

Before they were done, they found twelve.

2 EVE WENT THROUGH THE BUILDING SECTION by section. To the south wall first, where sweepers meticulously cut out a large square of gyp board, bagging some of its dust and chunks for analysis. Inside the narrow opening, three wrapped remains were stacked. She examined them along with DeWinter.

Females, between twelve and sixteen. As with the first two, some showed older injuries, none showed overt trauma that could be determined as cause of death.

With the remains, Eve found three studs and one small silver hoop.

The rest of the main floor held a handful of partitions, two small restrooms, long since stripped of fixtures.

By the time she, along with DeWinter, climbed the open iron stairs to the second level, the sweepers had found five more.

"Again we have a mix of ethnicity," DeWinter told her, "and

again, all female, all in the same age range. Some injuries I'd suspect resulted from childhood abuse, but none that determine cause of death. Whoever did this preyed on females past puberty, but far short of adulthood. Females of this age range, some of whom most likely experienced earlier physical abuse."

"It was, for a few years, a kind of shelter."

Eve glanced back at Roarke as she bagged what she thought might be a toe ring.

"What kind of shelter?"

"Documentation's spotty. It was used as a kind of shelter for children and teenagers during the Urban Wars, those who'd lost their parents. A kind of makeshift orphanage."

"These bodies haven't been here since the Urbans."

"It's possible," DeWinter disagreed. "I'll be able to determine how long, within a reasonable time frame, once I have the remains back in my lab."

"Not since the Urbans," Eve repeated. "The concealing wall wasn't built that long ago. And there would've been no need to keep them here like this. People died in droves during the Urbans. You want to kill a few girls, need to get rid of the bodies? Just take them out, leave them on the street. And," she continued before DeWinter could speak again, "how the hell do you kill them, wrap them up, stack them up, then build walls to hide them when the place is full of people? You need time, you need some privacy."

"Yes, I see you're right. I only meant, forensically, the remains could be from that time period, and we won't know until tests are run to determine."

Eve straightened, handed the evidence bags out to Peabody. "Any documentation on how long the place housed Urban orphans?"

"I'm working on it," Roarke told her. "This level and the one above were converted into dormitories, loosely. There were two communal baths, second floor, third floor."

"Best I can figure," Pete put in, "they went up toward the end of the Urbans, or right after. That's going by material, and most of what was in them's long gone. Nobody bothered with permits, inspections, codes back around then. What I can see of the plumbing that's left, the wiring and basic infrastructure looks like it was scavenged, cobbled together. Same with the kitchen on the first floor, the two johns downstairs."

"No upgrades?"

"Ah." He scratched his head. "Some patchwork, some jury-rigging here and there. Done on the cheap. It's why we didn't think squat-all about the walls. We could see they weren't part of the original structure, but it's had a lot of half-ass fiddling over the years."

"Dorms." Stepping out, Eve surveyed the big, open space, imagined it crammed with cots and narrow beds, cheap, boxlike dressers or chests for belongings.

She'd lived through the experience of a state-run dorm—housing for disadvantaged, disenfranchised, and troubled kids. She supposed she'd been all three. But remembered, most of all, the days and nights of misery.

"You could fit twenty, twenty-five in here, double with bunks."

"Be tight," Pete commented.

"These kinds of places always run tight, and usually run cheap."

She walked out, leaving DeWinter to her exam, studied the space across a narrow hall.

"Another dorm, maybe," Pete suggested.

No, she thought, probably the "group" room, where you had to go for talk therapy, to listen to lectures, to receive duties or assignments. More misery.

She walked down into what had been the communal bathroom for the floor.

And flashed clearly back to the one she'd dealt with.

Room for six stalls, maybe seven in a pinch, she decided. One tub, considered a privilege, open showers, maybe three showerheads that offered a piss-trickle on a good day, three sinks.

She tuned back in, heard Pete's rambling voice.

"Stripped the old copper clean out, but you expect that. Helped themselves to some of the plastic pipes. Punched some holes in the old walls to get to it. Hauled out the johns, the tub. Had to be a tub over there, from what I can see of the rough plumbing. Mostly the same as this in the one on the third floor."

"Girls on one level, boys on the other, most likely. Especially if there were teenagers." At least that fit with her experience.

"Lieutenant." Dawson walked to her, his face drawn now. "We found more."

So there were twelve, wrapped, stacked, and hidden between walls. Some with a glitter or two among the bones to speak of the life once lived.

When she'd done all she could do, she stood out on the sidewalk with Roarke. The cold, the noise, the rush of life blew away some of the film, gyp dust and death, that seemed to cling to her face, her mind.

"We're heading into Central. Any data you can find on the place, the time lines, owners, usage, send it—however minuscule. We'll springboard off it, find more."

"I've copied what I do have to your units, including the sellers." He watched the way she studied the building. "You don't like leaving them to DeWinter—your dead."

"She's the expert. And no," Eve admitted, "I don't. But I can't look at their bones and figure out what happened to them. She can. Or I have to hope she can."

"She's very skilled. Will she work with Morris?"

Eve thought of the chief medical examiner, another who was very skilled. And one she trusted completely. "Yeah, she will. I'll make sure of it. Twelve," she mused. "In four different hidey-holes on three floors. Why spread them out? That's a question. All the same basic types, but with a spread over racial lines. But height, age, all close. Maybe body type, too. Sloppy enough, or just didn't care enough to remove all the body adornments.

"Anyway," she said, pushing that aside for now. "They'll seal the place up until we clear it, and I can't say how long that'll take."

"It's not a concern of mine. I want to know their names."

She nodded, understanding. "So do I. We'll find them, and we'll find out what happened to them. And we'll find who did it to them."

"You're the expert." He pressed a kiss to her forehead before she could evade, because he needed to. "I'll see you at home."

She skirted around the hood of her car, slid in behind the wheel. And there let out one long breath. "Jesus Christ."

Beside her, Peabody let out one of her own. "I can't get past them being kids. I know we have to, but I can't get past the fact a dozen kids were wrapped up and dumped in there like garbage."

"You don't have to get past it. You use it." Eve pulled out, wove through traffic. "But I don't think it was like garbage, not to the killer."

"What then?"

"I don't know, not yet. The way they were wrapped, the way he spread them out through the building, stacked some of them together. Does any of that mean something? We'll bring Mira in on this," she said, referring to New York Police and Security Department's top profiler and shrink. "And we start working, straight off, with the data Roarke has on the building. We dog this DeWinter like hungry hounds."

"Did you see her *boots*?" Peabody's dark eyes rolled like a woman in the throes of ecstasy. "They were like butter. And the dress? The cut, the material, and the really cute little buttons running all the way down the back?"

"Who wears butter boots and cute little buttons to a crime scene?"

"It all looked really good on her. And the coat was totally mag. Not mag like yours, a more girlie kind of mag."

"My coat's serviceable, practical."

"And magic," Peabody added as it was lined with sheer body armor. "But still. Plus I got from Dawson she's like a bone genius. I think he's got a crush on her, which I get because she looks amazing, but he says she can find more answers in a finger bone than a lot of lab rats can in a whole body."

"Let's hope he's right because we've got nothing but bones, a handful of cheap jewelry, and a building nobody apparently gave two shits about for years."

"Wall material," Peabody added. "Lab rats may be able to date some of the gyp board, the studs. Maybe even the plastic."

"There's that. Cheap," Eve considered. "The plastic looked cheap to me. The kind you buy by the big-ass roll to toss over things you don't want to get wet, or throw down on a floor when you're painting or whatever, then just dump. Same with the wallboard. Not much of an investment, but decent enough work—carpentry work—so nobody poked at the walls before this."

"So the killer had some construction skills."

"Enough to construct walls nobody looked at and thought: What the hell is that doing there? That blended in. But why the hell hide bodies there? Why not find a better way to dispose of them? Ditch or hide the bodies—taking them out and burying them's easier—but hide them because you don't want them found. They might connect to you. But you've got to have easy access to the building, so that connects to you. Yet you keep the bodies there."

"To keep them close?"

"Maybe you want to visit them."

"That's just more sick."

"The world's full of sick," Eve said, and contemplated on just that as she drove into Central.

She zipped into her slot in the garage. No IDs, no faces, no names—but that didn't mean they didn't dig in hard.

"I'm going to start the book and board," she said, striding to the elevator. "You take whatever data Roarke's sent on the building itself, the history of it, get more." She stepped into the elevator. "I want to know everything there is to know about its use: who used it, who owned it, worked in it, lived in it. Primarily post-Urbans, but not exclusively."

"I'm all over it."

"We take the probability DeWinter's on-scene estimate's close, and the time line that's most likely—" She broke off to shift over when more people piled into the car. "We start at fifteen years, after the building was shut down. But we need to know who had a connection to it or interest in it prior, and after."

The next time the doors opened, two uniforms hauled in a very fragrant sidewalk sleeper. Eve opted out, Peabody in her wake, and headed for the glide up.

"She seemed to know her stuff, and not just fashion-wise."

"We're going to find out." She hopped off the glide, continued to Homicide. "Everything, Peabody," she repeated. And she'd do a little digging on Dr. Garnet DeWinter.

She stepped into the bullpen and the clashing scents of really bad coffee, processed sugar, and industrial-strength cleaner. The smells of home.

Detectives manned 'links and comps at their desks, uniforms did the same in their cubes. She noted the empty desks of Detective Baxter and his trainee, Officer Trueheart. Remembered after a quick mental search that they'd both be in court.

She split off from Peabody, shrugging out of her coat as she made the short jog into her office. There, in her small space with its single narrow window, sat her AutoChef with the perk of real coffee, most excellent coffee, thanks to Roarke.

She tossed her coat on her excuse of a visitor's chair. The ass-numbing chair, plus coat, should discourage visitors. Then she programmed coffee, dropped down at her desk.

She wrote her report first, copying her commander and Dr. Mira, adding a request for a consult to Mira's copy.

Then she tagged crime scene photos to her board. Twelve remains, she thought.

Young girls, who if DeWinter's gauge was accurate, would be adult women now, close to her own age. Women with jobs, careers, families, histories, lovers, friends.

Who'd stolen all that from them? And why?

"Computer, search and list any and all Missing Persons reports, New York area, for females between twelve and sixteen years. Subjects not found. Search parameters 2045 through 2050."

Acknowledge. Searching . . .

That would take a while, she thought.

And it took time to kill a dozen girls, barring group slaughter, mass poisoning, or the like. She didn't see that here. A mass killing would have resulted, most logically, in a mass grave, not scattered hiding places.

So one or two, possibly three at a time, with the added burden of concealment.

A closed or abandoned building would afford the time, the privacy needed. Nail down the TODs, then find who had opportunity and access—and the necessary skills to build the walls.

It grated a little, she could admit it, to depend on someone else to determine TOD—someone not within her usual team. But she studied the board, and reminded herself those girls, who would never have jobs, lovers, families, demanded she work with anyone who could provide answers.

But that didn't mean she shouldn't find out just who that anyone was.

She did a quick run on DeWinter.

Age thirty-seven, single, no marriage, one offspring—female, age ten. No official cohab on record. Born Arlington, Virginia, both parents living, both long-term cohabs, both scientists. No siblings.

The educations listing ran endlessly, and okay, Eve thought, were pretty damn impressive. She had doctorates in both physical and biological anthropology, both from Boston University of Medicine—where she sometimes served as a guest lecturer—master's degrees in a handful of other related areas like forensic DNA, toxicology. She'd worked in a number of facilities, most recently The Foundry in East

Washington where she'd headed a nine-person department of lab rats.

Earned the price of her fancy coat and boots on the lecture circuit, Eve deduced, after scanning the list—and consulting on digs and projects all over the world. That list ran from Afghanistan to Zimbabwe.

Arrested twice, Eve noted. Once at a protest rally against rain forest development, and once for . . . stealing a dog.

Who stole a dog?

Both times she pleaded guilty, paid a fine, and did the required community service.

Interesting.

She'd started to look more deeply into the criminal charges when Mira knocked on her doorjamb.

"That was fast." Automatically, Eve rose.

"I was on an outside consult and read your report on the way in. I thought I'd come by before I went to my office."

"I appreciate it."

"Those are your victims."

Mira walked to the board.

Eve didn't think of Mira as a fashion plate. She thought of her as classy. The pale peach dress and matching jacket set off Mira's sweep of sable hair, the soft blue eyes. The sparkle of little gold beads around her neck echoed in eardrops, and both the peach and gold merged in a swirling pattern on the shoes with their needle-thin heels.

Eve could never quite figure out how some women managed to match and merge that way.

"Twelve young girls," Mira murmured.

"We're waiting for data to ID them."

"Yes. You're working with Garnet DeWinter."

"Apparently."

"I know her a little. An interesting woman, and unquestionably brilliant."

"I keep hearing the second part. She stole a dog."

"What?" Mira's eyebrows lifted in surprise, then knitted in curiosity. "Whose dog? Why?"

"I don't know. I just did a run on her. She's got an arrest for stealing a dog."

"That's . . . odd. In any case, her reputation in her field is exemplary. She'll help you find out who they were. May I sit?"

"Oh, yeah. Let me . . ." There were visitors and there were visitors. Eve scooped the coat off the chair, then gestured to her desk. "Take that one. This one's brutal."

"I'm aware." And because she was, Mira took the desk chair.

"Do you want some of that tea of yours? Or coffee?"

"No, thanks. I—oh, I *love* the sketch."

Rising again, Mira walked over to admire the sketch of Eve, in full kick-ass mode.

"Yeah, it's good. Ah, Nixie Swisher did it for a school project or assignment. Something."

Little Nixie, who'd survived, by chance, luck, fate, the brutal and bloody home invasion that had killed her entire family.

"It's wonderful. I didn't realize she was so talented."

"I think she got an assist from Richard."

"Regardless, it's excellent, and captures you. She'd be so pleased you put it in here."

"I told her I would on Thanksgiving, when she gave it to me. Anyway, it reminds me. Even when the worst happens, when you think you can't take another step you can. You can survive."

"I only saw her briefly when Richard and Elizabeth brought the children to New York, but I could see she's done more than survive. She's begun to thrive."

She turned away, glanced at the board again. "They never will."

"No. The preliminary indicates the victims cross ethnic lines,which means it's unlikely they shared coloring or facial resemblance. That leaves age and possibly body type as physical links. My first instinct," Eve continued as Mira sat again, "at this point, is the ages of the victims were more important to their killer."

"Young, probably not fully developed physically or sexually."

"And small in stature, which would indicate even those who may hit the top of the age scale may have, and likely did, appear younger. Again, on the preliminary, there was no sign of violence immediately before death. Any sign of it was well before death, and healed."

"Yes, I saw in the preliminary prior abuse suspected on several of the victims. Young girls already used to violence," Mira said, "don't trust easily. Given the nature of the building during the most probable time frame, they, or some of them, might have been runaways."

"I've started a search using Missing Persons reports. It's—" Eve glanced over when her computer signaled. "That should be it. Computer, number of results."

Three hundred seventy-four unresolved reports on subjects fitting the criteria.

"So many," Mira said, but from her expression, the number didn't surprise her any more than it did Eve.

"Some of those are kids who poofed—of their own accord. Slid through the cracks, got themselves new ID."

"Some," Mira agreed, "but not most."

"No, not most. It's possible we'll find our vics among these. Certainly we should find some of them. Then again, not every parent or guardian bothers to file a report when a kid goes missing. Plenty are just fine with it if a kid takes off."

"You didn't run."

"No." There were few Eve felt comfortable speaking to about her past. Mira was one. "Not from Troy." Not from the father who'd beaten her, raped her, tormented her. "It never occurred to me I could. Maybe if I'd had exposure to other kids, to the outside, it would have."

"They kept you confined, separated, Richard Troy, Stella, so the confinement, the abuse, all of it was your normal. How could you know, especially at eight, it was anything but?"

"Are you worried about me, with them?" Eve gestured to the board.

"Only a little. It's always harder when it's children, for anyone who works with death. It will be harder on you considering they're young girls—a few years older than you were, and some of them abused, most likely by parents or guardians. Then someone ended their lives. Perhaps more than one person."

"It's a consideration."

"You escaped and survived, they didn't. So yes, it'll be hard on you. But I can't think of anyone more suited to stand for them. With only gender and approximate age, it's not possible to give you a solid profile. The fact that there was no clothing found may indicate sexual assault, or an attempt to humiliate, or trophies. Any number of reasons. Cause of death will help, as could the victims' histories once identified. Anything you're able to give me will help."

Mira paused a moment. "He had skills, and he planned. He had to access both the building and the material, and find the girls. That takes planning. These weren't impulse kills, even if the first might have been. The remains show no physical signs of torture or violence, though there may have been emotional torture. None of them were hidden alone?"

"No."

"Not alone, but in pairs or small groups. It might be he didn't want them to be alone. He wrapped them, a kind of shroud. And built them a kind of crypt. It shows respect."

"Twisted."

"Oh yes, but a respect for them. Runaways, abused girls, buried— in his way—in a building with a history of offering shelter to orphans. That's an interesting connection."

Mira rose. "I'll let you get back to work." She glanced back to the board again. "They've waited a long time to be found, to have some hope of justice."

"There might be others. Did the killer stop with these twelve, or even begin with them? Why stop? We'll look at known predators who were killed, died, or incarcerated around the time of the last victim—once we have that. But, too many aren't known. Still, we'll look for like crimes, known predators. A lot of times girls this age run in packs, right?"

Mira smiled. "They do."

"So it's likely one or more of the vics had friends, maybe were friends. It's possible we'll find someone who was friends with a vic, and saw or heard something. We don't have names, yet, but we have lines to tug."

She sat again when Mira left, looked at the list of missing girls.

And began to tug.

She'd eliminated a handful—too tall to match the recovered remains—when Peabody poked in.

"I've got a couple names."

"I've got hundreds."

Confused, Peabody looked at the screen. "Oh, missing girls. Man, that's just sad. But I've got a couple of names associated with the building during the time in question. Philadelphia Jones, Nashville Jones—siblings. They ran a youth halfway house/rehab center in the building, according to what Roarke dug up, from May of 2041 to September of 2045. They moved to another facility, one donated to them by a Tiffany Brigham Bittmore. They're still there, heading up the Higher Power Cleansing Center for Youths."

"First, who names somebody after a city?"

"They have a sister, Selma—I'm thinking Alabama—who lives in Australia, and had a brother, Montclair, who died shortly after they switched buildings. He was on a missionary trip to Africa, and got mostly eaten by a lion."

"Huh. That's something you don't hear every day."

"I've decided being eaten alive by anything is my last choice of causes of death."

"What's first choice?"

"Kicking it at two hundred and twenty, minutes after being sexually satisfied by my thirty-five-year-old Spanish lover, and his twin brother."

"There's something to be said for that," Eve decided. "Who owned the building during the Joneses' time?"

"They did, sort of. In that they struggled to pay a mortgage on it, and the bills that come with a decrepit building in New York. They defaulted, and the bank took it over, eventually. Then the bank eventually sold it. I've got that name, too, but it's looking like this little company bought it with the idea of pulling in investors so they could rehab it into a handful of fancy apartments. That fell through, and they eventually sold it at a loss to the group Roarke bought it from, who also lost money on the deal."

"Bad luck building."

Peabody looked at the board, the crime scene photos. "It sure as hell seems like it."

"Well. Let's go talk to Pittsburgh and Tennessee."

"Philadephia and Nashville."

"Close enough."

Higher Power Cleansing Center for Youths made its base in a tidy, four-story building just below the hip edge of the East Village. The short stretch on Delancey had rejected the Village's artistic edge, and just missed the Bowery's late twentieth-century facelift— and the bombings, pillaging, and vandalism that had infected its neighbors during the Urbans.

Most of the buildings here were old, some rehabbed, some gentri- fied, others defiantly clinging to their shabby urban shells.

The whitewashed brick building boasted a tiny courtyard where a scatter of short shrubs shivered in the cold. A couple of teenagers, impervious to that cold, sat on a stone bench playing with their PPCs.

Eve passed them on the way to the front entrance. Both wore HPCCY hooded sweatshirts, sported various face and ear piercings, and identical expressions of suspicious disapproval.

Street vets already, smelling cop, she concluded.

At her steady gaze, their expressions shifted to cocky smirks, but she noted the girl—or she assumed girl—slid her hand into her companion's.

She heard the hoarse whispers, the quick giggle (definitely female) behind her as she and Peabody climbed the trio of steps to the front door.

Security there included cam, palm plate, and swipe unit. She pressed the buzzer, over which a sign helpfully advised: PLEASE PRESS THE BUZZER.

"A clean and healthy day to you. How can we help?"

"Lieutenant Dallas, Detective Peabody, NYPSD. We're here to speak with Philadelphia and Nashville Jones."

"I'm sorry, I don't see your names on Ms. Jones's or Mr. Jones's appointment books today."

Eve pulled out her badge. "This is my appointment."

"Of course. Would you please put your palm to the plate for verification of ID?"

Eve complied, waited for the scan.

"Thank you, Lieutenant Dallas. I'm happy to buzz you in."

There was indeed a long buzz, followed by the clack of locks opening. Eve pushed the door open, entered a narrow lobby with an offshoot of rooms and hallways presumably to other rooms on either side, and a set of stairs jogging up.

A woman rose from a desk at the rear of the room, smiling as she crossed a buff-colored tile floor.

Matronly was the only description given her old-fashioned bubble of shoe-black hair, the dowdy pink sweater over a floral dress, the sensible shoes.

"Welcome to Higher Power Cleansing Center for Youths. I'm Matron Shivitz."

Fits, Eve thought. "We need to speak with Jones and Jones."

"Yes, yes, so you said. I'd love to be able to tell them what you're here to speak to them about."

"I bet," Eve said and let the silence hang a moment. To the left the door held a plaque for Nashville Jones. The one to the right named his sister.

"It's police business."

"Of course! I'm afraid Mr. Jones is in session at this time, as is Ms. Jones. Ms. Jones should be free shortly. If you choose to wait, I'd love to bring you some tea."

"We'll wait. Hold the tea, thanks."

Eve wandered deeper, looked through an open door where three kids worked comps.

"Our electronics area," Shivitz explained. "Residents are allowed access to complete certain assignments, or research for assignments. Or if they've earned the privilege for free time."

"How do they earn the privilege?"

"By completing tasks and assignments, participating in activities, earning merits through good work, kindness, generosity. And, of course, remaining clean in body and spirit."

"How long have you worked here?"

"Oh, fifteen years, since the home opened. I began as an assistant matron and lifestyle coach, part-time. I'd be happy to arrange for a tour of our home, if you like."

"Sounds good. Why don't we—"

Eve broke off when a door shoved open and a girl barreled out of Philadelphia Jones's office. Flushed, teary-eyed, her hair a swirl of purple and orange, she bolted for the stairs.

"Quilla! Inside pace, please."

The girl shot Shivitz a furious look fired out of molten brown eyes, added a defiant middle finger salute, and stomped up the stairs.

"I guess she's not earning privileges today."

Shivitz only sighed. "Some young spirits are more troubled than others. Time, patience, proper discipline, and reward eventually open all doors."

So did a few hard kicks, Eve thought, but Shivitz was already hurrying to the still-open office door.

"Excuse me, Ms. Jones, but there are two police officers here to see you and Mr. Jones. Yes, of course, of course." She turned back to Eve and Peabody. "Won't you come right in? I'll let Mr. Jones know you're here as soon as his session is over."

Eve stepped over. She scanned what she thought of as a simple, straightforward office with a sitting area. The sitting area, she concluded, would be used for "sessions," and visitors.

Child Protective Services, guardians, and the occasional cop, maybe a donor or two.

At a U-shaped work area, a woman with glossy brown hair pulled back in combs sat working on a computer. Her profile showed a strong, sharp chin, a generous mouth pressed now in a hard line, and the glint of a green eye.

"Just one moment, Officers. Please, have a seat," she added without looking up.

Since she didn't want to sit, as yet, Eve just walked toward the workstation, leaned against one of the two low-back chairs facing it.

"I apologize," Philadelphia continued. "A little difficulty with my last session. Now. What can I do for you today?"

She swiveled around, faced Eve, a polite smile on her face.

Then she shot up out of the chair, a tall, rail-thin woman with horror in her eyes. She clutched at her throat.

"Someone's been murdered. Someone's dead!"

Intrigued, Eve lifted her eyebrows. "More like a dozen. Let's talk about that."

3 PHILADELPHIA JONES ROCKED BACK ON HER heels as if Eve had punched her.

"What? A dozen? My kids!" She zipped around the workstation, would have barreled straight through Eve for the door if Eve hadn't thrown up a hand to stop her.

"Hold it!"

"I need to—"

"Sit down," Eve interrupted. "First explain why you jumped straight to murder."

"I know you. I know who you are, what you do. What's happened? Is it one of our kids? Which one?"

The Icove case, Eve thought. When you had a bestselling book and a major vid based on one of your cases, people started recognizing you.

Well, that, and being married to Roarke.

"We're here about murders, Ms. Jones, but not recent ones."

"I don't understand. I should sit down," she decided, and worked her way over to the sitting area. "It's not about my kids? I'm sorry. I apologize." She took a couple steadying breaths. "I'm not usually so . . . reactionary."

"Why don't I get you some water," Peabody began.

"Oh, thank you, but I'll ask the matron to bring in some tea, and she should reschedule my next session."

"I'll tell her."

"You're so kind."

"No problem." Peabody slipped out.

"Please sit," Philadelphia told Eve. "Again, I'm so sorry. I read the Icove book, of course—and slipped out just the other night with a friend to see the vid. It's all very fresh in my mind, so when I saw you, I jumped to the worst possible conclusion."

"Understood." Eve took a chair, and Philadelphia's measure. Calmer now, Eve thought, but still shaken.

Middle forties, she judged. Conservatively dressed, simple hair, small studs in the ears.

Like the room: neat, tidy, and nothing fancy.

"You and your brother once ran this organization out of another location."

"No, HPCCY has always been housed here. You must mean The Sanctuary. That's what we called our original home. Oh, we struggled there," she said with a ghost of a smile. "In every way. Not enough funding, not enough staff, and the building itself a maintenance nightmare. We weren't able to keep up the payments—we rushed into buying that building, I'm afraid, without clearly thinking it through. It housed war orphans during the Urbans."

"Yeah, I know."

"It seemed like a sign, so Nash and I rushed in. We found out there's a reason angels fear to tread," she said with that wispy smile again. "But we learned quite a bit, and with that, God's grace, and the generosity of our benefactor, we were able to create this home, and offer the children who need us much more than a sanctuary."

Peabody slipped back in. "Tea will be right along."

"Thank you so much. Please sit. I was just explaining to Lieutenant Dallas how Nash and I—my brother—were able to expand our horizons when we relocated here. Fifteen years ago last September. Time goes quickly, sometimes much too quickly."

"What do you do here, exactly?" Eve asked her.

"We offer children between the ages of ten and eighteen a clean, safe environment along with the necessary mental, spiritual, and physical aids to help them conquer addictions, to help them learn to make good choices, and build strong character. We're a route for the children, and their guardians toward a protective and contented life."

"How do you get them—the kids?"

"Most are enrolled by their guardians—either as day residents or full-time—some through the court system. Our children come to us troubled, many addicted to a variety of substances, all certainly with poor self-control, self-image, a plethora of bad habits. We give them structure, boundaries, group and individual therapy, and spiritual guidance."

"Is that what you did in the other location?"

"We weren't able to as effectively assist in addiction rehabilitation as we didn't have the proper staff. At The Sanctuary we were, I fear, little more than a holding pattern for most of the children. A place to come in out of the cold. Many were on the street—runaways or abandoned. Lost children. We tried to give them a safe place, a warm bed, healthy food, and guidance, but we were hampered by lack of funding until Ms. Bittmore, our benefactor, stepped in. She donated this building to us, and a financial trust to help us with the considerable expenses.

"Oh, thank you, Matron."

"I'm happy to help." Shivitz carted in a tray with a simple white teapot, three white cups. "Is there anything else I can do?"

"Not right now, but please, send Mr. Jones in as soon as he's able."

"Of course." Shivitz backed out, quietly closed the door.

"I'm happy to talk about HPCCY." Philadelphia poured the tea as she spoke. "And I'd love to give you a personal tour if you have the time. But I'm puzzled by your interest."

"This morning, the demolition stage of rehab on the building on Ninth began. Your old building."

"They're finally going to do something with it. That's good news. I have fond memories, as well as nightmares about that building." She laughed a little, lifted her tea. "The plumbing couldn't be trusted, the doors jammed, and the power would go out without explanation. I hope whoever owns it now has deep pockets. I suspect a true rehabilitation of that property will cost a great deal."

She looked over as her door opened. "Nash, come meet Lieutenant Dallas and Detective Peabody."

"My pleasure." He strode in, a striking man with a mane of white-streaked black hair, a prominent nose, his sister's sharp chin. He wore a suit and tie and shoes polished to mirror gleams.

"I'm aware of you, Lieutenant," he said with a firm handshake, "due to your connection with Roarke. And of both of you," he continued, giving Peabody the same businesslike shake, "through your reputations as police officers—and the Icove case particularly."

"Let me ask Matron to get another cup."

"Don't bother on my account." Nash waved his sister's offer away, joined her on the couch. "I'm a coffee man, and Philly won't allow caffeine in the house, even the faux sort."

"Especially the faux sort. All those chemicals." She made a disapproving face with a shake of her head. "You might as well drink poison."

"But such satisfying poison. So what brings two of New York's finest to HPCCY?"

"The lieutenant was just telling me that rehabilitation's begun on our old building, Nash. The Sanctuary."

"Rehabilitation's a byword around here, but that old place was, and would be still, beyond our limits. It was a happy day when we moved here."

"And lucky," Eve added. "It's not every day someone donates a building to you."

"Ms. Bittmore is our angel."

He sat back, a man at ease, with his eyes—a shade or two sharper than his sister's—direct on Eve's. "It's well known she lost her husband during the Urban Wars, then years later, lost her youngest son to addiction, to the streets. She nearly lost her granddaughter as well, generation following generation down that dark path. But Seraphim came to us—came to The Sanctuary."

"We were able to reach her," Philadelphia continued. "To help her turn off that dark path, back into the light, to reunite her with her family. Ms. Bittmore came to see us, saw what we were trying to do, and what we were up against. She gave us this building as a tribute to her granddaughter, who happens to be one of our counselors now. We're very grateful to both of them, and to the higher power for bringing us all together."

"Is Seraphim in-house today?"

"I'm not absolutely sure of her schedule, but I think this is her afternoon off. I'd be happy to check with Matron."

"We'll get to that. As I was saying, during demo on the building on Ninth, several false walls were discovered."

"False walls?" Philadelphia's brows drew together. "I'm not sure I follow."

"Walls constructed a short distance out from the originals, leaving a gap between the two."

"Is that why it was so drafty?" She shook her head. "We could never afford much more than emergency repairs, and even then we had to jury-rig more than we should have. I suppose someone might have built out the wall as the original was in such poor shape."

"I don't think so, but concealment was the purpose."

"We painted, tried some minor—very minor," Nash emphasized, "updating in the baths and kitchen, but we never put up walls. Concealment, you said? Hiding valuables—ill-gotten valuables? I can assure you if we'd had anything valuable we'd have spent it to keep The Sanctuary above water rather than hiding it away. What did you find? Cash, jewels, illegals?"

"Bodies," Eve said flatly, and watched both for reaction. "Twelve."

The teacup slipped out of Philadelphia's fingers so the cup bounced on the rug and pale amber liquid ran out in a thin river. Nash simply stared, his face going pale and absolutely blank.

"Twelve." Philadelphia choked it out. "You said—when I thought—you said a dozen. Do you mean, oh, merciful Jesus, did you mean twelve bodies?"

"What are you talking about?" Nash demanded.

"Twelve bodies," Eve said, "found between the original wall and the one constructed to conceal them. More accurately, twelve skeletal remains, preliminarily identified as females between the ages of twelve and sixteen."

"Girls?" As the kid on the bench had done, Philadelphia slid her hand into her brother's. "But how? When? Who could do something like that? Why?"

"All good questions. I'm working on getting the answers. Again, preliminarily, we calculate the victims were placed in that concealment, all wrapped in plastic, approximately fifteen years ago. About the time you left the building and moved into this one."

"You think that we—" Philadelphia leaned forward now, eyes intense. "Lieutenant, Detective, we've dedicated our life to *saving* young people. From themselves, from their environment, from destructive influences. We could never . . . we could never."

"It couldn't have been done while we were in there." Still pale, Nash picked up a teacup he'd refused, gulped down the cold contents. "We'd have seen. And if that isn't enough, there were residents, staff. It couldn't have been while we were in there. No."

"How did you leave it?"

"We just walked away on the advice of our attorney. We took what was ours. Furniture, equipment—what little we had. The extra clothes we kept on hand for those who came to us with little to nothing. That sort of thing. We just packed up, and moved everything we could here.

"You cried," he said to his sister. "Even though the place became a disaster, a stone around our necks, you cried leaving it."

"I did. It felt like a failure. It wasn't. We did good work there, with what we had. People would say we lost our investment, and we could ill afford it. But I believe we gained more than we lost. And then we were given this amazing gift. This terrible thing had to have been done after we left."

"Who had access, after you moved out the residents?"

"We did, for a short time." Nash rubbed his hand over his face as a man might when waking from a strange dream. "I suppose some of the staff or even some of the kids could've gotten in if they'd wanted to. Our security there wasn't very good. Another reason we needed to relocate."

"Again, on legal advice we didn't surrender it immediately to the bank." As she spoke, Philadelphia rose, took some napkins from a drawer. She blotted up the spilled tea, set the teacup aside. "We had to file papers, and we were told to simply let the bank foreclose. That it generally took some time to do so. We were actually still there for nearly six months after we stopped paying the mortgage. We could've stayed longer, but it felt like . . ."

"Stealing," Nash murmured. "You said it was like stealing. We were preparing to close up, thinking we were finished with our mission, then Ms. Bittmore offered us this building. It was like a gift from God. We believe it was, God's work through her."

"How long before the bank shut the place up?"

"I think at least six or eight months after we left. At least," Philadelphia repeated. "We'd have the notification of foreclosure, all the paperwork on file."

"I'd like to have copies."

"I'll see that you do. Anything you need."

"A list of staff, handymen, repair and maintenance. All of them. And a list of residents. You have records?"

"Of staff, yes. Most of the repairmen, yes. Our brother, Monty, did some of the minor repairs. And I tried, Nash is hopeless with tools.

Monty was killed in Africa several years ago. We'd have a list of the children, though our rules were less structured there. We were licensed, so we were given the responsibility of housing some children through court order. But we also took in what you could call strays. I'm afraid any number of them might have given fake names, and a great many were only there a night or two, or sporadically. But I'll see you have copies of everything we have."

"Twelve girls," Nash said under his breath. "How can this be?"

"And they may have been *ours*." Philadelphia's knuckles went white as she gripped her brother's hand. "They may have been girls who came to us, Nash, then came back looking for us. We weren't there, and someone . . . someone preyed on them."

"Are we responsible?" He shielded his face with his free hand. "Is this terrible thing on our souls?"

"I don't believe that." Philadelphia shifted closer, wrapped her arm around his shoulders. "I don't. Do you?" She lifted pleading eyes to Eve. "Do you?"

"The person responsible is the person who killed them."

"Are you sure they—of course you're sure." Nash dropped his hand, straightened his shoulders. "Wrapped in plastic, you said, hidden behind a wall. Of course this was murder. But how were they killed?"

"I can't give you that information at this time." Eve pushed to her feet. "I appreciate your cooperation in this matter. If I could have those copies, and speak to anyone on staff now who worked or lived in that building, it would be very helpful."

"I'll get Ollie started on that—Oliver Hill," Philadelphia explained. "Our office manager. He wasn't part of The Sanctuary. We could barely afford an office much less someone to manage it. Our matron—Brenda Shivitz—she worked part-time there, for the last year we were in that location, then came with us here, on a full-time basis. Seraphim, as I said. Oh, and Brodie Fine. He'd just started his business, and often did work for us. He's still our handyman. He's got his own company, a small service company. We call on Brodie for any number of things."

"I'd like his contact information."

"You'll have it. If you'll excuse me." Philadelphia pushed off the couch. "I'll take care of this right away."

"Anything you can add?" Eve asked Nash as his sister left the room.

He stared down at his hands. "There's nothing more I can tell you. I'm so very sorry. Will you tell us their names? I might remember them. I feel I should remember them."

"I will when it's cleared. If we could speak with the matron now, get that out of the way."

"Yes, I'll get her. Please use this office, for privacy." He started out, turned. "I hope their souls are long at peace. I'll pray they are."

"Quick take," Eve asked Peabody the minute they were alone.

"They come off dedicated, maybe a little pious, but not extreme, and really close-knit. On the other hand, either or both of them had the best access to the building, and likely to the victims, of anyone we currently know."

"Agreed, on both counts. They also don't seem stupid, and it would be stone stupid to hide bodies in a building you're giving up. They'd have been the first ones looked at if the bank had done any demo fifteen years ago. They're the first we're looking at now."

"Sometimes desperate equals stupid."

Eve nodded in approval. "Damn right it does. Let's find out more about the dead brother, and the sister. And we'll give a hard look to anybody who worked at The Sanctuary, even the occasional repair people."

"Her reaction especially came off as genuine. Real shock and horror."

"Yeah, but if I worked with teenagers every single day for years, I'd have developed exceptional acting skills just so nobody knew I often wanted to nail them to a wall and light fire to them."

"Ouch."

"I'm just saying." Eve turned as Shivitz stepped into the doorway.

"Mr. Jones said . . . He said you wanted to talk to me. He said—" She stopped there, her already streaming eyes flooding more tears.

Knowing her job meant taking point with emotional witnesses, Peabody walked over, put an arm around the woman's shoulder, led her to a chair.

"I know this is a terrible shock."

"It's—it's *unspeakable!* Someone killed twelve girls? And they might have been *our* girls? And then just left them alone in that terrible place? Who could do that?" Shivitz pounded her fist on her thigh. "What kind of godless monster did that? You find him. You *must.* God will punish him, I believe that. But the law of man must punish him first. You're the law."

"Can't argue with that." Since fiery anger burned off the tears, Eve moved closer. "Think back. Is there anyone you remember who concerned you, who maybe paid the wrong type of attention to the girls at The Sanctuary—or even here, especially in the early days?"

"It wouldn't have been allowed. We're responsible for the safety of the children who come to our home. We'd never allow anyone near them who would cause them harm."

Peabody sat in the chair beside Shivitz, leaned over conversationally. "Sometimes people do good work, appear to live good lives, but something about them gives you a little feeling. Just a feeling something may be off, somewhere."

"I know exactly what you mean." Nodding briskly, Shivitz poked a finger in the air. "I used to shop at this market, but the man who ran it gave me a bad feeling, so I switched to another. Then I heard the man who ran the first market was arrested. For"—she lowered her voice—"bookmaking! I knew there was something wrong with him. I had that feeling you mean."

"Okay then." Eve wondered just how high on the sin list bookmaking ranked in Shivitz's world. "So anyone from The Sanctuary give you that feeling?"

"Not really. I'm sorry, but—oh, wait." Her lips pouted and pooched as she concentrated. "Brodie Fine, our handyman. Oh, I don't mean Brodie himself. He's a lovely man, a good family man, and very reliable. He's even hired a couple of our kids after they graduated. But he did have an assistant—a helper, I think he called him, for a little while back when we were in the other building. And that one gave me a bit of that feeling. Twice I heard that man use coarse language, and there's no place for coarse language, most particularly around children. And I'm *sure* I smelled alcohol on his breath a time or two. He only came a few times, but I didn't like the feel of him, to tell the truth."

"Do you have a name?"

"Oh goodness, I don't remember. But he was a strong-looking young man, and, yes, when I think about it, there was a look in his eye. What I'd call feral."

"All right. We'll check it out. Anyone else?"

"We're so careful, and it was so long ago. Oh, those poor girls!"

The tears brimmed back, so Eve rushed through another question before the flood.

"What about visitors? Parents, guardians?"

"Back then, it was a rare thing to see hide or hair of a parent. The sad thing is most of the children had run away from home either because it was a bad place, or because they themselves had made bad choices. Now and again parents would come to take a child back home, and if the courts hadn't said otherwise, we couldn't stop them. And in truth there were some who were doing their very best, and the child was recalcitrant. I do remember, now that you mention it, one set of parents who came to take their girl home. The mother, she was quiet and weepy, but the father! He made a terrible scene. Stood there shouting, and accusing us of being a *cult*!"

She slapped a hand on her heart, patted it there as if the beat might stop at the shock of the accusation.

"Of encouraging his daughter to defy him, allowing her to run wild and so on when we were doing no such thing. Oh, I remember him—Jubal Craine—because I thought he might use his fists on Mr. Jones, or even Ms. Jones, and I'm sure as God's my witness he'd used them before on that girl, and probably his wife. From Nebraska they were. I'm sure I remember that right. Farm people, and the girl had run off, ended up here."

She hesitated.

"And?" Eve prompted.

"Well, I'm sorry to say she'd sold herself more than once for food, for a place to stay. Her name was Leah, and we did our best by her while we could. Oh, oh, and he came back, yes, he did, a month or so later, as Leah had taken off again. He wanted to tear through the place looking for her, even though she wasn't there and we told him so. We called for the police that time, and they took him away. And now that you mention it, that was right about the time we were packing up to make the move."

"That's really helpful, Matron Shivitz." Peabody boosted encouragement into her tone. "Is there anyone else?"

"Those are the ones that come to mind, but I promise I'll think more about it. Just to think I might have known who did this terrible thing, it's going to keep me up at night. But the fact is, Miss, we're— that is, Ms. Jones and Mr. Jones—are so careful about who works here, who comes into the home, has any interaction with the children, I just don't know how this could be."

"The children aren't always in the house, are they?" Eve put in. "They go out. You don't confine them twenty-four/seven."

"Of course not! It's important they have some sort of normal routine, a healthy balance, and learn to cope well with the outside world. It's vital to build up trust. And they have assignments, of course, that take them out. Marketing, field trips, free time. Oh! I see! Someone from the outside. It had to be someone from the outside who did this. Lured the girls back to the other building. From the outside," she repeated on a long breath of relief. "Not one of our own."

Maybe, Eve thought. And maybe not.

"We appreciate your help. If you think of anything or anyone else, contact us."

"I can promise you I will. You don't know their names." She rose. "Mr. Jones said they were only bones. Will you tell us when you know who they are? I try to build relationships with all the children. I try to know who they are, who they hope to be. I've always tried. When I know who they are, I can pray for them better."

"We'll let you know when we can. Is Seraphim Brigham in-house today?"

"Not this afternoon. She only had morning sessions and duties today. She doesn't know yet." Shivitz pressed a hand to her heart again. "This will be very hard for her. She was one of them, you see. One of the girls."

"I don't mean to interrupt." Philadelphia hesitated in the doorway. "I have what you asked for." She held out discs. "They're all labeled. It's everything we could think of."

"Thanks." Eve took them. "Would you know where we could find Seraphim?"

"I know she usually has lunch with her grandmother on her free afternoon. Sometimes they visit a museum, or go shopping. She's seeing someone, fairly seriously, so she may also have a date."

"You don't approve?"

"Oh, no, it's not that." Philadelphia flushed a little. "I didn't mean to sound critical. He's a very nice young man. An artist. He's offered to do sketches of the children, and that's very kind of him."

"But?"

"He's a Free-Ager."

Behind Eve, Free-Ager Peabody cleared her throat.

"It's only that we try very hard to instill clear boundaries about sex, and, of course, while we're open to all faiths, we do try to impress a more, well, traditional Judeo-Christian structure. Free-Agers are more . . ."

"Free?" Peabody suggested.

"Yes. Exactly. But as I said, he's a very nice man, and we want only the best for Seraphim. Lieutenant, I feel I should tell the rest of the staff, the children. Have some sort of gathering of respect. I know the children, with their attachment to their e-toys, will hear of this. I want to protect them, but I want to be open with them."

"That's up to you. We'll be in touch when we have more information to give you. Please contact us if you think of anything that might relate."

"I don't think any of us will be thinking about anything else. I hope what we've been able to give you helps."

She led Eve and Peabody toward the door. Feeling a little tingle, Eve glanced back, up the steps, and saw the girl—Quilla, she remembered—sitting on them, staring holes through her.

Once outside, she walked to the car, then just leaned on it. Waited.

"Do you want me to track down this Seraphim who has the bad taste to date a Free-Ager?"

"Untwist your panties, Peabody. A lot of people consider Free-Agers a little out in the weird."

"Because we believe in personal choice, in acceptance, in respecting the planet and everything, everyone on it?"

"There's that," Eve said easily, enjoying the moment. "And the weaving your own cloth, living in communes—or mostly—growing sheep and carrots and paying homage to the Goddess Moonglow for the harvest."

"There is no Goddess Moonglow."

"Well, it's an easy mistake since half of Free-Ager women are named Moonglow. Or Rainbow. Or Sundrop."

"I only have one cousin named Rainbow, and my cousins are legion." In a huff, Peabody leaned on the car as well. "You're fucking with me."

"Nice mouth, Free-Age Girl. And yeah, some. Philly in there? She's all about talking the inclusive talk, and might believe she means it. But her idea of what everybody should believe, God-wise, would fit in a pretty small box. With a very tight lid."

"Okay, yeah, that's true. And she strikes me as the type who doesn't mean to dismiss others' belief systems, or even their lack thereof. It's just she's so unshakably sure hers is right—and more, the only right one."

Peabody paused a moment. "What are we waiting for?"

Eve jerked a chin toward the building as the front door opened. "Her."

Quilla squeezed out the door. She paused at the palm plate, pulling something out of her pocket, shoving it underneath. Then she strolled very casually down the short steps, turned toward the bench, now empty, in the tiny courtyard.

Then suddenly veered off—cam blind spot, Eve guessed—jogged to the fence, vaulted over it.

And strutted up to Eve.

She said, "Hey."

"Back at you."

"You're completely the Icove cops."

"We're New York cops," Eve corrected, and got a big eye roll.

"You get me."

"What did you put on the plate, the security, to get clear?"

Quilla shrugged. "It's a jammer. We've got a couple of e-geeks in group. I paid one of them to make me one. You came because of all the dead girls they found this morning, right?"

"What dead girls?"

"Shit, get off. The ones that were all dead to the bone up in Midtown. In the fuck same building Ms. Jones used to have. So you're here about all that."

"Let's start here. How do you know all this?"

"I can see cops, can't I? And I recognized your faces from all the hoo-rah-rah about the vid. So after Ms. J's latest bitch-fest I did some research. I know how to research. I'm a writer."

"Is that what you are?"

"And I'm going to be a good one, once I shake out of this place. How'd they get dead?"

"Why would I tell you?"

Quilla shrugged. "I could write about it. You don't have to tell me, I'll find out. Like I said, I can research. But if you figure Ms. J or Mr. J killed them, you're not much of a fucking cop."

"Why is that?"

"They're too holy. And sure, some people play like they're holy, and they'll stick a hand down your pants first chance they get." Now Quilla stuck her hands in the kangaroo pocket of her hoodie. "But they're not playing at it."

"How old are you?" Peabody wondered.

"Sixteen."

Eve cocked her head. "Maybe you will be. In a couple years."

The girl tossed her colorful hair in a kind of head shrug. "A year and a half, so what? Doesn't mean I don't know what I know. Writers gotta observe, a lot. Those two are complete PITAs, but they couldn't kill a bunch of girls. That's what I'm saying. All you gotta do is squint, and you can see the halos." She circled her finger over her head.

"Didn't notice that myself. Why do you care what we think about the Joneses?"

"No skin off my ass. I'm just saying. I gotta get back." Another eye roll. "I don't get outdoor privileges until I complete my 'educational assignments and domestic tasks.'" She parroted the words, giving them a prissy edge. "But I'll be watching, so you should ask me when you want to know something."

She took a couple running steps, vaulted back over the fence. "I can write it up," she said again. "I can write it as good as the reporter wrote up the Icove shit, but with a different angle. Because I'm like them. I'm like the dead girls."

She cut toward the bench, veered back, disappeared back inside.

"What do you think?" Peabody asked.

"A lot, but first I think most every group of kids has at least one decent geek. If they've got one skilled enough to jam reasonably good security, it's a good bet the group at The Sanctuary had one who could get in and out of the crappy security there. Food for thought."

She started to walk around to the driver's side. "And what the hell does that mean? Why would you serve food for thoughts, and what kind of food? If you serve spinach, do you get healthy thoughts? If it's ice cream and candy, is it fun thoughts? Why do we say stupid sayings?"

"They're in our idiom?"

"Idioms for idiots," Eve muttered, and slid behind the wheel. "Let's go harass DeWinter."

"I'm game, but can I have some food for my thoughts? They're pretty hungry, and I know this deli that's not too far from here."

"Of course you do."

Peabody narrowed her eyes. "Is that a dig on my appetite?"

Eve only smiled. "Consider it food for thought."

4 EVE RARELY VISITED WHAT WAS NOW DEWINTER's sector of the lab, but she remembered how to make her way through the maze—the down glides, through corridors, past check-ins and security stations to a wide set of reinforced glass doors—and a final security check.

The ample, two-level space held a honeycomb of labs, testing areas, machines, and equipment. Techs, rats, and supervisors, walked from area to area or worked at counters, behind more glass. They dressed in lab coats, protective gear, street clothes—and in one case what Eve was fairly sure were pajamas.

Someone, somewhere played music. She felt as much as heard the throbbing beat pumping against the walls. Unsure, she aimed right, glanced through an open door where a woman with dark skin, an upsweep of silver hair, and a snowy white lab coat appeared to be performing an autopsy on a really big rat.

She lifted her gory scalpel, gave a friendly nod. "NYPSD, right? Supposed to expect you. Are you looking for Doc D?"

"If that's DeWinter, yeah."

"Up the steps, make a left, then a right, then her lab's straight ahead. Do you need me to show you?"

"I think we can find it, thanks. Why are you cutting up the rat?"

"To find out if he and his pals ate this guy's face off, and when. We got rat turds to analyze, too. The fun never ends."

"Sounds like a party." And one she'd be happy to miss, Eve thought as she headed for the steps.

"You see a lot of terrible things when you're a cop," Peabody said.

"And there's always worse things tomorrow."

"Yeah, but I'd still rather do the job than cut open a rat to look for pieces of somebody's face."

"I'm not going to disagree." She turned left past another lab where a clear jar of maggots wiggled obscenely, turned right past another area—where the music banged—holding computers, what she thought was a holo-station, monitors, and a large board covered with sketches of faces.

Then straight ahead where she saw bright lights, steel tables, more equipment, and shelves holding various skeletal parts.

Closer—and farther from the music—she heard voices. DeWinter's, and another much more familiar to her.

She stepped to the opening where the glass pocket doors tucked into the walls and saw DeWinter hip-to-hip with Chief Medical Examiner Morris.

She wore her body-skimming black, and Morris one of his steel gray suits. He'd paired it with a shirt a click or two lighter, had his inky hair in a single long braid.

Together they made a glossy plate of high fashion as they studied the white skeleton on the silver table.

A second skeleton rested on a second table; monitors displayed various individual bones.

Morris fixed microgoggles over his dark, slanted eyes to study the arm bone DeWinter lifted from the table.

"Yes," he said, "I agree."

Then his gaze lifted up, met Eve's. He smiled.

"Dallas. Peabody. Welcome to the Bone Room."

"Morris. I didn't know you'd be here."

"Garnet and I agreed it would be more useful to consult here. You've met, I'm told."

"Yeah." Eve stepped in, nodded to DeWinter. "What have you got?"

"I've started on the first two found. Remains One and Two. We recorded them, cleaned them, recorded again, and began the examine and analysis. Li and I agree the injuries to the remains were sustained much earlier than TOD. Some months prior, some years. Remains Two's injury pattern is consistent with a pattern throughout childhood of physical abuse, beginning, we believe, with this broken tibia near the age of two."

Would the bone snap, Eve wondered, such a young bone? Hers had six more years of growth before Richard Troy snapped it like a thin twig.

"A comparative analysis of the skull sutures and epiphyseal fusion sets Remains One at thirteen years of age, Remains Two the same. I can give you their weight. One between ninety-five and a hundred pounds, two between one-oh-five and one-ten. Both, as stated on site, are female. Li?"

"We'll draw DNA from the bones and run that. It will take some time. Much less if we're able to get a facial match, and test blood relatives. We're also running a variety of tests that should help us determine COD, will give us some data on the health and nutrition of the victims, and may even give us the general area where they grew up."

"From the bones."

He smiled again. "I'm a flesh-and-blood man myself, but yes, a great deal of information can be gleaned from bones."

"Our age, our sex, how we moved, our facial structure, how we ate, and often what we did for a living. It's in the bones," DeWinter claimed. "Victim One led a healthier and less traumatic life than Two. Her single injury is most likely the result of a childhood accident. A fall from a bike, a tree limb. It's cleanly and well healed, and was surely professionally treated. Her teeth are straight and even, and were, again, professionally treated, most likely on a regular and routine basis, while Two's are crooked, contain four cavities.

"Though it's only based on best probability, I would say One grew up in a middle-class or above household, while Two lived nearer poverty level, or below."

"The toes." Morris gestured. "You see how they're slightly curled, slightly overlapped?"

"From shoving them into shoes that were too small."

DeWinter beamed at her. "Exactly! Poverty or neglect, and likely both."

"This is helpful, but I need faces. I need names. Cause of death."

"And you'll have them. Elsie may have something for us. Elsie Kendrick does our facial reconstruction, and will very likely be faster than the DNA extraction."

"Faster's what I'm after. Can you tell when they died—from the bones?"

"Yes, within a reasonable span. They've been working on determining the age of the wall, the materials, in Berenski's area."

Dick Berenski, Eve thought, known as Dickhead for a reason, would get the work done. It also occurred to her that he'd likely been sitting in a pool of drool since he'd gotten a load of DeWinter.

"Give me a range."

"Given the method and material used to wrap them, the variance in temperature inside the building seasonally, the—"

"Just a range," Eve repeated.

"There are factors," DeWinter insisted, just a little on the testy side. "My initial analyses indicate a range of fifteen to twenty years. Berenski's initial tests indicate twelve to fifteen."

"That's good enough. It's going to be on the low side of yours, the high side of his."

"We haven't yet determined—"

"It's what makes sense. The last tenants vacated fifteen years ago last September, and that opens opportunity. At least some of these vics are going to connect to that last tenant—a shelter for kids— runaways and wards of court. It's what fits."

"It does." Morris nodded. "You'll find, Garnet, Dallas excels at finding the fit."

"All well and good, and most certainly possible. But TOD is yet to be verified by the science."

"You go ahead and verify," Eve invited. "And if it's not right about fifteen years, let me know. Where's the reconstructionist?"

"I'll take you. I'm having more tables brought in," DeWinter continued as she started out. "I feel it will be helpful to have them all in one space as we continue the work."

She turned into the music. "Elsie! How can you think with this so loud?"

"It helps me think. Mute music." Elsie levered herself out of a chair, set the sketchbook and pencil she held aside. She wore her blue-streaked blond hair in dozens of thin braids that ended in tiny beads. She looked about sixteen in an ankle-skimming dress swirling with color, if you overlooked the fact that she was hugely pregnant.

"How are the twins?"

"Active." Elsie rubbed her belly the way Eve had observed pregnant women did.

"Sit."

"No, I've got to move around, too."

"But not overdo."

"Don't say overdue!"

"How far along are you?" Peabody asked.

"Oh, I'm sorry. Detective Peabody, Lieutenant Dallas, Elsie Kendrick."

"Welcome. I'm at thirty-three weeks, four days. I'm going to start counting hours soon. I feel like I'm carrying a couple of small, frisky ponies." She pressed a hand to the side of her belly. "Wow. With really strong hooves. It's taken me a while to get started, so sorry right off. Hormones, I guess. Reconstructing little girls. Mine are both girls. I had to have a little meltdown first."

"Children always hit harder," Morris said.

"Boy, don't they? I was just finishing the first sketch. I always do a sketch, kind of a tribute, after a reconstruct. Let me show you the first girl."

"Victim One?" Eve asked.

"Yeah, Garnet said to start in numerical." She moved to the holo-table, tapped buttons. I got a ninety-six and change probability on her, so this should be close. It'll be close enough for a match run."

The hologram shimmered on.

Slim face, deep gold skin, dark Asian eyes, a short wedge of straight dark hair, full lips, strong nose, softly curved chin.

A pretty girl, Eve thought, with the potential of true beauty that would never be realized.

"Her racial profile weighed more heavily Asian, so I went with the probability of straight hair. Her facial bones and structure were both fine and even. Excellent bones. I added the nose stud, as Garnet said you found one, but I can take it out."

"It doesn't matter. This is good, really good. We need a copy. We'll start running for a match."

"We're working on establishing TOD. It's tricky to get a real pin-point on that."

"Fifteen years—in that area," Eve said. "If you can narrow it more, it'll help, but we're reasonably sure of that. You said this one likely came from a solid middle-class or better." Eve turned to DeWinter. "Had good health, good medical care. So it's probable we'll find a Missing Persons on her. What about Two?"

"I have the basics started." Again, Elsie tapped buttons. "I'm going to want to work with it, adjust the data. But here's what I have so far."

The holo, much less refined here, showed a fuller face, slacker. Smaller eyes, Eve noted, thinner mouth. Not a particularly pretty girl, not at this point in any case. Pale skin, somewhat sallow, a broader nose.

"We'll do better than this with more time. I'll send you a copy of the final."

"Good. We'll take what you have for now, get started."

"This one was sad." Elsie laid her hands on her belly again. "You can just feel it. And she didn't have time to get happy again."

When Elsie's belly jerked, visibly, under her hand, Eve took a definite step back. Peabody took one in.

"Can I?"

"Sure." Elsie turned her enormous belly toward Peabody's reaching hands.

"Awww." The cooing sound matched the sappy look on Peabody's face.

"I know, right? They're going to settle down soon, running out of room in there. It's crazy considering how many times a day they punch or kick me, but I'm going to miss it."

"Have you got names?"

"Daddy and I are still arguing, but I'm pulling for Harmony and Haven."

"Pretty."

"Okay, well," Eve began.

"Oh, let me make you a copy of both holos, and I'll update the second image as I refine it. I can probably get a third started today," Elsie continued as she programmed copies. "And possibly complete three to four tomorrow. I hope to have all of them for you within three days. I just think of the parents, the not knowing. It has to be torture, even after so many years."

"I don't want you upsetting yourself, Elsie," DeWinter warned. "Adding stress to your life at this stage."

"It's not, not really. I feel like I'm doing something for them, bringing their faces back, and that leads to giving them their names back. They shouldn't be numbers. None of us should ever just be a number."

She handed Eve the disc.

"You do good work. I'll be in touch, Dr. DeWinter. See you later, Morris."

"I'll be back in my own house before the end of the day if you need me."

She headed down, worked her way back out of the maze. When they were clearly out of anyone's earshot, Peabody spoke up.

"They look good together."

Lost in thought, Eve frowned. "What? Who?"

"Morris and DeWinter?"

"What?" Eve repeated. "Get out."

"No, they do. I don't see that *hum* between them like he had with Detective Coltraine, I just meant on a kind of visual level. Both of them kind of exotic and artsy. I always wonder if McNab and I come close to looking good together," she went on, speaking of her main man and one of the Electronic Detectives Division's aces.

"I mean, I'm kinda short and—it's Be Kind to Myself Day, so I'll say zaftig."

"Zaftig?" Eve muscled her way out the door, strode toward her car. "What language is that?"

"It's fancy language for full-bodied. And McNab's all bony and beanpoley."

"You look right together, which is better than good."

Completely stunned, Peabody stopped in her tracks. "That's the totally, absolutely nicest thing you've ever said about me and McNab."

Eve just shrugged. "I've gotten used to you. Mostly. Get in the damn car."

With her cheeks flushed with pleasure, Peabody obeyed. "Do you really think we look right together?"

"You're stuck together at the erogenous zones every chance you get, so why wouldn't you? Now, just for the hell of it, maybe we can focus on solving twelve murders."

"The facial reconstructing is really going to help. Elsie is totally iced at it. Oooh, and twin baby girls. How adorable is that? You should've felt the . . ." Hunching at the hard gleam in Eve's eyes, Peabody yanked out her PPC. "I'll start the search for the first reconstruction now."

"Really? What a fine idea. I don't know why I didn't think of that."

Wisely Peabody said nothing until she had the search under way. "Where are we heading?"

"To talk to the handyman. I want a sense of him, and I want to run down this helper type the matron had that *feeling* about. Then maybe we can run down Brigham and her grandmother. We're going to need to run all the staff at Higher Power, have a chat with anybody who overlaps with the other building. We can't—"

"Holy shit! Holy shit, Dallas! I've got her. I've already got a hit."

"Vic One?"

"I've got her. Look—wait—I'll put it up on the dash screen."

And there she was, Eve thought. The dark, almond-shaped eyes, the curve of chin, the full lips, the ebony hair glossed to a sheen. Not a wedge, but a long fall.

A professional and posed shot, Eve decided. A studio photo taken for official ID where the thirteen-year-old Linh Carol Penbroke stared soberly—with a touch of defiance—at the camera.

Missing since September twelfth, 2045.

The report gave her height, which matched Victim One, and a weight of ninety-seven pounds—so DeWinter hit on that as well, Eve calculated. Small girl, petite frame, pretty face with those glimmers of unrealized beauty.

"It lists both parents," Peabody said. "Two older sibs, one male, one female, and a Park Slope address. Affluent."

"Run it. See if the parents, or either of them, have the same address or another one."

"Searching now. Same address, for both of them."

Eve made the next turn, then the next, and headed toward Brooklyn.

"We're going to do a notification."

"I think they've waited long enough," Eve answered. "And I think they'll give us DNA samples. Like Morris said, we'll verify quicker with a parental swab to compare."

"Yeah. I've never done a notification on a long-term missing. Have you?"

"A couple of them. They're no easier."

"I didn't think so. Both parents are doctors. She's an OB, he's a pediatrician. They have a joint practice; it's attached to the home," Peabody read, "which I guess makes sense. Two sibs. The brother's also a doctor. Cardiologist, also in Brooklyn. The sister's a musician, first violin for the New York Symphony. I'm not finding any dings here on the criminal side. Finances are—whoa—doctors make a sweet living. They also have homes in Trinidad and the Hamptons. First and only marriage for each, into the thirty-fifth year.

"Everything says affluent, stable, and successful."

"If you don't count the dead daughter."

"Yeah." Peabody blew out a breath. "If you don't count that."

The house said affluent, stable, and successful as well. It took up a corner of a line of old and elegant townhomes. Eve assumed the Penbrokes had expanded the property at some point, incorporating the neighboring house into one large unit to accommodate two professionals and three children.

She spotted a Christmas tree in the tall trio of front windows, gave a fleeting thought to the fact Thanksgiving was in the rearview mirror, and they were barreling straight into the next holiday.

Shit. She had to shop.

With Peabody, she took the tidy brick steps to the front door, pressed the bell.

Seconds later, the door opened.

"Frank, I didn't mean you had to— Oh, sorry, I thought you were my neighbor."

The man wore cutoff sweats, a tank, and a gleaming layer of sweat over a pretty impressive build. Eyes a few shades darker than his skin skipped from Eve to Peabody, then back again, as he shot forked fingers through his close-cropped hair.

"Can I help you with something?"

"Samuel Penbroke?" Eve asked.

"Yeah. Sorry, I just finished a workout." He used the towel slung around his neck to swipe at his cheek.

"I'm Lieutenant Dallas, and this is Detective Peabody." Eve drew out her badge. "NYPSD. Can we come in, Dr. Penbroke?"

She saw it, the change on his face, in his eyes. From polite curiosity to a terrible blend of hope and grief.

"Linh? Is it Linh?"

"It would be easier if we came inside."

The hope died as he took an unsteady step back. "She's dead."

Eve stepped in to a wide, welcoming foyer scented by the bold red lilies on a stand. Peabody closed the door.

"We have some information, and some questions. Can we go in, sit down?"

"Please just tell me, is it Linh?"

"Yes, sir, we're here about Linh."

"My wife—" He had to stop like a man catching his breath. "She's still in the gym. I need you—she should . . ." He walked slowly to a house intercom. "Tien. Tien, there are people here to see us. You need to come."

It took a moment, then two, before a female voice, quietly annoyed, responded. "Sam, I haven't done my meditation. Ten minutes, and—"

He cut her off. "Please come out now." He turned toward the right where the big, sparkling tree stood in front of the windows. "Please, this way. We'll sit down. My wife—that is—it's our day off. We take a day off together."

He glanced toward a grand piano, and the family photos arranged on it. Among them stood the one of Linh they'd used for the Missing Persons report.

"My family," he began, and Peabody took his arm to guide him to an oversized chair.

"You have a lovely family, Dr. Penbroke. Are those your grand-children?"

"Yes. We have two grandchildren. A boy, he's four, and the baby is just two."

"They must be excited about Christmas."

"They are very excited. They . . . Tien."

She was petite, like her daughter, and trim, but with a wiry tough-ness Eve recognized.

She wore the wedge cut Elsie had imagined for Linh. Her eyes, a strong green that made a compelling contrast with the golden skin, still carried that quiet annoyance though she smiled politely as she came into the room.

"I'm sorry. We were using our gym. We're barely fit for company."

"Tien. They're police."

It came again, that flipped-switch change. Tien reached for her husband's hand. "Linh. You found her. You found our daughter."

"I'm sorry to inform you," Eve began.

"No." And here, in a mother's voice, a mother's face, the grief after fifteen years was as fresh as it might have been at fifteen seconds. "No."

"Here, Tien. Here." Samuel simply drew his wife down, into the big chair with him, hugged her. "You're going to tell us our illusions are finished, that the hope we've clung to all this time is gone. That our little girl is never coming back to us."

There was no easy way, and a fast and clean cut was best.

"Dr. Penbroke, we discovered several remains of females between the ages of twelve and sixteen. We believe we've identified one of them as your daughter."

"Remains," Tien echoed.

"Yes, ma'am. I'm very sorry. You could help us confirm her identity. Did your daughter have any childhood injuries? Did she break any bones?"

"She fell," Samuel said. "Airboarding in the park. A bad fall. She broke her arm, just above the elbow." He clutched his own. "She was eleven."

"Peabody."

At Eve's unspoken order, Peabody drew the hard copy of the reconstruction from her file bag. "We were able to approximate her face."

Samuel reached out, took the picture. "Linh" was all he said.

"It's my baby. It's our baby, Sam. But the hair's wrong. She had long hair, beautiful long hair. And . . . and her nose, the tip of her nose turned up just a tiny bit. She had a little beauty mark at the top right corner of her mouth."

"Tien."

"It should be right!" Tears fell in silent rivers down her face, but she pushed on. "It should be right. She was very proud of her hair!"

"We'll see that it's right," Eve told her. "We'll make it right."

"Twelve, there were twelve," Samuel murmured. "I heard, this morning, in the city you found twelve. She was one of them?"

"Yes."

"When? How? When did she die? How did she die? Who did this to her?"

"I can promise you, both of you, we're doing everything possible to find out. I can tell you that at this time, we believe she died about fifteen years ago."

"All the time." Tien turned her head, pressed her face to her husband's shoulder. "All the time we looked, and prayed and waited. She was gone."

"This is very hard, I know," Eve continued. "Can you tell us why she left home, what happened?"

"She was very angry. Young girls have an angry time, a time they're unhappy and rebellious. She wanted a tattoo, wanted to pierce her eyebrow, wanted to go with boys, not do her schoolwork or chores. We let her have the little nose stud—a compromise—but she wanted more. It's a time, a phase many go through," Tien said, with a plea in her voice. "They grow out of it."

"She wanted to go to a concert," Samuel explained. "We said no, as she'd skipped her classes, twice. And had behaved poorly at home. She said we were unfair, and hard things were said by all. We restricted her from her electronics as discipline. It was difficult, but . . ."

"It was normal," Peabody put in.

"Yes. Yes." Tien managed a smile through the rain of tears. "Her brother and sister had both had this stage. Not as dramatic as Linh, but she was always more passionate. And she was the youngest. Perhaps we indulged her more."

"On the morning of September twelfth," Samuel continued, "she didn't come down for breakfast. We thought she was sulking. I sent her sister upstairs to get her. Hoa came down, told us Linh wasn't upstairs, that some of her things were gone, and her backpack."

"First we searched the house, then called friends, neighbors. Then the police."

"Did she have friends in the city?" Eve asked. "In Manhattan?"

"Her friends were here, but she liked to go to the city. She loved it." Tien paused to compose herself again. "The police looked, and we hired a private investigator. We went on screen, offered rewards. They found, finally, she'd taken the subway into the city, but they couldn't find her."

"She never contacted you, or any of her friends?"

"No." Tien wiped at the tears. "She didn't take her 'link. She's a very smart girl. She knew we had a parental tracer on it, so we'd know where she was. She didn't want us to know."

"She would have bought another," Samuel said. "She had money. She had five hundred dollars. Her sister told us, when it became clear Linh had run away, that Linh had saved money and hidden it in her room, made her sister swear not to tell. We were glad she had money, glad she had enough to pay for food. And we thought . . . we thought . . . she'd come home."

"But she didn't. She never came home."

"We'll bring her home now." Samuel pressed his lips to his wife's hair. "We'll bring our baby home now, Tien. We need to see her."

"Dr. Penbroke—"

"We're doctors," he said. "We understand what happens to the body. We understand you'd only have her bones. But we need to see her."

"I'll try to arrange it. We're working to identify her, and the others. If we could take DNA samples from you, it would quicken the process for Linh."

"Yes. They're on record," Tien explained. "But take fresh ones so there can be no mistake. Did someone hurt her?"

Navigate carefully, Eve warned herself. "I think someone kept her from coming home to you. We're working to find out who. I can promise you we'll do our best for her, for all of them."

She glanced at Peabody again, and her partner took two DNA kits from her bag.

"Just a few more questions," Eve began as Peabody rose to get the samples.

5 "TAKE THE SAMPLES TO DeWINTER," EVE told Peabody when they left the Penbrokes. "Let's get this confirmed asap. And give the reconstructionist the long hair, the beauty mark, the bit about the nose. Let's make it right."

"I will. We will."

"If there's a completed reconstruction of the next vic, make sure I get that. Take a good, hard look at the Missing Persons report and investigative notes. If there's a hole, we're going to plug it. So contact the detective who headed it up, have a talk."

"Okay."

"I'll take the handyman and the donor, her granddaughter. If you finish what I'm giving you, do a run on this Jubal Craine, and get me anything you find. We do an immediate search for match on every face as it comes to us. Whatever you find, I know about it when you do."

"Same goes."

"Same goes," Eve agreed, then looked back at the house. "She had a good family, from the way it looks. A well-off one, but a normal one. Rules, chores, responsibilities, an airboard, a sister who'd keep a secret."

"I think she'd have passed through the phase where everything her parents said, wanted, expected was—or seemed to be—exactly the opposite of frosty. And you really want to be frosty at that age."

"She made a mistake—I'll show them I can do what I want when I want. I'm not a kid, they can't boss me around—and she never got a chance to fix it. That's how it feels."

"But you're going to dig down into the Penbrokes anyway."

"They loved their kid, and never hurt her. But . . . you talk to the detective who caught the case, and I'll poke a little deeper. It's better to be sure."

She dumped Peabody two blocks from the lab, continued on—then considered.

She used the in-dash 'link to contact Roarke.

He answered, and quickly. "Lieutenant."

As she'd suspected, whatever meeting he might be in, whatever meetings he might have next, his mind—like hers—was focused on the girls.

"I appreciate the data you've been feeding to us. We're using it. Wanted to update you. We think—hell, I'm sure—we've ID'd the first victim."

"What was her name?"

He would ask that, first. He would want to put the name in his memory. "Linh—that's L-i-n-h—Penbroke. The probability it's her is very high. I've just come from notifying her parents, and getting DNA samples so we can confirm. But—"

"As you said, you're already sure."

"Yeah, I am. I'm heading north now to talk to a potential wit/suspect. I've got Peabody on other angles, so if you're interested in standing in, have the time—"

"Give me the address. I'll meet you."

She beat Roarke there, but opted not to wait. Instead she used her master to buzz her way into a sturdy four-level building, veered past the gate of the elevator, and took the stairs up to the third floor, southwest corner unit.

And knocked.

When the door opened, Eve adjusted her eyeline down.

The kid—male—was in the neighborhood of ten, she calculated, and boasted a solar system of freckles over his round face—and some sort of purple goo at the corners of his mouth.

"I don't know you," he said, firmly, and started to close the door.

Eve stuck her foot in, which resulted in causing the kid to holler, top of impressive lungs: "Mom! Mom! Some lady's breaking in!"

"I'm not a lady. See?" Eve jerked out her badge as running footsteps pounded from the upper level of what she saw was a spacious loft-style that took up two floors.

"Mom! There's a police lady!"

"Trilby, get back!" The woman, blond ponytail, carpenter pants, plaid work shirt, nudged the kid away as she glanced at Eve's badge. "Go wash your face, for God's sake, Trilby, you've got grape jelly everywhere. And go finish your homework. Leave your sister alone."

"Jeez! I gotta do *everything*!"

"Yeah, your life stinks. Sorry," she said to Eve as the boy sulked away. "Can I help you?"

"I need to talk to Brodie Fine."

"We just got in, and he beat me to the shower." She glanced around to check on her son, lowered her voice. "Is this about the building on Ninth? The bodies? We heard on the news," she said when Eve said nothing. "Brodie and I were sort of half-ass dating when he did handiwork there. We've been talking about it most of the day. I'm one of his carpenters," she explained. "And his wife. And the mother of his children."

"I'd still like to talk to him."

"Sure. Sorry. I don't mean to keep you out in the hall. You can—" She paused as Roarke walked up to Eve.

"My consultant," Eve explained.

"Nice. If you don't mind me saying. Come on in. I'd rather talk about this when the kids aren't around, but what's the point? Kids hear everything anyway. I was just about to have a beer. You want?"

"I wouldn't mind one," Roarke said, sliding into the ambiance of the homey loft the way Eve imagined he slid into a boardroom.

"Civilian consultant," he reminded Eve. "She won't have one, being a cop on duty. You've a lovely space here—is it Mrs. Fine?"

"Yeah, I went traditional, but you can call me Alma. Brodie and I did the place ourselves. It's taken us six years so far, but it's coming along."

"Beautiful workmanship." Roarke ran his fingers down some beaded trim. "It's chestnut, isn't it?"

"You know your wood." She studied him. "My grandpa had a farm down in Virginia. Had a bunch of chestnut, so we stockpiled it, me and Brodie, cleaned it up, planed it down. Worth the work, we figure. Not many opportunities to work with real wood. Sure is a pleasure."

"I imagine so."

"Have a seat. I'll get the beer. You want something else?" she asked Eve. "I've got water, sure, but I can make coffee, or I got some Coke stashed away—hidden from the kids."

"Actually, a Coke would be great."

"You got it."

Eve glanced around. Roarke had it right: It was an impressive space. Family-with-kids messy maybe, but that added to it. They'd fashioned an open floor plan, using clever placements of counters or breakfronts to define living area from dining, dining from kitchen, and all of it from a play area.

A second floor circled three sides, again open with a decorative rail that looked sturdy, and was formed with pickets too close together to allow even a small head to shove through.

Lots of wood against lots of color, she noted, and all accented by big windows that would let in plenty of light.

Anyone who could do this kind of work, she thought, could certainly build some false walls that blended in without a seam out of place.

"Mom! Trilby's in my face!"

"Trilby, what did I tell you?"

"I'm not doing nothing to her!"

"You're not doing *anything* to her," Alma corrected as she brought out the drinks. "And don't, or there'll be no *Max Adventure* on screen tonight for either of you."

This time there came a stereo: "Mom!"

"I mean it. Sorry."

"No problem," Eve told her. "Your husband?"

"Sure, I'll go up and tell him to put some clothes on. Just give me a minute."

"What's all the racket?" The man's voice boomed, but didn't sound threatening. It sounded amused. "No *Max Adventure* tonight?"

"Dad!" More stereo.

"Better straighten up, or we'll never know what happens to Max and Luki on Planet Crohn. Hey, babe, can you . . . Hey, sorry." He stopped at the landing as he looked down, spotted Eve and Roarke. "Didn't know we had company."

"It's cops, Brodie."

His easy smile faded as he nodded and started down.

His hair, a curly brown mop, still dripped a little from the shower. He wore jeans, a long-sleeve brown tee, and thick socks.

"I wondered if you'd come by. Alma and I talked about if we should go in, offer to give a statement. We were going to talk about it more after the kids go down tonight. It wasn't a mistake? The media report?"

"No, it wasn't."

"I'll get you a beer." Alma brushed her hand down his arm.

"Thanks. I guess we should all sit down."

"I'm Lieutenant Dallas," Eve began. "Primary on this matter. This is my consultant."

"Roarke. I recognized you," Brodie said. "I've done a little work on a few of your places."

"Have you now?"

"Yeah, here and there."

"If your work for me is as fine as the work you've done for yourself here, I'm sure I'm very pleased with it."

"Well, you paid well, and on time. Can't say the same for everybody."

"What kind of work did you do in the building on Ninth, for The Sanctuary?" Eve asked him.

"Mostly slap and patch." He pushed at the damp mop of hair in what looked to be an absent habit. "They couldn't afford much, and I gave them the best break I could, seeing as what they were trying to do for the kids. I was trying to start my own business, just getting it going, so what I did for them was mostly on my own time, on my own."

"Did you build any walls?"

"No. Patched a couple."

Alma came back, sat on the arm of his chair, handed him a beer.

"Painted a few, but I didn't charge for that. Mostly they painted themselves, save the cost, you know? I did what I could with the plumbing. Rewired some stuff. I'm going to tell you I wasn't licensed to do the plumbing and electrical back then, but they couldn't afford someone who was. And I knew what I was doing."

"He can do anything," Alma said. "God's truth."

"So can you, that's why I married you."

"I'm not worried about code violations or licenses," Eve told them. "When's the last time you were in the building?"

"Oh, man, let me think." His hand went to his hair again. "It was right after they got the new one, and were still moving stuff out. They asked me to do a walk-through, just see if there was anything in there that would get them in dutch once the bank came through. I patched a couple more things, just in case. Alma was with me. Remember? We were dating."

"Half-ass dating."

"I got you, didn't I? Anyway, that was it. I started doing handiwork on the building they're in now. Sweet property that one. Good shape, solid bones. Nothing like that poor old dump. Somebody ought to gut it out, take it down to the bones and save it. I'd do it myself if I could. It's a damn shame to see it just die the way it is."

"But you said you haven't been in it recently?"

"Haven't, but I've seen it from the outside. We did a job in that area about six months ago. Heartbreaking, if you ask me, and just plain wrong. Boarded windows, all broken up, tagged all over. Roof probably won't last another year from the look of it. Anyway, not my business."

"If Brodie had the scratch," his wife said, "he'd save all the buildings in all the world."

"We'd start with New York."

"You had a helper at some point, who did some work with you on the building."

"Oh, yeah. Clip," he said to his wife who expressed her opinion by casting her eyes to the ceiling. "Jon Clipperton. I toss him work now and then, but I don't keep him on the crew."

"Because?"

"He's a good worker, when he's sober. Even when he's half sober."

"Which is the second Tuesday of every other month," Alma put in.

"He's not that bad. But close," Brodie admitted. "I used him more when I was first getting started. The drinking wasn't as bad, and I couldn't afford much better. But he only worked for me at The Sanctuary two or three times. Because . . ." he said when Eve just looked at him. "Well, because he showed up a little less than half sober and . . ." Brodie shifted as if he'd sat on a pile of rocks. "Well, he could be kind of a dick when he'd had a few."

"Brodie, he's a dick when he breathes. He's a total asshole when he's had a few."

"You stopped taking him to work at The Sanctuary because he came to work drunk, and acted like a dick. Why don't you describe the dickishness?"

Brodie winced at Eve. "It's just, you know, a couple of guys on a job might make some comment about a good-looking woman walking by. Maybe you could say a sort of crude comment sometimes."

"Please." Alma punched him in the shoulder, laughed. "We all do it. Depending which side of the fence you're on, some icy type comes in view, you remark." She shrugged. "Time-honored tradition of the trade."

"Yeah, well, the thing is, Clip remarked, but we're talking kids, you know? Okay, we were younger then, but old enough not to make . . . remarks about girls that age. I told him to knock it off. It was, you know, inappropriate. He mostly did, but I'd catch him giving them looks, or talking to some of them a little too . . . close, I guess, when he was supposed to be on break. It just didn't sit right with me, so I pulled him off there, gave him some other work."

"What kind of remarks?"

"I don't remember exactly, honest to God," he told Eve. "I just remember I didn't like it, and didn't like the idea he was sort of hitting on teenagers."

"He hit on me," Alma announced, and had her husband's jaw dropping.

"What? What? When?"

"Back then a couple times, a couple times since."

"Son of a bitch."

"You think I can't handle myself, babe?"

"No, you can handle yourself. But—son of a bitch."

"He was always pissed-faced drunk. Hell, he hit on Lydia. She's eighty-three," Alma explained. "She does our books. He's a dog, no question, and I can see him trying to cop a feel as long as it's female. Age not an issue. But I can't see him hurting anybody. Ever."

"No, no, he'd never hurt anybody. He's an asshole, but—cop a feel? Did he try that on you?"

"Remember that mouse he was sporting after the Fourth of July cookout about six, seven years back? Who do you think popped him?"

This time both hands went to his hair. "Alma, jeez! Why don't you *tell* me this stuff?"

"Because then you'd've popped him, and I already had. And it was the last time he tried to mess with me. He apologized when he sobered up. What I'm saying, Lieutenant, is say you're sitting at a bar, waiting for somebody or just trying to have a quiet drink. He's the type who'd be all over you, thinking he's witty-like or sexy or whatever, when what he is? Drunk and stupid and annoying. But he's not the type who'd follow you out of the bar and get physical or get riled up and start something when you tell him to blow. You know what I'm saying?"

"Yeah, but I want to talk to him. I'd appreciate his contact information."

"Sure. Yeah. Crap." Brodie boosted up a hip, pulled out his pocket 'link, then read off the data. "Right now I want to punch him in the face, but I have to say, he'd never do anything like this. He wouldn't have done anything to those girls. I mean, yeah, he might've gotten drunk enough back then to try for some touch, but he wouldn't have killed anybody."

"Okay. Did you ever see anyone come around, or notice anyone who worked there who gave you a bad feeling?"

"I can't say I did, or remember. I was juggling a lot of small jobs back then, trying to get a good toehold. It wasn't like I was there every day or anything. Sometimes I'd be there a few days running, but mostly it was spotty. They'd call me in for some little thing they couldn't fix, or to fix something they'd tried to fix and screwed up more than it was screwed up to begin with. I got more work out of it—doing stuff for some of the staff, doing stuff for people Nash and Philly recommended me to."

"Impressions, on any of the staff, including Nash and Philly."

"They were doing good work, still are, and it takes a lot of doing from what I can see. There's no clocking in and out."

"One more thing." Eve brought Linh's image on screen. "Does she look familiar?"

"Wow, really pretty kid. No." He glanced over at his wife, who shook her head. "Is she one of the . . ."

"She is."

"God." He scrubbed his hands over his face, angled, took another, longer look. "She doesn't ring any bells. I don't know if I'd remember after all this time, but she's got a really distinctive face, you know? A stunner waiting to happen."

"We appreciate the time." Eve pushed to her feet. "If anything comes to mind, contact me."

"I will—we will," Brodie assured her. "I hate thinking about those girls."

Eve figured she'd be doing little else but thinking about them, especially when the second reconstruction came through as they left the apartment building.

"Got another face."

Roarke looked at her screen, studied the thin-cheeked, sad-eyed image. "Would you like me to run a search?"

"Peabody's doing it on the preliminary we got earlier, now she'll run it on this. But hold on. Wait here, I'll be right back."

She dashed back into the building, left him on the sidewalk. To pass the time, he took out his PPC, did some research of his own.

She was back inside five minutes.

"He recognized this one. He seemed pretty confident, even added an eyebrow hoop they didn't have on the image. And said she had crazy hair—purple, pink, and green. She had tats—full sleeves—and he figured her for no more than about twelve or thirteen tops. He remembers all this because he was working right there when she jumped one of the other kids. He doesn't remember why, just that it took several members of the staff to yank them apart."

"Which tells you she was in the building, as a resident, had at least one physical altercation, and from the description wasn't the quiet, retiring type."

"You can't get tats at that age without a legal guardian signing off, showing ID, and being in attendance. Her remains indicate she'd been knocked around regularly so I don't see her legal guardian taking the time to do something that stupid with her. And that tells me she was likely on the street awhile, had connections. Maybe she'd been picked up a few times. We'll get her ID'd. We'll have her name."

"Are we off to talk to the rarely sober asshole while Peabody finds her?"

"Not yet. I'll get to him, but whoever did this probably wasn't drunk. Probably *isn't* a drunk as they tend to mouth off and make stupid mistakes, like hit on the boss's wife."

"Some bosses' wives," Roarke said, tapping the dent in her chin with his finger, "handle themselves."

"Yeah. Anytime one of your half a zillion employees puts a move on me, I'll deck him. Don't worry."

"Not a worry in the world, about that."

"Right now, I'm more interested in a former resident, current staff member, and granddaughter of the woman who donated the new building. Seraphim Brigham, granddaughter of Tiffany Brigham Bittmore."

"I know of Tiffany Bittmore." As she didn't want him running a search, Roarke walked around her car to the driver's seat. "Philanthropist, with particular interests in children and addictions. She worked as a general dogsbody for a political activist organization where she met and married Brigham when they were quite young I believe. Early twenties, and had two children with him before his death—a shuttle crash some fifteen or so years later. He was wealthy—family money—and political with a strong liberal leaning."

He slid into a stream of north-bound traffic as he spoke.

"She married again some years after his death. The Bittmores were even wealthier. They had two more children—I believe—before he was killed during an earthquake in Indonesia, where he'd gone as an ambassador for a global health organization."

"That's knowing a lot about."

"I supplemented my knowledge since this morning. She's known for being generous with her time, money, and influence when the cause speaks to her. She lost a son—that would be this granddaughter's father—to an overdose. Apparently his daughter was determined to follow in his footsteps before ending up at The Sanctuary. Bittmore showed her appreciation with the donation of the building and a trust for operating funds."

"And now Seraphim works for Jones and Jones."

"And is a respected therapist with a solid reputation. And is recently engaged."

"Huh. I'm just thinking I have to make sure my next husband's a rich bastard, too. But I'm not sure I can snap a richer bastard than you. The pool's pretty shallow."

"Maybe it'll be deeper in eighty or ninety years."

"Well, that's something to consider. How do you know where we're going?"

"You said you wanted to interview Seraphim Brigham. Anticipating that when you tagged me, I tugged a few lines and learned she's scheduled for drinks and dinner at her grandmother's home—her New York home. Not so far, really, from ours."

"I've said it before, but I'll say it again. You can be handy."

He shot her a glance. "You should also consider your richer bastard, should you fish one out of the pool, needs to understand cop brains, and have the right connections."

"Those are going on my list." She shot him a glance in return. "Would you go for another cop in eighty or ninety years?"

"Absolutely not. The next time I'm after a nice, quiet woman, perhaps one who does watercolors and bakes scones."

"My richer bastard bakes pies. I like pie."

"I like pie, too. I'd like to meet him."

"Wait a few decades. What's he been doing for fifteen years?"

She wasn't thinking of her fictional richer bastard now, Roarke mused. How her thought process fascinated.

"How did he stop killing? Did he? Did he find another way to dispose of the bodies? Did he die, end up in a cage, find God? He killed twelve. Probably within a few weeks or months. You don't just stop cold. I keep asking myself, where is he? What's he doing? I did a run on like crimes, and sure, you get a couple pops here and there for girls in that range, for the plastic wrap and other elements. But none that fit this, not this. Multiples, the time and effort to hide them, the lack of violence. How the hell did he kill them?"

"I think you need to give DeWinter a bit of time there."

"Yeah, yeah. She and Morris have their heads together on it."

Frustrated, Roarke concluded, that she didn't have the data, couldn't start using it to narrow her track toward the killer.

"We notified the parents of the first vic we ID'd. Solid upper middle-class—upper-upper. Both doctors, long-term first marriage, two other offspring—grown now. Nice home, stable, affluent. No signs of abuse on the remains, and every sign the victim had been well cared for, medically, physically."

"Was she abducted?"

"No. At least not from home. Got pissy about a concert. Was going through a pissy stage, which apparently is pretty normal. Took off for the city—from Brooklyn—had money, so my best guess is she lived it up for a couple days, tried the walk on the wild side, liked it fine. She wasn't like the girl he wrapped up with her though. If she'd stayed clean, she wouldn't have stayed on that path. She'd have gone home. The other one? The last place she'd have gone was home because that's where they hurt you."

Roarke simply covered her hand with his. It's all he had to do.

"It's not like me," Eve murmured. "There was never a home in the first place, and maybe that was an advantage. I didn't expect someone to look out for me. And I didn't know, until he was dead, I could run. Even after, I didn't manage to run far. Running's what killed her, or put her on the path to being a victim."

She yanked her 'link when it signaled, read the text from Peabody.

"Shelby Ann Stubacker. She's got a name now."

"Tell me about her."

"She was thirteen. Father's doing a dime in Sing-Sing—his second for assault. Mother's got a sheet, mostly for illegals. They didn't file a report, so we wouldn't have found her there. She was picked up a few times. Truancy, shoplifting, did some juvie time, and some court-ordered rehab as she was picked up stoned, and in possession of illegals. She was nine the first time she got busted. Born here, died here. She'd have a file with CPS, but what's the point. The system failed her, everybody failed her."

"You won't."

Roarke pulled up in front of a gold-trimmed white building with seas of glass sparkling. Considering the low-end look of the vehicle, it wasn't a surprise to Eve to see the doorman's chin jut up, his mouth tighten, and his feet beat across the royal blue carpeting that stretched from sparkling glass door to curb.

Now, she thought, Roarke would get a load of what she put up with. Looking forward to it, she squeezed her way out on the street side.

The minute Roarke stepped out on the sidewalk, the doorman went from protective terrier to welcoming hound.

"Sir! Are you visiting someone at The Metropolitan this evening?"

"As it happens, I'm accompanying Lieutenant Dallas inside. I'm sure she'll appreciate you keeping her vehicle in place until she's completed her business."

"I'll see to it personally. Can I notify anyone for you?"

"If you'd let Ms. Bittmore know Lieutenant Dallas is here to see her on NYPSD business."

"I'll let her know. You'll want the first bank of elevators, on the left side of the lobby. Mr. Bittmore's main entrance is on the fifty-third floor, number fifty-three hundred."

"Thank you."

Eve scowled her way inside. "How much did you slip him?"

"A fifty."

"I don't bribe doormen," she said with some righteousness.

"No, darling, you reduce them to quivering puddles of fear and awe, but this seemed quicker and cleaner."

"He recognized you anyway. I saw it. You don't own the damn place, do you?"

"I don't, no." He glanced around the spacious gold and white lobby, turned to the elevators. "Pity. It's quite nice."

"Next time I want the quivering and the awe."

He let her step in the elevator first, so he could give her a light pat on the ass. "Next time."

**6** A HOUSE DROID MET THEM AT THE DOOR OF an elegant little foyer with a lush grape arbor, complete with rustic stone benches, cleverly painted on its walls and ceiling. The droid, sober in a simple gray dress and low heels, requested identification.

Eve held out her badge, watched the droid scan it.

"Please come in. Mrs. Bittmore and Ms. Brigham are in the living area."

The area couldn't be called spacious, but it hit those elegant notes again with the play of light-colored fabrics against walls the color of good burgundy. Art leaned toward the old world with classy depictions of misty forests, quiet lakes, blooming meadows.

Two women rose from a wheat-colored love seat backed by a pair of glass doors and a short terrace—then the view of the great park.

The older one stepped forward. Tiffany Bittmore had allowed her hair to go white, but Eve decided the decision had elements of vanity as the perfect sweep of it resulted in the same sort of classy elegance as the decor.

Her eyes might have been a dreamy shade of blue, but they held a sharp shrewdness. Her face, dewy and smooth despite her years, wouldn't have been called beautiful, but arresting.

The curve of her lips did nothing to soften the stiletto blades of her cheekbones.

"Lieutenant Dallas, it's a pleasure to meet you. And, Roarke, another pleasure. Your reputations and deeds precede you."

"As do yours," Roarke returned, with a charm he could wear like a silk tie. "It's truly an honor, Mrs. Bittmore."

"The gods gifted you with looks designed to stop women's hearts. I'd have drooled over this one," she told Eve, "back in my day."

"I've learned to step around the puddles."

With a laugh, Mrs. Bittmore gave Eve a friendly slap on the arm. "I think I'll like you. Come meet the light of my life, then we'll have some coffee. I've read *The Icove Agenda* and seen the vid, which I rarely do, so I know you've a fondness for real coffee. Clarissa?"

"Yes, ma'am, I'll see to it right away." The droid eased out of the room.

"My granddaughter, Seraphim."

"It is a pleasure. It would be more of one, I'm sure, if we hadn't heard the media bulletin." She offered her hand, a woman with her grandmother's eyes in a softer, less dramatic face. "I contacted HPCCY when we did, and spoke briefly with Philadelphia. She told me you'd been in to see her, and Nash."

"You work at HPCCY, and were a resident of The Sanctuary," Eve began.

"Please, let's sit." Mrs. Bittmore gestured to chairs. "This is a horrible thing, and it's distressing for Seraphim."

"I might've known some of them," Seraphim said before she lowered to the love seat. "I almost certainly had to know some of them. The report didn't give any names."

"They didn't have any to give." Eve debated a moment, which angle to play first. She took out her 'link, brought up one of the ID photos. "Is she familiar?"

"Oh Lord." Seraphim took a deep breath, then reached for the 'link, and the photo of Linh Penbroke. "It was years ago, but I think I'd remember her. She's so pretty. I don't. I don't think I've ever seen this girl before. But I lived in The Sanctuary for months. So many came and went . . . Still, I think I'd remember this face."

"Okay." Eve took back the 'link, brought up the second image. "How about her?"

"Oh! It's Shelby. Yes, I remember this girl. Shelby . . . I don't know if I knew her last name. She was in residence with me. A year or so younger, I think, but years tougher. She scored me zoner. Sorry, Gamma," she added with a glance toward her grandmother.

"It was long ago."

"The first few weeks I was there, I was really only looking for a place to sleep. I didn't have any intention of getting clean, or changing my attitude, just paid lip service to all that."

"You were so angry," her grandmother added.

"Oh, I was *pissed* at everyone and everything." She gave a soft, almost wondering laugh, kissed Tiffany's cheek. "Especially you because you just wouldn't give up on me."

"Never."

"So I went to the sessions, did the assignments—because I got a bed and food out of it. I figured they—the Joneses—were suckers, and I snuck illegals, alcohol, whatever I could when I wanted. But it wasn't as easy as I'd assumed, because they weren't suckers. I traded a beaded bracelet I had for the zoner. Everybody knew Shelby could get whatever you wanted, smuggle it in, if you gave her something she liked, and a little time."

Seraphim paused when the droid brought in the coffee, and left just as quietly as she'd come.

"The staff didn't know?" Eve asked Seraphim.

"She was very clever. No, *canny*'s a better word. Shelby was very canny. She got caught for minor things a time or two—and looking back, looking back not only as an adult but as a therapist, she very likely let herself get caught. Minor things were expected, and the punishments easy to get through. We outnumbered the staff probably ten to one easily back then. They were doing what they could to keep us safe, off the streets, out of sex trades, to help us. But to us, a lot of us? They were just marks."

"What about a carpenter's helper? Jon Clipperton."

"I don't remember his name, and may not have known it, but I remember the man Brodie brought with him a few times, in those last weeks we were in that building. Some men look at you," she said to Eve, "and you know they're seeing you naked. Sometimes that's okay, you're seeing them naked, too. And other times it's insulting. Or it's worse. I was young, but I'd been on the street awhile. I knew the way he looked at me and some of the other girls. And it wasn't okay."

"Did he do more than look?"

"I don't know. I think he got some beer to Shelby, but she never said. We weren't tight. I was, to her, an occasional customer. How did they die?"

"I can't answer that yet. Did you ever go back inside that building after you'd changed locations?"

"No. I never wanted to go back there. I changed, before the move. Things changed for me, a transition. The talk therapy I paid lip service to so I'd get that bed, food, it began to get through, even though I resisted. Philadelphia worked with me one-on-one—whether I wanted her to or not and despite the blocks I put up, she began to get through the anger and self-hatred. She finally convinced me to speak to Gamma—my grandmother."

"And you donated a building, and funds to the Joneses."

"I did," Mrs. Bittmore confirmed. "I can't say they saved Seraphim's life, but they helped her come home, they helped her discover who she really was."

Tiffany patted Seraphim's knee as she sipped her coffee. "They were doing their work in an inadequate space in a subpar building, and couldn't afford the loan on that building much less proper maintenance, repair, the right staff. They'd given Seraphim a chance. I gave them one."

"Ms. Brigham, you said Clipperton gave you a bad feeling. Was there anyone else who gave you that kind of feeling, or made you uneasy?"

"Some of the boys who came and went. You'd learn who to avoid. Lieutenant, we were a house of addicts and emotionally damaged children. Some of us, as I was for a time, were just looking for a free ride and a way to score. If the staff found illegals, alcohol, or weapons, they were confiscated. No one was ever asked to leave, not while I was in residence. That was the point. It was a sanctuary, and the risk of that is giving safe harbor to those who want trouble. But the benefits outweigh that risk. They saved me, or put me on a path where I could save myself. I'm far from the only one."

"Does anyone stick out? Anyone you can think of who had reason to cause Shelby harm?"

"She scared the hell out of me, and a lot of others," Seraphim said with a hint of a smile. "I thought I could handle myself. The arrogance of youth, the few months I'd spent on the street, most of that high. But even at my worst, I wouldn't have taken her on. She had enemies, no question, but they tended to give her a wide berth. She could fight. I saw her take down another girl who probably had twenty pounds on her, and wasn't a wilter. But Shelby was just fierce."

She paused a moment. "My anger," she said slowly, "I see now, again as an adult, as a therapist, paled beside hers."

"Who did she hang with?"

"Ah . . . there were a couple of girls, and a boy. Let me think." As she sipped coffee, Seraphim rubbed at her temple as if to stir up the memory. "DeLonna—skinny black girl," Seraphim continued, closing her eyes. "She could sing. Yes, yes, I remember her. She had an incredible voice, a true gift. And another girl who was Missy or Mikki. I think Mikki. A bit plump, hard eyes. And a boy everybody called T-Bone. Smart, a little spooky. He'd just drift around like smoke. He'd steal your molars and you wouldn't know it. Old burn marks on his arms—he covered some with tats, but you could see, and a scar down his cheek.

"They weren't always together, but they hung together more than not, and more than any of them did with anyone else."

"Did anyone on the staff have trouble with Shelby, or these others? Did anyone threaten them to your knowledge?"

"They were in trouble often, and I'd say, with Shelby in particular, it was a constant battleground with the staff. It's frustrating and difficult work, Lieutenant, full of conflict and struggle. And incredibly rewarding. I would imagine you often feel the same about yours."

"I guess I would. Do you know anything about a Jubal Craine? His daughter, Leah, was a resident."

"I knew Leah. She was quiet, kept her head down, not only stayed out of trouble, but tried to be invisible, if you understand me."

"Yeah, I do."

"I remember her, very well, because she was, in essence, my transition."

"How was that?" Eve asked.

"We were in a class. I can't remember what class, but we had to put in a certain number of hours a week on educational requirements. We were in a class when I heard him—Leah's father. He was shouting, raging really, shouting her name, telling her she better get her lazy ass out there. Shouting at the staff. She went sheet white, I remember that. I can still see the look on her face. First the terror, the kind I'd never felt, then the resignation, which was almost worse. I remember all that, and the way she just got up, no protests, no pleas, and walked out."

Seraphim put her coffee down, gripped her hands in her lap. "It was the saddest thing I'd ever seen, the way she just stood up, walked away. I remember that moment because I thought of the things Philadelphia and I talked about in one-to-ones. I thought of how scary it was on the street when you're broke and hungry, cold, and when you hear stories about rapes and beatings. And I started thinking how Leah didn't have anybody outside The Sanctuary but this man who was shouting how he was going to whip the sass out of her, and that sort of thing. I thought of Gamma, and how she'd never hurt me. Not ever. And I started thinking I wanted to have somebody who'd take care of me, who'd protect me. That I *did* have somebody. And Leah didn't.

"They had to give her to him, you see. He was the legal guardian, and she wouldn't say he hurt her. She just said she'd go home with him."

"Poor thing," Mrs. Bittmore murmured.

"The next time I saw her was months later."

"She came back?" Eve demanded.

"I don't know, actually. I saw her on the street. I was shopping with a friend. Gamma trusted me—*I* trusted me by then. Or had started to. I saw Leah getting on a bus. I nearly called out, but I'm ashamed to say I didn't want my friend to know I knew this girl with her torn jacket and bruised face. So I didn't call out. But she looked at me. For just a moment we looked at each other."

Tears shimmered in Seraphim's eyes. "She smiled at me. Then she got on the bus, and I never saw her again. But I did think, even then, I thought: She got away. At least she got away from him again."

"I was told he came back, too."

"I didn't know that. I must have been home by then. He wouldn't have found her at The Sanctuary. She didn't go back there, at least not while I was there—and, honestly, I believe she was smart and scared enough not to go back to where he'd found her. It wasn't long after I went home, to my grandmother, that they changed locations."

"I had the building," Mrs. Bittmore explained. "And when I went back to thank Philadelphia and Nash, the others, I'd already made arrangements to donate it, if they wanted it. I'd done my due diligence," she said with a sharp smile. "So I knew they were legitimate. I asked if they'd be willing to let my lawyers and money people study their books and records, and they were. We were satisfied. I had my granddaughter back. I was more than satisfied. You never told me about this girl. This Leah."

"No. I felt ashamed, I suppose, that I hadn't gone up to her, spoken to her."

"We could look for her, find where she is now."

"Leave that to me," Eve advised. "Thank you," she said as she rose. "You've been very helpful."

"Have I?" Seraphim rose as well. "You must have already known Shelby's name."

"You gave me a better picture of her."

"Any one of them could have been me. Any one of the twelve. I'll do anything I can to help you."

"I may take you up on that."

Eve rolled it around as they rode down to the lobby. "She's lucky she had someone to go home to. Not the money, the privilege, but somebody who didn't give up on her, and wanted her."

"Too many aren't lucky." He had been, Roarke thought. Summerset had taken him in—some bloodied street rat—and for reasons he didn't understand to this day, had wanted him.

"Should I look for Leah Craine?"

Eve glanced at him. "I wouldn't mind knowing where she is. We can hope she's not in DeWinter's lab."

"She got away," Roarke said, and because he could picture that terrible resignation too well, he wanted to believe she'd stayed away. And safe. "We'll have some faith she made a life for herself."

"Data's better than faith."

"Such a cop."

"Yeah, and since I am I want to take a pass at Clipperton before we call it."

Anticipating it, Roarke took her hand, gave her arm a playful little swing. "I do enjoy intimidating drunk gits in the evening."

"If Brigham's right, he scored booze for a minor, and maybe got sex in return with said minor. He might've done it more than once, might've developed a sick little relationship there."

"Which leads to him murdering her and eleven others."

Eve checked her notes, rattled off the address before she got into the car. "She was a fighter, a badass. Had a rep for it, and had what sounds like a little crew. But they tell me there's no violence according to her bones, near TOD. All injuries well before that. You don't kill a scrapper without leaving some marks."

"Unless the scrapper trusts you."

"That's right. Maybe you get said scrapper drunk, take her out during her payment. Smother her maybe, or maybe you scored something more than some brew and she ends up ODing on you. Now what the fuck do you do?"

"Build a wall to hide the body?"

"Stupid, extreme, but . . . where'd the other kids come from? That's a question."

"Why kill all the others? If it did start with this Shelby, why kill eleven more?"

"Every serial killer has to start somewhere. There's always going to be a first. He killed the one, thought, 'Wow, that was fun, let's do it again.'"

She tapped her fingers on her thigh as Roarke drove. "He knew this victim, and had to know some of the others. He had to have access to this victim to get her the brew. He knew the building, he had the tools and know-how to build the walls. The Fines may say, Yeah, he's a dick but he wouldn't kill anybody. People who know killers rarely think they know a killer."

She pulled out her PPC. "He's had some bumps, mostly alcohol-related. D&D, disturbing the peace, vandalism, destruction of property. And two hits for sexual misconduct. Pleaded down on all, did a little soft time, some community service, some court-ordered therapy."

"The rap sheet of a dick."

"Dicks kill as much as anyone."

"I do try to keep mine nonviolent."

The smirk that crossed her face felt good. "It's got some punch."

"Thanks, darling. I'd love to punch you later."

"You always want to punch me."

"That's love for you."

Amused, she angled her head, studied him. "Maybe I'll punch you back."

"Here's hoping."

"And here's something else on the dick—not yours, the carpenter's helper dick. His listed address is less than three blocks from my crime scene. Which leads me to ask what in the hell are you planning to do with that dump?"

"It won't be a dump when it's done."

"Okay, what are you planning to do with what won't be a dump?"

"I thought we'd create something to connect with Dochas."

The abuse shelter he'd built, she thought. And the place he'd first learned about his mother.

"Connect how?"

"It's a cycle, isn't it, very often a cycle. The young, lost, or abused, ending up with someone who hurts them. Or becoming an abuser themselves. I've talked of it with the staff at Dochas, and a bit with Dr. Mira."

"Is that so?"

"I like to know what I'm about. The plans are to build a proper facility for children, those who get sucked into the system through no fault of their own, but are mistreated or neglected by those who should tend to them."

As she had been, Eve thought.

"And the others—the lost, you could say—who end up on the street trying to find a way just to survive."

As he had.

"We'll work with CPS, educators, therapists, and the like. Not that different, I suppose, from what it was when Seraphim was there. Maybe it's the building's fate to house the troubled and lost, to give them a refuge, a chance. We didn't have one, you and I."

"No, we didn't have one."

"They'll have a safe place, but with boundaries, with structure. Rules, as you're so fond of rules. They'll have therapy, medical treatment, recreation—as I think fun's important and too often left out. Education, of course, with the opportunity to learn practical skills as well. Summerset gave me that."

"He taught you to steal, too."

"He didn't, as I already knew how. Though he may have polished a few rough edges there." He grinned at her. "Still, they were practical skills of a sort. We won't have classes in lifting locks or wallets, Lieutenant."

"Good to know." She thought a moment. "It's a lot to take on."

"Well now, I'll have those trained in all those areas to do the taking on once we're up and running."

But your hand will be in it, Eve thought. You won't just dump the money, then walk away.

"Do you have a name for it?"

"Not yet, no."

"You should call it Refuge, since that's how you think of it. And you should stick with the Irish, like Dochas. What's Irish for Refuge?"

"An Didean."

"That's what you should call it."

He took a hand off the wheel to lay it on hers. "Then we will."

She turned her hand under his, linked fingers. "I guess I'm definitely punching you back later."

"Praise Jesus."

He found a spot, street level, within a half block of Clipperton's building. Eve deduced not many people parked their vehicles along this block or two if they wanted to come back and find it in one piece.

She wasn't worried, not with the shielding and theft deterrents on her DLE.

"You ought to buy this building," she said as they approached it. "It's more of a dump than the other one."

"I'll keep it in mind."

"Just don't . . . Okay, we got lucky. That's him, coming out of a dive to head to his dump."

Roarke saw the man in a padded canvas work jacket stumble out of the door of a place called Bud's, make a weaving turn in their direction.

"Apparently he's made good use of the dive," Roarke commented.

He was obviously impaired, his balance iffy, but apparently his vision and cop radar wasn't affected. He spotted them halfway between dive and dump, did a flash take, a fast, wobbling one-eighty. Then beat feet.

"Seriously?" Eve shook her head and sprinted after him.

He shoved through pedestrians, succeeded in knocking a woman and her bag of groceries to the sidewalk. A trio of anemic oranges rolled out. Eve jumped over them.

"Take care of her," she shouted to Roarke. "I've got this."

Her target opted to veer right at the corner, or his upper half made the turn while his bottom half tried to catch up.

He tripped over his own feet and skidded along the sidewalk, taking out another pedestrian.

Eve pressed her boot to the back of Clipperton's neck, glanced over at the stunned pedestrian sitting on his ass clutching a tattered briefcase.

"You okay?" She pulled out her badge. "Are you hurt?"

"I . . . don't think so."

"I can get medical assistance if you want it."

"I'm hurt!" Clipperton shouted.

"Shut up. Sir?"

"I'm okay." The man pushed to his feet, shoved a gloved hand through his hair. "Do I have to give a statement? Honestly, I'm not sure what happened. I think he more or less fell into me, and I was off balance."

"That's fine. Here." She managed to pull out a card and increase pressure with her boot when Clipperton wiggled under it like a snake. "If you need to contact me regarding this incident, you can reach me here."

"Oh, thanks. Okay. Um. Then I can go?"

"Yes, sir." She unclipped her restraints, bent down, and clapped them on Clipperton.

"Was he running away from you?"

"He was more stumbling away from me."

"Is he a criminal?"

Eve gave the bystander a last glance. "We're going to find out. Up you go, Clip."

"I didn't do anything."

His breath was cheap brew and ancient beer nuts. To avoid at least the worst of it, Eve shifted slightly to the side. "Why did you run?"

"Wasn't running. Just . . . walking quick. Gotta 'pointment."

"You've got an appointment with me now. At Central."

"Whafor? Get off me."

"You knocked down two people, and are even now attempting to immobilize an officer with your incredible breath."

"Huh?"

"Drunk and disorderly, pal. You've been here before."

"I didn't do anything!"

"That's him!" The woman with the oranges pointed an accusing finger. "He knocked me down."

"Did not."

"Do you want to press charges, ma'am?"

"Oh, come on!"

The women eyed Clipperton balefully. "I guess not. This nice gentleman helped me up, helped me get my groceries. And said you'd make this one apologize."

Eve flicked a glance at Roarke, then poked an elbow into Clipperton's ribs. "Apologize. Apologize," she said in darker tones, "or we add assault."

"Jesus, okay. Sorry, lady. I didn't see you, that's all."

"You're drunk," the woman said severely. "And you're stupid and rude. You're a gentleman," she said to Roarke. "Thank you very much for helping me."

"You're very welcome. I'd be happy to walk you home."

"See, a gentleman." She gave Clipperton the evil eye, then turned to sunshine when she looked back at Roarke. "Thanks, but I'm just in the next block." She beamed a last smile over Roarke, then carried her bag, anemic oranges and all, up the block.

"Let's go, Clip."

"I don't wanna."

"Ain't that a shame?" She quick-walked him to the car, maneuvered him into the back. "If you puke in this vehicle, I'll make you eat it."

He didn't puke—lucky for him—but he whined a lot, and bitterly muttered about someone named Mook. The whining spurted up toward panic when Roarke pulled into Central's garage.

"Listen, listen, it's all bogus, man. Her tits were right out there."

"Is that a fact?" Eve muscled him out of the car.

"Fucking A," he assured her, wobbling his way as she dragged him to the elevator. "And she's got some big-ass cha-chas, you know? They were right in my face."

Eve pulled him into the elevator, called for her floor and sector.

"Come on, man." He turned, appealing to Roarke. "A bitch has her major tits in your face, you're not going to grab a taste?"

"I take the Fifth."

"I'd take a fifth, I had the scratch for one. Come on."

"And Mook objected to you taking a taste of her major tits?" Eve suggested.

"Got real pissy, started carrying on, said it was like rape or something. I never had my dick out. I got witnesses. I never took the slugger out of the dugout, but she says she's going to call the cops. Next thing I know, you're coming for me. How'd you get there so fast?"

"I'm like the wind."

More cops, more Clip types piled on as the elevator climbed, but Eve stayed on, taking the time to work out her game plan.

She'd settle for a conference room if the interviews were booked, but when she hauled him along the corridor, she found A empty. She pulled him in, pushed him into a chair.

"Sit there," she ordered, and went out again.

"That's your prime suspect?" Roarke asked.

"He fits some of the bill, and yeah, he seems pretty stupid. But he's drunk. Either way, I need to go a round with him."

"I'll occupy myself and arrange to have your vehicle fumigated."

"You always do—and good idea. He's too drunk for this to take long."

"Understood. Just let me know when you're done."

"Before you occupy yourself, how about getting me a tube of Pepsi. And yeah, I'm still boycotting Vending. Those machines hold a grudge, but they've got nothing on me."

He obliged, handed over the soft drink tube. "If you're reasonable with them, they're reasonable with you."

"Not in my experience." She pulled out her comm, officially booked Interview A as Roarke wandered off.

Clipperton could sit and sweat a few minutes, she decided, and went to her office, put together a file.

By the time she walked back into Interview, Clipperton had his head on the table. His snores pulled the ugly paint from the walls.

"Record on. Dallas, Lieutenant Eve, entering Interview with Clipperton, Jon. Wake up!" She sat across from him, set her files down, gave his arm a brisk shake. "Wake up, Clipperton."

"Huh?" He lifted his head, stared at her with droopy, blood-shot eyes.

"Do you need or wish the assistance of Sober-Up before we begin the interview?" She rattled the small tin she'd brought in with her.

"I'm not drunk." He attempted to poke out his chest in outrage. "I'm just tired. A guy works all day like me, he gets tired."

"Yeah. Do you understand refusal of this aid, as offered, negates any future claim that this interview was conducted while you were impaired?"

"I'm not impaired, okay? Can't a guy take a quick nap after a hard day?"

"Your choice." She set the tin aside. "I'm going to read you your rights, for your protection. You've been down this road before. You have the right to remain silent," she began.

"I didn't do anything!" Clipperton claimed.

"We'll talk about that. Do you understand your rights and obligations?"

"Yeah, yeah, but—"

"Were you employed as a carpenter's helper by Brodie Fine fifteen years ago?"

"Done some work for Brodie, sure. Did some a couple weeks ago."

"And did this work—fifteen years ago—include a building on Ninth Avenue, then known as The Sanctuary?"

"Huh?"

"The Sanctuary, a shelter for youths in need."

"Oh, the dump over on Ninth. Sure, we did some repairs and crap there. So what?"

"How many times did you go there without Mr. Fine?"

His face, sallow, soft—perhaps once reasonably attractive—pulled into really hard lines as he thought.

"Why would I do that?"

"To see the pretty young girls, Clip. Like Shelby, the thirteen-year-old you bartered brew for sex with?"

"I don't know what you're talking about. If she said I did, she's a liar."

"Like Mook?"

"Yeah. Fuckin' A."

Eve leaned forward. "I've got witnesses, on both counts, Clip. Lying to me isn't going to help, and with your record, I can send you away for a good, long stretch."

"Wait a minute. Just wait. I told you Mook had her tits right out there. That was just a misunderstanding. That's it."

"And Shelby?"

"I don't remember her name."

"So there was more than one minor you traded brew for sex with."

"No. Jesus. And it wasn't sex. It was a bj. That's not sex."

"You're stating that a minor female in residence at The Sanctuary fifteen years ago preformed fellatio on you in exchange for alcohol?"

"It was a blow job." He looked momentarily and sincerely horrified. "We didn't do nothing weird like that thing you said. It was a straight bj."

"In exchange for alcohol."

"It wasn't alcohol. It was just a couple brews."

She wondered why this go-round half amused her, but tried to shortcut it to the point. "Let's put it this way. The minor female gave you a blow job in payment for a couple brews."

"Yeah. That's all it was." He sat back, obviously relieved all was clear. Then jerked up again. "And wait. It was like all that time ago, right? So there's like a statue of limits on that, yeah?"

"That would be statute of limitations." She slid the ID shot of Shelby Stubacker across the table. "Is this the minor female?"

"I don't know how I'm supposed to remember—oh yeah! Yeah, this one. She was a steamer. And she asked *me* about the bj and brew."

"She was thirteen."

"Said she was fifteen." Folding his arms over his thin chest, he nodded in satisfaction. "Told you she was a liar."

"And that makes such a difference, that you solicited oral sex from a girl you assumed was fifteen."

"She already had a nice little rack on her."

Eve simply stared at him until he blinked.

"How many times did you trade her a couple brews for a blow job?"

"A couple. Maybe three."

The way he cut his eyes away had Eve leaning in again. "How many other girls, Clip? She wasn't the only one."

"There was just the one more, and this one here brought her into it. Plus she wasn't any good at it. Kinda fat girl—the hefty kind. Kept giggling, you know. I barely got off."

"Where did these famous blow jobs take place?"

"Right there. I mean right outside the place. Kid knew how to get in and out, how to get around security. She was a steamer, like I said. And if she's trying to come back at me for it now, that's bullshit. She asked *me*, and there's the statue."

"Some things have no *statue*, Clip. Like being a revolting shit, such as yourself."

"Hey!"

"And things like this."

She shoved the photo of Shelby's remains across the table.

"What the hell is that?"

"That's Shelby Stubacker."

"Uh-uh. This is." He nodded toward the first photo. "That looks like some old skeleton, like for Halloween or something."

"This is what Shelby looks like now, after being murdered, then rolled up in plastic, and hidden for fifteen years behind the wall you built."

"You're fucking with me, 'cause we didn't build no walls in that place. Patched a few, painted some, but we didn't build none. And if we did, and we didn't, we sure as hell woulda seen that. You ask Brodie. We didn't see nothing like that. Just ask him."

"I didn't say you and Brodie built the wall. I said you built it, after you killed this girl and eleven others."

"You're shitting me now." His face died from sallow to pasty gray. "What the fuck? I never killed that girl. I never killed anybody. I just got a couple bjs, that's it. Just a couple blows."

"How many times did you go back to that building, meet this girl after they shut down that location?"

"I never went back there, not after Brodie pulled me offa the job. No reason to go back there. You can get a bj lots of places. Sometimes for free even."

God, she thought, a genuine moron. But she pushed through. "It's convenient though, just a couple blocks away."

"I couldn'ta gotten in if I'da wanted. The kid's the one came out to me. I didn't even know they left that place, not for months until I went by it one night. It was all boarded up, and dark, and I thought, 'Hell, the bj girl's gone.' I never went in, hand to God. I never saw that kid again after Brodie pulled me offa the job. I never killed nobody."

7 EVE FOUND ROARKE IN HER OFFICE. SHE dumped the files on her desk, went straight to the AutoChef for coffee, then dropped down in her chair.

Waiting until she had, Roarke slid his PPC into his pocket. "Well then?"

"The best I could do was dump him in the tank on the D&D. He deserves a hell of a lot more, but I don't think he killed those girls. He's too damn stupid for one thing. I'm talking deeply and sincerely stupid."

Roarke merely nodded. "Are you done here? At Central," he continued. "Is there anything left to do you can't do at home?"

"I guess not."

"Then we'll go home, and you can fill me in on the way."

He listened. She'd grown used to having someone who listened and, even better, understood without every *i* dotted.

"Sick fuck. He actually believes there's nothing wrong with getting his dick sucked by a goddamn child. Nothing wrong with paying a thirteen-year-old kid a couple of brews for going down on him—and, hey, her idea."

"But you don't believe the sick fuck killed her, or any of them?"

"No. He deserves to have his dick tied in a knot, covered with acid, then set on fire while thousands cheer, but—"

"You do have a way with imagery."

"But he didn't kill them. He's a sucking boil on the ass of mankind, but he doesn't have killer in him. And he's a complete moron. A moron didn't do this. I took him over, under, back, forth, pushed, shoved. He doesn't know a damn thing. We're going to keep an eye on him, not only in case I'm wrong on this, but eventually he's going to put hands on someone else, potentially another minor. Then he can whine in a cage for a few years."

She sat back, hissed. "I've got nothing."

"You know that's not true, you're just disappointed you couldn't set this one's dick on fire. You've eliminated, or certainly bumped down several people on your suspect list. And more, you have the names of two girls."

"I didn't have a hell of a lot to do with that part."

"Is that it?" He glanced at her as he turned through the gates that opened to home.

"I don't know." She shoved her fingers through her hair. "It's not going to be," she said. "It's just not going to be. I'm not a scientist. I can't look at bones and figure out who they were. It's stupid to resent getting that data from another source. An expert."

"And you're not stupid, even shallowly and insincerely."

That made her laugh a little. "I'm not stupid, and those girls deserve having every resource I can tap on this."

She looked at the house, the wonderful sweep of it, the towers and turrets, the countless windows. And thought of young girls—herself among them—who lived or had lived in cramped dorms, shared dingy bathrooms, who yearned for freedom and dreamed of somehow making their own.

Too many never made it.

"Too many never made it," she said out loud.

"Let me tell you about one who did."

When he pulled to a stop, she looked over at him. "What? Who?"

"Leah Craine. Leah Lorenzo now. She married nineteen months ago—a firefighter with a large Italian family. They're expecting their first child in the spring. She's a teacher—elementary school level. They live in Queens."

"You found her while I was dealing with the moron."

"I did. She made it, and from all appearances, has built a solid and happy life. Will you interview her?"

She sat for a moment, just sat. "If I have to. Otherwise I'd like to leave her alone. But . . . you might send her information to Seraphim Brigham."

"I already did."

"Okay." He'd waited, she realized, waited to tell her the good until after she'd finished her frustrated rant. Points for him. Big ones.

"Are you going to show me your plans for that dump you bought? How you're going to turn it around?"

"I can, of course."

When they got out of the car, he took her hand. "I asked myself today what might have happened if I hadn't bought that place. Those girls might have been there years yet. Then I thought, no, not at all. It was meant to be now, and me, and you."

"You're awfully damn Irish sometimes."

"Meant to be," he said with a shrug. "We know those children, and aren't so far from being them once. So we'll neither of us stop until we find who they are, what happened to them, and who took the rest of their lives from them."

"Whoever did it walked away from it for fifteen years."

"And now?"

"We're going to take the rest of his life away from him by putting him in a cage."

She stepped inside where Summerset, the scarecrow in a black suit, and their fat cat, Galahad, waited.

She'd walked out of the big, airy foyer that morning. Now she walked into Christmas. The scent of pine and cinnamon, the pretty dazzle of little lights roping up the banister, the clever arrangement of those big plants—what were they?—poinsettias into a pretty white tree.

And the twinkle, now that she paid attention, from the front parlor where a quick peek showed her the massive tree stood fully dressed in lights and sparkle.

"Where are the elves?"

"Gone for the day, I expect," Roarke told her. "They'll be back tomorrow to do the exterior."

"You might have seen some of them if you'd arrived home in anywhere near a timely fashion."

Eve gave Summerset a stony stare. "We've been out sledding and drinking brandy and discussing what not to get you for Christmas. Nothing but fun for us."

"Yet all that fun has done little to improve your mood or manner."

"Ah, the warmth of homecomings." Roarke shook his head,

started to shrug out of his coat as the cat pranced over to rub against his legs and Eve's. "Always such a pleasure."

"I didn't start—" Eve broke off, yanked out her signaling 'link. "They have another face," she said, dashing up the stairs as she called for the image.

"Twelve, the media said."

Roarke nodded at Summerset. "Yes. No more than children."

"There are ugly pieces to the puzzle of the world."

"She'll find them, put them where they belong."

"I've no doubt. It's a cold night. There's beef bourguignonne on the menu. Some red meat would do both of you more good than the pizza she'll think of first."

"I'll see to it. Thanks."

When he got to Eve's office Roarke found she already had the reconstruction image on screen.

Younger, he thought. This girl seemed younger than the other two.

"I'm going to run her against the list I have from Higher Power. If she was registered there, it'll be quicker than a broad Missing Persons search."

"Go ahead. I can set up your board for you. I know how you prefer it," he said before she could object.

"Okay, thanks. It'll save time."

He went to work as did she. Dinner, he thought, would wait a bit longer.

They'd put the little tree by her window, he noted. The one he'd ordered as it was simple and traditional, and his wife often thought herself both. Though she was far from either on most levels.

A simple, traditional woman wouldn't spend her evening searching for the names of dead girls. She wouldn't work herself to exhaustion—body, mind, heart—to find who'd killed them.

As difficult, as frustrating, as painful as it sometimes was, he thanked God he hadn't fallen for a simple, traditional woman.

"I've got her."

He stopped what he was doing to look at the wall screen. She'd split it, putting the images of the reconstruction and the ID photo of a minor female side by side.

"Yes, you found her. Only twelve years old?"

"That's according to her ID. I'm checking background and Missing Persons."

Lupa Dison, he read. It listed a New York address several blocks north of the building where she'd been found, and her guardian as her aunt, Rosetta Vega.

Tragic eyes, he thought. How did someone so young earn such tragic eyes?

"Missing Persons filed by the aunt. It's looking like her parents were both killed in an accident, the mother's sister—the only living relative in the States—named as guardian."

"A scatter of maternal relatives in Mexico."

As she continued to scan data, Roarke went to the wall unit for a bottle of wine.

"Okay, okay, the aunt worked as a maid for the Faremont Hotel, West Side. She was mugged on the way home from work, badly beaten, sliced up some, too. Had to spend a few weeks in the hospital and in rehab. She requested the kid be registered at The Sanctuary; she knew someone who'd had a kid in there. Court granted the temporary stay. She goes in, comes out, goes back home. And three weeks later, goes missing. Missing on September seventeenth. Five days after Linh Penbroke."

"Lured back."

"Could be. She went missing fifteen days after The Sanctuary changed locations. The place was empty. She'd never been in any trouble, neither had the aunt. Running the aunt for current data now."

"She wasn't a runaway," Roarke said. "Troubled, yes, but by the loss of her parents." There, he thought, the reason for the tragic eyes.

"The aunt's married. Ten years to a Juan Delagio. She's now head housekeeper, day shift, at the Antoine Hotel, tony East Side employment now. She's on the East Side, too, not an especially tony area, but a decent one."

"That's one of mine—the hotel."

"Well, we couldn't get around that for long." Eve glanced up. "Do you know her?"

"I don't, but I can get a full employment record from the manager."

"Not yet anyway. She and Juan have three kids. He's on the job, out of the two-two-six." She swung to her 'link, then frowned at the glass of wine Roarke set in front of her.

"I'll see about dinner," he said.

"But I—"

"We'll eat, and we'll sort through all this while we do."

"Fine, okay. Fine. This is Lieutenant Dallas out of Central," she began as Roarke walked back down to the kitchen and the AutoChef.

When he came back in she was talking to someone—he assumed whoever had caught the Missing Persons case—taking notes.

He left her to it, used the little table to set down the meal.

"Appreciate it," she said. "And yeah, I'll keep you in the loop on her."

She clicked off, frowned at the wine again. But this time she picked it up, sampled.

"I caught the detective who headed the investigation. She's got a solid memory. She said she remembered this one especially as her daughter was the same age at the time."

"Come eat, and tell me."

She thought how much easier a slice of pizza would've been since she could've kept working while she chowed it down. But still, reviewing what she had with him couldn't be considered a waste of time.

She went over, sat across from him. "Another reason she remembers is she and the aunt keep in touch. At least once a year one of them contacts the other, just to touch base. What I get is the kid was pretty shattered when her parents were killed, but it helped some she was tight with the aunt. They got counseling, and the kid seemed to be coming along."

"It must be crushing, even with a close family member able and willing to care for you, to lose both parents that way."

"Had to go to a new school, too, as the aunt didn't have enough money to move and keep her where she'd been. But according to the aunt, and the detective believed her, still does, the kid was doing better. Then about a week or so before she went missing, she started coming home late from school. The aunt had to work, but she had a neighbor keep an eye out for Lupa, and she started coming in just before her aunt was due home."

"This is really good," she said after another bite.

"Thanks. I slaved over the AutoChef for minutes."

Grinning, she ate some more. "When the aunt called her on it, the kid claimed she was just hanging with her new friends, doing her homework with them. But she was evasive, and the aunt didn't push. Felt she needed some room. Then one day she didn't come home at all."

"From all you said, she doesn't sound like a runaway."

"I don't think she ran away. I think she was lured or enticed into that building, killed there. I think, most likely, those few days before she poofed, she met the killer, or someone who connected her to him. She—the kid—started asking a lot of God questions."

"Excuse me?"

"You know, how come God this, or why doesn't God that. They're pretty serious Catholics, according to the primary, but during the investigation, they found she'd been reading about alternative religions and—what would you call them? Philosophies? Using the house comp, as they could only afford the one, late at night after the aunt was in bed."

"It doesn't seem unusual behavior for a young girl, especially one who'd suffered a major loss."

"No, but I think about that higher power stuff, and I wonder. It's another possible connection to HPCCY."

She gestured with her spoon, then used it to dig back into the stew. "Say the kid was meeting somebody from The Sanctuary—resident or staff. Someone she knew from her time there, had a connection with. They've never been able to track down where she spent that time, after school, before getting home. Could be someone used that spiritual angle to hook her. Why did God do such a shitty thing? Here are some answers."

"She might've walked by the building going to school," Roarke suggested.

"She's the second vic who was in residence there. It's not going to be coincidence, it's not going to be happenstance. She wasn't doing illegals, no sign of that anywhere."

"A good girl," Roarke put in, "with hard and sorrowful circumstances."

"Yeah. She went to school every day, and her grades were solid. She got counseling, both separately and with the aunt, and nobody saw her as runaway material. She and the aunt hadn't fought. Added to all that, she took nothing with her. She had school stuff, the clothes on her back. A kid doesn't take off without hauling some of her stuff."

No, Eve thought, no. A kid does what Linh did, packs up some of her things.

"She had a little money saved—just a little bit from doing chores or errands, that kind of thing. She didn't take it either. Nobody looked at this as a runaway once they got the ball rolling. And nobody came forward claiming to have seen anybody lurking around. I'm getting the case file, but my sense is this detective put in the time and effort, and maybe more than most would."

"But you have two of your victims in residence at The Sanctuary, at the same time."

She drank a little more wine as she considered.

"Of the three we've ID'd, we have an experienced street kid, an impulse runner from a good family, and a kid from the working class who was, by all reports, well behaved and learning to cope with loss. What they have in common is age, size—and, in two, confirmed connection to the crime scene."

"From what you know, age and size will remain common traits."

"So it follows the other commonality will hold true for the twelve. It just reaffirms the killer connects to The Sanctuary, and likely HPCCY."

"Another resident?" Roarke suggested. "Have you considered this may have been done by another child?"

"I'm running it around. An older kid. They took them, supposedly to eighteen, but they may have had a few that bumped over that."

"Letting it slide a bit," Roarke agreed. "Maybe having those who hit the age limit but still had nothing do a bit of work around the place in exchange for room and board."

"They'd be the type to do that," Eve agreed, thinking of her impression of the Joneses. "A boy. Girls that age might trust an older girl, but aren't they pretty stupid about boys in those years?"

"I've never been a teenaged girl, so I couldn't say for certain. You were."

"Me? Hell, I was never stupid about boys. Until you anyway."

He laughed into his wine. "That's so sweet."

"I had too much going on to get stupid about boys. I wouldn't even have had sex except I was curious what was the big deal. Turned out, at least back then, it wasn't all that big."

He laughed again, just enjoying her. "How old were you? I can't believe I've never asked."

"I don't know, about seventeen probably. Everybody else, or mostly, was banging like hammers, so I figured I should find out why. How about you?"

He lifted his wine. "I believe I'll take the Fifth, once again."

"Oh no, you don't. It's got to be in the marriage rules. I tell you, you tell me."

"Rules are so . . . confining, but all right then. About fourteen. The Dublin streets and alleys were colorful, we could say."

"I bet. Wait." She lifted a finger. "Is that accounting for you finding out you're a year younger than you thought?"

She watched his face go blank a moment—a rare event. "Ah well. Ha." He rose, began gathering the dishes.

"Thirteen? Seriously?"

"In my circumstances, it was grow up fast or pay the price. In any case, darling, think of all the practice I had before we met."

She angled her head. "You really want me to think about that?"

"Maybe not. Instead consider you're the only one I want to be with for all the rest of my life." He leaned over, kissed her knuckles.

"Good save."

"It was indeed, and also pure truth. I'll deal with these dishes so you can get back to it."

"Appreciate it."

She looked over at the board he'd begun. Yeah, he knew her system. She had another face to add now, and rose to add Lupa Dison to the others. She added the aunt, Rosetta Vega Delagio, as a connector, the primary investigator's data, the time line—or what she had of it.

Then began, systematically, adding the staff of The Sanctuary.

"That's considerable," Roarke said when he joined her.

"They all need to be run. Peabody should have started on it." She shot him a glance. "Do you have stuff?"

"This and that, nothing pressing."

Which likely meant more this and a whole bunch more of that than most people handled in a week.

"If you've got time, and feel like it, you could contact her, see how far she's gotten."

"And take a few off her hands?"

"You probably shouldn't, technically, but it would save time."

"And I do love poking in other people's business. I've time to do a bit of it."

"I really want to go through the list of residents who fit the pattern. I can eliminate any I find who're alive and well, or on record as deceased."

"And get a clearer idea who might be among the remaining nine." He touched a finger to Lupa's photo. The sad eyes. "Will you notify the aunt?"

"Tomorrow. It's not going to change tonight for anyone. And I'm going to take a pass on the residents—older, male. Maybe I'll ring some bell."

"Then I'll play with Peabody." But he drew Eve against him first, just held her. "It already rings bells, for both of us."

"Yeah." She closed her eyes a moment. Held on. "It could've been me. And cross the ocean to some building, it could've been you."

"Were we just too smart? Or just too mean?"

"A little of both, but even the smart and mean can fall through a trapdoor. Still." She lifted her face, kissed him. "Let's stay smart and mean."

"We couldn't be otherwise."

He went to his adjoining office, left the door open.

She went back to her desk, rubbed her hands over her face. And got down to it.

Within an hour she'd eliminated all but eighteen on the list. Some had gone on to lead what appeared to be normal, even productive lives. Others had served time, or were currently serving it as guests of various states or the feds. Some were dead, and everyone who'd died had done so violently.

Some of those eighteen, she imagined, had changed their names, forged IDs, and some had just dropped off the grid altogether.

She'd enlist EDD, or maybe Roarke, if she needed to hunt for them. But for now, she'd work with what she had.

Using the back of her board, she posted what she thought of as potentials.

She decided to copy DeWinter and the reconstructionist—maybe it would boost things there. Then she settled in to take a hard look at the male residents.

Children killed, she thought. Maybe not as often, rarely as cleverly as most of their adult counterparts. But they killed.

She'd done so herself at eight.

Not the same, she reminded herself. Stop pulling that into the mix. She shook it off, started digging into the male residents.

She was on her second hit of coffee, had made her first dent in the list, when Roarke came back in.

"Peabody had a good start," he began, "so we've got the lot done." He laid a disc on her desk. "She'll send your unit a copy, but I thought you'd want this as well for the file."

"Tell me."

"There are twenty-four who work or serve at HPCCY, on either a staff or volunteer basis, either full- or part-time. Six of them worked or served when it opened fifteen years ago, and four of them came to HPCCY from The Sanctuary."

"Smaller staff at The Sanctuary, not as many to pull from."

"Yes, and the bulk of 'staff' at The Sanctuary were volunteers, not paid staff. Of those—staff and volunteers from The Sanctuary on through HPCCY, or who've left that employment—criminal records are clean for all but five for between eight and twenty-six years."

"Give me the five."

"I thought you'd say that. Three illegals busts, with rehabilitation. One drunk and disorderly, again with rehab, and one vandalism. Estranged wife spray-painted obscenities on her husband's vehicle—charges dropped. None of them have anything that shows violence against children or young girls."

"Doesn't mean it's not there."

"It doesn't," he agreed. "A good portion who worked at The Sanctuary and who work at HPCCY have a sheet. All involve illegals arrests or arrests stemming from use. Of that faction a few have assault charges as well, but nothing on children. There were a few petty larcenies, shopliftings, petty thefts—all again connecting to illegals.

And all who were hired or accepted as volunteers had completed re-habilitation, had a minimum of two years clean, and passed physical and psychiatric evaluations."

"Things slip through."

"They do." He sat on the corner of her desk. "What I'm saying is, on the surface at least, it appears the heads of the former organization and the current did exactly what should have been done in hiring. We'll be doing much the same for An Didean."

"Your screenings won't be surface."

"They won't, no." He looked at the back of her board. "And those?"

"Eighteen who aren't recorded as alive and well or deceased. We've probably got some living with fake identification, dropping off the grid, and it's likely at least one or more is dead and hasn't been found or ID'd. That's the probability."

She picked up her coffee again. "Eleven out of the eighteen came from physically abusive homes. Three were chronic runaways. The others were doing rehab for illegals and/or alcohol use."

Since the cat knocked his head against Roarke's leg, Roarke hefted the not insubstantial cat up to stroke him.

"Eleven out of eighteen. That percentage is a poor testament to the state of the world."

"Some people shouldn't be allowed to procreate. At least some of our remaining nine victims are there. It's logical. As for the other residents, I'm hitting a lot of bad boys. And a lot of those bad boys went on to be bad men. I've run twenty . . ." She checked. "Twenty-eight. Nineteen of the twenty-eight served time as adults. Seven of those nineteen are either still serving out that sentence, or are serving for a second offense—one is a three-time loser. Could be the other dozen out of that nineteen learned their lesson, or got smarter."

"Such a cop."

She only shrugged. "One of the dozen wrote a book on being bad, the pain of incarceration, and the joys of living a clean life, and what it takes to do so. He's on the lecture circuit. Pulls in ridiculous fees. I don't like him."

"As the killer?"

"In general."

When Roarke set the cat on her desk, Galahad sprawled across it as if it were a patch of green summer grass in the sunshine.

Eve let it go—for now.

"I skimmed some of the interviews he's given," she continued. "He's got that pompous fucker vibe thinly covered with sticky humility. Lemont Frester. I'm going to track him down. He has a place in New York. His pied-à-terre he calls it, and that alone says pompous asshole to me."

"I'll be sure to refrain from using the term at any time."

"Good. Of the nine who never served time. One's a cop in Denver— he's got a strong record, but I'm going to poke deeper. Two work in social services, another's a lawyer, one's an MT, one owns a bar in Tucson, and the others are in what you'd call your average mid-level job. The twenty-eight procreated . . ." She checked again. "Thirteen offspring—out of the twenty who so procreated. Of those, ten actually live in the same household as said offspring. And of the twenty-eight— whether or not they are currently incarcerated—nineteen have New York as their primary residence."

"How many more do you have to go?"

"Triple it," she said and pressed her fingers to her eyes.

"Put it on auto. No, it's not that late," he said before she could protest. "At least not in our world, but you can come back fresh to the new data in the morning. You've been at this more than twelve hours."

"Without a single, solid lead."

"But with reams of information, with three of the girls identified, with several eliminated either as victims or possible killer."

"Okay." She rubbed her face again. "It feels like nothing but data crunching at this point anyway."

She needed to find more, eliminate more, she thought as she ordered her machine to continue the current tasks on auto. Talk to more people, look them in the eye, she told herself as she walked out with Roarke. Go back to the crime scene, go back to DeWinter's sanctum, talk to Lupa's aunt, track down the pompous fucker. And take a good, hard look at any male resident who was serving a long-term sentence that began after the murders.

You can't keep killing young girls from a cage.

She started working the theory in her head while the cat streaked out of her office.

A boy, she speculated, a few years older—charismatic. Wouldn't he have to be? Luring girls into that empty building. How?

Some, at least some, had to know him, trust him, maybe be attracted to him.

He gets them in there, subdues them.

How?

Drugs? So many of them had substance abuse problems, and the street smarts to score. Maybe he drugged them, then killed them.

How?

As much as she hated it, she had to wait for DeWinter to tell her.

Frustrated, she stepped into the bedroom.

The tree stood by the front window, as it had now for three holidays. The room smelled of pine, and the applewood that simmered in the fireplace.

The cat was curled up dead center of the bed—as if he'd been there for hours.

"We don't have to do it tonight," Roarke told her.

She looked at the stack of boxed decorations, shook her head. They'd done this tree together twice before. And they'd continue that tradition for a zillion years if she had her way.

"Tonight's good. Tonight's right." She took his hand, squeezed it. "How about we pour some more wine and get that sucker dressed?"

"How about we pop champagne?"

"Even better."

**8** THE FIRST TIME SHE'D WALKED INTO THE BED-
room to see a Christmas tree had been a little over-
whelming. Now it was simply tradition. The elves
could take care of the rest of the house, drape it in lights and tinsel,
put up a dozen trees—she wasn't sure she'd ever counted all of
them—but this was theirs.

So with the fire simmering, champagne bubbling, and hokey
Christmas music playing in the background, they decorated their
personal tree.

The cat uncurled, sat for a moment or two to watch. With a decided lack of interest he stretched—ears to tail—turned his habitual
three circles, then settled down for another nap.

"The whole city's like holiday on Zeus," Eve commented. "And
it's only going to get worse. Then we'll have the B and Es where, as
traditional as Santa, the Christmas Burglar swoops in, snatches all the
presents under the tree, and has them fenced by dawn."

"Bah humbug."

"Yeah, that's his version of ho, ho, ho. Then there's the shoplifting, the pickpocketing as the tourists flock in with their wallets practically jumping out into the pickpockets' hands."

"Ah, happy memories," Roarke said. "December was always a busy month when I was a boy on the hunt for those jumping wallets."

"I bet. Back when I was in uniform, you couldn't keep up with the incident reports on muggings, purse snatchings, and lifted wallets in December."

She hung a jolly Santa with an overflowing pouch. "Then it gets closer to Christmas and you start getting the domestic disputes, the drunk and disorderlies, the botched self-terminations, the murders, and the holiday favorite, murder-suicide."

"My cop," he said affectionately. "What cheerful thoughts she has on this festive occasion."

"I like it."

"Murder-suicide? Sorry, darling, I'll have to disappoint you. Maybe next year."

"No, Christmas. I didn't used to. When I was a kid—after Richard Troy," she qualified. "He'd go out, get plowed, and probably laid. That was a gift, come to think about it. Anyway, after it was always weird if I was in a foster house, and just fucking depressing in a group home, so it wasn't high on my list of holidays."

"It wasn't roasted goose and plum pudding in my memories either. I'd usually go over to a mate's or a few of us would go out, bang around."

"Hunting more wallets."

He sent her a cheerful look. "You have to celebrate somehow, after all."

"Yeah, you do. I used to take the extra shifts, so cops with families could get the break. And after Mavis and I hooked up, we'd do something." She studied a shiny silver reindeer. "Why are they reindeer? What kind of a name is that?"

"They need the reins for Santa to navigate the sleigh."

She slanted him a look. "Right. Anyway, with me and Mavis and Christmas, it usually involved a lot of alcohol."

"We can serve that tradition." He topped off her glass.

"She dragged me out ice-skating once." She brought the memory back, laughed and—what the hell—drank more champagne. "We were both pretty trashed by that time or she'd never have talked me into it."

"I'd pay good money to see that."

"She zipped around pretty good. God, she had this pink coat with purple flowers all over it, and she'd done her hair in Christmas red and green."

"That hasn't changed. I've wondered how Mavis came to have that ugly gray coat you borrowed." He drew out of his pocket the button he always carried, the one that had fallen off the unfortunate coat the first time they'd met.

"Holdover from her grifting days. A blend-and-be-dull deal, she called it."

"That explains that." He slid the button away again. "And how were you on the ice, Lieutenant?"

"It's just balance and motion. I stayed on my feet. She would have, but she kept trying to do those fancy spins, and she'd face-plant or fall on her ass. She had bruises everywhere, but I still had to drag her off the damn ice after an hour or something. Ice is freaking cold."

"I've heard that. We should try it sometime."

"Ice-skating?" She gave him a look of genuine shock. "You? Me?"

"Which makes we. Brian and I and some others liberated some skates one winter. We must've been fourteen or fifteen, around that. We had a go at playing ice hockey, Dublin rules, which means none at all. And yes, my God, the bruises were majestic."

"Hockey maybe." She considered it as she hung another ornament. "At least that has a purpose. Otherwise you're just strapping some blades to your feet and circling around on frozen water. I mean, what's the point?"

"Relaxation, exercise, fun?"

"I guess we had fun, but we were drunk. Or nearly drunk. I think I remember we finished getting all the way drunk back at my place. Her place now, hers and Leonardo and Bella's. That's kind of weird when you think about it."

"Life changes." He paused to tap his glass to hers. "Or we change it."

"I guess." She realized she was just a little bit drunk now, and that was just fine.

"Here we are decorating the tree. They've probably got one over at their place, which used to be my place. She used to bring over this skinny little fake tree, every damn year, and nag me until I put it up. She always took it back because she was smart enough to know I'd dump it if she left it with me. But I guess she was right. It added something."

Roarke draped his arm around her shoulders. "We should have them over, some preholiday drinks. Just the four of us. Well, five, with the baby."

"That'd be good." Leaning against him, she studied the lights, the shine, the symbol. "That's good, too. We're as good as the elves. We're having a party, aren't we? I mean, one of those bashes where a half a million of our closest friends come over to eat fancy food, drink enough to make them dance like lunatics?"

"We are. It's on your calendar, the one you never pay the slightest bit of attention to."

"Then how did I know we were having a party?"

"Good guess."

Because it was, she just laughed and turned so they were face-to-face, her arms around his waist. "You know what all this makes me want to do? The decorating, the memory street—"

"Lane. Memory lane."

"Street, road, lane, they all lead somewhere. All this, and the idea of having some big-ass party? It makes me want to punch you, and punch you hard."

She hooked her foot around his, shifted balance so they flopped back onto the bed. Galahad woke, gave them a hard stare of annoyance, and jumped off.

"How hard?" Roarke wondered.

"Really hard. Tell me when it hurts."

She took his mouth—an exceptional place to start—a nip, a graze of teeth before she sank in, met his tongue with hers.

Here was all she wanted in the world.

She could shed the miseries and frustrations of the day, even the grief she couldn't allow to surface and blur the job. Here, with him, the emotional fatigue that had dragged at her since she'd seen twelve young lives robbed of all possibilities and potentials lifted.

Here was happy, and she could take it, hold it, feel it bloom like roses.

The hard lines of his body under hers, his quick and clever hands already roaming. And one long, soul-searing kiss.

He felt her let it go, the tension, the worry that had dogged her even through her pleasure in the tree. The tether loosened, slid away, freed her.

Now just his Eve, just his woman, warm and eager over him. Drawing love in, pouring love out.

He tugged her shirt free from her waistband, wanting her skin under his hands—all that smooth skin on that long, narrow back.

And discovered neither of them had noticed she'd never taken off her weapon harness.

"Bloody hell," he muttered, shifting to find the release.

"Shit. I forgot. Wait. I'll get it."

"Got it." He shoved it off her shoulders. Ignored her wince when it thudded on the floor. "You're unarmed, Lieutenant."

"You'd better not be."

He laughed, rolled to reverse their positions. "Never with you around. My cop."

Now he nipped at her lip as his fingers got busy on her shirt.

"You've still got all this suit on," she complained, and fought off his jacket. "There are too many pieces."

"No rush."

"Speak for yourself."

"Is that the way of it?" Willing to oblige, he slid his hand down the trousers he'd opened, and shot her straight to peak.

When she cried out in shock and satisfaction, he lowered his lips to her throat. "Not as much of a rush."

He fed there, where her pulse hammered, then at her breast, so firm, so smooth, where her heartbeat thundered.

Her body was a constant joy and wonder to him. So slim, so tight. Satin skin over tough muscle. He knew where to touch to make her quiver, where to taste to loose a sigh in her.

He did both as they struggled themselves and each other out of clothes.

There, she thought, there he was, naked and hard and hungry for her. Everything about him so familiar and only more exciting for the knowledge. All that glorious hair sliding over her skin, those strong shoulders, the narrow hips.

She curled her fingers around him—hot, ready, as she was— would have guided him into her, but he pulled her up with him. Her arms locked tight around his neck to pull him closer.

And joined with him.

Shuddering, shuddering, she dropped her face to his shoulder. Impossible to feel so much, incredible to know there was more to give, to take.

The fire simmered, casting shadows and subtle light. The tree sparkled, casting joy.

Once again their lips met, clung.

She moved with him, surrounded him. Her hands came to frame his face in a gesture that burst through his heart.

Only with her had love and lust so perfectly twined. Only she met every need, every longing, every wish he'd ever made, every one he'd never thought of.

She bowed back, caught, caught on that final rise. Her hair streamed with the firelight, her skin glistened in it.

Once more he pressed his lips to her throat—a taste to take with him on the fall. And surrendered with her.

A ll the pretty young girls sat in a circle, cross-legged on the floor. She recognized three—Linh, Lupa, Shelby. All the others wore masks. All the masks were of Eve's face.

"We're all the same anyway," one of the Eves said. "Under it. We're all the same until you know."

"We'll find your names, your faces, who you were. We'll find who killed you."

"I just wanted to have some fun. My parents are so strict, so totally lame about stuff." Linh sulked, shrugged. "I needed to show them they couldn't treat me like a kid anymore. This wasn't supposed to happen. It's not fair."

"Fair's a bunch of shit." Shelby snorted out a bitter laugh. "Life sucks. Dead just sucks louder. You can't trust anybody," she told Eve. "That's the deal. You know the deal."

"Who did you trust?" Eve demanded.

"You have to trust people," Lupa insisted. "Bad things happen even when you're good. Most people are good."

"Most people are assholes, and just out for themselves." But even as she said it, a tear rolled down Shelby's face. "If I'd had a knife like you did, I wouldn't be here. You just got lucky. I never had a chance, not ever. Nobody gives a shit about me."

"I do," Eve said. "I give a shit."

"It's a job. We're a job."

"I'm good at my job because I give a shit. I'm what you've got, kid."

"You're just like us. Not even as much as us," Shelby shot back. Bitter, bitter. "They didn't even give you a name. The one you have's just made up."

"Not anymore. It's who I am now. I made myself who I am now."

And all the pretty girls sitting in the circle stared at her. And all of them said, "We'll never have a chance to be anything."

She woke with a jolt. Roarke sat, fully dressed, on the bed beside her, his hand on her cheek.

"Wake up now."

"I am. I'm awake." She sat up, stupidly relieved to have him so close as she shook off the sorrow of the dream. "It wasn't a nightmare." And still she was comforted by him, and by the cat who stopped bumping his head against her hip to worm his way across her lap. "Just my subconscious giving me a little mind fuck to start the day. I'm okay."

He cupped her chin, his thumb brushing lightly over the shallow dent in it as he studied her face. Then nodded as he could see she was. "You'll want coffee then."

"As much as my next breath."

He got up to fetch it, and to give her another moment to settle.

She sat, replaying the dream as she stroked the cat.

"All the vics, sitting in a circle," she told him when he came back in. "The ones we haven't ID'd had my face."

"Disturbing."

"Weird, but . . . apt, I guess. The lost and nameless. That's what I was." She took the coffee he brought her, drank some down—strong and black. "Mostly Shelby Stubacker had her say, being she's really pissed off. Who did she trust? Who did she trust enough he or she or they got by her defenses, because I'd think her defenses, her survival instincts would've been pretty sharp."

"Someone she trusted, or someone she thought she could manipulate. Like she did Clipperton."

"Looking to score. Yeah, it could've been."

She glanced over to the sitting area where the screen ran its financial reports on mute. "Been up long?"

"A bit."

"I better catch up. Thanks for the coffee service." She rolled Galahad over, gave his pudge of a belly a rub, then slid out of bed.

When she stepped out of the shower, warm from the drying tube and the cashmere robe, she found him on his pocket 'link with two covered plates and a pot of coffee on the table—and the stream of numbers and symbols still scrolling by on screen.

The man was the god of multitasking, she thought.

She sat beside him, cautiously lifted the dome over the plate. Then did a little butt-on-cushion dance when she found thick slices of French toast and a pretty bowl of mixed berries instead of the oatmeal she'd feared.

She popped a raspberry, poured more coffee—and he ended transmission.

"I thought a morning mind fuck deserved the French toast."

"It might be worth waking up with one every day. Did you just buy a solar system?"

"Just a minor planet." He passed her the syrup, watched her drown the bread. "Actually, just a quick conference with Caro, some schedule juggling."

His über-efficient admin could juggle schedules while balanced on a flaming ball. "You don't need to shift your stuff around for mine."

"I wanted a little more time this morning. You'll be starting in your home office, I assume."

"That's the plan."

"Mine's to do the same. Things can be rescheduled further if I can be useful. We can't resume work on the building until you close the case," he added. "And on a less practical level, I couldn't begin it until you close the case. These girls aren't mine, Eve, as they're yours. But . . ."

"You found them."

"And need to know their names, their faces, see their killer dealt with as much as you. What we hope to accomplish in that place is to keep the young, the vulnerable, the wounded safe. Those twelve girls epitomize the purpose."

She wanted to give him the closure, she realized, almost as much as the dead and those they'd left behind.

He wanted to build something good and strong and needed. She wanted to give him those names, so he could.

"It's going to be someone who lived or worked there. That's playing the odds, but they're good odds. It's not that big a pool. Added to it, it stopped—if DeWinter and Dickhead are right on the estimates, and the remains were all sealed in there approximately fifteen years ago. So the focus starts on someone who lived or worked there who died, relocated, or was put in a cage shortly after that time."

"Or moved his burial grounds."

"I thought of that." She ate while the cat watched her with a mixture of hope and resentment. "But why? It's working. It's locked up, no buyers, no plans. And it symbolizes the girls. It's where those vulnerable and wounded came. He knows how to access it, it's familiar. Why find another place that's not so well suited?"

"I hope you're right about that."

"If he had to relocate, for some reason, he would've found a place in his new area. But so far I haven't found any like crimes. And damn if I think he could create another mausoleum."

No, she thought, he didn't pull this off a second time.

"This one basically fell into his lap," she pointed out. "There can't be that many opportunities like it.

"Still, there are spaces in that theory," she admitted over a mouthful of syrupy toast. Take Lemont Frester. He's made some money, travels all over. If he's a sick-fuck predator he could be carrying on his sick-fuck predatory ways all over the world—and off it."

"Happy thought."

"I'm taking a look at him, but for anyone to pull this sort of thing off for this long? And someone like him, who puts himself in the public eye? It's hard to swallow it. Not impossible, but it doesn't go down easy."

"You'll interview him today."

"On my list. Along with nagging DeWinter and her team, notifying Lupa Dison's next of kin, and getting what I can there, maybe another pass through HPCCY and blah blah blah. Top of the list is ID the nine we have left. So I better get started."

She rose to go to her closet.

"The black jean-style trousers. The snug ones," he added, "with the black jacket, the cropped one with the leather trim and the zippers on the sleeves, black tank with a scoop neck, and the black motorcycle style boots. Wear the pants inside the boots."

She'd paused at her closet to listen to him as he reeled off the wardrobe.

"You're telling me to wear all black? You're always trying to paint me up with color."

"In this case it'll be the lines and the textures, as well as the unrelieved black. You'll look just a little dangerous."

"Yeah?" She brightened right up. "I'm all about that."

"I'll be in my office when you're done."

She grabbed what he'd listed, dressed, then curious, glanced in the mirror. Damned if he hadn't hit it again, she thought. She did look just a little dangerous.

Half hoping she had a chance to put the look to use, she went to her office.

Sitting at her desk, she called up the results of her auto-search.

She scanned the remaining sixty-three names, found four deceased within a year of the murders, and separated them as possibles.

She separated any who'd done time, with a subset for violent crime.

With all, she looked for any indication the subject had skill or interest in construction, then crossed them with the staff Peabody and Roarke had run.

"Could've been a team," she said when Roarke came in. "One to kill, one to clean up, or both together. I don't like that as much as it's a damn long time for two people to suppress the urge to kill, and for two people to keep their mouths shut about it."

"One or both could be dead or incarcerated."

"Yeah, it's an angle. Pairs like that usually have a dominant and a submissive." She drummed her fingers. "Older, trusted staff member exploits boy's dark side. Maybe. Maybe, but again it means keeping a secret for a long time, and two people don't keep them very well as a rule, especially when one of them's in a cage. Still, teamwork's efficient. You've got to get the girls, kill the girls, hide the girls. It's a lot of work."

"It's not work if you enjoy it."

She looked back at her board. "No, it's not, and he must have. You don't keep doing something unless you like it—or are compelled—until someone, something stops you."

She gestured to her screen where she'd put up three faces, three names. "The three chronic runaways. At least one of them. The odds again, but at least one of them is probably in DeWinter's lab. I'm going to send them to the reconstructionist, in case it helps."

"Why don't you give me a portion of the male residents to look at more closely? I can do that off and on today when there's time."

"Okay. I'll send you a few. If you don't get to them, just let me know. I've got to get going. I contacted Peabody to have her meet me at Rosetta Vega's. We'll get the notification done, see if she can add anything."

"Frester's booked to speak at the main ballroom of the Roarke Palace Hotel this afternoon."

Eve leveled a speculative look. "Is that so?"

"Excellent synchronicity, isn't it? It's a luncheon speech, the event runs from noon to two. I had no idea. I don't get into the weeds such as event bookings, but I thought I'd check on what he might be doing while in New York, and there you are. There's a twenty-minute question-and-answer period after his speech."

"Handy, as I've got some questions. Thanks. I need to go."

"Send me names for the girls as you get them, would you?"

"Okay." She laid her hands on his shoulders. "Go buy that solar system."

"I'll see if I can squeeze it in."

"Fair enough." She kissed him, then strode out to tell a woman any hope she'd clung to was gone.

U pscale neighborhood, Eve thought as she slid into a street-level slot. Nice, tidy townhomes, condos, glossy shops, and eateries. Dog walkers, nannies, domestics already bustled around on their early duties along with a few people in good coats, good boots on their way to work.

She caught the sugar and yeast scent from a bakery when one of the good coats slipped inside, and the chatter of kids, many in spiffy uniforms, marching along to school.

Then Peabody in her big purple coat and pink cowboy boots, clomping around the corner.

"I think it's not as cold" was the first thing she said. "Maybe. More like frigid instead of fucking frigid. I don't think . . ." She paused, sniffed the air like a retriever. "Do you smell that? It's that bakery. Oh my God, do you smell that? We should—"

"You're not going in to do a notification and interview with pastry breath."

"More like pastry ass. I think I gained a couple pounds just standing here smelling that."

"Then let's save your ass and get this done."

Eve walked up to the door of one of the pretty townhomes, rang the bell.

Instead of the usual computer security check, the door opened almost immediately in front of a pretty, attractive woman in a gray suit. "Did you forget your—oh, I'm sorry." She brushed back her dark curly hair. "I thought you were my daughter. She's always forgetting something when she leaves for school, so I—sorry," she said again with another laugh. "How can I help you?"

"Rosetta Delagio."

"That's right. Actually, I have to leave for work myself in a few minutes, so—"

"I'm Lieutenant Dallas, and this is Detective Peabody." Eve took out her badge. "NYPSD."

The woman looked at the badge, slowly lifted her gaze back to Eve's face. The easy laughter in her eyes died away, and what replaced it was old grief turned over fresh.

"Oh. Oh, Lupa." She laid a hand on her heart. "It's about Lupa, isn't it?"

"Yes, ma'am. I'm sorry to—"

"Please, don't. Don't tell me out here. Come in. Please come in. We'll sit down. I want to get my husband, and we'll sit down. You'll tell me what happened to Lupa."

9 "ALL THIS TIME." ROSETTA SAT IN A PRETTY, family-cluttered living area with her hand in her husband's.

Juan Delagio wore his winter-weight uniform squared away, his cop shoes polished. He had a striking face of sharply defined angles, set off by deep, dark-hooded eyes.

"I think I knew," Rosetta began. "I knew because she would never run away, as some thought she had. We loved each other, and for that time, had no one but each other."

"She stayed for a time at what was The Sanctuary."

"Yes. It was very hard for both of us. When I was hurt, there was no one to care for her. I knew of the place from a friend, so I arranged for her to stay there. They were very kind, and tended to her for only a small donation as I couldn't afford more. And one of the counselors brought her to see me in the hospital every day. But still, it was hard.

I knew there were troubled young people there, and my Lupa was so innocent—young for her age, if you understand? But I was afraid if they took her from me, into the child protection, they might not give her back."

"Was there a question of your guardianship?"

"No, no, but . . . I was very young myself, and not yet a citizen. So I was afraid, but I thought she would be safe at The Sanctuary, and she was. She did well there, though Ms. Jones told me Lupa had some fears as well, that I would leave her, too. We talked of it in counseling."

"The report states that when she came back, she began to come home late, and wasn't clear about where she'd been."

"It wasn't like her, the sneaking. She was an accommodating young girl. I thought maybe too much—afraid to do anything wrong or even a little bit wrong, afraid she'd be sent away. So I didn't punish her. I should have been more firm," she said and looked desperately at her husband.

He only shook his head, brought their joined hands to his lips.

"I said I wanted to meet her new friends, and we could have them over for pizza, or I could cook. She was evasive, just said maybe some-time. She was loving with me, and sweet, so I let it go. I thought she just wants something all of her own for a little while, and why should she sit alone in the apartment until I come home from work? She's a good girl, and she's making friends. Maybe it would help her with the grief. She had such grief, and still questioned why her mother and father died. Was it her fault? Had she done something? Had she not been good enough? Had *they* not been good enough?"

She glanced toward a table littered with photos. Eve picked out one of her sister—strong resemblance—young and smiling.

"For a time Lupa talked to our priest, but she still questioned, especially after I was hurt."

"She was mugged," Juan said. "There were two men, and they hurt her. Even when she gave them what she had without trouble, they hurt her. They cut her. You know how it can be, Lieutenant."

"Yeah, I do."

"A lady saw it from her window and called the police," Rosetta continued. "Then because I was hurt, and I couldn't come home or take care of Lupa, they had to take her. That's when I asked for her to be placed in The Sanctuary, and it was arranged. Lupa . . ."

She broke for a moment, then steadied again. "It scared her so, when I was hurt. And made her question even more. What had she done or not done? Why did terrible things happen to those she loved and who loved her?"

"It's pretty common," Peabody said, "for kids of that age to see themselves as the center. I mean, good things happen because they're good, bad things because they're bad."

"Yes, this was Lupa. So I thought friends, girls her own age, without such grief, would be good for her. Then, that evening, I came home from work, and she wasn't there. I tried her 'link, but she didn't answer. I waited and waited, I asked the neighbors, schoolmates, everyone I could think of. No one knew where she'd gone, where she was. I went to the police."

"Mrs. Delagio." Peabody spoke up gently when Rosetta's voice began to quiver. "You did everything right, and you did everything right for all the right reasons."

"Thank you. Thank you for that. The police, they put out the alert, and they looked for her. I looked for her. Neighbors looked, people were kind. But days passed, nights passed. She never came home. I never saw her again. She would have come home if she could. I knew it even then. She must have been afraid. I hate thinking of her afraid, wanting me, wanting to come home."

"Is there anything you remember, from looking," Eve began, "from talking to people? Anything that sticks out?"

"Some people would say they saw her here, others they saw her there. People called the . . . what is it?"

"Tip line," Eve supplied.

"Yes, and the police checked, but it was never Lupa. Detective Handy was so kind. We still talk now and then. I should tell her—"

"I've spoken with her," Eve said.

"I'll speak with her, too. She never stopped looking. She was my hope, even though we both knew, if she found Lupa, it would . . . it would be like this. I wrote down everything, every night for months. I have the little diaries I kept."

"Could we have them? We'll get them back to you."

"Yes, of course."

"I'll get them." Juan rose. "I know where you keep them. I'll call in for you, for me. We'll stay home today. Make arrangements."

She murmured to him in Spanish, and for the first time her eyes filled, overflowed. He answered quietly in the same language, then left the room.

"I hadn't met Juan when I lost Lupa. They would have loved each other. He loves her because I do, and he looked, too, long after she was gone. He knows we'll want to have a service for her. Is it possible to . . . can I have her for a service and burial?"

"It may take a while, but I'll see that you do."

She nodded, knuckled at the tears. "The other girls, the girls with her, do they have family?"

"We're working on that."

"We are, Juan and I, fortunate. We'd help with any of the girls who are . . . alone. Is that possible?"

When they stepped out on the sidewalk, Peabody dug in the cavernous pockets of her coat, pulled out a tissue. "Sorry." She dabbed at her eyes, blew her nose. "I handled it until she asked if they could help bury the other victims."

Eve said nothing until they'd gotten to the car, gotten into it.

"People mostly suck—it's the law of averages, I figure, especially when you're on the job. Then you cross paths with people like that. Bad shit's happened to them, seriously bad shit, but they still come out of it decent."

She handed off the diaries to Peabody. Old-fashioned ones, she thought. Small covered books you wrote in with pen or pencil.

"We'll take a look through these. Maybe she put something down she didn't realize was important at the time."

"McNab and I could take care of one of the vics. We could swing that."

"Peabody."

"It's not getting personally involved or losing objectivity," Peabody insisted, though she knew better. "It's being decent."

Eve let it drop as Peabody fumbled out a fresh tissue. "We're going to poke at DeWinter. We'll swing by Stubacker's last known address, see if anybody there remembers her, or has any fresh info."

It was like crossing a border from one country to another. Shelby Ann Stubacker's old neighborhood squatted with cheap post-Urban housing, or the crumbling remains of what had come before. Pawnshops and graffiti abounded alongside tat and piercing parlors, sex clubs and dingy-looking bars. Here people didn't hire dog walkers, but likely had attack-programmed droid Dobermans. Instead of carrying briefcases, they'd carry shivs.

Eve used her master to bypass the locks on the reinforced door of an eight-story building in the middle of the seamy squalor.

The entranceway carried the stench of old piss and puke under the chemically piney scent of the industrial cleaner some determined soul had used to try to eradicate it.

Not a chance, Eve thought as she started up the stairs. The stench was in the building's bones.

"She was in three-oh-five, living with her mother, and according to the records, a series of her mother's boyfriends, when the court took her out. We'll start there."

Screens blared behind triple-locked doors and paper-thin walls Eve imagined a determined chemi-head could punch a fist through.

Now she smelled what she identified—due to her exposure to Bella—as soiled diapers, mixed in with the scent of whatever someone had burned for breakfast.

"I'd need a portable air filter to live here," Peabody commented. Carefully she avoided brushing up against the wall, the sticky railing. "And a detox chamber."

A baby, maybe the one responsible for the crappy diaper smell, wailed like its feet were on fire. Some kind soul responded to the infant's distress by banging on one of the thin walls.

"Shut that brat the fuck up!"

"Nice." Peabody shot a hard look down the hall of the second floor. "I'd be crying, too, if I lived here. It must be absolute hell growing up in a place like this."

She'd been in places like it—and worse—in her first eight years, so Eve could attest. It was absolute hell.

On three, she used the side of her fist to bang on the door of the Stubackers' old apartment. It didn't warrant any electronic security, just a peephole and a pair of grimy dead-bolt locks.

She caught the shadow at the peep, banged again. "NYPSD." She held her badge up in plain sight. "Open the door."

She heard the clunk and rusty slide of a riot bar, then a series of hard clicks before the door opened a few inches on a hefty security chain.

"What the hell do you want?"

What she could see of the woman's face didn't look promising. It still wore yesterday's makeup, thoroughly smudged from sleep. Eve imagined the woman's pillow resembled one of those strange abstract paintings she would never understand.

"Lieutenant Dallas, Detective Peabody. We'd like to ask you a few questions."

"I don't gotta talk to you unless you got a warrant. I know my rights."

"We just have some questions about the former tenant of this apartment."

Something sly came into the woman's raccoon eyes. "You paying?"

"That depends on what you have to sell. Did you know the former tenant?"

"Sure. Worked with Tracy up at the club, VaVoom, back when we were dancers. So what?"

"Do you know where we can find her?"

"Haven't seen her since she blew town. Been easy ten years back. I sublet this dump, fair and square. Got rent control on it."

"Did you know her daughter?"

"The brat, yeah. Took off long before Tracy did. Had a mouth on her, the kid did, used to steal, too. Lift stuff in the dressing room at the club. Tracy tried to beat the wild outta her, but it didn't take. Some kids're born bad, and that's that. Got so Tracy had to hide any booze or brew she might have around or the kid would drink it. Told me how she came home one night, found the kid pissed-face drunk, probably no more than ten, eleven years old, and she's all over Tracy's boyfriend. Tried to say he gave her the brew and got all over *her*. Kid lied every time she opened her mouth."

"Tracy sounds like mother of the year," Eve said coolly.

"She did the best with what she had. Kid was no good. One day Tracy comes into work with a busted lip and a shiner. Kid did it. And what happens? You people come and say Tracy abused the brat just because the kid had some bruises on her. A woman's got to defend herself, and got a right to discipline her own."

"Did Shelby ever come back, after she was taken out of the home?"

"Who—oh, right, that's her name. Not that I know of, and Tracy would've told me. The kid was a freaking thorn in her side. They took her off, put her in some sort of group home, and that was the end of that. A few years later, Tracy took off with this guy. He played the ponies, hit pretty good on a trifecta or whatever the fuck. They took off, said they were going to live in Miami or somewhere. Never heard from her again. But I got rent control."

"Lucky you. Did you know any of Shelby's friends?"

"Why would I? Don't know as she had any. Piece of work, that girl. If she comes around here like you, looking for her ma, I'll tell her just what I think."

Eve tried a few more questions, and realizing the well ran dry, passed the woman a twenty through the gap.

She tried a few more doors, but stepped back out with little more than she'd gone in with.

"What a horrible excuse for a human being." Peabody dropped into the car, snapped her safety belt. "Not just the bitch on three, but the vic's mother by all accounts. I just don't get how a woman can treat her own kid that way. Knocking her around, neglecting her, and just walking away when . . ."

It struck her, obviously and visibly, so she cringed.

"Sorry. Sorry, Dallas."

Eve shrugged. "At least I didn't have about a dozen years with mine."

"Sorry anyway."

"The question is, if Shelby didn't go back to her mother—the bitch of a wit could be wrong about that, so see if you can dig up any record of her being placed back here—why didn't Jones and Jones file a Missing Persons on her?"

"I didn't think of that."

"That's why you're not the lieutenant. Dig, and while you're digging we'll go get all up DeWinter's ass."

"She's got a really good one."

"Jesus, Peabody." Amazed, Eve slid out into traffic. "You checked out her ass?"

"I check out everyone's ass. It's a hobby."

"Get a new one. Like . . . bird-watching or something."

"Bird-watching? In New York?"

"You could count pigeons. It would take the rest of your life."

"I like ass-watching." Peabody settled herself in comfortably.

"When I see one bigger than mine, it makes me feel good. When I see one smaller, it helps me resist eating a whole bunch of cookies. It's a productive hobby, my ass-watching. And there's no record on file rescinding the court order to remove Shelby Ann Stubacker from the home. No record of any petition filed by the mother to get her back."

"Which means, despite the notation in her records that she was placed back in the parental home, she went missing from either The Sanctuary or the new digs. Interesting."

"I guess Jones and Jones go back on the list."

"They were never off. But now they bump up to the lead."

She pushed and threaded her way through traffic, considering new angles. "Tag HPCCY, tell them we need the documentation on Shelby's court order. We need the CPS docs, the recommendation to send her back home."

"On that."

While she was, Eve parked again.

"Ms. Jones says she'll pull the files up out of storage," Peabody said as they went inside, worked through the maze to DeWinter's sector. "She asks if we've ID'd anyone else."

"Tell her that information will be forthcoming."

She found DeWinter—an emerald green lab coat today, open over another body-conscious dress, this one hot pink and white checkerboard.

She stood with Morris, who was just as snappily dressed in deep, dark plum. Together they studied a screen displaying indecipherable shapes—to her—in colors as bold as their wardrobes.

"It's cause of death," DeWinter said. "Do you agree?"

"I do."

"What's cause of death?" Eve demanded.

Both turned toward her so they stood with a trio of slabs, a trio of remains, between them.

"They drowned," DeWinter said.

"Drowned." Eve stepped in, looked down at the remains, up at the screen. "You can determine that, conclusively, from bones."

"I can. You see on screen a sample of the diatoms I extracted from the bone marrow of the third victim identified. That would be—"

"Lupa Dison."

"Yes. I also have similar samples from the first two victims, and the fourth. I'll continue to conduct the procedure on all the remains. But I can conclude for the four on which I've conducted the tests, these girls drowned. The diatoms here reached the lungs and penetrated the alveolar wall, and the bone marrow. Comparing these samples to samples of water I took from the crime scene—"

Eve tossed up a hand to stop the flow. "You went back to the crime scene? Without notifying the primary?"

"I didn't think it was necessary until I'd reached my conclusions, which indeed—in consultation with Dr. Morris—I have. Now, these unicellular organisms have a silica shell, and as you can see, truly gorgeous sculpturing. The aquatic diatom—"

"Stop." Eve held up a hand again, added the other, and caught Morris grinning out of the corner of her eye. "I don't want a science lesson. I need to know if you've found COD."

DeWinter just frowned at her. "As I just said, drowning, in city water. While certain additives have changed or been deleted from the city's water in the last fifteen years, the basic biology remains. Such as—"

"Stop there, too. City water? No chance of, say, pool water, river water, seawater?"

"No, again, aquatic diatoms—"

"Just no's enough. The bathtub then. It's not impossible to drown a girl in a sink, or just pour water down her throat, stick her head in the john. But with the lack of injury at or around time of death, the bathtub makes more sense. Plus, it's right there if you want to drown a bunch of girls."

She walked around the slabs as she worked it out.

"They'd have fought back if they could. Drowning's a hard way to go. You'd flail around, kick, knock your elbows, try to grab whoever's holding you under. They didn't do that, according to what you've seen."

"No, there were no fractures or other appearance of damage to the bones so far examined at or around TOD. However—"

"So he tranq'd them first. Just enough to make them go under easy. Enough so maybe he could bind their hands and feet, make it easier yet. Tranq them, maybe restrain them, then slide them in, hold their heads under. One at a time."

She studied the remains again, brought the bathrooms of the crime scene into her head. "You can't let one of the others see what you're doing. So one at a time. Maybe you've got another on tap, but you can't risk her coming around enough to make a fuss. When she's out, you undress her. That's practical, the clothes will add to the weight when they're wet. And it's more a thrill anyway, seeing that young, naked body. If she's out enough, maybe you rape her first. Slip her a little Whore or Rabbit, even something a little milder, she won't fight you."

She circled around the slab as she spoke, studying the bones, seeing the flesh and blood that had once covered them.

"When you're done with her, after you've watched her die, you take her out, put her on the plastic. You take the restraints off so you can use them on the next girl. And you roll her up."

Eve looked over at Morris, nodded. "That's how I see it. He'd probably already started the false wall, easier if he'd done that. Just leave a section of the board out. He'd put her back here, in the dark, out of sight, probably tack the board up. Nobody's going to come in, nobody but him and the next girl."

She shifted her gaze to DeWinter. "Does that work for you, fit with your conclusions so far?"

"Yes. Yes, it does. Though there's no way to conclude if they were restrained as there are no signs of damage from struggling against restraints on the wrists or ankles. And it's simply not possible to determine if they were raped."

"It's a theory. Let me know when you've done that diorama test on the others."

"Diatom."

"Right. And let me know if you plan to revisit the crime scene. The one about a killer returning to the scene of the crime's a cliché for a reason. See you around, Morris."

DeWinter took a long breath when Eve and Peabody left. "That was disturbing. It's disturbing to be walked through murder that way, as if by the murderer."

"It's a particular skill of hers."

"I can see them. The victims, the dead, through their bones. I can tell how they lived, how they died. But I wouldn't like to have their killer inside my head."

"Putting them there helps her find them."

"I'm very glad that's not my job."

"And she sees them, too, Garnet. She sees the dead, just as you and I do."

E ve saw them now, as she started out of the maze, the ones whose faces she knew.

"I hope you're right about the tranqing," Peabody said. "It wouldn't have been so painful and terrifying that way."

"Lieutenant!"

Eve stopped, looked back to see Elsie Kendrick waddling—that was the only word for it—down the wide steps to the lower-level lab.

"I'm glad I caught you. I have two more." She offered both disc and hard copies. "I should have at least another two by the end of the day."

"Fast work."

"I set it on auto for a few hours last night, just bunked here." She rubbed circles on her truly enormous belly. "I've never done so many from one case. I can't get them out of my head. Would you send me their names, like you did the others? I want their names."

"You'll have them when we do. Good work, and thanks."

She handed Peabody the disc as they continued out, and studied the computer-generated sketches.

"I know these two, they were on my Missing Persons search list. Pull up the file I sent you. They're both in there."

And two more of the pretty young girls had faces, had names.

10 SHE WENT BACK TO CENTRAL, TO HER OFFICE, to put those names and faces on her board. Both of them runaways, with LaRue Freeman fresh out of a stint at juvie for theft, and Carlie Bowen circling the foster system after being removed from an abusive home.

Their stories were all too typical, Eve thought as she scanned their files. A short, hard life with too much of it spent on the streets.

Neither of them had been registered at The Sanctuary or HPCCY.

Still, it didn't mean they weren't somehow connected. Street kids had networks, she thought as she began to run cross-checks. Networks could become gangs. But even on a lesser level street kids, like most kids, tended to form packs.

Both Shelby and LaRue had done time in juvie—not together, she noted, but . . . and there it was.

Both had had the same CPS caseworker. Odelle Horwitz no longer worked for CPS—nothing unusual there, Eve thought as she grabbed coffee while the current data generated.

Social workers burned out faster than a struck match.

Horwitz, age forty-two, on her second marriage, one offspring, now managed a flower shop on the Upper East Side.

Maybe she'd remember something, maybe she wouldn't, but it was worth the contact. She turned to her 'link.

She'd ended the interview, had grabbed her coat when Baxter rapped on her doorjamb. "Got a minute, boss?"

"About that."

He stepped in on his high-gloss shoes. The detective had a wardrobe more typical of Wall Street than Homicide, but she'd take him and his fancy suits through the door with her anytime, anywhere.

"Trueheart and I caught one yesterday, a double slice and dice in the theater district."

"Those auditions are a bloodbath."

He laughed. "Funny you should mention it, because it looks pretty much just like that."

He gave her a brief outline of two actors competing for the same part in a new production. Now one of them, along with his cohab, was in the morgue.

"The other guy, his alibi's solid. He was onstage playing Gino in a revival of *West Side Story*. Reviews are mixed, but there were a couple hundred people in the audience, plus the cast and crew who can all verify he was dancing with the Sharks at TOD."

"There's dancing sharks?"

He started to laugh again, then realized she wasn't kidding. "The Sharks—and the Jets. They're rival gangs, LT. The play's like a *Romeo and Juliet* takeoff, but set in New York. Rival gangs, first love, violence, friendship and loyalty, singing, dancing."

"Yeah, those street gangs are always breaking into song and dancing on their way to the next beat down."

"I guess you've got to see it to get it."

"Fine. So the competing actor's clear. He just got lucky?"

"We're looking hard at his boyfriend. He claims he was backstage during the performance, which would put him clear. And he's got some cover from some people who say they saw him. But the play runs a couple hours and he could've slipped off. We worked out the timing. Crime scene's a five-minute walk from the theater. Half that at a decent jog. He's got no priors, we've got no murder weapon, no wits. No security on the building. It's half a dump. But my gut, my nose—hell, my toned and manly ass—says he did it."

"Bring him in, sweat it out of him."

"Plan on it. I want Trueheart to take him."

She had a lot of respect for Officer Trueheart, despite the few smudges of green still left on him. "No wits, no weapon, a reasonable alibi, and you want Trueheart to get the guy to say he sliced up two people so his boyfriend could get a part in a play?"

"It's the lead." Baxter smiled. "And the thing is, the guy got that look in his eye for Trueheart when we interviewed him."

"What look?"

"The 'I'd like to take you out to lunch, eat the main course off your hard yet sensitive abs, and have you for dessert.'"

"I didn't need that picture in my head, Baxter."

"You asked."

Well, she supposed she had. "If you think Trueheart can bust him—and not because you think it'll look good when Trueheart takes his detective's exam next month—do it."

"He can bust him, and it'll look good. And it'll boost his confidence going into the exam. It's an all-around win." He paused a moment, looked at her board. "You ID'd two more."

"This morning, yeah. You keeping track?"

"We all are. And we're all up for OT if you need it."

"It's appreciated. Count on me letting you know. Now go wrap this guy up."

She walked out with him, signaled Peabody. "With me."

"I've got next of kin on the last two vics. Freeman, father unknown, mother doing her second stint for assault, with a side of illegals. This one in Joliet. There's an aunt in Queens, she's the one who filed the report."

"Yeah, I remember."

"The older sister filed the one on Bowen," Peabody added as she struggled into her puffy coat.

"Both parents have been guests of the state," Eve continued as they made their way down to the garage. "Older sister had filed for custody when she was only eighteen. It was working its way through the system, the kid in foster."

"The sister runs a sandwich shop with her husband." Now the scarf—a mile of bright green, wrapping, wrapping around Peabody's neck, then tucking into some sort of complicated twist. "Midtown spot. Two kids. Sealed juvie record on her, and a minor bump for him. They've been clear for about fifteen years."

"When her kid sister went missing. We'll talk to them, and the aunt in Queens."

"Sandwich shop would be an efficient stop—interview, lunch, all together."

Eve calculated the timing. "You do that. I'll drop you off at the sister's place on my way to check out this Frester character. You can contact the aunt, and we'll decide if it's worth doing a linkup with the mother. We'll hook up back at the crime scene. I want another walk-through."

"I'll pick you up some takeout. What do you want?"

"Surprise me."

The doorman at the hotel had obviously gotten the memo. He might have given a cop a little grief about leaving her vehicle in front of the grand edifice of the premier hotel, but for Roarke's wife, he rolled out the red carpet.

It was a little bit annoying.

Still it saved time, as did her stop at the front desk—memo also received. With a security guard as escort, she breezed through the checkpoints for the ballroom event, and straight inside.

Talk about grand. The glint of crystals dripping from chandeliers that managed to look Old World and futuristic at once, the gleam of white marble with silver veining, walls smoky gray to set off the black shine of trim and cornices.

About five hundred people at her estimate sat around big round tables draped in dark gray cloth with a navy underlayer. Servers moved silent as wraiths to clear dessert plates or serve coffee, pour fizzy water into glasses.

Lemont Frester stood on the wide front stage, a huge screen behind him showing him with various luminaries from Hollywood, music, politics. Mixed in were images of him speaking to prisoners, addicts, youth groups. Or pictures of him dressed for a hike with forested mountains around him, looking pensive and pious staring out at the roll of blue seas, on the back of a white horse in some golden desert.

They all had one common link. Lemont Frester was the focus.

His voice rolled out, as ripe and fruity as a basket of oranges. He practices, she thought: the rhythm, the punch words, the gestures, the expressions, the pause for a bit of laughter or approving applause.

He wore a three-piece suit, directly between the shades of the room's walls and table linen. She wondered if he'd had it made for just that purpose, along with the tie of pale gray chevrons on navy.

Too perfect a match for happenstance, which was usually bullshit anyway. And a man who'd order his wardrobe to coordinate with a speaking arena, or vice versa, had a towering ego, a tsunamic vanity.

She didn't like him. Didn't like the way his eyes glinted, his voice rolled, his suit matched. Didn't like the sense that he was on the same level as one of those pay-as-you-pray evangelists who banged the good-looking faithful on the side, and scammed the money from susceptible old women.

But not liking him didn't make him a murderer.

She listened with half an ear. He talked of not just overcoming his addictions, his flaws, what he called the dark child inside him—he'd triumphed over it. And the audience could, too. They could all lead strong, productive lives (that included world travel, Eve supposed, and fancy suits), could counsel others, even the darkest inner child, to win the desperate personal battle.

The answers, the solutions, the checklists were all handily contained in his latest book package, which included a disc compilation of homilies and highlights. And all that for the bargain price of a hundred and thirty-eight dollars, only twenty bucks more for the autographed package.

A steal, Eve thought. Oh yeah, Frester was robbing people blind, and not one of them appeared to mind a bit.

Her 'link signaled. She pulled it out, found a voice mail from Roarke, switched it to text only.

```
I'm between meetings, briefly, and assume you are
as well. Mavis and her family will be coming over
```

> tonight for drinks and a casual dinner. It'll do
> us all good. I've put it on your calendar, but
> as we both know I might as well write it on air.
>
> Take care of my cop until I see you, then I'll
> look out for her.

She had a moment of wondering why he'd asked their friends over when she was in the middle of a very ugly case, then remembered they'd talked of it the night before.

But that was then, with all the Christmas and champagne haze.

Still, she decided, it probably would do her good. Especially since Mavis had been a street kid, living on the grift for several years. An expert consultant, she decided, and immediately sent a text to her friend, asking if they could come maybe a half hour earlier and for Mavis to come up to her office.

> Couple questions on a case I'm working. Street
> kids. Want to poke in your memory for more
> insight. See you tonight. Dallas.

So, she'd combine hanging with friends with work. The perfect, for her, compromise.

She did a little more multitasking while Frester took questions, sending an e-mail to Mira, with DeWinter's findings on COD attached.

> Waiting to interview a possible suspect. Question. Murder by
> drowning, multiple cases—very likely in the tub of The Sanctuary

dorms. Not a practical method, comparatively. Possible kill thrill—
hands on, face-to-face. But possibly symbolic? Washed clean
maybe. Submerged. Listening to asshole speak on submerging dark
inner child, makes me wonder about that angle.

Some sort of ritual maybe?

Would you explore this area, or am I going off?

Dallas

Before putting it away, Eve began the laborious—to her—process
of using her 'link to order her office comp to begin researching ritual
drownings and submerging.

Then she walked to the side of the ballroom to work her way
down toward the stage as the time slotted for the Q&A section ran
down.

A hard-eyed female security type in a snug suit that set off an impressive rack stepped in front of her. Eve merely held out her badge,
returning hard eye for hard eye.

"You're not cleared. Mr. Frester is engaged directly after this event.
You'll need to contact his first assistant or his lawyer."

"Or I can make a cop scene right here, in the middle of said event.
I bet that'll cut into the sales of the inspirational packages."

"I'll need to speak directly with your superior."

"Here and now I am my superior. Now step aside or I'll arrest you
for interfering with a police officer in the course of her duties, with a
side of obstruction of justice and a sprinkle of being a pain in my ass."

Hard eye grew harder. "We're going to take this outside."

She clamped a hand on Eve's arm.

Eve smiled, toothily. "Now you've done it. You just added assaulting an officer to the menu of choices."

With her free hand, Eve swung the woman toward the wall, took an elbow in the gut with enough force behind it to make her grunt. And to make her think just how much she'd enjoy knowing Big Rack Security Bitch did some time in holding.

"You're now officially under arrest." Eve put some force behind her own next move, and shoved the woman's face to the wall, then grabbed the wrist of the hand that reached down for the stunner clipped to her waist.

"And it gets better and better," she said as people at the nearby tables began to react with alarm and movement.

"Police," Eve said clear and firm, as she yanked the woman's arms behind her back. "You're going to want to stay in your seats."

The woman had some skill, or so Eve thought when she managed to shift her weight, get one arm free, and use it for a back fist Eve couldn't quite avoid.

It glanced off her cheekbone and sent out some angry sparks of pain.

"You're just asking for it."

She kicked the woman's feet out from under her, planted a knee in the small of her back, and restrained her arms behind her.

She glanced up as a beefy male security type trotted up.

"Police," she repeated, and since it was the easiest way, and a little more dignified, she rose, exchanged knee for boot, flashed her badge.

The man's demeanor changed instantly. Another memo received, she imagined. "Lieutenant Dallas. What can I do to help?"

"Hotel security?"

"Yes, sir."

"I'd say this event is over. If you could see that Mr. Frester is brought to me in whatever room or area is most convenient, and systematically clear this room, I'll arrange for the prisoner to be transported to Central."

"She attacked me!" Big Rack bucked under Eve's boot. "I was doing my job, and she attacked me."

Eve simply pointed to her aching cheek, then drew out the grip of the stunner she'd managed to dump in her coat pocket during the scuffle. "Hers, which she tried to draw on me. You'd have security feed in here. My arrest will hold up."

"I'll take care of it right away."

With a nod, Eve pulled out her communicator and called for the closest unit to report to her location for prisoner transport.

All in all, she decided, it made up nicely for the doorman's red carpet treatment.

They set her up in a meeting room that held a round table with a half dozen chairs, a two-seater sofa, a jumbo wall screen, and a nice view of the great park in its current frigid glory.

They'd brought in coffee service, so what the hell, she poured some, drank it while she went over her notes.

Frester glided in—flanked by two suits, one male, one female. All three were polished to high gloss—with him the shiniest.

He radiated smiles and good fellowship, which just put her off.

"The famous Lieutenant Dallas!" He shot out a hand accented by a gold pinky ring with a fat ruby.

She didn't get pinky rings or people who wore them.

He pumped her hand three times, firm grip, soft palm.

"I wasn't in town for the vid premiere, but I enjoyed the book, and watched the vid at a private screening last month. Marvelous! Clones." He lifted his hands toward the ceiling, palms up. "I'd have sworn it was science fiction, but you actually lived through the entire thing."

"Just another day on the job. Have a seat, Mr. Frester," she said when he let out a barking laugh. Eve gave his two companions a once-over. "Do you feel the need for bodyguards during this interview?"

"Standard procedure, I'm afraid." He did the hand lift again, pulled out a chair. "Those of us in the public eye, as you know, can draw the wrong kind of . . . enthusiasm, we'll say. Greta is also an attorney, so . . ."

Eve only lifted her eyebrows as he trailed off. "That's fine, simple. Since you have a legal rep in the room, I'll just read you your rights, then we're all covered."

"My rights? Why—"

"So . . ." She mimicked him, then recited the Revised Miranda. "Do you understand your rights and obligations in this matter, Mr. Frester?"

"Of course, of course. I assumed this had to do with Ingrid's over-protectiveness. I'm told you had her arrested. Let me apologize. I feel responsible as she was only doing her job."

"It's her job to draw her weapon on a police officer?"

"Of course not! No, indeed." Very subtly, he slanted a look toward his companions. One of them slid soundlessly from the room. "I'm sure there was just a misunderstanding."

"The security feed will make it very clear as your boy—the one you just sent to review it—will find out. You're free to post her bond, should bond be granted. In the meantime, I'm here to talk to you about The Sanctuary."

"Ah, my crossroads."

He folded his hands, pinky ring glinting, leaned forward just a little—just enough to communicate earnest connection.

Oh yeah, he practiced.

"It was there I began to see there was another path open to me, to everyone. That I had only to accept a power, an entity, a hand in all things bigger—and certainly wiser—than myself, to accept that and take the first steps on the path."

"Good for you." Eve opened the file bag, took out photos. "Do you recognize any of these girls?"

"I can't say I do." He pulled at his bottom lip as he scanned the photos. "Should I?"

"Some of them were residents at The Sanctuary when you were."

"Oh. Well, let me look again with that in mind. So long ago," he murmured. "But such an important part of my life, I should . . . This girl. Yes, yes." He tapped a finger on Shelby Stubacker's photo. "I remember her. Tough exterior, and clever—though not in a positive way—but those of us there, at least most of us there were at first so troubled, so angry. Shelly, was it?"

"Shelby."

"Shelby. Yes, I remember her, and I think this girl. She sticks in my memory. A quiet girl, I think, studious, which was rare as hen's teeth, so I remember her. I don't know if I ever knew her name, but I'm fairly certain she was there only a short time. Then the facility moved to its new and current location. Is that helpful at all? I don't see why . . ." He paused again, then sat back with his face dropping from curiosity to concern.

"I heard bodies were found in the empty building, the old building. I never connected it to us, to The Sanctuary. Are these girls . . . were they the bodies found?"

"Remains," Eve corrected. "We've established these girls who've been officially identified and seven others who have not yet been identified were murdered approximately fifteen years ago, and their bodies hidden in the building where The Sanctuary was based."

"But that's—that's just not possible. Murdered? Hidden? Lieutenant Dallas, I can promise you the girls would have been missed. Philadelphia and Nashville Jones were dedicated, diligent. They'd have been missed, and searched for. It was a fairly large building considering, but it simply wouldn't have been possible to hide twelve bodies."

"The facility moved, the building was empty."

"I don't—oh. Oh, dear God." Clasping his hands together, he bowed his head a moment, as if in prayer. "There was some confusion in the move, of course, but if any of us had been unaccounted for, there would be a record. You've spoken to Philadelphia and Nashville, I assume."

She ignored that. "Did you ever go back to the old building?"

"Yes. When I was writing my first book I wanted to walk through, stir up memories, try to bring it all back clearly so I could mine all that for the work. About eight—no, nine—years ago, I believe. I contacted the owners. I'll admit I prevaricated a bit, let them think I might be interested in purchasing the building or leasing the space. I walked through with their representative, though she let me have plenty of space and time. It did stir up the memories."

"Anything strike you different?"

"It seemed bigger without all of us in it, without all the furnishings, the equipment, supplies. And yet it seemed smaller at the time. It had been let go, if you understand me. They'd had break-ins—the rep gave full disclosure. The bathrooms had been gutted of anything useful or sellable. You could see there'd been some squatting."

He pressed his lips together. "A terrible, stale smell to the place that would never have been permitted with Philadelphia in charge. I heard mice in the walls. Or it might've been rats. I went from bottom to top and back again. I wouldn't, couldn't have missed bodies. They must have been put there later."

"Do you ever do any handiwork around the place? Any repairs."

He laughed again, wiggled his fingers. "All thumbs. I remember being on painting detail once, and hating it. I bribed another boy to take my duty. We were required to do work around the building. Cleaning, painting as I said—and were encouraged to work with the handyman—what was his name? Brady—no, Brodie—and with Montclair."

"The brother who died in Africa."

"Yes, a terrible and tragic end to a quiet and simple life."

He paused for a beat, as if in respect for the dead.

"We were encouraged, as I said, to help, and would be given more training if we showed an aptitude for plumbing or carpentry. Which I certainly did not."

Another barking laugh at the thought.

"One of the staff played the piano and brought in a keyboard. Ms. Glenbrook—I had a terrible crush on her," he said with a dreamy smile. "She'd give music instruction, which I took due to the crush, but again, I had no talent at all. Another gave basic art lessons, or more involved lessons for those who had interest. We had a couple of staff who had solid e-skills, so we had that. It was, even in the sad old building, a well-rounded experience. Whether we wanted it or not, and many of us—including me for far too long—didn't. We just wanted to get high. That was the goal for some of us."

"And you scored?"

"We'd find ways. The addicted always do. We were caught— nearly always—but it didn't matter to us, not then. For some, it would never matter."

"And the staff? Did they use?"

"No. Certainly not to my knowledge, and I would have known. Zero tolerance. Any staff member, anyone who volunteered or worked there would be shown the door immediately, and the police notified."

"What about sex?"

"Teenagers, Lieutenant." He unfolded his hands long enough to lift them in a what-can-you-do gesture. "Sex is another kind of drug, another kind of high. And the forbidden is always the most exciting."

"Did you try out any of these girls?"

"You don't have to answer that, sir."

The bodyguard who doubled as a lawyer spoke up, her face carved in dispassion.

"It's all right. I've long accepted and repented my many sins. I don't remember ever having relations with any of these girls, but if I'd been high, I might not remember. Still, they look young. Younger than I was. There's a pecking order, if you will."

But Eve saw his gaze linger on Shelby's photo, and thought he re-membered her and her bj bargaining chip well enough.

"Any of the staff hit on the kids?"

"I never heard about anything like that and you'd hear. I know I was never approached, and I'd have given up my cache of zoner if Ms. Glenbrook had crooked her finger in my direction."

He leaned forward again, just a bit more this time, held out his hands. "We were given what we needed at The Sanctuary. Shelter, food, boundaries, discipline, reward, education. Someone cared enough to give us what we needed. And when we moved locations, became the Higher Power Cleansing Center for Youths, we were given more of it, in a better place, because they had more funding. Without what I was given, without the opportunity to see the path, to accept the higher power, I would never have seen or lived up to my own potential, or had the courage to offer a new way to others."

"These girls never had the chance to find out what their potential might have been," Eve reminded him. "Somebody cut all of that off, shut off their lives."

He bowed his head a couple respectful inches. "I can only believe they're in a better place."

"I don't see dead as better. Save the higher power," she told him before he could speak. "This is murder. Wherever they are, nobody had the right to put them there."

"Of course not, of course not. To take a life is the ultimate sin against all life. I only meant with the pain and trouble and hardship these girls likely knew, they're at peace now."

Eve sat back. "Is that what they taught you at The Sanctuary, at HPCCY? That being dead at peace is better than living a hard life?"

"You misunderstand."

He pressed his palms together, aiming the tips of his fingers toward her, and spoke earnestly.

"Finding your life, the light in it, the peace and richness in that, no matter how difficult, is what lifts us above the animals. Offering a hand to those in need, a kind word, a place of shelter, a chance to spread the light and guide us on our path, and when the path ends, there is even greater light, deeper peace. It's that I wish for these unfortunate girls. I'll hope for the same for their killer. That he accepts what he's done, repents it, offers his contrition."

"I'll take his confession, he can keep his contrition."

He sat back with a sigh, one lightly tinged with pity. "Your work takes you into dark places. Greta, get Lieutenant Dallas a complimentary package."

"Thanks all the same." As she rose Eve thought she'd rather have a sharp, burning stick jammed in her ear. "We're not allowed to accept any gifts. Thanks for your time. If I have any more questions, I know how to find you."

He looked momentarily nonplussed at being so abruptly dismissed. "I hope I've been of some help." He got to his feet. "I'll wish you clear-sightedness on your path."

He glided out as he'd glided in, but she thought she'd dulled that shine a little.

She decided it made her a small person to take pleasure in that, but she was fine with it.

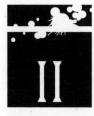**II**

EVE STOOD ON THE SIDEWALK STUDYING THE crime scene, imagining how the building looked fifteen years ago. Not quite as shabby, she thought, no boards on the windows. From her sense of the Joneses, they would have assigned staff, kids, themselves to scrub off any tagging.

Maybe this time of year there had been some holiday wreath instead of a police seal on the door.

The buildings around it would have changed a little here and there. Owners selling, tenants moving out, moving in.

She considered the tat parlor and the bargain electronics shop with the going-out-of-business sign that had likely been up since it opened. Then scanned over to the small, anemic market on the other side.

According to the canvass the tat parlor had only been in that location for seven years, but apparently the market had been struggling along for more than twenty.

The uniforms she'd sent out hadn't gotten much from the owner . . . Dae Pak, she confirmed from her notes.

She crossed over, stepped inside. It smelled earthy, the way she imagined farms did. A guy of about twenty with ink-black hair hacked into an airboarder chop at the counter. A dragon tat he might have gotten a couple doors down circled his left wrist. From his sullen expression, she deduced he wasn't in love with his work.

She ignored him and walked up to the old man with a face the color and texture of a walnut who methodically stocked bags of instant noodles on a shelf.

"I'm looking for Mr. Pak." Eve held up her badge.

"I talk to cops already." With an expression as sullen as the counter boy's, he pointed a stubby finger at her. "Why you not come around when the kids steal me blind? Huh? Huh? Why you not here then?"

"I'm Homicide, Mr. Pak. I work murders."

He held out his arms to encompass the market. "Nobody dead here."

"I'm glad to hear it, but twelve girls were killed in the building next door."

"I hear all about it, don't know nothing. You come in here, you buy something."

She dug for patience because he looked about a million years old, and the kid at the counter was snickering at him. She walked over to the cooler, yanked out a tube of Pepsi, snagged a candy bar at random, then slapped them on the counter in front of the snickerer.

He scanned them, and under her baleful stare stopped snickering. She paid, stuck the candy bar in her pocket, cracked the tube of Pepsi.

"I'm a paying customer," she told Pak.

"You bought, you paid, you go."

"I'm amazed you're not packed with paying customers with all this cheerful, personalized service. Twelve dead girls, the oldest we've identified from what was left of them was fourteen, the youngest twelve. You've been in this location a long time. Some of them must have come in here. You'd see them walk by, hear their voices. Whoever killed them left them to rot away to bones, with no respect, with families who searched for them."

He only scowled, jammed packages on the shelf.

"Every day when you opened, when you closed, when you stocked your shelves, swept your floor, they were over there in the dark. Alone."

He tightened his walnut face. "Not my business."

"I'm making it your business." She glanced around the market. "I could probably find some violations around here if I wanted to play hard-ass like you are. Or I could put in a request for an extra beat cop to patrol this area. Which way do you want it?"

"I don't know about dead girls."

Eve gestured him to the counter, took out the photos, and laid them out with the boxes of gum and breath mints at point of purchase. "Anyone look familiar?"

"You all look the same." But for the first time he cracked a little smile. "They come in here all the time, the girls, the boys, steal from me, make noise, make mess. Bad girls, bad boys. I think when they leave there it stops. But there are always more. I work, my family work, and they steal."

"I'm sorry about that, but these girls sure as hell won't be stealing from you. They're dead. Look at them, Mr. Pak. Do you remember any of them?"

He huffed out a breath, adjusted his stance, leaned over until his face was only inches away.

"Hasn't had his eyes fixed in over a year," the boy said.

"My ears work. Go finish stocking. This one. Trouble."

He jabbed the stubby finger on Shelby's face.

"She steals. I tell her she can't come in here no more, but she sneaks. I go over, talk to the lady, and she is polite. She gives me fifty dollars and says she is sorry, she will speak to this girl and the others. She is gracious, and it is better for a little while. This girl."

Eve's eyes narrowed as he pointed at Linh Penbroke.

"Are you sure?"

"She is dressed like a bad girl, but she has good family. It shows. I remember her because she didn't steal, and she paid for what this one, the bad one, took."

"They were together? These two?"

"Late, near when I close."

"Was this before or after the group next door left the building?"

"After, but not long. I know this because I thought I would not be troubled by this one again, but she came back. I tell her get out, and she gives me the rude finger. But the other girl pays, and she says, 'Sorry,' in our language. This is polite, it is respectful. I remember her. She is dead?"

"Yes, they both are."

"She has good family?"

The polite girl, the good family, made a difference to him, Eve noted. And used it.

"Yes, she does. Good parents, a brother and a sister who looked for her, and hoped, all these years, to find her. She made a mistake, Mr. Pak, and shouldn't have died for it. Was anyone with them?"

"I can't say. I only remember they come in, before I close. I remember because this one gives me so much trouble, and this one is Korean, and is respectful."

"Did they talk to each other? Do you remember anything they said, if they were meeting anyone, going somewhere?"

"Girls chattering is like birds." He fluttered his fingers at his ears. "You hear only the notes."

"Okay, how about the others? Did they come in here?"

"I can't say," he repeated. "They come in, go out. These two only I remember."

"This one." She tapped a finger on Shelby's picture. "Who else did she come in with? Who did you see her hanging with?"

"Most times with little black girl, big"—he held out his hands to indicate a hefty build—"white girl. Skinny boy, too, brown boy. The black girl sings with a voice like . . ." He struggled, called out something in Korean to his now sulky counter boy.

"Angels."

"Yes, like angels. But she steals. They all steal. Are they all dead?"

"I don't know. Thanks for your help."

"You'll do what you said. More cop?"

"Yeah, I'll do what I said."

She walked out, strode over to the building, bypassed the police seal.

He'd connected two of the vics, the first two found together. Killed together? she speculated. One had been a resident, one hadn't. One a girl of good family, the other from an abusive home who'd churned her way through the system.

But they'd been together before they died, and right next door to where they'd been hidden away.

She stepped inside. Just stood.

Linh hooks up with Shelby *after* The Sanctuary moves out. A runaway, looking for some excitement before she goes home, a street kid who knows where to find the excitement. And the two of them end up all the way back here.

Because the building was empty, Eve thought.

Street girl says to runaway: I've got a place you can flop. We can hang, we can party.

Easy enough to get in. Maybe street girl had keys or passcodes, or a way she'd found before to sneak in and out.

Maybe Shelby's looking to score, Eve mused. Looking to barter the old bj for something good. Maybe Linh's just a mark to her—a mark with money—or maybe not. Eve doubted either one of them lived long enough to decide.

Was the killer already here, or did he come in after? Was it a meet or just bad luck?

He had to know Shelby, at least, would come back. So he watched, waited. Arranged?

Were they the first? DeWinter's magic might not be powerful enough for them to ever know which of the twelve died first, or last.

She heard the door behind her, turned, and pulled it open so an off-balance Peabody stumbled inside.

"Whoops. Hey." Cheeks pink from the hike from the subway, Peabody held out a takeout sack. "Got you half a spicy turkey sub. I had the other half, and it's pretty good. Hey, what happened?"

"About what?"

"About the bruise on your face."

"Oh, that. Little tussle with a rabidly enthusiastic private security skirt. I won."

"Congrats. I've got a med pack in my field kit."

"It's nothing."

"Well, I've got it if you want it. You got a drink. Good, 'cause I forgot that, and they're not lying about the spicy."

"Thanks. Did you get anything else?"

"You wanted chips or something? Oh, oh, the notifications and interviews. Not a lot. First the aunt—LaRue Freeman."

Peabody took out her notebook.

"I don't think she knows anything. The kid didn't live with her, but she filed the report when she found out—from her sister's neighbor—the kid had run away again. Mostly she just sounded tired and resigned."

"All right. I didn't expect much there."

"Carlie Bowen," Peabody continued. "The sister was a little shaken, but it felt like she'd already resigned herself she wasn't seeing Carlie alive again. They were tight, them-against-the-world kind of thing. She knew when Carlie poofed, something happened to her. The vic didn't really have friends, couldn't have anyone over, was embarrassed to hang when she'd have bruises or a busted lip half the time since she was in and out between foster and the home. She stayed with the sister every chance she got. Went to school, went to church, kept her head down."

"What church?"

"Ah . . ." She swiped the notebook to the next entry. "Different churches, according to the sister. She didn't want to draw any attention so she spread it around. The foster family she was with had a good rep, no violations. They reported she was doing well, and with some encouragement had joined the school band. Was learning to play the flute. She went to practice, left at about five-fifteen, went to the school library to study in this after-hours group, also approved."

Lowering the notebook, Peabody looked back at Eve. "Basically, Carlie was doing everything she could to have the normal, to keep it steady until she could move in permanently with her sister. She contacted the sister the night she went missing, asked if she could come over, got that cleared. She left the library just after seven on the evening of September eighteenth, according to the log-outs and wits at the time. And that was it."

"Just two days after Lupa didn't come home. This Carlie, she'd have walked by here on the way to the sister's?"

"It's the most logical route, yeah."

Eve nodded, absently pulled out the sub, took a bite. "I'll fill you in on Frester later. The guy who runs the market next door put Shelby and Linh together."

"He did? After fifteen years?"

"Shelby was a regular troublemaker over there. He remembered her. Linh came in with her—was a contrast. Polite, spoke to him in Korean. It puts them together here, and shortly after The Sanctuary closed."

She took another bite, enjoyed the heat, then washed it down with Pepsi. "Shelby brought Linh here, that's the way it plays. Ran into her on the street, hooked up. Picked up some stuff at the market. Linh paid, so maybe Shelby was after the soft touch there, but she brought her over here."

She wandered as she thought it through.

"It's empty. That's a thrill. Shelby knows the place, can show her around, tell her stories. It's echoey, dark. She'd have a flashlight or a light stick. No point in stumbling around in the dark. She's probably staying here, flopped here after she took off from the new place. It's a decent shelter, especially since nobody's here, since it's empty. It's all hers now, until she shares it. She probably likes having the company, this new girl who doesn't know shit about crap. Probably has some blankets, some bedding. She knows how to steal, how to take care of herself."

"It'd be kind of frosty at first," Peabody considered. "Like camping out."

"Everything's at first, everything's now. Tomorrow's for grownups. Linh didn't act out in the market. Could be she was starting to miss home. It feels good to have a friend right now, and a place off the street. Maybe she'll go home tomorrow. They'd come get her, take her home. They'd cry and they'd yell, but they'd come. But she doesn't want to look lame in front of her new friend. She'll just hang awhile in the spooky old building."

Eve started up the steps. "He could already be here. Shelby knows him. She's not afraid of him. Maybe she barters sex for drugs with him. Maybe they get high. It's a way to pass the time, have some fun, show off for the new girl."

"It's a way to tranq them."

"A little something in the zoner or whatever he gives them. Just a little something extra. Then they're compliant. Not unconscious, what's the point in that? Where's the thrill in that? But just stoned, limp, stupid. Undress them—one at a time—do what he wants to do. Fill the tub. Warm water, cold might shock them straight enough to put up a fight. Under they go. They might struggle a little, it's instinct, but not enough.

"Sit down over there like the tub was still there."

"Huh?" Peabody's eyes widened, then blinked twice. "What?"

"In the pretend tub, I want to try something."

"I don't wanna get in the pretend tub."

"In," Eve ordered, dropped her sandwich back in the bag, set it and the tube aside.

"Oh, man. I'm not stripping. Even if you hurt me."

"I don't want you naked, I just want you in the damn tub."

Grumbling, Peabody sat between the old rough-in pipes.

"I think he tied their hands and feet, but not tight. Just enough to keep them from kicking around. Then all he has to do is—"

She took Peabody's wrists in one hand, pressed the other on her head.

"You'd go right under, without any real traction to pull up again. Holding your arms up like this, you slide down. Too woozy to push hard enough with your bound feet to surface. From here he can watch your face as the panic cuts through. You can scream, but from here it's sort of soft, almost musical. Then your eyes fix, and that's the moment, the moment he knows it's done."

She released Peabody's arms, picked up her sandwich bag again.

"It's creepy. Seriously creepy." With some rush, Peabody pushed to her feet.

"Carlie went to churches. Lupa went to church. This was sort of a faith-based place, right? Frester all about turning it over to a higher power and all that. Bad girls."

"Who, the vics?"

"That's what Pak—the market guy—called them. Bad girls, bad boys. Isn't there that whole thing about washing sins away?"

"You mean like baptism?"

"Maybe." Frowning, she studied the scarred floor, the broken pipes, imagined the old white tub. "They dunk you, right?"

"I think, some religions do the dunk. Free-Agers aren't into that kind of thing. You're thinking some twisted ritual?"

"It's an angle. If you're going to hide the bodies anyway, there are lots of ways to kill. He doesn't experiment from what we can tell. No broken bones, no bashing, no strangulation. Just a slide under the water. It's almost gentle."

She took another bite of turkey, paced around. "It doesn't seem like he keeps them for long. He has choices. He could drug them, bind them, keep them for days, playing with them, torturing them, entertaining himself. Think of McQueen."

"I'd rather not. Sick bastard."

"He kept all those girls chained up, weeks, months, some even longer. He had a high old time with them. But this guy doesn't do anything like that. This is his place. Are they his girls when they come here? His to cleanse and kill?"

"I think they drowned witches."

Puzzled, Eve stopped pacing. "Witches?"

"I mean women they decided were witches, back in the Dark Ages and stuff. And Salem, like that. I think they hanged them, burned them, too—depending. But they drowned them. They loaded them down with stones, tossed them in the water. If they sank, they weren't witches—just dead. If they didn't sink, they were witches and I guess they'd have killed them some other way—the hanging or burning. Only women just drowned."

"Bad luck. That's interesting. It was like a test?"

"I guess. Sick, ignorant, but yeah, like a test."

"That's interesting," Eve repeated. "And another angle. If they were evil—witches we'll say—they wouldn't drown when he held them under. Or, alternatively, if they were pure enough they wouldn't drown. Hmm. All sorts of angles. Let's go another round with the Joneses."

Eve rolled half her half sub back in the takeout bag.

"You're not eating that."

"It's big. It's good, but it's big." Eve held it out. "You want it?"

Like a woman warding off evil, Peabody turned her head, held her hand in front of it. "Stop it, put it away. I'll eat it otherwise. Find a recycler before I do."

"The vic's sister makes a good sandwich." On her way down, Eve polished off the Pepsi. "Let me tell you about Lemont Frester," she began.

Matron Shivitz wore black, and dabbed at tired eyes. "I couldn't sleep, not a wink, all night." She sniffled, dabbed. "Thinking of those girls, those poor girls. Have you found out who they are—were?"

"We've begun identifying them. We'd like to speak to Mr. Jones and Ms. Jones."

"Ms. Jones is off campus. One of the boys cut himself while on kitchen duty, so she took him to urgent care for treatment. She shouldn't be much longer. Mr. Jones is leading a round table. I'm afraid he'll be about twenty minutes more. If it's an emergency—"

"We can wait. How well did you know Shelby Ann Stubacker?"

"Shelby Ann, Shelby Ann . . . Oh! Shelby, yes, yes." Shivitz lifted both hands, shook them in the air. "A challenge. She presented a constant challenge, always testing the boundaries. Still, a personable girl when she wanted to be, and bright. I remember being relieved—I'm not ashamed to say—when they were able to place her in foster care."

"I need the documentation on that. The when and where and who. I contacted Ms. Jones to let her know."

"Oh, dear, she must've forgotten to tell me, with Zeek cutting himself, and the argument. Two of the girls had to be separated and—"

"Matron. Let's stick with Shelby Stubacker, foster care and when, how, where."

"Yes, yes. My goodness, so long ago." She patted her bubble of hair. "I seem to recall, yes, I'm sure it was during our transition. We were moving in here when her paperwork came through. I wouldn't remember where she was placed, even if I'd known at the time. Is it important?"

"It's important because there's no record of her being placed anywhere."

"But she certainly was." Shivitz smiled patiently, as Eve imagined she did at residents who required careful explanations.

"I distinctly remember speaking with Ms. Jones about it, and helped process Shelby myself. We always send our children with a going-home pack of books, a house pin, an affirmation disc and so forth. I put it together myself. I always tried to do that, and always added a container of cookies. Just a little treat."

"Who picked her up?"

"I . . . Someone from CPS, I'm sure. Or one of us took her to her new family. I don't know. I'm not certain I was here, I mean right here, when she left. I don't understand."

"I want to see your copy of her paperwork on the court order, the release papers."

"Oh my, that may take just a little doing. It was years ago, as I said, and during the upheaval of the move. I'll have to look for it."

"Yeah, you will."

The smile turned into a firm, flat line. "No need to be testy, young lady. We keep all records, but it would be archived. Fifteen-year-old records aren't something we have at our fingertips. Why would we when . . ."

Eve watched her put it together, saw the mild insult turn to sick realization. "Shelby? She was one of the . . . One of them?"

"I need to see the paperwork."

"I'll find it!" She jogged off on her sensible shoes, shouting for an assistant to pull up the archives.

"Get an earful, Quilla?" Eve asked without turning around.

Quiet as a snake, Quilla glided down the stairs.

"I'm a challenge, too."

"Good for you."

"Hey, somebody punched you in the face."

"That's right. Now she's in a cage thinking about how much time she'll get for assaulting a police officer."

"In the face is a bitch," Quilla commented with the casual knowledge of one who'd been there often enough to know. "So anyway, everybody's talking about the dead girls. The wardens closed themselves up in the office for like an hour."

"Wardens?"

"They might as well be. It's like half past zero around here with Matron crying and everybody has to make these black bands for their arms even though we didn't know any of the dead girls, and they've been dead already forever. Then we're stuck with extra meditation so we can help their spirits cross over."

"Cross over where?"

Quilla circled her finger toward the ceiling. "Or wherever. I fucking hate meditation. It's boring. Plus I heard Mr. Jones say—" She broke off, glanced toward the stairs.

"Say what?"

"Hey, Ms. Brigham," Quilla said.

"Hi, Quilla." Seraphim appeared at the top of the stairs. "Lieutenant, Detective," she said as she continued down. "Is anyone helping you?"

"Matron Shivitz is getting us some files."

"We're all a little off our stride today." She stroked a hand down Quilla's shoulder. "Quilla, aren't you supposed to be in class?"

"Maybe. I saw them hanging here and didn't want them to have to just stand around."

"That's very polite and thoughtful. I've got it from here, you go on to class."

"Okay." She slanted Eve a look before she scurried off.

"She's curious," Seraphim began. "Most of the kids are. It's all more mysterious and exciting to them than tragic. It's a normal reaction for the age. Though I'm told a couple of the more sensitive girls had nightmares last night."

"You didn't tell the matron about Shelby being identified."

"No. I didn't tell anyone, was I supposed to? I'm sorry," she continued before Eve could speak. "I'm so used to keeping a confidence, I just kept it to myself."

"That's fine. It's not your job to notify. I was just curious why you hadn't."

"You came to see me at my grandmother's. To me, that equaled what we spoke of as in confidence."

"Got it."

"And it's the same reason—that trained circumspection—that had me hesitating to ask if I can get you a cold pack for that cheek. It looks painful."

"It's okay. Thanks anyway."

"All right. Lieutenant, I wanted to thank you for looking for Leah Craine, for finding her."

"Roarke did the finding."

"I know, but it meant a great deal to me to know she's well, happy. I contacted her. I couldn't decide if I should, but Gamma and Jack—my fiancé—convinced me. I'm so glad they did. We're going to have lunch next week."

"That's nice."

"It feels nice." Her smile bloomed all the way to her eyes. "I should tell you we spoke about the girls. Just briefly, but she'd heard about them, too. She did tell me she'd never gone back to The Sanctuary when she ran away again. She was afraid to go near it, in case her father looked for her there."

She paused a moment, glanced toward the stairs just in case. "I think we knew—but didn't say, either of us—that if she had, she might be among those girls. Instead, she has work she loves, a man she loves, and her first baby on the way."

"You could tell her if she remembers anything from her time here that may apply, to contact me."

"We talked about that, too, a little. I gave her your information, but as I think I told you, she really kept her head down in those days."

"Okay. If you've got a minute now, we have more identifications."

"Let's sit down. The children should all be in class or activity at this time of day—including Quilla." She glanced at the stairs again, down both hallways before she took one of the seats near Shivitz's station, accepted the printouts.

"God, they're so young. Were so young. I don't remember these girls. They don't seem familiar. Do you know what happened to them, to all of them?"

"The investigation's ongoing." Eve drew out her 'link when it signaled, studied the image and text. Switching it to image only, she held it out to Seraphim. "What about this girl?"

"Another? I hate to think . . . Yes! Oh, this is Mikki—I told you about her yesterday. Shelby, Mikki, T-Bone. Mikki . . . I don't remember her full name."

"Mikki Wendall."

"Yes, that's it. But she was placed back in the parental home. I remember that. I remember because it was right after they'd moved here—or a week or so, I'm not sure. I remember because I came with my grandmother to see this new place. I was so nervous," she murmured with a small smile. "Seeing everyone again, and I heard—DeLonna told me—both Shelby and Mikki were gone. Shelby to foster, Mikki back home."

She'd seen the Wendall paperwork, Eve thought now. But no Missing Persons report had been filed on Mikki by the custodial parent. "Peabody, get the data on Mikki Wendall. Do you know if she had contact with Shelby after they left The Sanctuary?"

"I'm sorry, I don't. I was working hard to turn that corner, to rebuild myself, to keep myself straight so I could stay with my grandmother. I didn't keep in touch with any of the girls here."

With a last look at the printouts, she handed them back to Peabody. "I wouldn't have with Shelby in any case. She was, and it sounds harsh now, but she was trouble. I'd had enough trouble. Mikki was—it's easier to see now with adult hindsight and training—she was needy, so wanted to fit in. She'd have done anything for Shelby's approval, and did. I'm not sure she ever had a friend before Shelby and DeLonna, and T-Bone."

"We found it!" Shivitz bustled back in, waving a disc and hard copy. "Oh, Seraphim, I'm just that upset. It all seems like too much."

"It's a difficult time, Matron." Seraphim rose, wrapped Shivitz in a hug. "Difficult and incomprehensible. But the children depend on us."

"I know it, I know it. One was Shelby Stubacker. You must remember her. She was a hard one to forget."

"Yes, I know."

"But she was *gone*," Shivitz insisted, and pushed the documenta-tion at Eve. "She'd been placed in foster care. It was after you left, Seraphim, and right in the middle of the move. In fact, the paper-work still has The Sanctuary information."

"Uh-huh." Eve studied the hard copies, shook her head. "It's a half-decent fake."

"Fake!" Shivitz bristled with outrage. "What do you mean fake? That's absurd."

"So is spelling borough b-u-r-r-o-w. One of those spell-check errors, I'd guess. A couple of other things, but that's the big tell."

"Let me see that." Shivitz snatched it away, peered down, and went dead pale. "Oh dear God. Oh Lord. I don't understand this. I don't know how this could happen."

"Sit down now. Sit down and catch your breath." Seraphim eased Shivitz into a chair.

"How did the paperwork come in?" Eve demanded.

"I don't know. I honestly don't know. It must just be a mistake. Can't it just be a clerical mistake?"

"I don't think so."

Seraphim glanced back as doors began to open, voices carried down the stairs, clumping feet sounded above.

"Can we take this in Mr. Jones's office? I'll go find him. He needs to know, he may remember something."

"Let's do that." She signaled Peabody. Her partner nodded, crossed toward the office while she continued to talk on her 'link.

"What do you remember?" Eve asked Shivitz.

"I just don't, not really. We were carrying boxes and tables and chairs, and so many things. Inside, upstairs, downstairs. Somebody told me—I'm not sure who—Shelby was going into a foster home. I remember thinking we might be able to start off more peacefully in *our* new home."

"What seems to be the problem?" All business, Nash Jones clipped into the room, eased the door closed.

"The paperwork removing Shelby Ann Stubacker from your care and putting her in foster care is a forgery."

"I'm sure that can't be." He took the paperwork, carried it around to his desk, sat. "It certainly looks to be in order. I'm not sure what you . . ."

"Caught it?"

He leaned forward, pushing at his hair as he studied it again. "How did this get through? This isn't my signature. Matron, Seraphim, it's not my signature."

Seraphim moved closer, read over his shoulder. "It's not. It's close, but it's not your signature."

"We can and will have that verified," Eve told him, "but for now, what the hell happened?"

"I have no idea. Let me think. Let me think." He shut his eyes, breathed slow and deep in what Eve assumed was some form of meditation. Another minute of that would, she knew, piss her off. But he stopped, opened his eyes.

"I remember. Matron—not you, dear," he said to Shivitz. "Matron Orwin telling me Shelby's paperwork was on my desk in my office, which had yet to be organized. We were still moving in—we had abbreviated classes and group, we'd divided up staff and residents into teams, so everyone had a part in making up our new space. We were excited, all of us—the newness, the larger space, excited, grateful."

"We were." Shivitz twisted her fingers together as she nodded. "So excited and grateful."

"We were so busy," Nash continued, "but it was a good confusion, if you understand me. I said something to Philly about it—about Shelby, that is. We discussed it as we worked. Both of us had some concerns, but we are, after all, only a temporary haven. Later, Philly and I had a bite to eat in our new quarters—a jumble, but still ours. She mentioned she'd found Mikki Wendall—she and Shelby were friends—she'd found her crying in her room. Because Shelby was gone. We talked about what we could do to make the transition easier for Mikki. I assumed that Philly had taken care of the transfer, but this is an attempt at my signature, not hers."

"You didn't see her leave, didn't connect with the CPS rep who should have escorted her?"

"No. I assumed Philly had, or Matron. Or Montclair. Our brother was with us then. Did I ask about the paperwork at some point?" Still pale, he rubbed at his temple. "I must have."

"I think Matron gave it to me to file," Shivitz told him. "That would have been the usual procedure. We were trying to get all the files and comps in order, and I must have filed it. I never really looked at it."

"We'll need to speak to your sister."

"Yes, yes. Let me contact her, tell her to come back right away. There were so many people," Jones murmured as he turned to his 'link. "All the staff, volunteers, the e-company who'd come in to set up the equipment, all the children. It was so busy, so happy. Hopeful."

Eve imagined Shelby had had her own hopes—and reaching for them had ended them.

EVE SPENT THE BEST PART OF AN HOUR TAK-
ing them all back through the steps. Nashville, Philadelphia when she arrived on the run, Shivitz, and
two staff members who were there when Shelby walked out the door
for the last time.

She left unsatisfied, and left them in considerable turmoil.

"I can't decide if they're worried about being sued—though who's
going to bother?—about getting fined or cited—and I can't figure
out how that would work, exactly—or if they're guilty they might
have abetted a murderer."

"I think it's some of all of the above." Peabody settled into the car.
"Do you want the line on Mikki Wendall?"

"I do."

"The mother had a substance abuse problem that resulted in neglect, unemployment, and eventually eviction for nonpayment of

rent. They ended up on the street where the mother did some unlicensed prostitution for food, shelter, and more often illegals. Got herself bashed up a few times and the kid got busted for stealing. CPS finally stepped in, and Mikki ended up in The Sanctuary with the mother doing a short stint and obligatory rehab."

"Where'd you get all this?"

"From the source, the mother. She didn't put any bows on it, Dallas. She was a junkie, whored herself, let the kid run the streets, encouraged her to steal what she could. She skipped out on the rehab the first round, got busted again, got the shit kicked out of her in jail, and had herself a personal epiphany. Stuck with rehab, did a full ninety days in with follow-up meetings, got a job cleaning offices at night, and worked days in a sweatshop off the books, saved up for an apartment and petitioned to get the kid back."

"How quick did they pass the kid back?"

"It took the best part of a year, with the mother taking regular pee tests, regular counseling, and CPS visits. It sounds like she was one of the success stories."

"They're rare."

"Yeah, so it stands out. During the year she was saving up, working, getting the supervision, going to meetings, she met this guy. Worked maintenance at the office building where she cleaned. Straight-arrow type, and they ended up cohabbing."

She shifted. "I ran him just to tie up the ends, and he's clean. He passed muster with CPS, with the court, and they granted her custody. Kid comes home."

"Where it doesn't end up a little happy family."

"Nope. Kid won't go to school, won't pull her weight. Sasses, sneaks out at night, steals from them. The mother found illegals—which she flushed—and a knife hidden in the kid's room. The knife scares her, but they're going to stick it out, get more counseling."

But the kid's done with that, Eve thought. Done with all of that.

"And the mother finds out she's pregnant. Sees it as another chance. She's going to do it right this time. She's clean, going to stay clean.

"She catches the kid coming in stoned, middle of the night, still has a twist of zoner on her. They fight about it, and the kid runs out, mother runs after her. Tries to pull the kid back upstairs, and the kid shoves her down them."

"The kid pushed her pregnant mother down the stairs?"

"She didn't know she was pregnant, but yeah. Left her there, and just kept going. She was hurt pretty bad. I checked on the medical, and she told me straight. It was touch-and-go on the baby for a couple days, pretty touch-and-go all around. And she said she made a choice, and let Mikki go. Hated herself, but she was afraid of her own kid. She didn't file a Missing Persons, didn't file charges because she didn't want the kid sent back to juvie. She said Mikki said they weren't family, that she had family and she was happy with them, to leave her the hell alone."

"So she did."

"Yeah, she did. She spent two weeks in the hospital, another four on doctor's orders bedrest at home. The guy went out looking for Mikki when he could, but they never saw her again. They've got two kids now, a boy about the age Mikki was, and a girl a couple years younger."

"She fucked the kid's life."

"And she knows it. She tried to fix it, Dallas, and she couldn't. Now she's got to live with knowing her daughter's been dead all this time."

"Mikki didn't go back to the new home—to HPCCY—so they weren't the family she spoke of. Shelby, I guess. And the old building where they formed that family. Shelby, DeLonna, and T-Bone. We need to find the other two, dead or alive."

"They're off the grid. I can't track either of them. Records show they were with The Sanctuary, then with HPCCY. DeLonna got into a work/study program at sixteen, then poofed. So unless that's bogus, she wasn't one of the remains. T-Bone stayed until he hit eighteen, then just vanished into the city. No data on him after he left."

"Pass them to McNab," Eve ordered. "If he can't find them, I'll give them to Roarke."

"I'm all over that. Are you buying this clusterfuck deal with Shelby?"

"I haven't decided. I can see how it could happen—shoddy, but the kid had some smarts. Timed it when everything was messed up, mixed up, and the doc looked legit if you didn't look real close. I want to verify the signature. If it's not his, Jones looks a little clearer on it."

"You have to wonder why she wanted out all of a sudden, getting better digs and all that."

"Better digs, but not hers. Not her rules." She'd had decent digs in the state facilities, Eve remembered. Mostly three squares. And she'd wanted out as much as she'd wanted to live.

"Somebody offered her something she wanted more. Or she saw the chance to take what she wanted more. Freedom. No rules but her rules, do what she wants when she wants. Eat what she wants when she wants. It's not like family, Peabody—most of where you end up if you're a kid without a safety net—it's okay, it's decent, and they're trying to help. But it's not family. It's two slippery steps up from prison."

"Did you ever run?"

"In the early days, yeah. And I know I was lucky they caught me. I'm lucky I realized pretty quick juvie's only a half a slippery step up from prison. So why not take the extra steps, do the time, take what you can out of it?"

Eve shook it off. "But she risked getting caught, getting dumped in juvie instead of a group home because it was all shit to her. I knew plenty like her, and most of those, I can guarantee, ended up slipping down that half a step into a real cage."

"I guess some of it is shit," Peabody considered. "It's just the best shit we've got."

"She wanted out, and she knew how to bargain, probably black-mail, cheat, steal, whatever it took. But somebody helped her get out, and I'm going to take a leap and say the probability's high the person who helped get her out killed her."

"Well, here's a thought. If Jones or his sister are psycho kid killers, they've had their pick from a garden variety for years. Unless those specific kids were specific targets, or there's some meaning in the number twelve."

"Yeah, I'm going around on that. The brother was there."

"The dead brother? The lion lunch brother?"

"That's the one. Try this on," Eve said with a glance at Peabody. "Say he's a psycho kid killer. He has access to the vics, at least we can be sure he had access to the ones connected to the home. He had access and knowledge of the building. They dropped that he helped with repairs now and then, so maybe he can build a few walls."

"Then why did he go to Africa, unless he wanted to become an international psycho kid killer? We should check to see if any kids went missing over there before he got eaten."

"We'll do that. But as to why, what if they caught him? The siblings—the do-gooders? Or maybe it doesn't go that far, but they catch him behaving inappropriately with one or more of the girls. Can't have that. Ship him off, time for a missionary stint. And the king of the beasts takes care of him."

Eve didn't like the ending. "We're sure he and the lion went a round?"

"I verified the report, the death certificate, the cremation, and the transportation of the ashes back to New York."

"Rather have a body," Eve muttered. "Better, I'd rather have a live killer so we can bag his sorry ass. But we're going to play with psycho dead brother some."

"It's hard to see either one of them covering for him if they found out he'd killed those girls."

"Blood. Water."

"Okay, maybe so. But they don't strike me as stupid, or as gamblers. Would they just leave the bodies there?"

"Not if they knew about them, and I'm tripping over that one, too," she admitted. "So, like I said, maybe it didn't go that far. And maybe this is a dead end and the dead brother was just another do-gooder who provided a lion with a tasty meal."

"Like the Christians. You know how the Romans fed them to lions to the cheers of the crowd?"

"Why did they do that?"

"Bloodthirsty?"

"I don't mean the Roman guys, that I get."

Peabody blinked. "You do?"

"Bloodthirsty," Eve repeated. "Better you than me. Power. But I don't get the Christian guys. Why not say, why yes, Roman asshole who can feed me to the lions, Luigi or whoever is a very fine god."

"Luigi?"

"Whoever—then run away to the—what do you call them, the caves."

"Catacombs?"

"Yeah, those. Run off there and have some wine, plot out your rebellion, and organize to kick some Roman ass."

"I'm still kind of stuck on the god Luigi, but I think they were peaceful."

"Yeah, and where did that get them? Lion dung."

"Eeww."

"Exactly." She turned to the dash 'link when it signaled. "Dallas, on screen."

The next girl smiled out at her.

"There's a missing on her," Eve said. "Cross-check it. I remember seeing her."

"Cross-check going. Kim Terrance, age thirteen. Runaway from Jersey City, New Jersey. Filed by the mother. Father incarcerated at the time for assault."

"Get the current data."

"It's coming up. Mother remarried, two years ago, relocated with spouse to Vermont where they run a small resort. Spouse has two grown offspring. Quick background shows pattern of abuse by first husband, and a restraining order. He's doing another stretch now—assault and rape, second wife. She's got a regular flag in her file for the Missing Persons, with comp-generated age enhancements."

Peabody brought the latest one up, showing a woman in her late twenties.

"She's still looking, Dallas."

"I'll make the notification. Let's see if we can dig out any connection to The Sanctuary, HPCCY, any staff or residents."

"This makes seven of them," Peabody said as Eve pulled into Central's garage. "Five more left. It doesn't get easier."

Eve added the new faces to her board. The last, Terrance, hadn't had a chance to grow into the comp-generated face. She'd been stuck forever at that awkward between-stage when the teeth seemed too big, the eyes too wide.

She wasn't on the resident list Philadelphia had given her. To be sure, she contacted CPS, then wheedled, browbeat, and nagged the overworked and unlucky social worker who answered to dig into the archives.

There'd been a file on Kim Terrance—some truancy, some shoplifting. Counseling for her and her mother both times the mother had run with the kid to a women's shelter.

And both times the mother had gone back, dragging the kid into the hot hell their lives must have been. A pattern, Eve thought, too often repeated. At least the vic's mother had finally broken the chain, but not until she'd lost her kid to the streets, scraped herself off the bottom of her personal barrel.

And all too late, Eve thought, too late for the kid to trust the woman who'd boomeranged back to the man who beat her, who took swipes at the child they'd made together. Too late for the kid to care about the fear and self-loathing that kept a woman tied to an abusive man, too late to care about breaking the pattern, turning the corner.

Too late for her to ever grow into her face.

She finished up her notes. Not a churchgoer like Lupa or Carlie. Not a girl taking a shot at rebellious independence like Linh. Not, from the accounts, as hardened or tough as Shelby.

More like Mikki, Eve supposed. Sick of it all.

She spent some time on the 'link, tugging some threads, snipping off others. Then, because it nagged at her, checked Peabody's data on Montclair Jones.

The youngest of the four, he'd barely made it to twenty-three. Seven-year gap between him, Eve noted, and Philadelphia. Home-schooled like his siblings, but unlike Nash and Philadelphia he hadn't taken a spin through the public sector for the certification in social work.

Unlike sister Selma, nearly thirteen years his senior, he hadn't traveled, then planted himself far away, made a family.

She dug back, shoved forward, shoved sideways.

When Peabody came in, Eve held up a hold-on-a-minute finger, continued to talk on her 'link.

"I appreciate the help, Sergeant Owusu."

"It is my pleasure to assist you in any way."

Peabody angled her head to see the face that matched the crisp and musical voice. "I will speak with my grandfather and my uncle. If there is more information I will contact you. Good evening to you, Lieutenant."

"And to you, Sergeant."

"What was that? Who was that?"

"Sergeant Alika Owusu, of the Republic of Zimbabwe Police and Security Department."

"No freaking shit! You were talking to Africa?"

"A small part of it."

"What time is it there? Did you hear any lions or elephants or anything?"

"She was on the night shift, which was lucky considering I don't know what the hell time it is there because I'm here. I didn't hear any roaring, or anyone screaming as they were being mauled by the local wildlife."

"I'd like to see an elephant," Peabody said thoughtfully. "Not in a wildlife refuge, but in its natural habitat. And I'd like to hear a hyena, even thought they're supposed to be mean and crazy. I'd like—"

She finally caught Eve's stony stare.

"Anyway enough about that. You're on the idea of Montclair Jones."

"I want more clear intel on it, that's all. I managed to track the sergeant down. She was a girl when the whole lion-eating-man deal happened. She remembers Jones a little—remembers better what was left of him after the lion, which her grandfather killed."

"Aw." The romantic safari building in Peabody's head shattered. "I know, man-eater, but still. It's just the nature of the beast, right?"

"Rogue man-eating lion, small village with tiny, tiny children, slow old ladies, and hapless pets. Lion loses."

"I guess. But she confirmed Jones was lion chow?"

"She confirmed there was an incident, and a missionary named Montclair Jones who worked in the area was attacked and killed."

"Which jibes with his siblings' story, and the official data."

"Yeah, yeah." She drummed her fingers on the desk. "It bugs me, that's all. Biggest sister Selma, goes off on missions, finds her place in Australia, marries a sheepherder. Why do people herd sheep?"

"You're wearing a wool jacket."

"I am?"

"Soft," Peabody said reverently as she snuck a stroke down the sleeve.

"Hands off. Anyway, she's herding sheep, making babies, and younger brother and younger sister are getting college degrees, doing missions, and eventually pooling their resources to buy the building on Ninth and found The Sanctuary.

"Some of those resources, FYI, come from a small inheritance, and a share of the sale of the family home after the mother's suicide, and after the father sells the home to go on a mission."

"I saw the self-termination in the file," Peabody commented. "It looked, from what I scanned, she'd had bouts of depression since her final pregnancy."

"Popping one out when you've got three—one's a teenager—and you're rounding the bag to fifty sounds depressing to me."

"I don't . . . On second thought," Peabody considered, "it kind of does."

"So both mother and youngest son have some treatment for depression, anxiety. And baby brother sticks close to home until Mom opens the veins in her wrists. After, he lives with Jones and Jones. He didn't go for any higher ed or certification—did one youth group mission to Haiti at eighteen. And never went to any out of the country again."

"That all sounds depressing, too."

"Probably, but the mother had a history of emotional and mental challenges, ending with her offing herself with the classic slit wrists in the bathtub."

"It's less messy, and the hot water helps numb. But bathtub." A little glint shone in Peabody's eyes. "I didn't go back that far."

"It's a standard self-termination style, especially for females, but the bathtub's a little bell. From what I can tell he did mostly scut work at The Sanctuary. Some cooking, cleaning, repairs, assisting in classes or groups. No real authority."

She rose, tapping the old ID photo of Montclair Jones she'd put on her board. "Then, about the time we've got twelve dead girls tucked between the walls at The Sanctuary building, his sibs send him off to Africa.

"He'd traveled before that one time, on the missionary trail, but never again out of the States, never alone, never without one of the sibs or an experienced associate." Eve shook her head. "The timing sure is interesting."

"But if they knew, they'd have gotten rid of the bodies," Peabody insisted. "And I don't know how they could've just kept quiet all this time, or gone cruising along knowing all those girls were in that building."

"Hangs me up a little, too. But the time line . . . If he were here, if he still lived and worked here, he'd be number one on my list. So, for now, he's number one on my look-a-little-harder list. What did you get?"

"A big goose egg. There's no connection I can find linking the latest two vics ID'd with The Sanctuary, HPCCY, Nash, Philadelphia, any of them."

Eve nodded, as she'd laid the same goose egg. "We have the Korean market linking Shelby and Linh. We're going to find other connections, just that nebulous. I'm taking this home. I need to spread it out, shuffle it up, look at it from other angles."

"Did you notify next of kin on the latest?"

"I talked to her mother. She didn't know any of the other vics, never heard of The Sanctuary."

"How'd she handle it?"

"Glazed over some," Eve said as she packed up what she wanted. "But toughed it out. She'll claim the remains when we're clear with them. I backtracked, too, and got the data on Jubal Craine. His wife killed him, set their barn on fire with him in it."

"She must've been very upset."

"Apparently she got a little ticked off when he beat the crap out of her, yet again. But according to everything I can find, he was alive and well, and in fricking Nebraska during September of 'forty-five. And since his daughter didn't slip the leash again until November of that year, he didn't have any reason to come back here."

"You didn't really think he'd killed them."

"No, mostly because I don't think he'd have spent all that time in godless New York, or if he had, any of those girls would've gone with him without a serious fight." She yanked on her coat. "But it was a loose end."

"McNab's on the hunt for DeLonna and T-Bone. We'll probably take that home, too."

"If he finds them, either of them, I want to know asap."

She carted the file discs, headed out.

Deliberately, she drove home through the insane circus of Times Square. She studied the packs of teenagers, the packs of girls she gauged to be on the cusp of their teens or just over the line.

She'd never sought out a pack, alone had suited her. Too much bouncing from place to place in the beginning in any case, she thought, even if she'd been inclined to the pack mentality.

But she understood she represented the exception.

They looked alike, she noted, streaming along under the flooding, jittery light that kept the dark away and invited everyone to the endless party. Their coats, hats, scarves, gloves might be different colors, but a definite style ribboned through most. Clunky boots that must have weighed like anchors, bright pants worn tight, bright coats worn big, hats with long ties flopping.

They sucked on tubes of fizzies, yammered on 'links, chowed on warm, soft pretzels they tore apart and shared.

And they stuck together as if hooked by invisible wires.

Boys scattered through some of the groups of older girls, but the younger ones—the vics' age range—largely stuck with their own kind. Not only gender, she saw now, but class.

She picked out huddles of cheaper boots, thinner coats, most of them hatless with streaks of color through their hair rather than their wardrobe.

She spotted one helping herself to some scarves while her two partners kept the vendor busy on the other side of the stall. She watched the handoff to the girl doing a brisk walk-by before Light Fingers wandered around to her friends, all innocence and empty pockets.

Would they wear them, sell them?

Then the light changed, and she drove on.

You couldn't pull them all in, couldn't chase them all down, couldn't wrap them all up in the system so they came out the better for it.

Some, as Roarke had, were just surviving, taking what they could from the streets so they'd have food in their bellies or enough to catch a vid. Others just looked for a quick thrill, some noise, some movement, with them so much in the center.

And all of them thought they'd live forever.

She left the crowds, the noise, the jittery lights behind, and drove toward home.

The elves had definitely paid another visit, she thought as she studied the house. It looked like some elegantly wrapped gift with its starry lights, countless wreaths, flowing greenery.

A long way, she thought, a long, long way from the single spindly tree Mavis had pushed on her every year.

"Mavis." She said it out loud. "Crap, crap. I forgot." She glanced at the time, winced, then grabbed her file bag.

If they were already here, Summerset would have something snide to say. Hell, he'd have something snide to say anyway, but she'd deserve it—a little—if they were already here.

And she needed a few minutes to get upstairs, update her board. A few minutes to just sit and think.

She stopped herself from dashing inside—it would look as if she knew she ran late—that she *cared* she ran late. Instead, she sauntered in.

He stood there, of course, looming in black—but she didn't hear voices.

"Fortunately for you, your guests are running a bit late," Summerset told her. "And had the courtesy to contact me to let me know."

"Not a guest." She shrugged out of her coat, tossed it over the newel post so he could scowl at it. "Don't answer to you."

Grateful they were later than she was, she saved any insults on cadaverous looks for another time, and jogged up the stairs with the cat on her heels.

She went straight to her office, hit the house search. "Where's Roarke?"

Roarke has not yet arrived.

"Even better."

With some luck she'd get her board updated, get one hit of coffee while she studied it, and let her brain circle around.

She tried a new system, live girls front, remains back.

On the front she pinned parents, guardians, the staff of The Sanctuary.

She connected Shelby and Linh, Shelby and Mikki. Shelby, Mikki, and Lupa, as they'd all been in residence together whether or not they'd interacted.

She pinned Seraphim as a girl, and as an adult. Another connection.

She got the coffee, sipped while she circled, changed photos, took another hard look at the tubs, the bathroom areas where she believed the girls had died.

She sat at her desk, propped up her boots, and studied some more.

Mikki went looking for Shelby, that played for her. Had Shelby already been dead? They didn't die together or they'd have been hidden together. No, Shelby and Linh, they'd died together, and very likely on the night, or near to it, they'd stopped in the market next door.

Lupa, Carlie Bowen, LaRue Freeman. Next group, stacked together. Had he killed them all in one night? Why the rush? And a lot to take on.

But it's his sanctuary now, so there *is* no rush.

Time line again. Three days between Lupa going missing and Carlie Bowen. Not killed together, concealed together. With LaRue possibly between. She was listed as Victim Four. After Lupa, she thought, before Carlie.

But no other connection between them yet come to light.

What did he—

She glanced over as the cat jumped off her desk, and watched him pad his pudgy way over to Roarke.

"You're later than me."

"So I've been told." He studied her face as he crossed to her, then stroked a fingertip gently down her bruised cheek. "As I was told about this?"

"Huh? How? Oh, your security guy?"

"Yes. One of Frester's private security, was it?"

"She objected to my presence. I objected when she put hands on me and actually tried to pull her stunner. She objected when I pushed her face to the wall—and she got in one lucky backfist—just caught the cheekbone."

"So I see." Now he brushed his lips over the bruise.

"She really objected when I put her on the ground and cuffed her. So I won."

"There's the upside," he said. "Still, it could use a cold pack."

"Maybe later. Mavis should be up here soon. I wanted to talk to her about street kids, girl packs. Girl packs now, ice packs later."

"Hmm. You've identified more, I see."

"Yeah. I was going to update you, but I guess it should wait for later. We've still got five more outstanding. I've made some connections, and I'm trying some new angles."

"Such as this." He tapped Montclair Jones's photo. "Lion fodder."

"Yeah. The timing bothers me, so I'm just playing around with it. The timing, his lack of real work or apparently any desire for it. His mother's suicide—slit wrists, bathtub. His treatment for depression like his mother."

"He's your top suspect. I can hear it."

Damn it, she thought when she jammed her hands in her pockets, he was.

"He just fits. But I can't interview him, I can't look at his eyes. I can't know it. I can tell you Shelby Stubacker forged docs to skip out of the home. Jones claims he didn't sign the doc, and I'm having the signature tested. Nobody knows who took her out, if she walked out on her own, what. It was all moving-out-and-in confusion."

"You think she had help."

"I think she was pretty canny, but where does a kid get the document paper, because it looked legit at a glance. How does she know what documents, what paperwork? The judge's name on it, real. The caseworker, real. I think a girl who knows how to trade blow jobs for brew knows how to trade for information and documentation. Montclair Jones was early twenties, young enough to be stupid. Well, men are stupid about blow jobs."

"It's difficult to resist challenging you to prove that. I believe my intelligent quotient can stand the test."

"Even you, pal, lose brain cells when your dick's involved. But let's stick with Jones, the younger. She bartered bjs for favors. He could have gotten her the doc paper, the names. Nobody's going to say anything if he goes into his brother's office, right?"

"I'm sorry, I'm having difficulty understanding. I was thinking about my penis."

"Funny. And probably true."

She got up again, circled again. "You ran with a pack. Would you have just ditched them, taken off on your own?"

In the end, he supposed he had. "Some are more loyal than others."

"Yeah, I get that, too, but the instinct, if you've formed a pack, is to keep it. I wonder if she planned on getting the others out. Could she have had the idea they'd all flop back in the old building? Familiar place, but without the rules, the supervision. Before she can follow through, she's dead. This one gets reinstated with her rehabilitated mother."

Eve tapped Mikki's photo. "The last thing she'd want if she had plans to hunker up with her friends. Before long, she takes off from there, and violently."

"And if she'd been meeting or intended to meet Shelby at the building . . ."

"She'd walk right in, and she's dead."

She circled again. "Still . . ."

"We're late!" Mavis bounced in on thigh-high platform boots as red as Rudolph's nose. Her hair, a twisting, curling, corkscrewing mass of sunshine covered with silver glitter, tumbled around a face that lasered out smiles.

She danced over, a high-on-the-thigh skirt of Christmas green scattered with silver stars fluttering as she tossed her arms around Roarke, then Eve for hugs.

"I'm totally juiced you thought of get-together time, because we haven't—just us—in a while. Leonardo's down with Bella, but you said I should come up, Dallas. The house looks ultra mag Santa time. Bellamina's seriously dazzled. And—"

She broke off, frowned at Eve's board.

"Work. I was just finishing up. I just wanted to ask you a couple questions about street life, girl packs, street packs, flops, chain of command. Anything I can get."

"It's work," Mavis said slowly, in an un-Mavis-like tone. "The girls in the building on the West Side. Their bodies, in the old building. I turned off the screen because I didn't want to hear about it."

"Sorry, but I wanted to pick your brain a little," Eve began.

"They're all dead, these girls? All of them?"

"Yeah." Eve didn't like the way the rosy glow in Mavis's cheeks died to sickly white. "Let's go downstairs and talk about it."

"A case. Your case. But I knew them. This one, and this one. This one, too."

"What?" Eve gripped her shoulder. "What do you mean?"

"I knew her." She gestured to Shelby. "And her." Now Mikki. "And her." And lastly LaRue Freeman. "I knew them, Dallas. Before you. I knew them before you."

She turned her face to Eve's with tears shimmering. "They were friends of mine."

**13** "you're sure?"

"Yes. You don't forget . . . They're dead. They've been dead all this time. That's why they never came back."

"Came back where?"

"To The Club. That's what we called it. They never came back."

"Mavis." Eve took her by the shoulders, shifted a little to block the photos on the board so Mavis would look at her instead. "When did you know them?"

"Before. Before I met you. I told you how it was before."

"Yeah." But she'd given Mavis a lot of leeway on details. No point pushing for them when they could make you wonder how many times you could arrest your best friend on prior bad acts.

"I'm going to need you to tell me more now."

"I need . . . a minute. It's all still there. You think it's not. You figure you've dumped it, or at least packed it all away. But it's all still there." She leaned on Eve a moment, all the bright clothes and hair. "You know."

"Yeah, I do."

"We were just kids, Dallas. They were just kids." She shuddered, eased back. "I want Bella, for a minute. I want Bella and Leonardo."

"We'll go down," Roarke said. He brushed off Eve's protest before it happened, simply giving her arm a squeeze as he drew Mavis away. "You could do with some wine, darling, and a bit of time to gather your thoughts."

"I guess. I'm upside down, or inside out. Maybe both. I thought they took off." She leaned on him now as they went downstairs. "A lot of us did, or got picked up, swallowed up. But a lot just took off. People don't always stay, even when you want them to."

"They don't, no." He led her into the parlor where Leonardo and Summerset, with equally besotted smiles, watched Bella bang enthusiastically on some sort of colorful plastic cube. One bang and it played a rapid guitar riff, another trumpets blasted like New Year's Eve on Zeus.

While it riffed, blasted, drummed, tweeted, Bella laughed like a loon and shook her hot pink ruffled butt.

"Look what Summerset gave Bella." Beaming over the cacophony, Leonardo, a glittering silver vest flowing over a sapphire shirt, rose from the sofa. "She has your musical talent, moonbeam."

His smile faded as he focused on the sheen in her eyes. "What's the matter?" He started toward her, but she shook her head, glanced down at Bella.

"Oh, that's just mag!" Mavis dropped down by Bella to poke the image of a keyboard. "It's the total ult. You can play backup for Mommy! Thanks, Summerset."

"I thought she'd enjoy it. Music's in the blood." Though his voice held as much cheer as Summerset's ever did, the amusement had gone out of his eyes.

But for Bella, still shy of her first birthday, the world was bright lights and music.

She spotted Eve and Roarke, squealed with boundless joy.

"Das!" As fast as her chubby legs could manage, she toddled over to Eve, and her pretty face glowing with desperate love, lifted her arms. "Up!"

"Oh, well, I—"

"Up, up, up! Das."

"Okay, okay." Flustered, Eve reached down. Bella took it from there, all but climbing into Eve's arms, then clapping both hands on Eve's cheeks while she jabbered in the foreign language of baby.

"'Kay? 'Kay?" She made an exaggerated *mmmm!* sound as she pressed her lips to Eve's.

"Yeah, sure." It was hard not to grin around a kid just that pretty and happy, but the timing . . . But when Eve tried to set her down again, Bella clung like a burr, dropped the foreign tongue to a hissy whisper in Eve's ear. Then laughed deep from the belly at the joke only she knew.

And with a bounce, she twisted in Eve's arms, gave Eve a hot moment of sheer panic before she tried to fly across to Roarke.

"Ork!"

"Good idea. Great idea." Mentally swiping sweat from her brow, Eve shoved Bella at Roarke.

He received similar treatment—hands, jabber, kiss—and his reaction slid along the same lines as Eve's, until Bella tilted her head to one side and batted her lashes like a pro.

Despite it all, he laughed, found she seemed less likely to slip out of his hold when she settled on his hip. "And look at you now, quite the flirt already."

She smiled, just a little sly, played with his hair.

"Men are her playthings." Mavis's voice trembled a little before she sipped the wine Summerset offered her.

"Perhaps she can keep me company for a while." Stooping, Summerset picked up the toy.

"She'd like that," Mavis began. "If she gets in the way—"

"Pretty girls are never in the way." Smoothly, Summerset plucked her from Roarke, balanced her on his bony hip with an ease of motion that baffled Eve. Bella launched into a fresh spate of babbling, feet cheerfully kicking in fuzzy pink boots.

"I think that can be arranged," Summerset told her as he carried her out.

She patted his cheek, said something that sounded like "some shit." Eve found herself puzzling over it, until she put it together.

Shum shit. Summerset.

Now that she could appreciate.

Bella grinned over his shoulder, waved a hand. "Bye-bye! Bye-bye!"

"Someshit—that's her name for him. You gotta love it. Did he actually understand her?" Eve wondered.

"She was flirting for cookies," Mavis said, then just sat, closed her eyes.

"Mavis, what happened?" Leonardo sat beside her, cuddled her as he would a child. "Tell me what's wrong."

"The girls. We heard the media blast, remember? All those girls. Roarke's building. They said it was your building."

"Just recently, yes."

"I think, sometimes, I think maybe it's all a big, wicked loop. Who you know, what you do, where you are. I knew some of the girls, Leonardo. Some of the girls they found in Roarke's building. The girls on Dallas's dead board upstairs. His building, her case. My friends, from another life."

"I'm sorry. I'm so sorry." He pressed his lips to her hair, rocked her.

"I don't know why it's screwing me up like this. It was a million years ago, and I hardly thought about them, ever. But . . . seeing them, and knowing, and they looked like they did. Mostly like they did."

"What can you tell me about them?" Eve began, and Roarke put a hand on her shoulder.

"Eve."

"Look, I'm sorry." Instead of taking a chair, Eve sat on the table directly facing Mavis. "I know it's rough, but if you knew them, even a million years ago, something you know might help me find who killed them, and why."

"They wouldn't get you. I did. Do you ever wonder why? I got you, almost from the bounce—or the bust. You were so *official*, and so grumpy in your uniform."

Those hard black cop shoes, Eve thought. God, how she'd hated them. She probably had looked grumpy.

"And you looked like some kid playing fairy princess dress-up, even with your hand in that mark's pocket."

"I didn't even have his wallet yet."

"And tried to tell me you were just trying to get his attention. Bogus."

"I was pretty good at the lift, even though I mostly ran cons. But now and again you'd see some tourist just asking for it, you know? You know?" she repeated to Roarke.

"I know very well."

"You ever think about that, Dallas? Your man and your best girl, thieves and grifters."

"Night and day."

With a watery laugh, Mavis leaned her head against Leonardo's arm a moment. "My moonpie here, he knows it all, all the way back. When you love somebody, they've got to know who you are, even if you're not exactly who you were. Did she tell you about me—back then?"

"No," Roarke said, "not, I think, all of it."

"You wouldn't." Mavis looked at Eve, and saying nothing told her she, too, kept her friend's secrets. "Some's in the bio. It plays okay, former grifter, turns it around and scores on the music charts. The before that? Wouldn't ring so sweet, so I twisted it around some."

"Yeah, I noticed." And on that, too, Eve had kept her silence.

"We do what we do, right? Let me spread it all out, okay, so we're all up on it. And maybe it'll help settle the jumpies."

As Mavis was beginning to sound more like Mavis, Eve nodded, then rose to take a chair and the wine Roarke handed her.

"Start wherever you want," Eve told her.

"Okay, well, big entrance. My mother was a drunk and a junkie. She'd drink, smoke, pop, and stick anything when she was rolling. The father wasn't around much, then not at all. I don't remember him very well, and I don't think she did either. We lived mostly around Baltimore. Sometimes she worked, sometimes she didn't. Sometimes we'd skip out on the rent in the middle of the night because she'd snorted it up. It made her crazy, but when she was using she mostly left me alone. It was better when she was using."

She paused a moment, seemed to gather herself. "But she'd get busted, maybe I'd get shuffled out unless I slipped the leash. Then we

were in the rehab cycle, and when she was in that mode, she'd get re-
ligion. The kind where she'd have me by the neck twenty-four/seven,
preaching weird stuff, not your basic God stuff, the hellfire crap."

She sighed a little, nuzzled into Leonardo. "I don't get why some
people want God to scare the shit out of you. Anyhow, she'd throw
out all my things—my clothes, my discs if I had any, the lip dye I'd
probably shoplifted. Everything. "New broom sweeps clean," she'd
say, and make me wear these dresses—always brown or gray, high
neck, long-sleeved, even in the summer. And—"

She stopped to swallow, to breathe out. "She'd cut my hair—
shorter than Dallas's—especially when I started to bud some. She'd
whack it off, so it wouldn't tempt men. If she caught me at anything
she didn't like, she'd take a belt to me, beat out the devil kind of
thing. And I'd have to fast, no food for however long she figured."

Saying nothing, Leonardo shifted her just a little closer. And that,
Eve thought, said everything.

"Then she'd start using again, and it was better. Until it wasn't.
Round and round, you never knew who she was going to be on any
given day. Am I taking too long? It's a messy memory lane deal."

"You're not." Roarke topped off her wine, brushed his fingers
down her cheek, then sat again.

"It's just—I was afraid, for a long time, it was like passed down.
Like the whole gene thing. I was never going to get totally about a
guy or have kids."

Her voice broke, and while she struggled to control it, Leonardo
pulled a blue hankie with silver snowflakes out of his pocket, dabbed
at her eyes himself.

"As if I could help it," she added, "once I found you. But it wasn't
the gene pool thing. She'd messed herself up, fried her brain, fucked

it up good. So one night, she woke me up. Middle of the night, middle of the winter. She was using again, but it was different this time. It was like the worst of both ways she could be. Hellfire and beat the devil, and that dead look in her eyes. She . . . Dallas."

"They were living in a flop," Eve continued. "Junkie flop. She had a couple of guys hold Mavis down while she cut her hair off again, and sold Mavis's clothes for junk. The others used her like a slave, and some of the men wanted to use her for something else. The mother didn't give a shit, and when she got offered some Zeus one of the fuckers claimed to have coming for Mavis, the mother made the deal, said it would be Mavis's initiation."

"That's when I was scared, the most," Mavis murmured. "That's when I knew I had to get away, all the way."

"Mavis was supposed to fast, purge, clean up—all this weird ritual prep. Instead she ran, grabbed whatever she could carry and she ran, all the way to New York."

"I was always going to run—I mean once things got really bad, and the flop was really bad. I was hiding some money, stealing it mostly. I was just waiting for better weather, but the idea of her selling me to that guy? Time to book it complete. I was going to go south, follow the sun, you know? But there were a couple of cops at the transpo station, and it spooked me. I got on the wrong bus, ended up here."

"Perhaps it was the right bus after all," Roarke said quietly, and made her smile.

"Yeah. Yeah, I guess it was. I did some sidewalk sleeping, changed my name. I did that legally—sort of—when I could, but I already had the name picked out. We had a neighbor once, Mrs. Mavis. She was nice to me. She'd say how she made too much food, and would I do her a favor and eat it, that kind of thing. And I just liked the way Freestone sounded, so I was Mavis Freestone."

"It's exactly who you are," Roarke said and made her smile again.

"It's who I wanted to be. I was scared for a while, and freaking cold, hungry. But I knew how to get by, and anything was better. I was doing some panhandling and pickpocketing in Times Square when I met a couple of girls. Not the ones upstairs, not then. They took me to The Club. I never told you much about that," she said to Eve. "I wasn't there that long really. Maybe off and on for a year, a year and a half."

"Where was it?"

"We moved around. A basement, a condemned building, an empty apartment. Nomads, Sebastian called us."

"Sebastian who?"

"I don't know. Just Sebastian, and I never told you about him because, well, because. He ran The Club. It was like the street academy, a school, a club, a place to hang. He'd teach us the ropes—pocket picking, handoffs, drops, simple cons, most short cons. Crying Baby, Lost Girl, Duck and Goose, like that. He made sure we ate, were outfitted—and pooled the take, of which he took a cut."

"Your Fagan."

Eve frowned at Roarke. "Her what?"

"Fagan. A character from *Oliver Twist*. Dickens, darling, only Fagan ran a gang of boys in London."

"Sebastian figured girls got less of the cop eyeball, and pulled off the cons better than boys. That's where I met Shelby and Mikki and LaRue. They didn't stay—Sebastian called them day-trippers. But they ran with us, and Shelby made noises about starting her own club. Somebody was always making noises about starting something, going somewhere, being somebody."

"This Sebastian, did he ever hurt any of you, go at any of you?"

"No. No!" Mavis waved a hand in the air. "He looked out for us—

not your way, Dallas, but it worked. He never laid a hand on any of us, not any way. And if any of us got in the stew outside, he fixed it."

"Forged documents?"

"He was pretty good at it, I guess you could say it was one of his specialties."

"I'll need you to work with an artist. I need his face."

"Dallas." Mavis just looked at her, waited a beat. "If you think he did that to those girls, you're out of orbit. He'd never hurt any of them. Nonviolence all the way. No weapons—ever. "Wit and speed," that's what he'd say. "Use your brains and your feet." Even after I went out on my own, I'd do jobs with him now and then."

"I need to talk to him, Mavis."

"Shit. Double shit. Let me talk to him first."

Eve eased back a little, nearly goggled. "You know how to contact him?"

"Triple shit. He helped me out, Dallas, when I needed it. He taught me—okay, not what you'd like, but still. He's sort of semi-retired. Sort of. Now I know why I never told you about him."

"Twelve girls are dead."

"I know it. I know it, and I knew three of them. Maybe it's going to turn out I knew more of them. It makes me sick inside. I'll talk to him, get him to talk to you, but you have to promise it's, like, not in that sweatbox deal. That you won't bust him for—just stuff."

"Christ."

"Please."

"Set it up, but if it leans a frigging inch that he killed those girls, it's over."

Mavis breathed out in relief. "It won't, so that's a deal."

"Tell me more about the girls."

"Shelby ran the show—with her crew. LaRue hung with them

more than anybody else, but she was more on her own. Mikki was, like, all about Shelby. I think she had the hots for her, too, and just didn't get it yet. There was another girl—kinda small black girl, with a great big voice. Really magolicious pipes."

"DeLonna."

"Yeah, yeah—I didn't really know her. She only came around with Shelby a couple times. And there was a guy, but Sebastian didn't allow boys in The Club. I think that's why Shelby didn't just bag it and stick with us. She had mega loyalty. They were hers, including the guy, so she just hung and ran sometimes, and talked about getting her own place."

"He didn't allow boys, but what about men?"

"It was just Sebastian. Actually, he, like, boosted us. Our self-esteem and all," Mavis explained. "He always said stuff like we were worth more than anything we could liberate. He used words like that instead of, you know, *steal*."

Mavis cocked her head at Eve. "Fancy words," she said in a reasonably decent impression of Eve, "don't make it less of a crime."

"Funny. Why are thieves so hilarious?"

"Stealing's kind of a funny business when you think about it. Anyway, he'd say how we should never give away what we had—meaning sex—or let anybody take it. And how we needed to wait until we understood all that stuff."

She looked down at her fingers, joined with Leonardo's. "He made me feel like I was worth something. No one ever had."

Not a bad ploy, Eve thought, for getting a bunch of hungry girls to steal for you. "He had to move merchandise. Had to have a fence, had to buy supplies."

"He mostly dealt with a couple pawnbrokers, but they never came around The Club—not while I was running with them anyway."

"Women?"

"No. He hooked with this LC, but he never brought her around either. Look, he wasn't—isn't—a sleezewad. We had rules, and okay, sure, they were pretty loose, but we had them. We even had to study, like in school. He said there was no excuse for stupid. No illegals or booze. If you wanted to screw yourself up, you did it outside. That was the thing with Shelby," Mavis remembered, circling back. "She had a taste for illegals, for brew. She wanted her own place so she and her crew could do what they wanted. That's why I figured—we all did, I guess—she just took off."

"How many girls?"

"It went up and down. Ten, maybe fifteen. More when the weather went sour. Some stayed a couple days, some stayed years."

"I've got some pictures I'd like you to look at."

"I saw them, on your board. I only recognized the three."

"We're still IDing. I have some pictures from Missing Persons reports. Can you look at them?"

"Oh." Mavis let out a long breath. "Yeah, sure. Yeah. If it could help." She turned to Leonardo. "I want to help."

He brought her hands to his lips, then kissed her cheeks. "I'll check on Bella."

"You're the biggest prize in the big, shiny box of prizes."

"Maybe the biggest." He touched his lips to hers. "You're the sweetest. I'll be right here."

"I know. Okay." She rose. "Let's do it. Thanks for listening," she said to Roarke. "And the wine."

He stood, stepped over to enfold her in a hug. "You're family."

She squeezed hard. "One of the top ten phrases. Right up there with 'I love you,' and 'For you it's free.'"

When she went out with Eve, he sat, looked at Leonardo.

"I need to give Summerset a break."

"Take a moment," Roarke advised. "I can promise you he's enjoying himself."

"Little shaky, I guess." Leonardo picked up the wine he'd ignored while Mavis had talked, while he'd held her through it. "I knew it all, but hearing her say it all again . . ."

"It makes it all real again. It makes you wish again that you could somehow go back and save her from all of it."

Leonardo let out an unsteady breath. "It does. It does just exactly that. Everything got brighter when I met her, and faster. Then, it stayed bright but it all settled in. I could've gone on just fine with my work, and the women, the parties. It seemed like enough. Now? All of that could go. I don't mean the women," he said, suddenly flustered. "I mean there aren't any women, not since Mavis. I mean *she's* the only . . ."

"I understand." The tangle made Roarke smile again. "Perfectly."

"I mean, it could all go away, because I have my girls. It hurts when she hurts."

"Yes. I understand perfectly," Roarke repeated.

I know this is hard on you," Eve began as they walked to her office. "I need to say—before—I need to say maybe I'd have been one of those girls if it wasn't for Sebastian. Or maybe I'd have ended up trading bjs for junk, like Shelby. She bragged about it. And maybe if I'd gotten through all that, maybe I'd still be grifting and getting nowhere especially if I hadn't met you, if you hadn't let me in."

"Couldn't keep you out."

"Yeah, you could've, but you didn't. And I'd never know this." She pressed a hand to her heart. "I'd never know what it really is without Leonardo. I'd never have something so amazing and beyond the mag of the mag like Bella, and have a chance, a real chance, to be a really, really good mother. I want to be a good mother, Dallas, so bad it scares me shitless thinking I might screw up."

"We both know about mothers who screw up, big-time. You're not one of those, and never could be. I don't know much about the other kind, not so much, but I know the kid's insanely happy. I don't know what the hell she's babbling about more than half the time, but she's happy as a monkey with a box of bananas. She's safe, she's not a whiner, and she already knows she can count on you and Leonardo for anything. That seems like it covers the job to me."

"I want another one."

"Oh sweet weeping Jesus."

On a bubbling laugh, Mavis threw her arms around Eve, did her bounce. "Not right away, but not way down the highway either. I want another baby, for me, for my moonpie, and for my Bellamina. I am good at it, and maybe having the weird wigs about being good at it makes me good at it. Whatev, I want a bunch of them."

"Define 'bunch.'"

"I don't know yet. More." She drew back, swiped her hands over her face as the mix of emotions had flooded it. Looking at the board, she sighed. "I'm so lucky, and they weren't. We got really lucky," she said, taking Eve's hand.

"Yeah, we did."

"I'm going to look at the pictures, then I want to go home with my man and my baby. I want to put my baby to bed and watch her sleep for a little while. Then I want to have crazy sex with my man. Because I got lucky, and I'm never going to forget it."

"They got pretty lucky, too, your man and your kid."

"Damn right. We're all stupid with happy."

"Can't argue. But before you go home to bedtime and sex, I need you to contact Sebastian, set up a meet."

"Crap."

"Sooner's better," Eve added.

R oarke came into Eve's office after seeing Mavis and her family off, found her at her desk with a mug of coffee. And noted the two new pictures on the board, one with a question mark.

"I had to stick with this," she said. "Mavis wanted to go home anyway, to put the kid to bed, then jump Leonardo."

"I see. She said she recognized two more."

"One for certain, one mostly for certain. I sent DeWinter and Elsie the data so they can confirm. The one she's sure of—Crystal Hugh—she did some time at The Sanctuary. Got shifted to foster, went missing from there. Too many lines lead back to that building, that place, those people for it to be just because."

"I'll agree."

"And now I've got four, possibly five, connected to this Sebastian character Mavis is rosy-eyed over."

"He's her father figure, Eve. She was a frightened, scared young girl, and he gave her structure, safety, a purpose."

"Structure? Flopping in basements and empty buildings? And the purpose was stealing and bilking."

"And yet."

"Yeah, you'd think that," she replied. "Seeing as."

"Summerset provided me with a very nice home, furnished. I already knew how to steal and run a con, he just added some polish."

He picked up her coffee, took a sip. "I wondered why I felt a kind of affinity with Mavis, always. I see now we traveled some similar roads. How old was she when she ran?"

"Around thirteen, I think." She stopped, met his eyes. "I wasn't holding out on you, not telling you all that. It's just . . ."

"It wasn't yours to tell, not even to me. Just as she's never told Leonardo yours."

"I told her she could." Eve shoved her fingers through her hair as the idea made her uneasy, even though it seemed right. "You know, balance it out."

He leaned over, pressed his lips to the hair she'd just mussed. "I adore you."

"Yeah, well, good. You're going to have to because you're going with me to meet up with this Sebastian." She glanced at her watch. "In two hours, at some seedy dive in Hell's Kitchen."

"You plan such entertaining evenings for me. Two hours? That's time enough for dinner. We'll make it pizza."

How could she argue with that?

SEEDY COVERED IT.

The hole-in-the-wall that had been named, fairly realistically, Belly Up slouched between a porn shop where a variety of strap-ons were featured in the dingy display window, and what had been in its latest and now-defunct incarnation a place called Bill's Quik Loans.

Just across the street, the dying neon on a sex club stuttered NAKED—SEX—DANCERS in a migraine-inducing loop.

In its intermittent blue lights, Eve clearly saw the illegal deal being transacted by a bulky dealer in a heavy black coat, and his skinny, shivering customer.

"Is he shuddering because he's jonesing," Eve wondered, "or because he's freezing his junkie ass off in that trench coat?"

"Likely both. If you're going to bust them, I'll wait."

"Only take a minute." She stepped to the curb, shouted over the dented hood of an ancient Mini, "Hey!" And waved her badge in the air.

Both bulky dealer and skinny junkie pounded sidewalk in opposite directions.

"You know they'll both just deal elsewhere."

"Yeah, but it's fun to watch them run when I'm not going to chase them. Let's go Belly Up with Sebastian—if he shows."

It proved as seedy inside as out with a trio of shallow booths and a pair of scarred tables lining the sticky floor. The short black bar boasted three backless stools, and occupants who looked like they belonged there.

The flabby bartender didn't look thrilled with his work, and after a flick of a glance toward Eve and Roarke appeared pissed off at the prospect of more customers.

The air smelled of cheap brew and centuries-old sweat.

The bony guy at the end of the bar slid off his stool as Eve passed, and strolled, desperately nonchalant, to the door and out.

She supposed he'd smelled cop even in the bad air.

She ignored the LC trying to make a deal with the man on the other stool, and walked to the back booth, and Mavis's Sebastian.

He wore a suit—unexpected—of charcoal gray. It didn't reach the heights of Roarke's custom tailoring, but it was a decent fit. He'd paired it with a black turtleneck.

A silver pen peeked out of the breast pocket.

With his artfully shaggy mop of brown hair, the quiet, pale blue eyes, and neatly trimmed goatee, he might've been mistaken for a college professor. He even had his hands neatly folded over a ratty paperback book.

Long, graceful-looking fingers, she noted—certainly adept at lifting wallets, flicking off wrist units.

He rose as they approached. Eve managed to watch his eyes and his hands at the same time, just in case.

"Lieutenant Dallas." He offered a hand—empty—and a smile as quiet and professorial as the rest of him. "Such a pleasure to meet you at last. And you." He offered the same to Roarke. "Mavis has told me so much about you, and I follow news of you in the media, of course. I feel I already know you."

"We're not here to get chummy."

"In any case." He gestured toward the booth. "Let me buy you a drink. The safest here is beer in the bottle. Anything else is suspect."

"On duty," Eve said briefly.

"Yes, I understand. Still, the bartender looks askance when there's no order on the table. There's bottled water to be had. If that will suffice, just give me a moment."

"What's with this guy?" Eve asked, sliding into the booth as Sebastian stepped to the bar.

"He hopes to make a good impression." Roarke angled his head to read the title of the book. "*Macbeth*. It suits the educated voice, the well-presented demeanor."

"He's a thief and an enabler of delinquent girls."

"Yes, well, we all have our flaws."

Sebastian came back, set down three short bottles. "I wouldn't trust the glassware either. I'll apologize for asking you to meet me in such a place, but you'll understand I feel a bit more comfortable on my own turf, so to speak."

He sat, looking comfortable, a man in his middle forties who kept in shape—body and mind.

"Shelby Stubacker," Eve said.

He sighed, nudged his book to the side. "I heard the reports on the girls you found. It's painful to me, on a human level, to know there are those who'd prey on the young. And painful on a personal level as Mavis said three had been mine."

"Four."

Shock flicked in his eyes. "Four? Mavis said three. Shelby and Mikki and LaRue."

"Add Crystal Hugh, and possibly Merry Wolcovich."

"Crystal." He slumped a little. "I remember her very well. She was only nine when she came to me, still wearing the bruises her father had put on her."

"Then you should've called the police."

"Her father was the police," Sebastian said with a snap in his tone. "There are beasts in every walk of life. She was hurt, hungry, and alone, with nowhere to go but back to the man who took out his frustrations on a child and her spineless mother. She stayed with us until she was thirteen. It can be a difficult age."

He paused a moment. "Crystal. Yes, I remember Crystal. Soft brown eyes and the mouth of a longshoreman. I appreciated the first, discouraged the second. As I recall, she'd started considering boys, as girls will at that age, and straining against the rules."

With a half smile, he lifted his bottle. "We do have them. She told me she was leaving and going with some friends. They were going to travel down to Florida. I gave her some money, wished her well, and told her she could come back whenever she wanted."

"You let a thirteen-year-old girl walk."

"They were only mine as long as they chose to stay. I'd hoped she'd gone to Florida, and sat on the beach. She deserved to. I remember Shelby as she was brash, rebellious—an interesting girl. A leader, but not always where others should be led. And Mikki because she would have followed Shelby into hell and back again. But the other you mentioned?"

"Merry Wolcovich."

"I don't recall right off. Fifteen years is a long time, and I've taken in a lot of girls over the years."

It put her back up, this *taking in girls* as if he were some selfless hero instead of an exploitive criminal. She leaned forward.

"Let's just lay this out. You train disenfranchised kids to steal, to break the law, to treat it like a game on one level, an avocation on another. So they run the streets, bilking people, taking money and possessions those people worked for, money they earned to pay the rent, to pay bills, or to blow at craps at a casino—because it's *theirs*. And you make a profit on your school of thieves and grifters. Mavis might see you as some sort of savior, but to me, you're just another criminal circumventing the law for his own gain."

Nodding, Sebastian sipped his water. "I understand your point of view. You've built your life around the law, have sworn to uphold it. And while you're neither naive nor rigid, your duty is your core. I'm a hard bite for you to chew and swallow, but you'll do it. On a personal level for Mavis, and on both a personal and professional level for twelve dead girls."

"Girls you might've killed. You helped Shelby get out of the new HPCCY, just as they were moving in."

"I don't remember doing anything of the kind. How did I help her leave there?"

"Forged documents. It's something you do."

"I may or may not forge documents. I'll tread softly there. But I never did so for Shelby. Not of any kind. She wouldn't have asked me."

"Why?"

"First, because she knew better than to offer her usual bartering system to me. I don't touch the girls sexually, despise any man who would, and she knew my line there. Second, it would have implied she needed me, and she was always out to prove she needed no one."

"Did you teach her how to forge official documents?"

"Not directly, as again, she'd have never asked me to teach her any skill. It's certainly possible she picked a few things up. She knew how to pay attention."

"Shelby planned to get her own place and had one in mind. A born leader, in your own words, she might've taken a big chunk of girls with her, threatening your operation, cutting into your profits."

He drank some water, watched her steadily. "I imagine you'll have to explore that possibility. I'm outside your lines for one, and connected to at least some of those poor girls. But you know, as I do, Mavis is a very sharp judge of people. She knows I've never hurt a child in my life, never could or would."

Now he leaned forward. "I don't have the inclination and you haven't the time to hear my long, sad story, Lieutenant. I'll just say that while we have different methods, even opposing methods, our goal is the same. To help those who've been hurt or discarded. Because of that, I'll do anything I'm capable of doing to help you find out who killed those girls."

He paused a moment, leaned back again, drank again. "Some of them were mine," he said quietly.

It pissed her off that she believed him. Saying nothing, she reached in her file bag, took out a photo, and set it on the table between them.

He nudged it closer and, brows drawing together, studied the face.

"Yes. Yes, I know this face. She came in—was brought in—by one of the others. With . . . give me a moment."

He frowned at the photo, then closed his eyes. "With DeLonna, of the siren's voice."

"DeLonna Jackson?"

"I don't know if I had DeLonna's full name as she wasn't really with us. Came and went, one of Shelby's friends. But it was DeLonna, I'm certain, who brought her to me, after she'd found the girl being hassled by some older boys. Some will always prey on the smaller and weaker—and though DeLonna was small, she was fierce." He laughed a little, at some memory. "In any case this girl . . . yes, Merry, but not the traditional spelling. She was very specific, M-e-r-r-y. Again, I don't know the last name. She only stayed a handful of days."

"Why?"

"I don't remember, right offhand, the particulars. I do remember her now. I remember her face. Do you have more? More photographs?"

"Not yet. What about girls who left during this time period. You said some came and went. Who went."

"Actually, there is one. After I spoke with Mavis, I thought of her. Iris Kirkwood. She'd been with us about a year. All too typical story. Father gone, abuse and neglect from the mother. In and out of foster homes, some of which were no better than the parental home, then back with the mother who simply walked out one day. Iris opted not to go back in the system, but went on the street. She was a terrible thief, clumsy fingers. I used her primarily as a pickup, or on the Lost and Found grift, something simple. She was . . . a little slow, if you understand me. A sweet smile when she used it, but far too eager to please. She liked to sit in church."

Eve's eyes sharpened. "What church?"

"None in particular. She said she liked them because they were quiet and pretty and smelled good. Is it important?"

Eve pushed past the question. "She was with you for a year, then she wasn't. You didn't think anything of it?"

"On the contrary, we looked for her. One of the girls told me Iris said she had a secret, but she couldn't tell or it wouldn't come true. Secrets are stock and trade for girls of that age, so I didn't think anything of it at the time. She had a stuffed dog she'd found somewhere. She called it Baby. She was very young for her age and circumstances. She took Baby with her when she left, and as she left during the night, after curfew—"

"Curfew?"

"There are some rules," he said again. "Since she left on her own, I had to believe she'd chosen to leave us. Still we looked."

"Back in a minute," Eve said to Roarke, and strode out of the bar.

"I believe I'll have that beer." Sebastian cocked an eyebrow at Roarke. "Are you sure you won't have one?"

"Yes, I'm sure, but thanks."

Sebastian went to the bar, came back with a bottle. "I admire your wife," he began.

"As do I."

"She's dedicated and ferocious, for all the right reasons. She'll find who did this."

"She won't stop until she does."

"It's an interesting life the two of you've made."

"I could say the same of yours."

"It's one that suits me. I think you understand the perspective of a certain fluidity of borders others, such as your lieutenant, must see as firm demarcations."

"I understand adjusting borders when needs must."

Sebastian looked down at his beer a moment, then just nodded to himself. "They have nowhere to go. Most will say they have to go into the system—the system will tend to them. It was created to tend to them. But we know, you and I and your lieutenant, that far too often the system fails. It fails, even with the dedication of ferocity of those who've sworn to protect, who do everything they can to fulfill that duty, it fails. When it does, the wounded, abused, and innocent among us suffer."

"I don't disagree. Neither would the lieutenant on the failure of the system, and the cost when it does. So she'll fight within the system to protect. And when she can't protect to work—ferociously—to see that justice is served for those who suffered."

"Even if it means dealing with me."

"Even that. Some of them, it seems, were yours for a time. All of them are hers now. They'll always be hers now."

She walked back in, eyes flat, stride brisk. And held out her PPC. "Iris Kirkwood."

Sebastian looked at the screen, at the image of the girl with straight, sandy blond hair, wide brown eyes, and lips curved in a small, sweet smile.

"Yes, that's Iris." He picked up the beer, took a slow swallow. "Is she one of them?"

"I don't know yet. Her mother's dead, beaten to death by the guy she lived with in North Carolina. April of 'forty-five."

"That would've been six or eight months after Iris came to me, and a few months before she left us."

"Any other girls who left about that time?"

"No, at least none who didn't go back to a parent or guardian. Which is encouraged—strongly—when they're spinning a tale as Merry did."

"As Merry did?"

"You've looked at her background by now, so you know—as I did—she came from an average family. No reports of abuse, no Double Ds—and yes, some of that often isn't reported. But I know when a girl's lying to me. And her claims of terror and misery at home were lies."

He paused to consider his beer again. "She paid far too high a price for it. If and when you have more photos, I'll look at them."

"He fished in your pool, and The Sanctuary's. Where was your flop during this period?"

"We had three on rotation that year, year and a half. As I assumed you'd ask, I've noted them down." He took a piece of paper out of his pocket, handed it to her. "All three buildings have been renovated and are occupied now, but at the time they were useful."

"Where's your flop now?"

He smiled a little. "I won't tell you the truth, and find myself reluctant to lie to you. So." He gave a small, elegant shrug, sipped his beer. "If you need to talk to me again, Mavis knows how to contact me."

Eve sat back, considered. She wouldn't break her word to Mavis and run him in on the stream of charges that came to mind. And for now, he might be useful.

"The other two in Shelby's crew. What do you know about them?"

"The boy, nothing. DeLonna . . ." He hesitated. "She's alive and well."

"I need to talk to her."

"It's awkward. I'll contact her, ask her to contact you. I can't do more without betraying her."

"She's very likely a material witness in multiple homicides."

"I very much doubt that, or she'd have said or done something. She loved Shelby, and Mikki. But I give you my word I'll contact her tonight, and I'll convince her to talk to you."

"Your word."

"Is good, which is why I rarely give it. How did they die? How did he—"

"I can't tell you at this time." She slid out of the booth again, hated that she saw genuine grief on his face. "But when I can, I will."

"Thank you."

"If I find out you had anything to do with it, the wrath of God has nothing on mine."

"I hope that's true. I hope when you find him, the wrath of a thousand gods comes down on him."

She turned to go, scowled when Roarke held out a hand to him. "It was good to meet you."

"And you. Both of you."

Eve kept her silence until they were out in the cold and the wind. "You're freaking polite."

"No reason for me to be otherwise."

"You *liked* him."

"I didn't dislike him," Roarke qualified, as he grabbed her hand and walked toward the car.

"He conceals girls from the authorities, teaches them to distrust, disrespect, and break the law, cheat people, steal from people when they should be . . ." She waved her free hand. "In school and whatever."

"They should be in school and whatever," he agreed. "They shouldn't be used as a punching bag, or worse, by a parent. They shouldn't be neglected and left to fend for themselves or exposed to violence, illegals, indiscriminate sex, and everything else they'd be exposed to in a bloody awful home."

He opened the car door for her. After one fulminating glare, she got inside.

"And just how many of the girls who've run through *his* system," she began the minute Roarke slid behind the wheel, "are in a cage, or dead, or working the streets because of the lifestyle he promoted?"

"I expect some are, and likely would have been with or without him. I also know at least one who's happy, successful, has a family, and a very fine life."

"Just because Mavis—"

"Where do you think she'd be, given how she was, where she was, her age, if he hadn't given her a place?"

"I think she'd have been scooped up, the cops and CPS would've interviewed and examined her, would've tossed her worthless, batshit mother in a padded cage, and put Mavis in foster care."

"That's possible," he said as he drove. "As it's possible someone prone to taking young girls would have raped her at the least, sold her, killed her. Many possibles, but the fact is she wouldn't be who she is, you wouldn't be more than sisters if not for Sebastian. Change something by a hair, darling, change it all."

"It's not right, what he's doing. I let it go because I needed her to get him to talk to me. And because—"

"You gave her your word you wouldn't arrest him."

"It's different now."

"You don't think he killed those girls."

Damn it, no, she didn't—and hoped to hell she wasn't being conned. "Thinking isn't proof, and he's connected. Liar, thief, con man."

"Are you speaking of him or me?"

She slumped down in her seat with a fresh scowl. "Stop it."

"Well now, I didn't run a gang of girls, but I ran with a gang. I lied, I stole, and certainly ran the occasional scam. You've learned to live with that, but it niggles now and then."

"You gave it up."

"Some for myself before I met you. The rest for you. For what I wanted for us. I had Summerset, or else the old man would've beat me bloody time and again until he did me in. You know, better than most, that the system does fail, however much those in it try. And that not all who take children in, within that system, do so with open hearts. You have your lines, Lieutenant, and I've my own. I don't think we're too far apart in this case. More a bit of a lean in two directions, but not far. Not with Mavis in the middle of it."

He reached over, rubbed her thigh. "Where's her mother? You'd have looked into that."

"In a facility for the bat-shit who carve an equally bat-shit up with a butcher knife. She's been in for about eight years now—before that she moved around, joined a cult, left it, did some time for trading sex for Zeus. Got out, got on the funk. She was wasted on it when she sliced up the woman she ran with—and was sleeping with by that point. Mavis was right. She just fried her own brain over time. She's mostly sedated."

"You haven't told her."

"I will if and when she needs to know. If and when she ever wants to know. She's pushed it all out, or had until tonight. Really pushed it out. She had some moments tying herself up in knots that she wouldn't be a good mother, but she figured out how to set it away, and be happy. Telling her just throws it back at her."

Eve leaned her head back. "And she was right. If her mother wasn't shit-house crazy, she'd never recognize the kid she knocked around in Mavis Freestone, music star and fashion . . . wonder. I often wonder about her fashion."

"That's part of the point, isn't it? Forced to wear dull clothes, having her hair whacked off. It's not just shoving it out, it's beating it with sticks and setting it on fire."

The image surprised a laugh out of Eve. "Yeah, it is. I wonder if she knows it."

"I suspect she did when she started experimenting with hair color, eye color, the clothes. Now? It's who she is."

He turned in the gates, toward the big, handsome house. "She didn't recognize Iris from The Club?"

"I didn't have an ID photo to show her. No Missing Persons ever filed on Iris Kirkwood, no alerts, not here, not where the mother died. She slipped through the cracks. Yes, the system fails sometimes, some of the worst times, but teaching adolescent girls how to run Take the Candy isn't the solution."

"I've never heard of that con."

"I made it up. I want some candy."

He parked in front of the entrance, smiled at her. "Let's go get some."

She went in with him, tossed her coat over the newel post.

"What do you intend to do with the addresses Sebastian gave you?"

"Send out some uniforms to canvass and dig up residents and merchants who were around when the girls went missing, show them photos. Poke, prod, pry. It only takes one person," she continued as they went upstairs, "just one to have seen one or more of the vics with someone. They'll have been friendly with him, trusted him. She had a secret," Eve murmured. "Iris."

"You believe she's one of them."

"She sneaks out of the place that's been her home, where she feels safe, takes her stuffed dog, and never comes back? They never find her, because I believe him when he said they looked. Somebody snatched her or lured her, and/or killed her."

Eve looked at the board as they walked into her office. "So she goes up. The question mark comes off Merry, and onto Iris. But it won't be a question mark for long."

"You've only two more."

"Yeah, maybe one of the last two hold the key. Or DeLonna. She poofed, too, but not until she was about sixteen and pretty clear of the system. But she's alive according to Sebastian."

"And well."

"I'll judge that when I talk to her—and I will talk to her," Eve said as she hunkered down beside her desk chair. "If he doesn't come through by tomorrow, I'll have to squeeze him."

"Which you wouldn't mind doing just on principle." She took a candy bar out of the desk drawer.

"In here? Really? I didn't know you kept a stash at home."

"It's not hidden from you. and I'll even share this time." She broke the bar neatly in two.

"Here's to that," he said and tapped his half to hers.

The chocolate gave her a boost—especially with the coffee she pumped in after it—so she worked until midnight.

Spinning wheels, mostly, she admitted. Covering and recovering the same ground. But sometimes you spotted something when you backtracked.

Someone they knew. And most if not all of them knew each other. Some lived together, or ran together. Same basic turf.

If Sebastian was to be believed, he hadn't forged Shelby's docs. Say he told that straight, Eve thought as she propped up her feet to study the board.

Could she have done them herself, catching on to how Sebastian did forgeries? Picking it up, as he'd said, because she knew how to pay attention?

Possible. Possible.

Eve brought Shelby's picture on screen, studied it.

Smart girl, tough girl, hard girl. But loyal. A born leader—and I bet you liked being in charge—who didn't like the rules. Not with the do-gooders, not with the grifters. Wanted your own.

"And didn't the place, the perfect place, drop into your lap when The Sanctuary pulled up stakes? That's what plays. It plays. It's familiar. It's empty. You know it top to bottom."

She rose, walked closer to the screen as Roarke stepped back in.

"I half expected to find you snoring at your desk."

"Caffeine works. I don't snore." Eve pointed at the screen. "She's the key."

He turned to study the screen with her. "Which is she?"

"Shelby."

"Ah, the leader, the one who walked out of the new facility with forged documents."

"Exactly. She knew the ropes, had an agenda. And she had a connection with somebody who knew how to forge."

"I don't see why Sebastian would deny doing so, at this stage."

"She could've done them herself, picked up the basics from him, just like he said. That would explain the misspellings, and the really bad attempt at forging Jones's signature. That data came through from the analysis," she added. "It's way off from Nashville Jones's signature.

"So . . ." Turning from the screen, she circled the board. "She's learning, planning, and Bittmore drops the bountiful in The Sanctuary's lap. Hey, kids, we're moving to big, pretty new digs! Pack it up."

"And she realized it's just the right time."

"Perfect time. Everybody's going to be busy, running around, distracted. More, she's smart enough to know what goes on, and what goes on is the old building's going to be empty. At least for a bit while the bank gets its act together, and that's already been hanging for months."

"A lifetime at thirteen. Would she even think about that really?" Roarke wondered. "Opportunity's there, grab it?"

"Yeah. Foreclosures, mortgages. Adult stuff. For her, it's just perfect time, perfect place. She'll get out, get in, set things up for her friends until she can get them out. Nice and tidy, with documentation so nobody comes hunting for them."

"It worked for her—the getting out."

"Yeah, it did. Did she have somebody inside, or outside? Did she use somebody? She'd have seen it that way, just another mark. And the mark turns. Maybe she lured him in, trading sex for whatever she needed or wanted. But that didn't work out for her, because she was the mark all along."

"Why kill her?"

"Need, desire, or a dozen more reasons. Iris had a secret, but I don't see somebody like Shelby taking somebody like Iris into her confidence."

"The killer?"

"Maybe, just maybe. She's no leader, but can be led. Iris went to church, like Lupa, like Carlie. Lots of churchy talk with Jones and Jones. Where does that fit in? Does it?"

When she rubbed her eyes with the heels of her hands, Roarke took her arm. "Let it sit for now. Get some sleep."

"I feel like I'm circling it, like I'm close, but not close enough to see it clearly."

"In the morning you might."

She shot him a look when he led her out. "You could find Sebastian's flops. You could," she pressed when he said nothing.

"I imagine I could."

"Just keep that on tap, okay? I won't ask unless I have to ask."

"Agreed, *if* I agree with the 'have to ask.'"

That had to be swallowed, though it was hard going down. "Good enough."

AGAIN, ALL THE PRETTY GIRLS SAT IN A CIR-
cle. More had faces of their own now, young and sad
in contrast with their bright clothes, bright hair.

They didn't chatter like the girls in Times Square, or giggle at
jokes only they could understand. They sat, they watched.

Eve thought they waited.

"I'm getting close," she insisted. "It takes time, and work—
and maybe some luck. There are so many of you. I only need two
more IDs."

And the two wearing her face turned and looked away.

"There's no point in being pissy about it."

"They don't like being dead," Linh told her. "None of us do. It's
not fair."

"Life's not fair. Neither's death."

"Easy for you to say." The girl named Merry sneered at her. "Your life's totally mag. You're sleeping in a big warm bed with the frostiest guy on or off planet."

"Her father beat and raped her when she was just a little girl," Lupa told Merry. "Younger than us."

"She lived through it, didn't she?" Shelby stood up, crossed her arms over her chest. "And landed in the prime. Now she's blaming *me* for everything."

"I'm not blaming you, for anything."

"Are too. You're saying it's *my* fault we're dead. That just because I wanted my *own* place with my *own* friends, everybody got killed. Like, what, I knew it was going to happen or something?"

"Listen—"

"So what if I sucked off a few fuckheads?" She threw her arms out now. "So the fuck what! I got what I wanted, didn't I? And shit for my buds, too. If you don't take what you want, somebody takes it first. No way I was going to be stuck in that 'holy higher power meditate your brains out' shit until some jerkwad who didn't know jack about me decided I could get the hell out. I decide for myself. Nobody was going to push me around again, ever, ever, ever!"

"Wow." Eve gave her a considering nod. "You really were a bitchy little whiner. Not that you deserved to die for it. Maybe you'd have grown out of it, or maybe you'd have been a bitchy grown-up whiner given the chance. But you didn't get the chance. And that's where I come in."

"You're no different than the rest of them. No better than the rest of them."

"I'm what you've got."

"Fuck you!"

"Sit down. Shut up."

Mikki hauled herself to her feet, hands bunched to fists at her sides. "You can't talk to Shelby like that."

"Sure I can. It's my dream, and I'm in charge here."

"I don't like when people fight." Iris put her hands over her ears, began to rock. "People shouldn't fight."

"Where's your dog?" Eve wondered. "Didn't you have a dog?"

"We don't have to listen to you!" Shelby shouted, running to each girl, hauling her up to stand. "We don't have to talk to you. We don't have to do anything you say. Because we're dead! And it's not my fault."

"Jesus. Shut up. Shut up so I can think."

"You're the one doing all the talking."

Eve blinked her eyes open, looked blurrily around the dimly lit room. "What?"

"That should be my question." Roarke stroked a hand over her hair. "Who needs to shut up?"

"Shelby. The girls came back. That Shelby. Bitching, whining, bitching. I probably would, too, if somebody drowned me in the tub. What time is it?"

"Early." He leaned over to touch his lips to hers. "Go back to sleep."

She sniffed him. "You're up, just out of the shower."

"Can't fool an ace detective."

"Your hair's still damp." She walked her fingers through it. "And you smell really good." And her detective skills told her he wore nothing but a towel. "I bet you have a 'link conference with Pluto and a holo-meeting with Istanbul or somewhere scheduled."

"And a mind reader as well. What a lucky man I am."

"You could get luckier." She skimmed a hand down his chest, down his belly, down. And grinned. "But I see you knew that."

"I've deductive powers of my own."

She used her other hand, tugged him down by his hair. "What else you got?"

"Apparently a randy wife." His hands got busy as well, skimming up and under the thin nightshirt she wore. "Pluto can wait."

"Now, how many people can say that?" She tugged again so his lips came to hers.

And in the thrill of the long, lazy kiss, wrapped her arms, her legs around him, holding him tight and close.

Because she was lucky, and wouldn't forget it. She had lived through it, all that had come before. And she was in the big warm bed with the frostiest guy on or off planet. The man who loved her, wanted her, tolerated her, and understood her.

Whatever the day brought when it dawned, she had this, she had him, to begin it.

"I love you." She tightened around him. "I really mean it."

"I love you." She felt his lips curve against her throat. "I really mean it."

"Show me."

She arched toward him. He slid into her.

On the slow rise, the slow fall, he watched her face in the quiet light. Happy, he thought, there in her eyes, in the easy, fluid move of her body, in the quickening beat of her heart.

Whatever had troubled her in dreams she'd set aside, for this, for him. For them.

He touched his lips to her cheek, then the other, her brow, then her lips. To show her.

Dawn crept closer as they gave pleasure and took it. She sighed, a simple sound of bliss, stroked her hands down his back, up again until her fingers tangled in his hair.

All as sweet and lovely as a walk in a summer garden.

As the heat built, as the need sharpened, he watched her still, saw that pleasure peak in the deepening of her eyes even as he felt her body arch up to reach it, to take it.

Her heart drumming now against the thud of his own, her sigh sliding into a long, throaty moan. And her eyes, her eyes going dark and blind for that moment, that sumptuous moment when she lost herself, surrendered herself to what they made.

Reaching, taking, he fell into her eyes, fell into her.

She lay under him, limp, dazzled. If she could wish a single thing for a single day, it would be to stay just as they were, all warm, all tangled, all content. She turned her face, nuzzled it against his hair to cover herself with the scent.

She could take that with her, whatever else the day handed her.

When she stirred, he pressed his lips to the side of her throat, then levered up to look down at her again. "Can you sleep now?"

"I think I'm awake. Just as well."

Rolling over, he drew her to his side.

"Don't you have Pluto on tap?"

"In a bit."

He thought he could lull her back to sleep, she realized, but her mind was already starting to churn.

"I don't blame the kid for it."

"Of course not."

"Figuring she might be the key isn't the same as thinking it's her fault."

"Got under your skin, did she?"

"I think I'm looking at her as a part of me I was still testing out at that age. Not the bjs and booze."

"Happy to hear that."

"It's the pushy little bitch part, the 'I want my own place, my own purpose' part. She, from what I know and the dots I connect from that, let all that right out. I mostly kept it under wraps."

"She was in a safe place, Eve, or what should have been. You rarely were."

"But I hated it, safe or otherwise. Hated all of it. I think she did, too—or am I projecting? I think she hated it, resented it, thought it was all bullshit. Even Sebastian's club. None of it was hers, and that's how it was going to be. Someone she knew used that. She thought— I'm probably projecting—she thought she was using him, but she was a child, and easily strung along. Figured she knew the score, but she was still just a kid."

"How does that help you?"

"I'm not sure yet. I'm trying to get a clear picture of all of them, and she's pretty clear at this point. Anyway, you should do your Emperor of the Known Universe thing. I think I'll get in a workout before I start all this."

"I'll be about an hour. I'll meet you back here for breakfast."

"That'll work."

They rolled out of bed, he to go to his closet for a suit, she to grab some sweats.

As she pulled on a tank, she frowned over at him. "It's not really Pluto, right?"

"Not yet." He smiled at her. "The day may come."

She let her mind roll around possibilities, speculations, avenues while she pushed her body into a good, muscling-pinging sweat. Satisfied, she took the elevator from the gym back to the bedroom, and straight into the shower.

Roarke hadn't come back by the time she got out, so she amused herself by hunting up the financial reports he habitually scanned in the mornings before she even opened her eyes.

She glanced down at the cat bumping his head against her leg. Suspicious, she hunkered down, sniffed.

"I know Summerset fed you. I can smell your kibble breath."

He merely stared at her with his bicolored eyes, then butted his head lightly to hers.

Okay, so she was a sucker. Rising, she ordered up a saucer of milk—a small one—and set it out for him. While the cat happily lapped, she grabbed pants, a sweater, a jacket she was reasonably sure she'd never seen before. But she liked the dark chocolate leather trim at the pockets, and the cloud-soft rest of it.

She started to swing it on over her sweater and weapon harness, caught the label.

"Cashmere. Jesus, Jesus, why does he do that?" she demanded of the cat, who merely continued fastidiously washing himself. "Watch, just watch. I'll get in a fight with some psycho and ruin in. Just watch."

With those dark thoughts she put it on because, damn it, she liked it—and it was his own fault if she destroyed it on the job.

As he was still with Pluto or whoever, she considered the Auto-Chef, then made her choices for breakfast for two.

She was sitting, as he usually was, the financials on mute, as she went over her notes and drank coffee when he came in.

"It took longer than I thought it would," he began, then stopped to smile at her, and the two plates, covered with warming domes, on the table in the sitting area. "You've done breakfast for me. What do we have?"

He lifted the dome. "Omelets, berries, toast, and jam. Nicely done."

"I figured you'd stick me with oatmeal. Beat you to it."

"An omelet does very well." He sat beside her.

"How are things in Roarke World?"

"Satisfying at the moment. I've some meetings later—"

"My shocked face." She opened her mouth and eyes wide.

Amused, he popped a berry in her mouth. "I can and will make time if you can use me for anything."

"I thought I already used you this morning."

"Aren't you the clever one today."

"Every day. I'll let you know. If Sebastian doesn't come through on DeLonna this morning, I may ask you to dig out his flops."

"I like to think he'll come through."

"We'll see."

He gestured toward her PPC. "How are things in Eve World?"

"I shot off some more notes to Peabody, to Mira. Figured I'd work here for an hour or so as I'm getting going so early."

She forked up some omelet—not bad at all.

"This will happen when you're waked by a group of unhappy girls, then want sex."

"I guess. It'll give me a jump anyway. She was unhappy," Eve said after a moment. "Not just pissed off and defensive. She picked up Linh somewhere along the line, but never took her to Sebastian's. Going to take her to *her* place. Get a few supplies first, take her newest bud to the place she was making for herself. And he kills them both. Did she know? Was she aware enough to know? Now I'm going to be dead, and so's Linh. I'm never going to have what I want. It's not fair."

She could picture that—the despair, the frustration, the guilt, the anger.

"It worked so well for him, he could do it again. Some, like Mikki, just walked right in, probably looking for Shelby. Others, he lured. Lupa and this Iris kid. A church-type thing for them, at least for them if not some of the others. Use what works? Vary it to suit. Or did he use the same basic ploy?"

It nagged at her, the not knowing. Shaking her head, she tried to focus on the food, but her thoughts kept circling.

She sat up. "The dog. Where's the dog?"

"I don't believe we have one. We have a cat."

"No, the toy dog. The kid's stuffed dog. She took it with her when she left The Club. It wasn't with any of the remains. He had to take it, like their clothes, out of the building. Did he toss it?"

"I would think."

"Maybe he kept it. A little souvenir. He might have other things. The jewelry we didn't find, e-stuff, backpacks. Yeah, he might have kept some of it, to remind him."

She shoveled in more omelet. "Something else to think about."

When she walked into her home office, she frowned at the board, studied it, then muttering to herself changed the arrangement again.

She pinned Nash, Philadelphia, Shivitz on one side, with the victims in residence at The Sanctuary below—connecting them in turn to Fine, Clipperton, Bittmore, Seraphim Brigham in one group, Linh Penbroke offshooting from Shelby.

Sebastian headed the other section, the victims from his club ranged under him.

Cross-matched were victims connected to both groupings.

Too many, she thought, too many crossed, and that meant the killer had knowledge of both pools to fish in both pools.

And however she arranged it, she still came back to Shelby as a key.

Considering, she moved Montclair Jones from ancillary to the head group with his siblings.

It had to flow from there, she decided. So turn it all over, start again at the top.

She went to her desk to review the runs on all three. She picked apart little details, poked through on education, activities, relationships, medicals, and financials.

Then got more coffee, and did it all again from another angle.

Despite the early start, the extra work had eaten up the time. Rising, she went to the doorway of Roarke's adjoining office.

"I've got to go in."

He paused at his work on screen. "I'll be leaving shortly myself."

"This new place you're starting when the building's cleared. What's the name again?"

"You inspired it. An Didean."

"Yeah, that. It'll be good works, socially conscious, blah, blah, but to some extent it has to be run as a business, right? Payrolls, overhead, job descriptions, supervisors, pecking orders."

"It would."

"Organized so people have schedules, duties, so bills get paid, supplies get bought and distributed. And like a home, too, with that kind of dynamic—chores, say. Somebody's got to take care of laundry, cleaning, food."

Interested, he sat back. "The concept is to have the residents take part in that. Assignments to cook and clean—to establish routine, discipline, and a sense of ownership."

"And when you don't have unlimited resources, you have to keep things pretty tight. You'd have a budget, and somebody has to keep a handle on that. And to keep within that budget, everybody has to pull weight, pull some extra when it comes down to it, and it's going to come down to it pretty regularly without solid outside funding."

"You run a department," he pointed out. "And have a budget to work within."

"Yeah, which got me thinking. I'm juggling all the time, or trying to mine what I have for a little extra. Shift this to open that, then you have to figure out how the hell to fill the hole you opened when you shifted. It's a pain in the ass, but it has to be done. The Joneses had the same deal. This is what we've got, and we have to figure out how to make it work."

Those wild blue eyes lit with interest. "Now you're following the money?"

"Kind of. Both Nashville and Philadelphia Jones got the training and degrees for the social work and counseling aspects. The older sister—the Aussie now—she got some of it, too. Philadelphia some business management, so you have to figure she was the one with the budget headaches."

"I wouldn't say she did a stellar job of it."

Eve pointed her finger at him. "That's exactly right. They pretty consistently swam in the red, right up until they were swamped by it before Bittmore built them a big, shiny boat. Now, many people like that run on good intentions and the hope that a higher power—one with deep pockets—is going to come to the rescue. But Philadelphia strikes me as more realistic than that. When you're the one trying to add up the columns and stretch the numbers, you have to be."

"All right. What does that tell you?"

"You sound like Mira," she commented. "Anyway, it makes me

look at the whole production, and the parts of it. Philadelphia's pulling a lot of weight; the older brother, he looks to be pulling pretty hefty, too—even did some outside work, part-time teaching, part-time preaching—to bring in a little more here and there."

"And the younger? Not pulling weight."

"It looks like he *was* weight. Didn't get the certifications, so he can't officially run any of the sessions or counsel or teach. Treatment for depression, and meds to deal with it. No specific training I can find. From my shuffling around in the financials, it looks like he had a little stipend from the mother at her death—just him, not the others—a portion of insurance there, but no stipend—which is also telling."

"She left what she could to the one she felt needed it most."

"Yeah. And for the rest, his siblings covered him. Even the Aussie sister sent them some money now and then," Eve added. "They paid baby brother out of the budget for general labor, and that's mostly a bullshit term to get around specifics when there just aren't any.

"That goes on for years. Then boom, they get that big, shiny boat. They're barely on board when they send him to Africa—and it wasn't first-class travel, but it cost them. They finally have a little breathing room in the budget, and instead of absorbing him into the new place, they ship him off."

"And you wonder, was it to just divest themselves of the weight, was it a sudden opportunity they believed would serve him, or did they get him as far away as they could because his mission wasn't to help young girls, but to kill them."

"That's just what I'm wondering. He's the one with all the loose time."

"And it would take time to lure, to kill, to construct the walls."

"Yeah, and where does somebody with a full schedule, with an armload of stuff to do, get that time? But he's got plenty on his hands. What do you do with that? Maybe you hang around the neighborhood, and you see where some of the kids—like Shelby—go when they get out and around."

"A kind of stalking," Roarke suggested.

"Maybe. Or maybe envying. Some people kill what they envy. If you're Montclair Jones, you know what they're doing, the girls, and maybe you let them know you know and you're okay with it. You build up that trust—we're all pulling something over on the do-gooders."

"Why kill them?"

"Don't know. Maybe you've got a stresser that breaks in. Moving to a new place, have this huge opportunity to do more good, and do it right. But the sibs lay it on the line for him. You have to straighten up, bro. We can't keep floating you the way we have. We can't squander this gift from the old higher power. So that's a pisser. Now he has to actually work? Have real responsibilities, and they're going to be on his ass. And who's fault is that?"

"The children."

"He could think so. And those girls—they sneak around doing what they want, but he's going to have to toe the line."

"And back to envy."

"Yeah, so screw that, screw them. Something like that," she said, not quite satisfied. "Because I'm not buying all the coincidence in timing, in cross-relationships. It all has a center. If Shelby's a key, maybe he's a lock. Put them together and it could open the center."

"You're going to have a busy day."

She cocked her head. "Am I?"

"You'll want to consult with Mira because talking it out with her will help you refine the theory. You'll want to talk to both Joneses—separately. You'll hope to get this DeLonna's contact information from Sebastian, otherwise you're going to squeeze me to find his HQ so you can put your boot on his neck until he does. And I imagine you'll be talking to someone in Africa."

He rose as he spoke, came to her, laid his hands on her shoulders. "My meetings pale beside your meetings."

"I don't have meetings," she insisted. "They're interviews, interrogations, consults. Meetings are for suits." She gave his tie a tug.

"You may not wear one, Lieutenant, but you're a suit with a badge."

"Insulting me so soon after we've had sex could mean it's the last sex you have for the foreseeable future."

He pulled her in, caught her mouth with his. "I like my odds," he told her, taking another quick nip before he let her go.

They were probably pretty good, she admitted as she headed down. She flipped her coat off the newel post, shrugged into it as she headed out into the frosty, ear-numbing morning. And as she engaged her in-dash 'link to contact Mira, she thought as she often did, if Roarke had turned right instead of left, he'd have made a damn good cop.

"Eve. You're moving early today."

"Yeah, I've got a full plate. I'm hoping you can make room for me on yours. I've got some thoughts on the Jones siblings I want to run by you. Get your sense."

"I have an hour now if you can come to my home."

"Oh. I don't want to push into your off time."

"It's not a problem. I was about to review the notes you sent me in any case."

"I'm on my way then. Thanks." She switched off, contacted Peabody as she made the first turn out of the gates. "I'm swinging by Mira's for a quick consult, then I want to hit Jones and Jones again. I want to talk to them separately."

"You want me to meet you there?"

"No. Arrange for the sister to come in. Play it nice, but firm. I want her in my space. Then we'll take her brother. While I'm with Mira, contact Owusu in Zimbabwe. I want—"

"I get to talk to Africa? Major score!"

"Glad I could start your day off with a bang. See if she's talked to her people yet about the younger Jones. And ask if she can—if she hasn't—get a sense of him. Did he put in the work? Was he good at the work? And get those details of the lion mauling. And if she can find anyone who has a picture of him from back then."

"I'm all over it, like a hyena. No crazy and mean. Like a howler monkey."

"Hold the howling and get a clear picture of him over there. I want specific details I can use in the interviews with the siblings."

"I'll get what's to get. Then you've got to give me the deep deets on this Sebastian. I can't believe Mavis knew—"

"Basics are in the notes. We'll get deeper later. Get me something from Africa."

Eve shut off, and began to hunt for parking.

She took the block-and-a-half walk in stride. Fast strides as the air froze her fingers and cheeks. Too early for the off-to-school brigade, she noted, but not for the domestics. Nannies, maids, cooks poured off maxibuses, streamed up from the subway, hoofed it over the sidewalk toward the day's work.

Owners, or those owners paid, walked a variety of dogs. She smelled fresh bread, chestnuts roasting, coffee, sugar-dusted pastries.

Not a bad place to call home, she thought as she walked up to the Miras' front door. Even before she rang the bell, the door opened.

As always when she saw the kind and dreamy eyes of Dennis Mira, her heart gave a little tug. Just something about him, she thought, with his cardigans and mussed hair, bemused smile.

"Eve. Come in out of the cold." He took her hand to draw her inside. "Where are your gloves? Your hands are freezing. Charlie! Find Eve some gloves."

"Oh, no, I have them. I just forget to—"

"And a hat! You should always wear a hat in the cold," he said to Eve. "It keeps the heat in." He winked at her. "Warms the brain. Who can think with a cold brain?"

In her life he was the only person she actively wanted to hug the minute she saw him. Just press up against him, rest her head on his sloping shoulder and just . . . be there.

"You can sit by the fire," he said, nudging her into the living area with its sparkling Christmas tree, its family photos, and lovely, lovely sense of home. "I'll make you hot chocolate. It'll do the trick."

"You don't—" Hot chocolate? "Really?"

"It's my secret recipe, and the best. Charlie will tell you."

"It's incredible," Mira confirmed as she came in—looking nothing like a Charlie in an icy blue suit and heeled boots in metallic sapphire. "We'd love some, Dennis." Then she tugged on the frayed sleeve of his cardigan. "Didn't I put this sweater in the donation box?"

"Did you?" He smiled in that absent way he had. "Isn't that strange? I'll make the chocolate. Where did I put the . . ."

"First cupboard, left of the stove, second shelf."

"Of course."

He walked off, little shuffling sounds in his house scuffs.

"I can't get him to let go of that sweater. It'll probably unravel on him one day."

"It looks good on him."

Mira smiled. "It does, doesn't it? Have a seat, and tell me what you're thinking."

Eve sat near the simmering fire to talk of the business of murder.

16

MIRA LISTENED IN THAT QUIETLY ABSORBED way she had even when Eve felt the need to get up and pace out the theory.

"There's no way it all slides in that neat," Eve concluded. "'Hey, we're moving. Listen, brother, you're going to Africa to spread the word.' And between those two events, twelve girls are drowned in the bathtub of the former digs, rolled up and walled up. It has to tie."

"The mother's history of mental illness, and her eventual suicide when the youngest child was still living at home."

"He never lived on his own."

"Yes, a dependency either innate or fostered. You're looking at the tub—the mother died in one, now the girls are killed in one."

"It's tidy."

"It's the wrong symbolism. The mother took her life, and it's a violent act. A blade through flesh, blood in the water. The girls were drowned, not—according to the forensics—bled out."

"The killer could have cut their wrists. It wouldn't show on the bones. And it's pretty damn annoying not to be able to just look at a body and *see*."

"I'm sure it is. Let's take the other route. This Sebastian—a fascinating character from your notes—do you tie him in?"

"I'm not sure where or how, just yet. My first instinct was he'd be top of the list, no matter how Mavis feels about him, because those feelings go back to when she was a kid and he played the center role in keeping her from going hungry and being alone."

She shoved her hands in her pockets. "But then you talk to him awhile, and the sense is he's sincere—in his warped way. That he has a code—it's screwed up, but it's a code—and he isn't capable of doing what was done to those girls. Then, with a little distance, you have to remember he lives and makes his living off the grift. He's not just a liar, he's a damn good actor with it. So, he's a possible, even if just a possible accomplice."

"Is that because you sense he is capable after all, or because you instinctively hate the idea whoever killed those girls may already be dead and beyond the reach of justice?"

"Probably more of the second." She dropped down again. "But—" Then stopped when Dennis shuffled in again with a tray loaded with cups, what looked like a bowl mounded with whipped cream, and a fat white pitcher.

"Here we are. Don't let me interrupt. I'll fix you up and be right out of the way."

"Sit down and have some with us," his wife instructed. "It's very possible for older siblings to feel a sense of duty and responsibility for a younger, especially a younger who falls short. They come from a family who based their lives, their work on faith, good work, and the mission to use that work to draw more into the faith. They could hardly exclude their own brother from that mission."

She shifted, crossed her legs. "Particularly after the mother's death, the suicide which would go against their tenets—suicide affects those left behind, and the younger brother was still a teenager when she died."

"It messes you up."

"Family and loved ones often feel anger and guilt after a suicide. And there's often a sense of abandonment."

"The father went off on a mission within the year, dumped the younger on his older brother and the sister. So they're responsible, right? That's the way it would work. They're responsible for him now. It's their job to take care of him."

"Yes, they would in a very real way have substituted for the parents. At the same time, repeated failures by a sibling or a refusal or disinterest by that sibling in sharing the load, doing the work, would begin to wear. No one rubs you quite as hard the wrong way as a sibling. And while you may criticize, protecting and defending from the criticism of others is common."

"He was a drain on the work," Eve began, then goggled at the cup Dennis offered her—and the frothy hillock of whipped cream, sprinkled with shaved chocolate topping it. "Thanks. Wow."

"You'll want this," he said, handing her a spoon.

"From what you're telling me, yes," Mira agreed. "He put a strain on the mission they both forged their lives to fulfill. It may very well be they found this post in Africa as a way to push him to contribute, and remove him from the immediate area while they reorganized in the new location."

"Could he have snapped?" Eve demanded. "If they gave him an ultimatum. We're shipping you out if you don't start pulling your weight?"

"There's so little known about him. The medical records are very general, and there aren't many. The treatment for depression indicates he was troubled, certainly, that he had some difficulty not achieving what his siblings had, suffered from anxiety, and as I said, those abandonment issues. But the doctor who treated him is deceased, and the treatment ended fifteen years ago with the patient's death."

"He was more isolated than his brother and sister. And I have to ask, is this legal?" Eve dipped her spoon into the cool cream and warm, rich chocolate again.

Dennis beamed at her. "In this house it is."

"It's really amazing. Sorry," she said to Mira. "What I mean is, being more isolated, having less opportunities to socialize with peers, like the others who went on to study and work outside the homeschooling and missionary stuff, wouldn't he have a harder time adjusting to that life outside? His mother self-terminates, his father goes off on a missionary gig, leaves him in the care of the older two. They were given a small but decent financial share of the sale of the family home, a kind of before-I'm-dead inheritance. But the younger got an allowance, you can say, in the mother's will. So much per month he could draw from rather than a lump like his siblings."

"Which indicates the parents, either together or separately, had decided he couldn't or wouldn't handle a lump sum well, and needed more guidance. And yes, that could have caused some resentment on his part. Could have caused some anxiety and depression. So depressed, anxious, in treatment for both, still in a way under the thumb of his parents, who are now represented by his siblings, he's pulled into their work as he has nowhere else to go, no particular skills, and from what it seems, no burning ambition."

"Ends too loose tend to tangle," Dennis said as he sipped his chocolate, and Mira nodded.

"Exactly. You want to know if it's a viable theory. Could this at-too-loose-ends young man—with emotional challenges, challenges that may very well have been compounded by his separation from socializing with others his age in school, in play groups with other viewpoints and faiths . . . this young man who lacked his siblings' skills, their drive, and perhaps their vocation, have become so troubled, so tangled, that even the change from one location, which would have been his home now as his parental home had been taken away, to another—yet another, where he was not given a true choice—have caused a psychic break?"

"Yeah, I guess that's about it."

"It's certainly possible. And the method, the drowning, at the place that had become his home? Perhaps a rebellion against the tenets he'd been raised on, or a terrible attempt to embrace them."

"A ritual baptism deal—either to screw with the whole basis of his siblings' world, or to try to prove he could be a real part of it."

"Yes." Through the hillock of whipped cream, Mira sipped the chocolate. "You lean toward the first of those. You'd prefer it if he acted out of malice. But in this scenario, if it falls along these lines in the end, I'd lean toward the latter."

"Why?"

"He seems sad, your tragic and doomed suspect. His life so restricted—the youngest is often babied too long, held too tightly. If they were raised traditionally, as I suspect, rigid tradition, I mean, the mother—also challenged—would have had more of the day-to-day care and tending. She may have held too tight to him, and as he approached adulthood, despaired."

"You'd feel sorry for him, even if he killed those girls."

"I'd see someone who wasn't given what he needed . . . emotionally, physically." She sat back, as if considering. "The older siblings are grouped closely together in age. Then the long gap, the late baby. It's very possible the mother clung to this last child, discouraged him from spreading his wings."

"Stay with me? I need you to be with me?"

"Yes. Now he's a teenager," Mira continued. "The instinct is to rebel, to push away, to try new things. Even in a healthy family it can be a difficult time."

"And maybe he did a little of that pushing away," Eve speculated. "The mother, already on shaky ground, gives up, chooses to end it."

"Does he blame himself? If he'd been good, would she still be alive? Rigid tradition again," Mira emphasized. "She sinned, went off the path. Did he push her off the path? And I'd wonder if his treatment only added to the problem, the fact both he and the mother were under the same doctor's care."

"And it didn't help with the mother."

"Even an excellent therapist can miss signs of suicidal tendencies. But I think I'll do some research on his doctor, and I may understand more through that. Still, the short answer is yes, I believe he's viable as a suspect. I'll want to know more about Sebastian before I say the same about him."

"I'll get you what I can. If Montclair Jones killed those girls, his siblings had to know."

"Considering how tightly their lives intertwined? I'd rate the probability very high on that."

"Then I'll push on it. Thanks. I should get going."

"Finish your chocolate," Dennis told her. "I'll be back in a minute." He wandered out.

"It's so calm here," Eve commented.

"Oh, here has its moments."

"Yeah, I guess everywhere does. But it's got a calm center—I've been thinking about centers. And calm's different from regimented. It strikes me that's maybe how the Jones house was. Even with all those good intentions, and from my look at the parents they aren't fanatics or burn-in-hellfire types. But the center was their particular beliefs, the mother's problems, and their children were kept in that center without much chance to walk around outside it. Maybe you raise really caring, good, selfless people that way, or maybe you don't."

"Parenthood always has its individual structure. And it's a risky business. You do your best."

"I've seen the worst come out of the best, and know the best can come from the worst. It's a hell of a crapshoot. I really appreciate the time," she said as she rose. "And this really amazing magic in a cup. He could open a shop selling only this stuff, and make a fortune."

"He enjoys making it for family, and thank God not very often or I'd gain fifty pounds every winter."

"Tell him thanks again," Eve said as she put on her coat. "And I'll—"

She broke off as Dennis came back in, with a pair of wooly red gloves and a bright blue ski cap. "Here now," he said, "put these on."

"Oh, well. I really—"

"Can't go around with cold hands," he continued, tugging the gloves on her hands himself as he might with a child. "And you'll need to keep that brain warm to figure everything out, won't you?" He put the cap on her head, adjusted it. "There. That's better."

When she said nothing, genuinely could say nothing, he just smiled. "I'm always misplacing my gloves, too. They should have tracking built in."

"Thanks," she managed. "I'll get them back to you."

"No, no, don't worry about it. The kids are always leaving gloves and hats and scarves and socks and everything else around here. We have a box full of them, don't we, Charlie?"

"Yes, we do."

"You keep them," Dennis said as he walked her to the door. "And stay warm."

"Okay. Ah, in case I don't see you before, Merry Christmas."

"Christmas?" He looked momentarily blank, then grinned. "Of course, it's nearly Christmas, isn't it? I lose track."

"Me, too."

She walked down, then onto the sidewalk with emotion clogging her throat. And looked at the gloves as she walked. Roarke gave her countless gloves for the exact reason Dennis had put these on her. Gorgeous, sleek, warm leather, which she promptly ruined or lost.

But she swore she'd make damn sure she didn't lose the silly red ones.

She made it to her car with warm hands—and maybe a warm brain.

When Eve walked into a buzzing bullpen she caught the scents of refined sugar, yeast, fat before she spotted Nadine Furst. Doughnuts, Eve thought, the cop's sweet spot. No one knew that better than the ace reporter and bestselling author.

Nadine, her excellent legs crossed, her well-toned butt perched on

Baxter's desk, chatted amiably with Trueheart, flicked a drop of jelly from the corner of his mouth. And made his young, handsome face flush when she licked it from her finger.

"Pitiful." Eve said it loud enough to penetrate the din. It quieted the voices, but didn't stop the scramble to stuff sugary fat in mouths. "Just pitiful. Every one of you."

Jenkinson swallowed a last bite of cruller. "They're still warm."

Okay, warm doughnuts was playing dirty, but still.

"Sanchez, you've got crumbs on your shirt. Reineke, for God's sake, wipe that doughnut cream off your face."

"It's Bavarian," he said with a satisfied smile.

"Peabody."

Since she'd just taken a big bite of glazed with sprinkles, Peabody shoved it into her cheek like a chipmunk, talked around it. "I, ah, contacted Philadelphia Jones, Lieutenant. She's coming in this morning. I was, um, about to book an Interview room."

"Chew that damn thing and swallow it before you do. Nadine, get your ass off Baxter's desk and into my office. Everybody else. Fight crime, for Christ's sake."

She strode off, relieved she'd thought to stuff the gloves in her pocket when she'd come into Central. The dressing-down would've been less effective while wearing red wooly gloves.

She considered tossing something over her board to conceal it, but knew very well—sneaky warm doughnuts aside—Nadine could be trusted.

"Saved you one at great personal risk." Nadine walked in with a little pink bakery box.

"Thanks." Eve considered trying to hide it, but the scent would guide a cop's nose straight to the concealment. And she didn't want to risk a hunt that might turn up her current candy hiding place.

"Those are the girls you've ID'd?" At home—and how did *that* happen?—Nadine tossed her fur-trimmed scarlet coat on Eve's visitor's chair, stepped to the board.

She studied it with her sharp green eyes. "All between twelve and fourteen?"

"So far."

With a sigh, Nadine studied the other faces and notes on the board. She might look glamorous with the streaky blond hair and angled face, both camera-ready, but under the sleek package lived a canny reporter who could dig up tiny pieces of a broken gem and fit them together to make a clean, shiny whole.

"You've been keeping a lid on the data pretty well, especially considering Roarke found the bodies."

"He broke through a wall—ceremoniously mostly—and discovered two of the twelve."

"I know the outline. The buzz is who are they, how did they get there—are there more—and the Roarke connection winds through it."

She'd basically ignored the media messages on her 'link, but there hadn't been all that many in the big scheme. But suddenly it occurred to her Roarke was probably dealing with more. A lot more.

"His connection's thin at best. The victims were killed about fifteen years ago, long before he bought the building."

"It's Roarke," Nadine said simply. "And it's you. I got word you're working with the fashionable and brilliant Dr. DeWinter."

"She's handling the remains."

With a little smile, Nadine sat on the corner of Eve's desk. "How's that working out for you?"

The question brought an annoying itch to the base of Eve's spine. "She's doing her job. I'm doing mine."

"When are you going to release the names?"

"When we have all twelve, and when any and all next of kin have been notified. I'm not dribbling them out, Nadine, to keep the media happy."

"It's a long time to grieve." Her gaze tracked to the board again. "I wonder, is it better to know, absolutely, there's no hope, or to cling to that thin, pale ray of it? You're looking at Jones, Nashville and Philadelphia? And weren't they lucky they weren't born in Helsinki or Toledo?"

"Consider Timbuktu, which I rarely do. I'm looking at everyone, Nadine. You know how it works."

"Siberia."

"What?"

Nadine grinned. "I thought we were playing. And yes, I do know how it works. And I know when you're not giving me anything, you don't think you can use me." In a careless move, Nadine shrugged. "Fair enough. My team's done some research on them, for the stories as they stand now, and to lay the foundation for later. Interesting about the mother's suicide."

"Interesting?"

"How the husband took the hard line. Suicide, ultimate sin, no consecrated ground for you. Her children had her cremated, scattered the ashes at sea."

That was interesting, Eve thought. And proved Nadine was useful even when Eve didn't have a particular use for her. But she said, "Sounds more fucked-up than interesting."

"Depends on your angle. And it's weird and wicked about the younger brother and the lion."

She nodded toward his photo. "But if I'm judging the time line, he was still alive, still in New York, when the twelve were killed."

No point in bullshitting, Eve decided. "Being dead doesn't mean he's not a suspect."

"With the king of beasts as executioner. Could be a nice twist. Anyway, we did our own due diligence on brother and sister. The sister in Australia, too. Even the New York sister's ex, though that was over before the murders, and didn't net anything interesting as he moved to New Mexico, remarried, and has a tidy little family. But you knew that."

"We call it doing the job."

"Me, too," Nadine said cheerfully. "Big brother's never hooked up legally, though he does date now and then. They were raised to save sex for marriage, which is why I figure the sister married young. But I have this nagging doubt they've stuck to that tenet." She smiled when she said it. "And one of the brother's former companions was willing to confirm that."

She hadn't bothered to go there, Eve thought, but had to admit it was good data to add to the mix.

"I don't much care about their sex lives, unless it pertains."

"Oh, I care about everyone's. And poking around in that area, I couldn't find anybody little brother dated."

Okay, that could be interesting, Eve thought. "He was only twenty-three when he died, and since you poked around, you know he led a sheltered life, had some emotional issues, add in my-mom-killed-herself issues. Could've been a late bloomer if he hadn't gotten snipped off the vine."

"You're looking at him."

"I'm looking at all of them."

"Dallas." All friendly amusement, Nadine pointed at her. "I know how it works, remember? And I know how you work. You're looking at the dead brother particularly."

The hell with it. "If he was alive, I'd have him in the box sweating him. And I don't want you running with that angle on-air, Nadine. I'm not ready."

"We're just chatting." She tapped the pink box with a pink-tipped nail. "Aren't you going to eat your doughnut?"

"I had breakfast, then I had the world's most amazing hot chocolate. Doughnuts pale." Which reminded her she still wore her coat.

Nadine nodded at the cap. "I like your hat," she said as Eve shrugged out of her coat. "The snowflake's adorable."

"The what?" Eve snatched the hat off, stared at the sparkling white snowflake on the front. "Shit. There's a snowflake on this thing. A glittery one."

"It's, as stated, adorable. But I digress. DeWinter's keeping a tight ship over in her world, but you should be aware she enjoys a good, frisky media conference. Once she gets to the point she's ready, she'll call one."

"She'll call one when I tell her to." But Eve made a note to make that crystal clear, and to use the commander if necessary.

"Just a heads-up, friend to friend."

"And you're being so damn friendly."

"I am. We are," Nadine added. "And before I move on to my not-so-secret agenda, I want to say I really, seriously, completely enjoyed Thanksgiving at your place, with the gang, with Roarke's family."

She angled to smile at the framed sketch on Eve's wall.

"That's great, you know. Not just that the kid thought of it, or what she wrote on the back, but that you'd hang it in here."

"I told her I would."

"And that mattered to her. You could see it on her face. Anyway, I know I was a little drunk—just a little—but what I said about being in love with Roarke's family remains true cold sober. If I wasn't a to-the-bone urbanite, didn't have to-the-marrow ambitions, a job I love, and so on, I'd move to Ireland, pick one out of the herd, and marry him. I may hold out for Sean," she said considering, speaking of Roarke's young cousin. "I might be ready to retire to Ireland by the time he's old enough."

"They have cows," Eve said darkly. "Practically in the backyard."

"I could live with that," Nadine decided. "In about twenty years. Until then, I'm writing my next book."

"Oh."

"Such enthusiasm!" Nadine laughed. "*The Icove Agenda* took everything up a level for me. I'm ready to dig into another. My working title is *Ride the Red Horse*."

"You're going to write about Callaway, about Menzini."

"It's a natural. A cult, a crazed leader harking back to the Urban Wars, a deadly weapon used to cause ordinary people to hallucinate and kill each other within minutes. The legacy passed on, the courageous cop who brought them down."

"Shit."

"Really, try to control your joy. I'll be tapping you, Roarke, the team from time to time while I'm drafting it out, and I'll be asking you to look over the finished manuscript, to make sure you're okay with it."

"They're going to make another vid, aren't they?"

"Bet your ass. While I'm working on that, I'd like to give the twelve girls some play—respect," she said before Eve could speak. "You'll do what you do to get them justice. I'll do what I do so people know they existed. To know their names, their faces, and that someone took their lives before they'd really begun. It matters, too."

It did, Eve knew. And no one did it better than Nadine because it mattered to her. "Get out your recorder."

Nadine fished into the suitcase she called a purse, pulled it out. "I can have a camera here in ten minutes."

"No camera, no interview. Just names." Eve listed them off. "You can't release them yet, but you can do some basic background—quietly—on them. I'll give you the others when we have them. I'll give you the green light when you can go with them. Until then, you're on red."

"Understood."

"Now go away. I've got work."

"So do I." Nadine scooped up her coat. "Looking forward to your holiday bash."

"My what?"

"I spoke with Roarke briefly. He said if I mentioned it to tell you to look at your calendar." Swinging on her coat, Nadine headed out.

She remembered now, with the mention of her calendar. But still. "Didn't we just have a bash? Isn't Thanksgiving a bash? Why is Christmas so close to Thanksgiving? Who plans this stuff?"

Since there was no one to answer, she got coffee.

Peabody barreled in. "I talked to Africa!"

"Kudos."

"Seriously, it was a big moment for me. Sergeant Owusu talked to her uncle, her grandfather, a few others. She was actually writing up a report on it, so you'd have it all laid out. She'll send it as soon as she's done, and digs up some pictures."

"Good."

"Meanwhile the gist she gave me is everyone agreed Preacher Jones—that's what they called him—was a lovely man of faith and goodwill. He spoke with respect, enjoyed trying their native dishes—even learned to prepare a couple. He also studied the language, and had humor when he made mistakes in speech. He was kind, and they believe his spirit has remained in Africa."

"So they liked him. How'd he get eaten?"

"He had a curiosity about everything. And liked to take photos, small recordings, for himself, talked of compiling them one day into some sort of book or documentary. He was out, wandering farther than was wise, to take photos of a watering hole at dawn. The lion came to feed, and he was the main entrée."

She'd read most of that in the incident report already. "Did they say if he habitually went on these photo shoots alone?"

"I didn't ask that specifically, but Owusu strikes me as thorough. If she got anything, it'll be in her report."

"I don't remember any interest in photography or animal life in Montclair Jones's background."

"Well, he'd never been to Africa before," Peabody pointed out. "If I went there I'd live with a camera. Basically, it sounded like he'd decided to make the best of it, was enjoying it. It makes sense—he was off the tether for the first time, and somewhere exotic and new."

Eve glanced at her computer when it signaled an incoming. "We have Iris Kirkwood confirmed as the tenth, and the ID on the reconstruct on the eleventh."

Eve studied the image—mixed race, she judged. Thin face, wide, wide eyes, sharp cheekbones.

"I recognize that face." Eve ordered the Missing Persons images, split screen. "There. There she is. Shashona Maddox, age fourteen. Went missing from the grandmother's residence. Grandmother custodial guardian. Mother took off when the kid was three, father unknown. Grandmother had custody of Shashona's half sister, same mother, father gave up parental rights, which wouldn't have been hard for him, most likely, as he was serving twenty to life for murder two at the time."

"We have another notification."

She did a quick search. "Yeah. Grandmother's still alive, still in New York. Half sister's a doctor, surgical resident at Mount Sinai. Grandmother, Teesha Maddox, lives and has lived for twenty-five years in an apartment on Eighth Avenue. A professional nanny, currently working Upper West Side. When's Philadelphia due in?"

Peabody glanced at her wrist unit. "We've got about an hour."

"Let's go see the grandmother. Tell the bullpen if we're not back, have her wait in the lounge."

As Peabody hurried out, Eve took the time to send a short, direct e-mail to DeWinter—copied to Whitney.

Appreciate the fast, efficient work. As per my reports, we're pursuing several investigative lines. Until we have all the victims identified, all the notifications done, and have interviewed all relevant parties, any media release or conference remains on hold. Dallas, Lieutenant Eve.

"Keep a lid on it," Eve muttered, then like Nadine, scooped up her coat, swinging it on as she walked out.

17

THEY FOUND TEESHA MADDOX WITH A BABY of indeterminate age and sex in a neat and attractive apartment. She took one look at Eve, at Peabody, nodded wordlessly. She pressed her lips to the baby's forehead, just held them there a moment, then stepped back.

"Please come in. You've come to tell me my Shashona's gone. One of those poor girls they talk about on screen."

"Yes, ma'am. I'm very sorry."

"I knew when I heard the report. I've known all along, but that's when I knew where she was. I was going to come in to the police station, but Miss Hilly—she's my lady. Hilly McDonald? She said, now, Teesha, don't put yourself through that. If they've found her, they'll come to tell you. And here you are.

"I'm going to put the baby down. She's all dry and fed and burped. I'm going to put her down in her crib awhile, with the monitor on in case she goes fussy. You have a seat here, and I'll be back in just a minute. I don't like to talk death with the baby. They take in more than some believe."

"Nice place," Peabody said quietly. "It has, I don't know, a nice, settled, comfortable feel to it. Totally stylish, but homey at the same time."

Decent view, Eve thought as she sat down, scanned the room.

A lot of photographs—baby, no, two babies, with one of them progressing to the small person a kid was. Maybe three, four? No way for her to know.

Pictures of a woman—Hilly, she supposed—and a guy who was likely the father. Together, with baby, baby, kid. And a shot of Hilly—a white-skinned redhead with Teesha, whose coloring made Eve think of Dennis Mira's amazing hot chocolate.

"She doesn't look old enough to be the grandmother of grown women," Peabody commented.

"She's sixty-four."

"Doesn't look it. And still really young to have grown grandchildren."

"I was seventeen when I had my girl. Didn't mean to eavesdrop," Teesha said as she came back. "I've rocked a lot of babies in my time. Rocking babies soothes the soul, and keeps the wrinkles away. I can fix something for you to drink," she offered. "Cold day like this, maybe you'd like some tea, or coffee. On the police shows they sure drink a lot of coffee."

"Don't trouble yourself," Peabody told her. "We're fine."

"Miss Hilly won't mind, so if you decide you want something, just say. I was seventeen," she repeated as she sat, neat and tidy as the room. "I was just stupid in love, the kind of stupid you can be at that age when it isn't love at all. But when you think you are—why, a boy can talk you into most anything. Sixteen years old when I got pregnant, and scared to death. I didn't even tell my mama until I couldn't hide it anymore. I told the boy, and he was gone like the wind. My mama stood by me, even when my daddy went a little crazy. But he came around. I learned when you do something foolish sometimes you spend your life dealing with it."

She sighed, looked toward the window. "I loved my girl. Love my girl still. I'm good with babies, with children. It's my gift. I did my best for my baby, and my mama helped. I worked, earned money, finished school at home, tended my baby. I raised her to know right from wrong, to be responsible and kind and happy inside her skin."

She sighed again. "It just didn't take with Mylia. She seemed to run wild no matter what I did, and she hated that I worked with other children to put a roof over her head, food in her mouth, to give her some fun or something pretty to wear. Anyway, she was barely older than I'd been when she started Shashona. I stood by her. I helped every way I knew. She took off awhile with the boy, but he left her, and she came home to me, had the baby a month later. That didn't take either. She just didn't have the gift."

"So you raised Shashona," Eve said.

"I did. Mylia, she'd come and go, leave for weeks, then come back. We had some fights over that, I'll tell the truth. Then another man, another baby. And she's off and gone again as soon as she could get out. Beautiful babies, Shashona and Leila. I did my best by them, too. I had to go to court after a while, and they made me legal guardian. The people I worked for then, nice people, sweet children, they were both lawyers, and they helped me."

At the slightest mew, Teesha's gaze shifted to a little screen on the table where Eve saw the baby sleeping on pink sheets in a white crib.

"She's just dreaming," Teesha said with a smile. "The truth is Shashona took after her mama. Had a wild side nothing seemed to tame. Smart girl, clever girl. I prayed on it, prayed she'd grow out of the wild some, make something of herself."

She took a long breath. "She was smart, ma'am, like I said. I believe in my heart she'd've turned that wild into a passion for something, maybe she'd've done something important one day."

Teesha pressed a fist to her heart. "That passion, that important? It was just hidden inside her, waiting for her to grow up a little more."

In all the pretty young girls, Eve thought. The life yet to come had been hidden inside them.

"What happened the day she went missing?"

"She went off to school just like usual, but she didn't come home that day, not after school, not after dark."

"Was that usual?"

"No, ma'am." Teesha shook her head slowly from side to side while her eyes trained on Eve. "She loved me, even with the wild, she loved me. I know that in my heart, too. She always let me know she wouldn't be home awhile, whether I said okay to that or not, she'd tell me. Not that day. I couldn't find her. She had a 'link, but she didn't answer. The crowd she ran with didn't know, said they didn't, even after the police came into it. She was seeing a boy. Thought I didn't know about him, but I did.

"Pretty girl like Shashona," Teesha said with a sad little smile. "Well, there's going to be a boy. He wasn't a bad boy either. Smart like her. I talked to him myself, and he said how they were going to the vids that weekend, on a date. How they'd gone and had some pizza after school the day she didn't come home, even though I'd asked her to come straight on home that day. And he'd walked her to the corner, gone his way. And hadn't seen her again."

"I have his name from the Missing Persons report," Eve said.

"He's a loan officer now, works in a bank. He's engaged to be married next spring to a fine, well-mannered young lady. We keep in touch. I knew he never hurt her. Do you know who did?"

"We're investigating," Eve said.

"Did she know the other girls? Do you know?"

"You might be able to tell us. We're not releasing their names yet. I have to ask you not to mention them to anyone."

"I can promise that."

Eve handed her a list. Peabody offered her photos. Teesha studied them, shaking her head.

"I don't know these names, or these sweet young faces. There's only eleven names here."

"We haven't officially identified the twelfth."

"Poor thing. She had a lot of friends, my Shashona. I don't know if I knew them all, or if she brought them all around, but I don't know these girls."

"Do you know if she ever went around The Sanctuary? The building where she was found?"

"Seems she may have. She knew about it. Once when we were arguing about how she wasn't doing right, she said she could just go live there. She said it to hurt my feelings, or rile me up. I guess it did both. But she wouldn't have gone there asking to be taken in. If not for me, and under it she loved me, but she wouldn't have left Leila. Her baby sister. Leila, she worshipped Shashona. Every year, on the day she went missing, I say a prayer for Shashona, and I say one thanking God Leila hadn't gone with her. I kept her home from school that day, took a sick day off work."

"Was Leila sick?" Peabody asked.

"She started her cycle. The night before she had her first period. I always let my girls stay home that first day of the first cycle, pampered them a little, so Leila wasn't with her sister. Now she's a doctor. She's going to be a fine surgeon. She's a beautiful young woman. She's safe, and she's happy. And our Shashona, she's found now. I'll have to tell Leila."

For the first time, her eyes sheened with tears. "I'll have to tell her. I'll have to tell their mama when she gets in touch again. She does, every now and again."

"Ms. Maddox, did Shashona go to church?"

She smiled a little at Eve. "Every Sunday, whether she wanted to or not. As long as they lived under my roof, they'd respect the Sabbath. She didn't mind church too much. Lots of singing. She liked singing. Had a fine, clear voice, too. When can I have her?"

"It'll be a little while longer," Eve told her. "We'll notify you. Did you ever see any of these people around Shashona, around the neighborhood?" At Eve's signal, Peabody drew more photos out of the file bag.

Teesha studied them in turn. Nashville Jones, Montclair Jones, Philadelphia Jones, Sebastian, Clipperton.

"I'm sorry, but I don't recall these people. Are they suspects? I do like watching the police shows on the screen."

"We're looking into anyone with a possible connection."

"I don't know why people do the things they do to each other. We're all here to live our lives, to do our work, to raise our families, to love who we love. We're all here for the same things, but some, they can't let that be. They can't be happy or content with that. I don't know what that is."

She handed the photos back to Peabody. "Do you?"

At a loss, Eve shifted. "No."

"If you don't, I don't suppose anybody really does."

S he must be really good at her job," Peabody commented. "The way she has. It's soothing. She was brokenhearted, even though she'd resigned herself her granddaughter was gone a long time ago, it hurt her to hear it. But she still had that soothing way."

"The kid probably would've turned out all right. Like Linh. She just never got the chance to grow out of the snotty phase. Another church connection."

"Kind of loose, but yeah."

"And the singing. If Sebastian comes through with DeLonna, maybe we'll connect that."

"A lot of connection, but no strong links."

Eve glanced at her communicator when it signaled. "Philadelphia's in the house. Let's go see if we can make a link."

S he sent Peabody along to transfer Philadelphia to the Interview room. More official setting, Eve mused, a little more pressure. Later, they'd repeat the routine with Jones.

She took her time, gathered props and tools, then started over to where Peabody stood outside the door.

"I got her a lemon fizzy," Peabody began. "She's a little nervous, and a little unhappy with the wait, but wants to help however she can. And so on."

"Nervous and unhappy works just fine." Eve walked in. "Record on. We need to record the interview, Ms. Jones, for the record."

"Of course, but—"

"Just one minute. Dallas, Lieutenant Eve, and Peabody, Detective Delia, entering Interview with Philadelphia Jones, in the matter of case file H-5657823. We appreciate you coming in," Eve said as she sat. "We're just going to read you your rights, for the record."

"I don't understand. My rights?" Philadelphia wore her hair swept up today, and smoothed a hand over it in a nervous gesture. "Am I a suspect?"

"It's procedure," Eve said briskly, and rattled off the Revised Miranda. "You understand your rights and obligations?"

"Yes, of course. I'm here to help however I can."

"We appreciate that. We've identified all but one of the victims whose remains were found in the building you owned at the established time of their deaths."

Eve laid out eleven photos. "Do you recognize any of these girls?"

"Shelby, of course, as we discussed before. And Mikki. Lupa, who was only with us briefly. I . . . This girl looks familiar, but I'm not sure." Her finger hovered over Merry Wolcovich's photo. "If you gave me her name, we could check our records."

"I have. She wasn't in residence at either of your establishments, officially."

"If she'd been one of ours, she'd be in our records." Shoulders stiff, she sat back. "We don't take our responsibilities lightly."

"But she looks familiar?"

"I . . . I just have this little flash of seeing her with Shelby, Shelby and Mikki—maybe DeLonna."

She lifted the photo, frowning at it until a vertical line formed between her eyebrows. "She . . . I'm not sure. It was years ago, but something seems familiar."

"Only this one?" Eve said.

"Yes, and I'm not sure of that. I—in the market!" She sat up very straight. "I went into the market, and they were all in there—with this girl. Dae Pak's market—oh, he was *such* an impatient man. He complained to me, more than a few times about the children coming in, stealing or acting up. I remember because I happened to go in, and, frankly, they were being rude. I ordered the girls—our girls—to apologize and come straight back with me. I remember because I asked the other girl her name, where she lived. She told me to mind my own business, only not that politely, and ran out. I remember," she repeated, "because I kept an eye out for her after that for a couple weeks, in case she came back. I had the feeling she might be a runaway. You start to get a sense when you work with them routinely."

"Okay."

"Was she? A runaway?"

"Yeah."

"And one of the girls who died." Closing her eyes, Philadelphia laid her hand on the photo. "I should have gone after her, called CPS. I only thought of getting our girls back, and I didn't follow through."

"You couldn't know," Peabody began.

"It's my work. I'm supposed to know. Shelby and Mikki, both of them were out of my hands when this happened to them. But some of the responsibility's mine, isn't it? Shelby deceived us, and she shouldn't have been able to. We should have been more vigilant with her, but we were distracted, so excited by our good fortune we let her slip through. Now we have to live with that, with knowing that. Mikki, I don't know what we could have done, but it feels like we could and should have been able to do something. Now they're both gone. Both of them."

She looked back down at the pictures, then sharply up again. "But not DeLonna. She's not there. They were so close, the three of them. But she didn't go with them. She stayed with us, stayed until she was sixteen."

"But you don't know where she is now?"

"No, and I admit, I expected, hoped, she'd keep in touch. Some of the children do, some of them don't."

"Did she ever ask about them? Ask to go see them or contact them?"

Philadelphia rubbed at her forehead. "It's a lot to remember. I've been reviewing my notes from that time, trying to see how . . ."

She shook her head. "I noted that DeLonna withdrew for a while, claimed to be unwell. Natural enough, when two of her closest friends left."

"Was she sick?" Eve asked.

"Lethargic, according to my notes, and my memory. Weepy, though she tried to hide that. In session, when I was able to get her to open up a little, she talked about being one of the bad girls. Everyone left her because she was bad; she didn't have a real home, a real family because she was bad. We worked on her self-esteem. She had such a beautiful voice, I was able to use singing to bring her out a bit more. But she never bonded with any of the other girls in the same way. And, as I said, she withdrew, went into a kind of grieving, which was natural, expected. She spent her free time in her room, and was, well, too biddable if you understand me. She'd simply do whatever she was assigned, then go back into her shell. It took nearly a year before she seemed to resolve herself."

"Didn't you question the fact neither of her friends made an effort to see her, to hang with her?"

"Lieutenant, children can be self-absorbed and their world is often . . . immediate. It's the here and now, so the bonds formed in-side The Sanctuary, or now HPCCY, can be strong, lifelong, or they can be tenuous, situational bonds, that dissolve once the situation changes."

"And you don't follow up?"

She lifted her hands—short, neat, unpolished nails, no rings, no bracelets. "We're a transitional home, and most often for a relatively short time. Often the children and their guardians prefer to leave that behind, start new. We don't interfere."

"So when they walk out the door, that's it?"

By the way Philadelphia's shoulders stiffened, the little barb struck a nerve. "We give the children in our care everything we can, physi-cally, spiritually, emotionally. We do everything in our power to see that when they leave us, they leave in a better state, and go prepared to lead a productive, contented life. We feel deeply for them, Lieuten-ant, and on a professional level we understand they're only ours for a short time, so we have to let go. For their well-being, and for our own."

"But you interact with them every day, basically live with them."

"That's correct."

"Who's in charge?"

"I'm not sure what you mean. My brother and I share duties, responsibilities. We founded both The Sanctuary and HPCCY to-gether."

"So you're partners, in a sense."

"Yes, in every sense."

"But you're the one with a business degree, with business manage-ment training."

"Yes, that's right."

"So you deal with the finances."

"At HPCCY, yes, primarily."

"How did you let the other place tank so bad you literally walked away from it?"

The faintest color spread over her cheeks. "I'm not sure how this applies."

"Everything applies."

"We overextended," Philadelphia said shortly. "Emotionally and financially. We simply believed in what we were doing, and wanted to do so much we neglected the practicalities. Actually, I got the management training during the last year we had The Sanctuary as we realized we were in trouble in that area."

"So before that, you just fumbled along. What, hoping for a miracle?"

Both her eyes and her voice went very, very cool. "I understand not all believe in the power of prayer. We do, even when the answer to that prayer isn't clear or seems hard. In the end, our miracle came. We've been able to help many more children, give them much more care, simply because we initially failed in a practical, business sense."

"Who handled the finances at The Sanctuary—before you got the training?"

Philadelphia made a short, impatient sound. "Again, I don't understand these questions. Nash did, for the most part. We were raised in a very traditional home. Our father earned the living, handled the money, the bills. Our mother kept the house. So we initially approached The Sanctuary with that dynamic. It was what we knew. But it became apparent to both of us that Nash simply wasn't gifted with a real head for business. I was. We also believe in using our gifts, so I got further training. It was too late to save The Sanctuary, but we accept that was the plan."

"Whose plan?"

"The higher power. We learned, we lost, we were given another chance, and we've succeeded."

"Handy. So you handle the finances now."

"For HPCCY, yes, along with our accountant."

"You'd each handle your own personal finances?"

"Of course. Lieutenant—"

"Just getting a picture," Eve interrupted. "What about your other brother?"

"Monty? Monty died."

"In Africa. Fifteen years ago last month. I meant before he died. What was his function? What were his duties, responsibilities? His share?"

"He . . . assisted wherever he could. He enjoyed helping with meals, doing small repairs. He helped Brodie now and then."

"You're talking about scut work."

Philadelphia's eyebrows drew together to form that deep crease between them. "I don't know what that means."

"No real responsibilities, no real job. Just picking up lower-level chores."

"Monty wasn't trained to—"

"Why not? Why didn't he get the training to be a partner, like you and your older brother?"

"I don't understand why that matters? Our personal lives—"

"Are my business now." Eve snapped it out so Philadelphia jerked in her chair. "Twelve girls are dead. It doesn't matter if you understand the question. Answer it."

"Come on, Dallas." Playing her good cop role, Peabody soothed her way in. "We need to know," she said to Philadelphia, "whatever we can know, so we can try to piece everything together. For the girls," she added, nudging some of the pictures just a little closer to Philadelphia.

"I want to help, it's just that . . . it's painful to talk about Monty. He was the baby." She sighed out the stiffness. "The youngest of us, and I suppose we all indulged him a little. More when our mother died."

"Committed suicide."

"Yes. It's painful now, it was only more painful then for all of us. She simply wasn't well, in her mind, in her spirit. She lost her faith, and took her life."

"That's a terrible thing for a family to go through," Peabody said, gentle, gentle. "Even more, I think, for a family of faith. Your mother lost her faith."

"I feel she lost her will to hold to that faith. She was ill, in her mind, in her heart."

"Your father took a hard line on that," Eve put in.

The flush returned, more temper than embarrassment this time, Eve thought. "This was, and is, a very personal tragedy. If he took a hard line, as you say, it was his grief, his great disappointment. My father's faith is absolute."

"And your mother's wasn't."

"She was unwell."

"She became unwell, or began treatment, shortly after giving birth to your youngest brother."

"It was an unexpected and difficult pregnancy. And yes, it took a toll on her health."

"Difficult and unexpected," Eve repeated. "But she went through with it."

Hands folded tightly on the table, Philadelphia spoke coolly.

"While we respect the choices each individual makes, the termination of a pregnancy, except under the most extreme conditions, was not a choice for my mother, nor for those who share our beliefs."

"All right. So an unexpected and difficult pregnancy, followed by clinical depression, anxiety, and ultimately self-termination."

"Why do you make it sound so cold?"

"Those are the facts, Ms. Jones."

"We don't want to miss anything." Peabody added the lightest touch of her hand on the back of Philadelphia's. "He was still living at home at the time of your mother's death, your younger brother?"

"Yes, he was only sixteen. He came to us—to Nash and me—a few months later, when our father sold the house, went on a mission. It was shortly after that we were able to buy the building on Ninth with our share, and begin The Sanctuary."

"So young to lose his mom," Peabody said, all sympathy. "He'd have been old enough to think about college, or practical skills training when you started The Sanctuary. I didn't see anything in the file on that."

"No. Monty had no drive to try college, or practical training, and honestly, no real aptitude—not for counseling or organization. He was good with his hands—that was his gift."

"But no training there either."

"He wanted to stay close to us, and we indulged that."

"He'd had treatment for depression," Eve added.

"Yes, he had." Resentment shimmered again as she looked back at Eve. "What of it? It's not a crime. Monty was an internal sort, more introverted than either Nash or I. When we were old enough to go on missions, or to seek more education, and our mother died, he became lonely and depressed. And help was sought and provided."

"Introverted. So not much for interaction with the residents and staff, when he joined you at The Sanctuary."

"As I said, when our father was called to mission, we took Monty with us, helped give him a purpose. He was somewhat shy, but enjoyed the children. In some ways, he was one of them. The Sanctuary was his home, too."

"How did he feel about losing it?"

"It was difficult for him, frankly. It was his first place outside the parental home, one he considered his own—as we all did. He was, we all were, understandably upset. Failure is never easy to accept. But that failure opened a new door."

"And right after you walked through the new door, you sent him to Africa. This shy, introverted younger brother."

"The opportunity came. We felt Monty needed to expand his world. To, well, leave the nest. It was hard for me, to be honest, but it was a chance for him. A door for him."

"Who arranged it?"

"I'm not sure what you mean, 'arranged.' The missionary in Zimbabwe wanted to retire, to come home to his family. It was a chance for Monty to see some of the world, as both Nash and I had, and to see if he had a calling after all."

"How'd he like it?"

"His e-mails were happy. He seemed to fall in love with Africa at first sight. I believe if he hadn't been taken from us, he would have bloomed there. He'd found his place, and a calling I'd doubted. The condolences after his death spoke of his kindness, his compassion, his . . . joy. It's both painful and freeing to know he'd found his joy before leaving us."

"How often did you talk to him?"

"Talk? We didn't. When first embarking on a mission, especially the very first on your own, it's too easy to cling to home, to family or friends. For the first few months, it's best to keep that contact somewhat limited so you can focus on the mission, consider that your home, your family. And serve them with a full heart."

"Huh. Sounds like boot camp."

She relaxed enough to smile a little. "I suppose it does, in a way."

"How about him and Shelby? How did they get along?"

"Get along?"

"You said he was like one of the kids."

"Yes, I just meant he was younger than Nash and myself, and younger in, well, spirit."

"How did he get along with them, Shelby in particular?"

"He was particularly shy around girls, but he got along well enough. I'd say he might've been a bit intimidated by Shelby. She was a big, and sometimes abrasive, personality."

"And with him being shy, and the little brother of the heads? I bet she took a few pokes at him. One way to get back at you, say, if you disciplined her or denied her, would be to poke at the most vulnerable."

"She could be a bully, that's true enough. Monty tended to give her a wide berth. He was more comfortable with the quieter residents. He did talk sports with T-Bone." She smiled as she caught that flutter of memory. "I'd forgotten that. Monty loved sports, any kind at all. He and T-Bone would talk football, or baseball. Reeling off all those stats . . . I can't understand how they remembered when they barely remembered to empty the recycler."

"So he interacted regularly with one of Shelby's crew."

"He was more comfortable and confident around boys, men."

"So no girlfriends?"

"No."

"Boyfriends?"

She shifted in her chair now. "While our father wouldn't have approved, both Nash and I would have been fine if Monty had developed a relationship with another young man. But I don't think he was physically attracted to men. And he was, at that point, just too shy to pursue a relationship with a woman."

"Girls might've been easier."

It took a moment, then Philadelphia's puzzled frown turned into the fire of outrage. "I don't like what you're implying."

"A shy guy, little to no social networking, homeschooled, indulged, as you said, and at the same time restricted. No serious responsibilities, a lot of time on his hands. And a house full of young girls—some of them, like Shelby, willing to exchange sex for favors."

"Monty would *never* have touched any of the girls."

"You said he wasn't gay." Eve leaned forward, pushed herself into Philadelphia's space. "He's young, just into his twenties, and all those girls, some of them just starting to bud. A lot of them with plenty of experience from the streets. And there's Shelby, happy to give a guy a blow job for a bottle of brew or whatever else she wants."

Philadelphia's face flamed. "We weren't aware of Shelby's . . . activities until Nash caught her stealing kitchen supplies, and she offered to . . . she offered to service him in exchange."

"So you were aware."

"She was put on immediate restriction, and her counseling was increased and directed at addressing the situation."

"Was this before or after she went down on Fine's helper, Clipperton, for some brew?"

"I wasn't aware." She stuttered a bit, and the fire in her cheeks died to ice. "I didn't know about that. The incident with Nash happened just before the move, just a week or so prior."

"You put her on restriction, yet she still managed to—how did you put it?—slip through."

"We failed her. In every possible way. But you have no right, no right, Lieutenant, to try to implicate Monty."

"Reality," Eve said flatly. "If she was ballsy enough to go for big brother, little brother would be easy pickings. I bet little brother could get her paperwork to forge. Who notices the shy guy? Little brother could help her access the old building, his first adult home. Little brother's handy around the house. Little brother could probably build a few walls."

"How dare you? How dare you sit there and insinuate my brother would kill? The taking of a life is against everything we believe."

"Your mother took her own life."

"You won't use our personal tragedy as *evidence*. My mother was ill. You're floundering around because you don't have a clue who murdered those girls, so you point your finger at my brother who can't defend himself."

"Here's where my finger's pointing: Little brother's boxed in, and suddenly the top's off the box when his father takes off. He's got substitute parents, a new home—in his siblings and The Sanctuary. He's a big boy now, a troubled big boy who still has no real responsibilities, no real job, no real purpose. But he's got hormones. He's got needs. All these pretty young girls, girls who know the score. Know how to score, like Shelby.

"She uses him. It's what she does. What she knows. Because she's been boxed in, too, and she's damn well going to have her own place, her own way, whatever it takes. Now there's that big, empty building just sitting there. She needs a way out, and a way in. Monty can help her get both. But once he has, she's finished with him. He's not one of her crew, he's not her friend. He was a means to an end."

"None of that's true." Philadelphia's breath came fast; her fingers flexed and released on the table. "None of it."

Eve drove on, hard. "She made him feel like a man, now she's made him feel useless again. She has to be punished for that. He knows how to get into the building. He'd know how to cop a tranq. He has to make her see what they had was special. She has to give herself over to him, and to the higher power. Accept. He'll make her accept."

"No."

"But she's with another girl. He hadn't expected another girl. She'll accept, too. They're not scared of him, the shy, awkward guy. Tranqing them's not hard. Then the rest is easy, too. Maybe it goes too far, maybe he planned to kill them all along, but either way, they're dead now. Gone to that better place, washed clean. But people won't understand, so he has to hide them, and what's handier than right at home? His sanctuary. It was all so easy, really, and how it made him feel? He's found his mission now. Found his true calling. He only has to find more girls."

"Everything you said is a lie. Everything you said is hateful."

"It may be hateful," Eve agreed, "but it sure is plausible. What I can't figure is when you found out, why did you just leave the bodies where they were? Or if you didn't know where he'd concealed them, why you didn't make him tell you before you shipped him off to Africa?"

"We found nothing out because he'd done none of the things you say."

"Or did you ship him off?" Eve leaned back with a thoughtful shake of her head. "That's another puzzler. The shy introvert wakes up in Africa and becomes a born missionary. That's long odds to me."

"Of course he went to Africa. It's documented. People knew him there."

"I'm working on that. He'd killed, betrayed everything you stood for, and had put your life's work on the line. Who would sponsor you now? What court would entrust children to your care now? Everything you'd worked for, over. That door that had opened, slammed shut. Will we find his remains, Ms. Jones? Was little brother sacrificed to your higher power?"

"That's enough." She lurched to her feet. "You have an ugly heart, an ugly mind. I loved my brother. He never harmed anyone in his life, and I would never harm him. Your world's a cold and ugly place, Lieutenant, filled with that."

She gestured toward the photos still on the table.

"I have nothing, *nothing* more to say to you. If you insist I stay in this horrible room, I want my lawyer."

"You're free to go," Eve said easily. "Peabody, why don't you show Ms. Jones the way out."

"I see the door." Spinning to it, she rushed out and away.

"Jesus." Peabody blew out a long breath. "Intense. Is that really what you think happened? Because it's not only plausible, but convincing."

"It's one way. It's most of the way. I haven't got all the threads knotted, but it's most of the way."

"Their brother killed the girls."

"He's the one who fits, and he fits just fine for all the reasons I hit her with."

"Yeah, convincing. But do you really think they killed their baby brother? I mean, who went to Africa if he didn't? Because she's right, it's documented."

"I don't know, but we're going to find out."

"*That's* why you said to ask Owusu to see if anybody in the village had a photograph taken of Jones—the younger—when he was there."

"Any kind of identification's out since he's cremated and scattered. He—whoever he was—took pictures. So I'm betting there's some photos of him. One thing I do know after that little session. However it went down, however the last of the threads knot, she didn't know."

"That's what I think, but you said—"

"I got a rise out of her, didn't I? Got the shock and outrage, and little bits of information that fill in some blanks. What I didn't get, once we got rolling, was fear or nerves. Guilt, some guilt over the girls, and I'd have looked at her sideways if I hadn't gotten some of that. But if I'm right, and little brother hooked with Shelby, and that connection forged the rest of the chain, she didn't know."

"But . . . then the Africa bit? Are you saying just a coincidence?"

"Hell no. She's got another brother, doesn't she? She's got a partner. Raised traditional—old traditions. Big brother, head of their little family. Yeah, it could play. We need him in here, Peabody."

"I'll make it happen."

When she started to rise, Eve's 'link signaled. She pulled it out, glanced at the readout, arched her brows. Then punched for the text. "Son of a bitch. Sebastian came through. My faith in humanity is . . . about where it was a minute ago. I've got a meet with DeLonna."

"No shit? When?"

"Now. Let's move."

 THE BAR AT THE PURPLE MOON GLITTERED
with stars. More stars twinkled in the ceiling and
would, Eve imagined, sprinkle light on dancers who
took to the floor when the place was open.

For now its purple booths and silver tables stood empty.

The couple who stood in front of the glittery bar turned when Eve
came in.

The man, rangy in good jeans and a white shirt, held both hands
of the woman with him. He had an excellent face of strong bones,
hard chin, framed by an artful tangle of dreads. Eyes green and hard
as the chin watched Eve resentfully as she crossed the room with
Peabody.

The woman looked up at the man who said something in an urgent undertone. She only shook her head.

"It's important, baby," she said, gave his hands a squeeze, then
pulled hers away to stand on her own.

Eve doubted she'd have recognized the skinny, not quite formed DeLonna in the curvy, exotic beauty.

She'd grown into herself, Eve thought, and knew how to make the most of what she had. The short, spiky cap of hair gave her face a lift, made the most of big, slanted eyes of rich chocolate.

She'd painted her lips stoplight red, and wore the same color in a short, snug dress.

"Lieutenant Dallas." Her voice was smoke.

"That's right." To keep it smooth, Eve held up her badge. "Detective Peabody. DeLonna Jackson?"

"It's Lonna. Just Lonna. Lonna Moon. This is my man, Derrick Stevens. This is our place."

"It's a nice place."

Derrick angled himself between Lonna and Eve. "She doesn't have to talk to you."

"Derrick."

"You don't have to do this."

"Oh, baby, you know I do. We've got a life, Derrick and me," she said to Eve, stepping to the side to stand unshielded. "We've got a place, and a life that's a long way from what was. He worries about me going back there."

"We're not here to bring you trouble."

"The trouble was already there," Lonna said to Derrick before he could speak. "It's hard to know it, but now I do. We should sit down. We can get you a drink. Derrick, I could use a fizzy water. How about some fizzy water all around?"

"That'd be great," Eve told her, and went with her to a booth. Eve and Peabody slid into one side. "You were friends with Shelby Stubacker."

"Best friends ever. Shelby, Mikki, T-Bone. I think I'd have faded away like air without them. Shelby and Mikki, they're dead, aren't they? Sebastian didn't say, not right out, but I knew when we heard about . . . about what they found in The Sanctuary, I knew. I thought they just left me, and it broke my heart."

"They didn't just leave you."

"It's worse. So much worse knowing that. But it helps, the knowing."

"You were going to have your own place, your own club—like Sebastian's—in The Sanctuary."

"How'd you know that?" Surprised, she stared at Eve when Derrick brought over a tray with tall glasses of water sparkling like the ceiling stars. "It's all we talked about for days and days when we found out we were moving out. I was so scared, but I couldn't admit it. Scared at the thought of being on our own, but excited, too. Best friends ever," she murmured, and sipped her water when Derrick sat beside her.

"Who helped her get the forged documents, the paperwork to get out?"

"You know about that, too? I don't know, not for certain. Shelby didn't always tell us everything. She was the captain. She had power, but she had responsibilities. She said things like that."

"She developed a relationship with Montclair Jones. The younger brother. Sexual?"

On a sigh, Lonna tipped her head to Derrick's shoulder. "She didn't see it as sex. She saw it as bartering, as currency. It took me a while to see it as different." She smiled over at Derrick. "It took some doing for Shelby to draw Monty out. He was a little scared of her, and awful shy, but he was fascinated, too. And he wasn't smart and straight like Mr. Jones or Ms. Jones. He didn't seem all that much older than us, though I guess he was. Shelby gave him his first blow job, and was proud of that."

On a wince, Lonna touched a hand to her heart. "God, that makes her sound awful. You have to understand—"

"I do. She'd been abused, over and over. She learned to survive in a way she thought gave her some control. She was a child who never had a chance to be one."

"Most of us were." The first tear slid down Lonna's cheek.

"Don't cry, baby."

"I have to, a little. Shelby never got a chance to be happy, like I did. And Mikki, she was so needy, so angry. But my God, she loved Shelby. Loved her too much, in a way I see now Shelby could never have given back. We followed her, and she gave us direction, she gave us . . . family. We'd hook up with Sebastian's club sometimes, for fun, for the company. And because you could learn a lot. He said you weren't going to hassle me about the things I did back then."

"I won't. I understand that, too." To cover it, she shifted her attention to Derrick, just for a moment. "Nobody's going to hassle Lonna."

"First time you do, I show you the door."

"Fair enough. You brought a girl to Sebastian," she said to Lonna. "This girl." And laid Merry Wolcovich's photo on the table. "Do you remember?"

"I do. I don't remember her name, and it turned out she was mean as a snake. But I brought her to Sebastian when I came across some boys giving her trouble. She was giving it back, but they had her outnumbered, so I stepped in."

"You always do."

She laughed a little at Derrick's comment. "I was a fighting fool back then. Shelby taught me how to handle myself, so I pushed right into those boys, went after the meanest one—you can always tell. Take him out, I figured, the rest'll run off. And that's how it was. Then I took her to Sebastian because she was alone."

She ran a finger over the edge of the photo. "She's one of them, too. In the building."

"Yes. You tried to help her, but she didn't stay with Sebastian."

"Mean as a snake," Lonna repeated. "But she was just a kid. She hung with us a little while—mostly with Shelby—but she left, and I didn't see her around anymore."

"Did she leave before or after Shelby?"

"Oh, let me think about that. It must've been after. I snuck back to Sebastian's a couple times, hoping to find Shelby there, but she wasn't. It seems to me this girl was, then she wasn't."

"Okay. How about this girl."

At Eve's signal, Peabody put Shashona's photo on the table.

"Not one of us," Lonna said slowly. "Maybe I saw her around— she's sharp-looking, isn't she? I wonder . . . did she sing?"

"Yeah." Connection, Eve thought. "Yeah, she did."

"That's it then. Sharp-looking girl, good voice. We sometimes snuck off to Times Square, and I'd sing for the tourists. They'd put money in the box. This girl here, I remember how she came by, sang with me. Just picked up the song—don't remember which—with the harmony.

"Shelby, Mikki, they couldn't carry a tune in a bucket. T-Bone was okay at it, but he wouldn't sing out on the street. But this girl stopped—I'd seen her around before, but more up our way, I think. And she'd seen me. I could tell, the way you do."

"You'd seen her before," Eve pressed. "Near The Sanctuary?"

"Seems like it. Always with a pack. Girlfriends, laughing, talking, going home or out somewhere. I envied that. She had nice clothes, seems they all did. I hated wearing those hand-me-downs, and I noticed clothes on girls around my age."

"Then you ran into her in Times Square."

"That's right. I was set up with my box, and truth be told Shelby was working the crowd for wallets. Telling the truth, back then it was fun, an adventure. We didn't have many. But this time, this sharp-looking girl here, she stopped, and we had ourselves a little duet. Then another, before she went off with her friends. I remember because it felt good to sing with somebody, and because I offered her part of the money, and she wouldn't take it. She said she hadn't done it for money, but for the song. And damned if she didn't put five dollars in the box."

"Good, clear voice," Lonna murmured as she studied the photo. "Gone now, too."

"She has a grandmother, who raised her, who loved her," Eve said. "It's going to mean something to her when we tell her that."

"Tell her . . . her girl could sure sing, and she had a kindness to her. Lots of girls that age with nice clothes? They'd look down on someone dressed like I was. She didn't."

"I'll tell her. Tell me a little about The Club. Sebastian's."

"Well, Sebastian saw we got food. I was getting fed just fine by the Joneses. They saw to it you ate healthy and didn't go hungry. But some of the girls in The Club would've gone hungry without him. You need to know that."

"Okay."

"We learned to street snatch, pick pockets, learned a few cons. It was exciting, and I was pretty good at it. I liked having a little secret money of my own, even though it belonged to somebody else. I'd never had my own. Couldn't do the bjs, and Sebastian wouldn't have liked it anyway. But I couldn't do them the way Shelby did, even though she tried to teach me that, too."

She laughed a little, gave Derrick a wink out of watery eyes. "Not then I couldn't. I was a little younger, and I told Shelby no way I was doing that. It was nasty. She just laughed, said I should think of it like medicine. Just get it done. But I wouldn't."

"Did you ever get caught?"

"Nearly, lots of times. It added to the thrill, I guess. Mr. Jones and Ms. Jones ran things pretty tight, but most of us had had some street time—and I was getting more of it—so we found ways around and through. And we always had each other's backs."

"Do you still? Do you know where T-Bone is?"

"He did the same as me, got his name changed. Then he lit out. He wanted to see the world, that's what he wanted. And he has. He got some education, and that's thanks to Mr. Jones and Ms. Jones and the rest. He got on a boat, worked on the crew and went all the way to the South Pacific. He's still seeing the world, and I hope you'll let him be. We talked after I heard about the girls, and he said he'd come back if I needed. I don't want him to have to."

"We'll let that stand for now. If it turns out he's needed, I'll want you to tell him, or give me a way to contact him, to talk to him."

"I can do that, but he's probably going to come anyway. We go back. You know how it is when you go back."

Not as far, Eve thought. But she thought she knew.

"Tell me about when Shelby left."

"We had it all planned. I still remember being so scared it wouldn't work, then so happy—and so unhappy—when it did. She got out, she'd set up our place, and would get the rest of us out. I'd have to go. Part of me wanted to so much, and another part just wanted to stay where I knew it was safe. And the new place? It was so nice. I'd never been in such a nice place.

"But she got out, just like she said she would. But then Mikki had to go back to her mother, right on top of it. That wasn't the plan. We had a meeting—Mikki, T-Bone, and me—and decided Mikki would need to wait it out with her mother for a few days, maybe longer, and we'd wait to hear from Shelby."

"And you never did."

"We never did. Now it was just me and T-Bone. And he got in trouble for mouthing off. He was wound up tight—we both were—because he usually knew how to keep a lid on it. He was on restriction and kitchen duty—and they really buttoned down the new place, so it wasn't easy to slip out like before. But we figured I had to. We had to find Shelby, get some direction."

She took a long drink now. "I was a skinny little thing. One night after bed check, I climbed out the window of my room. The windows only opened partway, just for that reason, but I wiggled my way out. Then I had to climb down, and I'm lucky I didn't fall and break my leg, or my neck. Then I ran to the subway. I'd taken Matron's swipe card out of her purse and I'd have to get it back. I'd have to climb back up, wiggle back in, but all that was for later. In that moment, I was free as a bird, and running to my best friend ever."

"To The Sanctuary."

"I took the subway, and I got off at the stop. It's just a couple blocks to walk, and I ran. I ran, and it was a nice warm night. I remember thinking Shelby would be so surprised to see me. She'd be proud of how I got out the way I did when the new place was so buttoned up. She'd laugh, and we'd laugh, and she'd tell me what to do next.

I thought of that. I remember thinking that, and how fast my heart beat.

"And then I don't remember. It's all a dark blur. I remember waking up in the morning, in my bed in my room, in the new place. Feeling sick and so tired. And scared, because I wiggled out and climbed down—I was sure I had—but I never remembered climbing back or wiggling in, or laughing with Shelby. And my window was closed tight and locked. I was wearing my uniform pajamas, and I hadn't been."

"Do you remember seeing anyone, talking to anyone?"

"I remember just like I told you. Except . . . I had dreams for a while. Dreams where I see myself walking around in there, calling out for Shelby. And everything gets dark, and in the dream I hear someone preaching about cleansing. The mind, the body, the spirit, sort of like what we talked about at The Sanctuary, but not. Cleansing for the bad girl, so . . . she could come home. It's mixed up. And I was cold, and I was naked, and scared, but I couldn't scream or run or move. I had that dream a long while."

She gave a little shudder. Instantly, Derrick put an arm around her, drew her into his side.

"Sometimes in them I hear shouting and yelling. Sometimes I feel like I'm floating, and not scared, just floating away with this soft, soft voice telling me it was all right, to just forget, to just forget."

"Whose voice?"

"I don't know. But now I think—" She gripped Derrick's hand. "Now I *know* what happened to Shelby and Mikki was going to happen to me. But it didn't. I don't know why it didn't, and how I woke up safe, dressed in my uniform nightgown, in bed with the window tight shut."

"No one ever asked you about that night?"

"T-Bone. I told him what I remembered, but he figured I'd dreamed it all. That I never climbed down at all. I started to think the same, and I felt awful about it. I'd been a coward and let down my friends. But they'd let me down, too. I held on to that so I wouldn't feel so ashamed."

She turned her head toward Derrick, just a little. He brushed his lips over her hair.

"Shelby abandoned me, like everybody, so I wouldn't care. I'd just get through it, get by. I'd do what I had to do to get through and get by until I was old enough to get out. Nobody was ever going to take me on—scrawny, skinny, odd-looking girl like me. I just had to get through until I could walk out. Then I'd be whoever I wanted to be."

She finished off her water. "That's what I did. I changed my name. I didn't do it legal, Sebastian helped me. If you do it legal, there's a record. I wanted to just be new, be me. So I was Lonna Moon. I thought it sounded like a singer. It's all I wanted to be. I did all right. Sang for my supper, and paid the rent singing, waiting tables, whatever. After a while, I didn't have to wait tables so much. Then I met Derrick. And I'm with Derrick. That's the best thing I've ever been. The only thing I ever want to be.

"Shelby and Mikki, they never got the same chance."

"I want to show you some other pictures."

Her hand tightened on Derrick's. "The other girls."

"We have all but one identified. I wonder if you remember any of the others. Peabody."

"I just want to say, Ms. Moon, I admire what you've done. I admire someone who can take the pain and the hard from the past, and make it into the strong and the good. I just wanted to say."

"Thanks for that. It feels good to hear that." Then she looked down at the rest of the pictures Peabody laid out.

"Oh God. Oh God! That's Iris there. Sweet Iris, oh God. And this one, she was in The Sanctuary with us. I don't remember her name."

"Lupa Dison."

"Yes, Lupa. She was nice. Quiet, but nice. I know these faces, almost all. Not names of the others. I think I knew some of them on the street, either with Sebastian or just on their own. Mostly they'd have street names or made up ones anyway. I don't remember this one at all."

Eve nodded when she touched Linh's picture. "Okay."

"I'm sure of Iris, and this one. Lupa. And the one I told you I brought to Sebastian, and the one I sang with. We looked for Iris. I helped when I heard she'd left. She wasn't . . . she was special, and Sebastian worried something would happen to her on her own. Something did."

"Yeah, something did. Lonna, would you be willing to work with a doctor? Someone who could help you remember what happened that night?"

"No." Derrick rapped his free fist on the tabletop. "She's not doing that. She's not letting someone poke around in her head, try to make her remember something that still makes her wake up crying some nights."

"I understand how you feel," Eve said. "I know what it's like to block something out, something bad and frightening. Something that comes back at you in dreams when you can't block it so completely."

"Do you?" Lonna murmured.

"Yeah. And I know what it's like to have a man who loves me just want to make it stop. Just want me to have some peace. I know it can tear just as much at the one who has to hold you when you wake up from it. But it won't stop until you pull it out, look at it square. It won't just stop until you can look at it, then learn to deal with it.

"You're the only one we know of who survived. The only one who might have something buried down deep that can lead me to him so he can pay."

She took out a card, wrote Mira's name and contact on it.

"If you decide to do that, to dig down for it, look at it square, you contact this woman. I promise you she's the best there is. She'll take care because she'll care."

"What I told you, what I do remember, is it enough to help?"

"It is. You don't have to give any more if you can't." She nudged the card closer. "This is for you, whether you talk to me again or not. Peabody's right, you've made something good and strong."

She looked up at the stars on the ceiling. "And you've got a nice place here."

"You can come back sometime, have a real drink, see it at night, when it really shines."

"I might just."

She slid out of the booth, waited for Peabody to do the same.

"Lieutenant? They were my friends. You have to find who hurt them."

"Working on it."

Outside as they walked back to the car, Eve tossed Peabody a look. "Your brain's buzzing so loud I want to swat it. Spill."

"I've got more than one thing, but I guess I want to start saying you don't usually—mostly ever—say something personal to a wit the way you did to her. About knowing what it's like to block out something terrible, and have it come back at you anyway."

Eve let it hang between them until they'd gotten into the car, into the warm. "It felt okay with her. Okay on my side of it, the right thing on hers. It is personal, but sometimes you use the personal to lever off the lid of something."

"Do you still have nightmares?"

"Not like I did." And it wasn't as hard to think about, Eve realized as she merged into traffic. "Hardly ever. I have weird dreams, talking to the dead."

"That's creepy."

"Not really, not always. And it's useful. Just another lever. See about Nash Jones. I want him in the box, and I've got just the lever to pry him open."

While Peabody tried to hook Nash Jones, Eve used the in-dash to contact Mira's office.

Mira's dragon peered coolly from the screen. "Lieutenant."

"I need a few minutes with Dr. Mira."

"The doctor is in session. She has a meeting directly after, followed by a consult. Her day is booked, Lieutenant."

"Five minutes. Twelve dead girls and I need five minutes."

"I'll get back to you when I find five minutes."

Eve bared her teeth at the screen as it went blank. "Who doesn't have five fucking minutes? You'd think I was asking for an audience with God."

"Mira is her god," Peabody pointed out. "And Nash Jones is also in session. Shivitz passed me to his assistant who said she'll have him contact me as soon as he's free. But also said his day was crowded."

"He'll just have to make room."

Since without Nash Jones or Mira *she* had five minutes, Eve detoured to DeWinter's lab.

She heard someone shouting as she walked in. Her hand went to the butt of her weapon, then released it again when she recognized elation rather than fear or violence.

From the other direction she heard what sounded like a muffled explosion, followed by hysterical laughter.

"What kind of madhouse is this?"

"I think it's kind of icy." Peabody peered through glass walls, craned her neck to see over equipment. "But maybe you have to lean toward nerd to think it."

"You have to be neck-deep in nerd to think it. Like nerd quicksand. And why is it called quick anyway? In the vids people and unfortunate animals just sink slowly."

"Actually, you wouldn't sink but float, unless you struggle."

Eve glanced to the left where some nerd—sex not quite apparent in the baggy lab coat and behind the fly-eye microgoggles—looked up from examining a jawbone.

"What?"

"Quicksand's just ordinary sand that's saturated with water to the point it can't support weight, and it's usually only a few feet deep. The grains lose their friction, being saturated. But if you can, just float on it because your body's less dense than the quicksand."

"Okay, good to know. Next time I fall into some, I'll remember that."

"But if the mixture contains clay, that's a problem. The clay acts as a gel, so if you fell into it, the force would cause the gel to liquefy and bond the clay particles together."

The lab rat slapped one palm on the other. A good look at the hands determined male lab rat for Eve.

"You could sink pretty deep. Then the force needed to pull you out would be about the same as to lift a car or small truck. The trick is to wiggle out, as the motion lets water seep in, so you're back to floating."

"Okay then. I'm going to have to write all that down. Just in case."

To avoid more quicksand data, she got moving. "How do people know that stuff? Why do people know that stuff?"

"Science," Peabody said. "You can't live without it."

Eve started to argue, then remembered she was on her way to nag a scientist.

DeWinter wore the same weird little microgoggles, but her lab coat would never be called baggy. Today's was hot pink and matched her skyscraper ankle boots.

"I wondered if you'd make your way here today," she said without looking up from the bones on her steel table. "This is our last victim. COD remains the same. I put her age again between twelve and fourteen. Closer to fourteen, I believe, as there are signs of malnutrition. Her teeth indicate she had little professional dental care. Six cavities, apparently untreated, and two lost teeth, several others chipped or broken. Her right wrist had been broken in early childhood, probably around the age of five. It healed poorly, and likely troubled her."

Eve stepped in, studied the bones.

"A more recent injury here. Hairline fracture, left ankle. Probably incurred a week to ten days prior to her death."

"Signs of abuse?"

"The wrist, and this hairline again on the right elbow. From a fall, landing on the right. Certainly possible she was pushed. There's considerable wear in the hips, the knees, for a person her age, indicating she did considerable walking, repetitive motion. And see the toes, how they overlap."

"Wearing shoes too small, like Shelby Stubacker."

"Yes."

"Street kid, and not a new one. She lived on the street for years."

"I tend to agree."

"How's the facial reconstruction going on her? She's the last of them."

"We can check. She couldn't have run on that ankle."

"No, but she probably didn't have the chance to try anyway."

"I got your e-mail," DeWinter began as she removed the goggles. "While we've kept the media feed thin, with this last ID, I believe it's time to open it up."

"I believe it's not."

"Lieutenant, cooperation with the media can be very useful. Not only does it keep the public informed, as is their right, but the exposure of relevant data can and does generate interest, and interest can and does lead to information that can and does provide new leads."

Eve let her wind down so she could wind her back up. "First, I don't care about keeping the public informed because right now, this is my business, not theirs. Second, I have a key interview yet to complete, and I don't want information leaked that could bump up against that. When we have all identifications," she continued, rolling right over DeWinter's next pitch, "and if there's any notification to be given to next of kin on the last vic, we can release their names."

She'd just make sure Nadine got the final names first.

"You can do the release, make a statement, but"—Eve paused to drive the point home—"no information on my investigation is to be released. No components of the investigation, no discussion of potential suspects, motives, no release of COD."

"I've done this sort of thing before," DeWinter said dryly.

"Then it shouldn't be a problem." Eve glanced at the bones again. "But she comes first."

"Lieutenant." Insult, with a thin coating of frustration, shimmered into her voice. "They matter to me, too. I hold their bones in my hands, I scrape at them, test them, incise them. To do that I have to keep . . ." DeWinter drew the flat of her hand down in front of her. "A certain separation. I have to focus on the science. But it doesn't mean they don't matter to me.

"I can tell you about her." She gestured. "How she walked and walked the streets in ill-fitting shoes, eating what she could find when she could find it. The pain her mouth gave her, those bad teeth aching and aching. The last week or so she lived, limping, her ankle swollen, bruised, miserable. I think she had a very, very hard life. Her death, the method of it, was almost kinder. Wrong and immoral and unfair, but almost kinder than the life she lived."

"Maybe it was. I can't disagree with you, but her death, the method of it, the mind and hands behind it, have to stay on top for me. The public's right to know doesn't even come close."

"You have a suspect," DeWinter realized. "You have someone in your sights."

"I need her face, her name. I need to complete an interview. With those, it's possible this will break. Until then, I have lots of suspects."

"I'd like to know who—"

"Why did you steal the dog?" Eve interrupted.

"What?"

"The dog. You were charged a few years back for dognapping."

"I didn't *steal* the dog. I released it from its neglectful owner who kept it chained outside, summer and winter, with no shelter, who often forgot to feed it or give it fresh water. *And*"—oh, she was wound up now—"who told me when I spoke to him about it to mind my own *fucking* business, using that word in front of my little girl."

"Nice," Eve commented.

"One day instead of taking food and water over to the dog when the abusive, ignorant, disgusting excuse for a human who owned it was out—probably getting drunk, again—I took over bolt cutters. Then I took the dog to the vet."

"You got charged."

"Because I refused to give the dog back to him. The dog needed to stay at the vet to be treated for dehydration, malnutrition, fleas, mange, among other issues."

"Aw." Peabody's dark eyes filled with sympathy. "Poor thing."

"Yes! I refused to say where the dog was, and the pathetic man called the police. I was charged with taking the dog, and when the dog was examined, *he* was charged with animal abuse. That was satisfying."

"What happened to the dog?" Eve wondered.

"We named him Bones, my daughter's idea." She smiled now. "He's healthy, sweet-natured, and enjoying living in New York."

She pulled out her pocket 'link, swiped, then held it up. On screen sat a sleek brown dog with floppy ears and a dopey look in his eyes.

"He's so cute!" Peabody exclaimed.

"He is now, and worth the arrest and the fine."

"If you'd've called the cops, you'd have avoided the arrest and the fine," Eve pointed out.

"Maybe, but I was too mad. And I enjoyed breaking Bones out of jail. So, now that we've settled that, about the media—" She broke off as her pocket 'link played a bar of—of all things—one of Mavis's current hits. "That's my girl's signal."

"We'll head over to Kendrick."

"I'll be a minute."

"Take your time."

"I hate when people are mean to animals," Peabody said as they headed out.

"The guy was obviously an asshole," Eve said, "but taking the dog that way? It's playing vigilante and shows a little problem with impulse control."

"Maybe, but Bones sure looked happy. You're really not going to tell her the theory?" Peabody glanced back as they turned toward Elsie Kendrick's area.

"I don't know her well enough to trust her, and don't know if I'll trust her when I do know her well enough."

She walked in to find Elsie working at a control panel. "Hey. I've just about got her. Just fine-tuning."

"These are really mag." Peabody turned from the sketches pinned to Elsie's board. "They're really beautiful. I wonder if maybe we could have copies for the ones who had somebody. Their parents or guardians, who cared about them."

"I can make copies, sure."

"That's a good thought, Peabody."

"Here's our last girl." Elsie set the controls for the holographic reconstruction.

Eve watched it shimmer into three dimensions.

Not such a pretty girl, this one. A thin face, a little hollow on one side—the missing teeth, she thought. The eyes seemed hollow as well, a little sunken.

"Peabody."

"Running it for match now, sir."

"She's not in the Missing Persons file. Nobody reported her, but then, from the forensics, she'd been on the street a long time."

"It looks like it," Elsie agreed. "She didn't have an easy time of it."

"Nothing's popping," Peabody put in.

"Keep running it. Elsie, can you make a copy of this, then do another? Can you do the reverse-age thing? Take her back about, let's say, three years."

"I can do that, good thought. Just hold on."

Eve took the copy, stuck it in Peabody's file bag, then watched as their Jane Doe morphed into a younger girl. Just a little more fat in the cheeks, a little more symmetry.

"Copy that, too. I'll run this one."

"I can do a lateral search and match while you are," Elsie told her. "One of us should hit."

But they didn't.

"Maybe I went off," Elsie began.

"I doubt it. You were on the nail with the other eleven. We'll widen the search. Peabody, copy both images to EDD, ask Feeney to do a global. It'll be faster going through EDD."

"I'll keep it running here, too. If you find her, send me her name. I feel—I don't know why—more with this girl."

"Maybe because it feels like she never really had anyone."

"Maybe." Elsie nodded at Eve.

Back in the car, Eve headed for Central. "Give Jones another push. He's got to be out of whatever he was in by now. No, I'll do it. Hit them with rank."

She used the in-dash, put cold cop on her face.

"Higher Power Cleansing Center for Youths. How can I help you today?"

"This is Lieutenant Dallas, NYPSD. I need to speak with Nashville Jones immediately."

"Oh! Just one moment, please, I'll transfer you. Have a positive day."

"Yeah, yeah. People are always saying shit like that," Eve complained to Peabody. "Have a good day, have a happy day, have a peaceful day or whatever. I'd rather have a kick-ass day."

"That should be your sign-off."

"Mr. Jones's office, this is Lydia. How can I serve you today?"

"You can serve me Mr. Jones, asap."

"Lieutenant Dallas, yes, I gave him the message. I'm afraid Mr. Jones had to leave. Something came up and—"

"What the hell do you mean, he left?"

"He had something come up," Lydia repeated. "He asked me to cancel the rest of his schedule for today. I'm sure it was very important. I'd be happy to leave him another message."

"Because the first one worked so well."

Eve clicked off before Lydia could wish her a positive day.

"Goddamn it." She zipped between a Rapid Cab and a panel truck—incurring the ire of the truck driver, switching lanes so she could make the turn.

Peabody clamped a hand on the chicken stick as Eve punched into vertical to avoid a minor traffic snarl.

"I take it we're going to HPCCA."

"You bet your ass. Son of a bitch!" Eve threaded another needle. Peabody shut her eyes.

19 EVE BARRELED INTO HPCCY, AND HAD SHIVITZ waving her hands, bouncing from foot to foot in distress.

"Please, please! You can't just barge in! You can't just push into Mr. Jones's office."

"I just did. Where is he?" she demanded of the wide-eyed Lydia.

"I-I-I—"

"Snap out of it! Where's the boss?"

"He didn't say. He just said he had to go and to cancel his book for the day. I was just—"

"You." She rounded on Shivitz. "You know everything. Where is he?"

"I don't know. I wouldn't presume to ask Mr. Jones where he intended to go. It's not my place."

"Where's his sister?"

"Ms. Jones is leading a circle group. If you'd just—"

"Get her."

"I most certainly will *not* interrupt her."

"Fine. Get the key to their quarters."

She audibly gasped. "I most certainly will *not*," she began again, then chased Eve to the stairs. "Where are you going? Where are you going?"

"To Mr. Jones's quarters. I have a master."

"You can't do that! It's an invasion of privacy. It's—it's illegal. You haven't got a warrant!"

Eve stopped on the stairs, caught a glimpse of Quilla from the corner of her eye before she froze Shivitz with one hard stare. "You want me to get a warrant? And while I'm doing that, I'll contact some people I know in the media, let them know this institution, and its founders, are now under investigation for the murders of twelve young girls."

"You can't do that!"

"Peabody, can I do that?"

"Oh yes, sir, Lieutenant, you can do that. Should I tag up Nadine Furst for you?"

"No, no, no! Just wait! Just wait! I'm going to get Ms. Jones. You wait!"

"Fine by me."

Eve leaned against the banister as Shivitz ran. She gave Quilla up to five seconds to slither out of her hole.

It only took three.

"Total drama. Completely better than a vid. You sure got Matron's skirt blown up."

"Specialty of mine."

"Is Mr. Jones in the heat?"

"He is."

"No way he killed anybody. He's too do-unto-others and crap."

"Killing's doing unto others."

"Yeah, but not that way," she said matter-of-factly.

"Ms. Jones, she was *steaming* when she got back a while ago. Red in the face absolutely, and she told Mr. Jones he had to come into her office *right now*. And she never does like that. So, you know, then they're in there and she's carrying on about you making shit up to screw them over—only she said it in fancy words. And he's, now, now, there, there, but not like the other day, after you left and they first found out about the murders and stuff. She was crying so he did the now, now bullshit. She was all—"

Quilla put the back of her hand to her forehead in the classic distress gesture. "Those poor children, those poor lost souls and all that, and he was, there, there, Philly, they're at peace now. It's not like our responsibility. We do our best, blah, blah, but she's watering up all over.

"This time it was more now, now, I wish you'd shut the fuck up so I could think, but he didn't say that. I just read between the words, like."

"How about that."

"And then—" She straightened like an arrow, glanced back. "Gotta blow."

"Bat ears," Eve murmured when Quilla blew seconds before Philadelphia came thundering down the second-floor corridor with Shivitz yapping at her heels like a corgi.

"This is outrageous."

"It can get more outrageous," Eve told her.

"You have no right to try to push your way into our private quarters. This is harassment, and I intend to contact our lawyers."

"Go ahead. I'll contact the PA, get the warrant, and while that's coming through . . . Peabody, go ahead and tag up Nadine Furst. She'll want to lead with this on the evening slot."

"Just one minute!"

"That's all you get," Eve snapped back. "Your brother is a person of interest in a multiple homicide investigation, and no one seems to know where he is. In fact, Peabody, let's get a BOLO out on Nashville Jones."

"What does that mean?" Philadelphia demanded. "I don't know what that means."

"Be on the lookout," Peabody said helpfully.

"As if he's a criminal! Stop it."

"Tell me where he is," Eve suggested, "and I won't have to have every cop in the city on the lookout."

"I don't know. For heaven's sake, he doesn't tell me his every move. He needed to go out, he went."

"He went after you came back from Interview, after you told him what we discussed, after receiving a message that I wanted him to come into Interview. Smells, doesn't it, Peabody?"

"Very fishy."

"He's upset. We're upset. Please just go—" She actually made a shooing gesture. "All this is disrupting our classes, our sessions, our residents. Just go, and I'll make sure he contacts you the minute he's back."

"Not good enough. I want to take a look at his quarters."

"Why? What do you think? He's hiding bodies in there?"

"Show me. Prove me wrong."

"This is so insulting." But she turned on her heel, strode to the next turn of the stairs, and clipped her way up.

A few doors were open a crack, and Eve imagined ears and/or eyes pressed close.

Total drama, as Quilla said.

Philadelphia produced a swipe card from her pocket, used it on a small security panel, then tapped in a code.

"Worried the residents will sneak in?"

"If they're not tempted, then they can't make a mistake." She stepped inside.

"Here. We share this living area and kitchenette."

Eve judged it modest, nicely appointed, but anything but fussy. She couldn't claim, from the looks of it, they funneled donation money into elaborate living.

"I have a bath, bed, and sitting room on this side, and Nash has his on that side. Both close off with panel doors if more privacy is wanted. As you see, they're open, as they usually are."

"I see." Eve started toward Nash's part.

Philadelphia rushed after her. "I don't want you touching his things."

"Then stick around, make sure I don't touch."

Cheeks pink, eyes fired, Philadelphia fisted her hands on her hips. "I'm going to want an apology from you, both of you, and your immediate supervisor. In writing."

"Yeah, we'll get right on that."

His sitting room held two chairs, a small desk with a minicomp, a couple inexpensive pictures on the wall, a carpet that showed considerable wear.

The bedroom mimicked the Spartan style. A simple bed, another small chair, one dresser with a photo of his sister—younger—flanked by him and their younger brother, standing outside the HPCCY building.

"Is that his 'link?" Eve asked, gesturing toward the dresser.

"What? I . . . oh. He left his 'link. That explains it. I tried to contact him when Matron told me you were here, but it went to his v-mail. He forgot his 'link."

"Uh-huh." Can't trace 'link transmissions if you don't make any, she thought. Can't triangulate your location with it if it's sitting on your bedroom dresser.

"Look in his closet."

"I certainly won't."

"Look in his closet," Eve repeated with more patience than she thought the woman deserved, "see if anything's missing."

"Of course nothing is missing. It's ridiculous." Incensed, Philadelphia pulled open the narrow closet. "You act as though he's in flight or . . ."

"What did he pack?"

"I-I didn't say he packed anything."

"Your face did."

"I never . . . Matron, would you go down, make sure the children are— Please, go downstairs."

"I'll be right downstairs if you need me." Shivitz gave Eve the fish eye. "If you need anything."

Philadelphia nodded, then walked over, sank into the little chair. "Something must have come up."

"So everyone's saying. What did he take?"

"I'm not sure. I'm not. It's just . . . he kept a small suitcase in the closet, as I do in mine. For quick trips. It's not there. He must have been called away, suddenly."

"And took off without telling you, without telling his assistant, without his 'link?" As Roarke would say, she thought, bollocks to that. "You're not a stupid woman. He's running. Peabody, get that BOLO out."

"He's not. I swear to you. I swear on my *life*, he's done nothing wrong. He couldn't."

"Where does he keep his cash?"

"What?"

"Everybody keeps a little cash hidden, for that rainy day. I say it's raining. Where does he keep it?"

Pressing her lips together, Philadelphia rose, walked to his dresser, opened the top left drawer. Carefully, she lifted some folded socks, then simply stared.

"It's gone."

"He may have moved it. He generally keeps some cash here. I don't understand. He's a good man." She turned back, her hands linked together as if in prayer. "I don't say that just because I'm his sister. I work with him, every day. I know him. He's a good man."

"Where would he go?"

"I don't know. I just don't know."

"Where do you go to relax, to get away for a few days?"

"Oh, Lieutenant, we haven't had a vacation in five years. Or six. I'm not sure. We've both gone on short retreats but they're work related. What you might consider a conference of peers and co-workers."

"We'll need a list of where you've retreated. And I want you to look through the quarters. I want to know what he took."

"There's an explanation for all of this. An innocent one."

"Let's start with the lists. And I want to see DeLonna's old room."

"DeLonna? DeLonna Jackson?"

"That's right. I want to see the room she had when Shelby left."

"I . . . God, my head. I can't remember. Matron will. She'll remember. I'm sorry, I have a raging headache. Just let me get a blocker. Nash has some."

She walked slowly into the little bath—shower only—opened a little cabinet.

Then burst into tears.

"He took his toiletry kit. Oh sweet God, Nash, where are you?"

"Take care of her, Peabody. I'll take Shivitz."

"Got it. Let's sit down a minute, Ms. Jones. I've got a blocker. Let's sit down, and I'll get you some water."

"This doesn't make sense. None of this makes any sense."

Wrong, Eve thought as she started out. It was making perfect sense.

She put out a BOLO, flipped the resentful Shivitz by suggesting she order a soother for her boss. With that humanitarian mission to distract her, Eve wandered to what had been DeLonna's room.

It was tiny, held two narrow beds, two skinny dressers. But she noted the occupants had been allowed to add some touches to bring in a little personality. Posters of music groups, a couple colorful pillows, stuffed animals. Each of the girls had a wall platform by the bed for a minicomp or tablet, a lamp—some girl debris. One of them had switched out the plain white shade on the lamp for one with purple polka dots.

The window still only opened about nine inches. But a small, thin girl could have wiggled through. The climb down . . .

You'd have to be determined, she noted, to risk it with only bits of guttering and a few chancy toeholds in the decorative brick facade.

But she could see it, just as Lonna had described. The dark, the thudding heart, the fingers and toes gripping even as they trembled. Then that final drop, just long enough to make the knees and ankles sing on landing.

"What's the what?"

Eve straightened from the window, shut it again, turned to Quilla. "What?"

And made the girl grin. "How come you're in here? Randa and Choo share this room, and they're chill. My roommate got fostered. She was a pain in the ass with that halo shining in my eyes all the time. I like having my own room, hope I can keep it. So what?"

"Do you actually ever go to class or session or whatever?"

"Sure. It's all huh and whoa right now 'cause Ms. Jones is twisted, and Mr. Jones is wherever, and Matron's completely whacked out. They all pretend everything's just like always, but the vibes, man, they're fucking bouncing. So what?"

"What is we want to find Mr. Jones."

"You're not going to find him in here. He mostly handles the boys' side, and Ms. Jones handles us. They wouldn't want to see anybody naked who didn't have the same parts."

She threw her arms up in the air, opened eyes and mouth wide. "Scandal!"

Eve figured the girl should give up the idea of being a writer and try acting. "The staff follow that line?"

"Abso-complete. Sometimes some of the older kids sneak in a bang, but it takes mad plans and mega luck. If Ms. Jones found out, she'd dump all kinds of shit work on them, figuring if they're busy they won't think about banging. As if. But if anybody from the staff tried anything, she'd rip 'em up like the lion ripped her bro. Fierce."

"You know about the brother?"

"Everybody does. There's like this plaque deal in the Quiet Room—you know, in his honor and all."

"The Quiet Room?"

"They don't call it a church or a chapel deal, but it is." She wandered as she talked, poking into the occupants' things. Since Eve would've done exactly the same in her place, she didn't comment. "No talking, no e-stuff. You're just supposed to sit and think or meditate or pray. Whatever."

"No" was all Eve said when Quilla started to slip some sort of hair clip in her pocket.

The girl only shrugged, put it back. "Anyway, Mr. Jones didn't kill anybody, that's for solid. He doesn't even hit or push or even yell. When you screw up you get this."

She mimed a sternly disapproving look.

"Or this."

Now one of strained patience that slid into sorrowful disapproval.

"And says stuff like: 'My dear Quilla, perhaps you need twenty minutes in the Quiet Room to consider your behavior, how it affects you and those around you.' Ms. Jones is more direct, you know? Screw up, the next thing you know you're scrubbing toilets. Which is way, way gross. Anyway, he'll lecture your brains out, and she'll just hand you a bucket or something. Mostly the bucket's better. So he didn't kill anybody, and especially those old dead girls, but something is bogus."

In a few sentences, the kid had given her a pretty good sense of house and sibling dynamics.

So she'd happily listen to the rest of the flood.

"What's bogus?"

"Something." She admired herself in various poses and expressions in the little mirror on the wall. "Since the day you first came he's been spending a lot of time in the Quiet Room, and more time in his quarters. More than usual. And he's taking a lot of walks. Once he walked all the way to the old place. It had the police tape on it and stuff. He just stood across the street and stared at it. Weirdo-city."

"How do you know he walked there?"

"I followed him. If you're quick, you can get out the side door when they're making deliveries. I'm quick, and I wanted to see. And he talks on his new 'link a lot, quiet, so you can't hear even when you try."

"What new 'link?"

"He bought one when he was walking. A toss-away."

"Is that so?"

"Yeeeah. So something's bogus, but he didn't kill the dead girls because of the halo. I think he feels really bad about them being dead, especially since he knew a couple of them."

"How do you know that?"

"I hear, I listen, I know." She turned a shaky pirouette. "He and Ms. Jones and Matron were all huddled in Ms. Jones's office about it. And crying some—him, too, which is totally whoa. And they're going to have a memorial thing. We're *all* going to have to go, even though we didn't know them and they've been dead forever already. But it's gonna be the big M for mandatory.

"Anyway, I think he's having sex somewhere, and they say in group health and well-being, you can feel guilty and conflicted about having sex if you aren't in love and committed to the one you're having the sex with, and the higher power, and all that fucking blah."

"Jesus Christ."

"Maybe he's your higher power, maybe not." Quilla shrugged.

"They don't push it. Anyhow, I think he's feeling really bad, and he's all that conflicted, so he probably went off to have a whole bunch of sex to get it out and done, and so he won't have to feel bad for a while."

After Eve's ears stopped ringing, she decided it actually made sense, or would under different circumstances.

"I'll look into that," she said, figuring it was the best response.

"Okay. I gotta get back before they miss me."

She zipped off, and the room suddenly felt bigger, quiet and still. Blowing out a breath, Eve sat on the side of one of the beds for a moment to let the quiet in.

The kid's brain was like one of those rat things—hamsters—on a wheel. Spinning, spinning. But she'd actually turned over considerable information, once you pulled it out of the maze of thoughts and jumbled words.

So she sat a moment longer, making a few notes now in case anything slipped away back into that maze.

She went back to Nash's quarters, found Philadelphia in the shared living space with Shivitz urging her to finish the soother, and Peabody on guard.

"Lieutenant, I want to apologize for falling apart that way. I'm generally more sturdy."

"No problem. Ms. Jones, I can get a warrant, and I'm going to have my partner start that process—now. Peabody."

"Yes, sir."

"But it would be better all around if you gave permission, on record, for my partner and me to begin a search. I'd like to start in the quarters. I'll have more officers come in, with the warrant, to assist with a search of the entire premises."

Eve figured the woman couldn't get any paler, but her voice dropped to an unsteady whisper.

"You're going to search the home?"

"With or without your permission, yes. It would be easier, all around, with your permission."

"You should contact your lawyer, Ms. Jones," Shivitz began.

"We have nothing to hide here." Straightening her shoulders, she patted the matron's hand. "I'll give my permission, and I'll contact my lawyer."

"Those are good choices," Eve told her.

"I think it's obvious now that my head's cleared, Nash just needed some time alone, away, to process all this. I know how much it's affected me, and he tends to hold things inside, to stand as the strong one, the head of the household. I think he just needed some time, especially when I was so emotional when I came back from talking to you. He must have found a retreat—there's always one going on, and he'll contact me as soon as he's settled. He'll realize he forgot his 'link, borrow one, and let me know where he is."

"I'm sure that's it." It was Shivitz's turn for a bolstering pat.

"Could you put together a list of current retreats for Lieutenant Dallas? Or it might be quicker, Lieutenant, if Matron checked herself if Nash registered for one today."

"Why don't we do both? Peabody and I'll get started up here."

"Do I have to stay?"

"That's up to you."

"I'd rather not watch you . . . search our things. I'll go down to my office, contact some friends, some associates. It might be someone knows Nash's plans. I'll feel much better when I know where he is, and we can straighten all this out."

"That's fine."

"I'll go down then. Matron."

"It's all going to be fine." Shivitz hooked an arm around Philadelphia's waist, led her from the room. "You'll see. You have faith now, and everything will be fine."

"What the hell was in that soother?" Eve wondered.

"I think Shivitz tipped a little liquor in it, and I think Philadelphia's just gone straight to denial. She can believe what she just said, and delete the rest. Otherwise, it's too much to deal with, and she has to deal. She's wired that way. She has a houseful of troubled kids to keep in line, to keep calm, so she has to deal."

"She's going to have a lot more to deal with. Set up Baxter and Trueheart to assist us, if they're clear. Trueheart's a nonthreatening presence. Toss in Uniform Carmichael and another uniform. It's a big place."

"I'll get it done."

"Meanwhile," Eve said as she moved to Nash Jones's bedroom, "I've got Quilla as a bottomless source. Things are bogus, according to her," Eve began and filled Peabody in as she started the search.

The small bedroom area and few possessions didn't take long. She learned Mr. Jones liked good fabrics, and was practical and thrifty enough to have his shoes resoled.

"Nothing out of line on his pocket 'link," she told Peabody when she checked it. "But it shows some recent deletions from the contact list. Let's get EDD in here, too; they can check all the e-junk, and see if they can dig out the deletions."

"McNab's coming in with Baxter and Trueheart. I figured we'd need an e-man."

"You figured right."

"You know, this all speaks of a pretty simple lifestyle." Standing beside the bed, Peabody took another study of the room. "A box of condoms—but tucked away in the bathroom, not in the bedside table. No sex here on site. The clothes, decent material—it wears longer. Somebody darns his socks."

"Does what?"

"Sews the toes, heels. You know how you can wear a hole in the toe or heel? Somebody darned a couple of his—repaired them."

"Like the shoes. A simple life, one where, from the looks of it, money and possessions don't drive the engine, doesn't mean the halo."

"The halo?"

"Quilla again. Her term for totally good. That's how she sees Jones. Maybe a hidey-hole somewhere." Hands on hips, she did a turn. "But I can't find it."

"If he had something to hide, odds are it's with him."

"Yeah. Left his bedside reader, discs and downloads—mostly halo stuff—some novels, some books on psychology, spirituality, dealing with addictions and low self-esteem, all what you'd expect. Let's move on."

The living area offered little more. The music and vids stuck primarily with the spiritual and uplifting again, with a few random secular options.

Healthy food in the little kitchen. No alcohol or illegals hidden away. Not even a secret stash of candy.

"Got your warrant, LT," Baxter said when he walked in. "Duly served to one Philadelphia Jones. The building's full of kids pretending to be bored the cops are tossing the place. I bet a princely amount of zoner's flowing into the sewer from here right about now."

"Maybe, but they run a pretty tight operation."

"We'll be the judge of that. Your love muffin's starting on main level e-shit, Peabody."

"He's not my love muffin. He's my lean, mean sex machine."

"I stand corrected. Where do you want us to start, Dallas?"

"Basement. Storage. Potential areas of concealment. Work your way up. We'll work our way down. Uniforms should give the residents' rooms a quick pass. I'm not looking for anything there, but we can't leave them out."

"Basement." Baxter sighed at Trueheart, looked down with a shake of the head. "I knew I should've changed these shoes."

"Be glad I don't make you darn your socks."

"Do what?"

"That's what I said. God, this is a snack? Ginger-flavored rice cakes. Cakes of rice are not a snack. I suspect them of evil deeds for this alone. Basement," she repeated.

They found nothing in the private quarters. Eve learned Philadelphia was slightly looser in her reading and personal music choices, mixing in more pure entertainment, with a lot of current options.

On which she made notes in her memo book.

So she could discuss what the kids watched, listened to, talked about, with some practical knowledge, Eve concluded.

She used birth control, skin-care products—a lot of those—and minimal enhancers. A couple of lip dyes, some hair gunk, some eye gunk.

It occurred to Eve, with some embarrassment, that she had more herself.

Not her fault, she thought. It got dumped on her.

 **THEY WORKED THEIR WAY DOWN TO THE** main level where she saw Quilla—the kid was everywhere—giggling over McNab's shoulder as he conducted what she assumed was a standard search on Shivitz's comp.

"Ah, she's crushing," Peabody said quietly. "Who can blame her? He's so cute."

Eve frowned, studied the little tableau. Quilla in her house uniform—but yeah, she'd slicked something shiny on her lips. McNab, his long blond hair in a straight, streaming ponytail down the back of his screaming pink shirt with a purple elephant emblazoned on the front. He wore his usual complement of silver ear hoops. She caught a glimpse of purple airboots under the desk.

Next to Quilla's dull and simple uniform, he looked like the opening act of the circus.

Next to anything, Eve corrected.

They continued down; Quilla Bat-ears glanced up. And yeah, Eve concluded, she had that dewy, dopey, love-struck look in her eyes.

"McNab said I could watch."

"McNab's not in charge. If you get caught meddling in a police search, you'll end up doing time in the Quiet Room."

Though Quilla only shrugged, McNab caught Eve's eye, nodded. "Hey, Quill, this is thirsty work. Any chance of getting a fizzy around here?"

"Zippo. Not allowed in the house."

"Sad."

"Totally sad. But I can ask if I can get some at the market. It's right next door."

"Ask," Eve said, then dug in her pocket for the price of fizzies. "If it's cleared, get a variety pack, and a tube of Pepsi."

"Completely." She took the money, rushed back to the kitchen area.

"That'll keep her busy."

"She's cute and funny," McNab commented. "Smart, too. What's she doing in here?"

"The same as a lot of them. Shit for parents, kicked around, picked up repeatedly for truancy, shoplifting and so on. She's better off here, which doesn't say much for the shit parents. What have you got for me?"

"Not much. I went over the suspect's e-stuff first. I'm taking it in to give it a deeper look, but honest, Dallas, it's mostly for form. Nothing pops. It's all work, work, work. Some correspondence, but nothing funny. Some pictures in files—some personal of him, his family, with some going back a ways. Pictures of some of the kids, but nothing perv-oriented. Some interoffice stuff, kinda jokey with his sister now and again, but mostly just straightforward."

"No searches for transportation, tickets, accommodations?"

"No, not in the last ten weeks. Some of that prior, a booking for some deal in northern PA. He's got all that in a file, too, with some speech he wrote for it, and some notes about a workshop."

"A retreat."

"I guess." He flipped the notebook he had on the desk. "Yeah, the Reaching Inward Retreat. The list I got from the sister says he has the office comp, and they each have a mini upstairs. He has a PPC, a pocket 'link, a memo book. The office comp's all that's in the office."

"He left the 'link."

"I got it." Peabody handed over the 'link, sealed in an evidence bag.

"I took a look, and there's nothing overt," Eve began. "But it looked to me like a couple of contacts had been recently deleted. And your new girlfriend tells me he bought a new disposable in the last couple days."

"She's my little playmate. I've only got one girlfriend." He reached over, wiggled his fingers against Peabody's. "I'll check out the 'link. No PPC on site?"

"Not found. He must have taken it and the memo book with him. I scanned through the minis, didn't see anything, but take them with you, too."

"Will do." McNab dug some gum out of one of the many and copious pockets of his purple baggies, offered it. With no takers he popped one of the little green squares into his mouth. "So the sister's is the same, but she's got budgetary stuff on there, revenue, expenses, a list of benefactors. Admin stuff. Some of that's on here, too. And files for each kid, circumstances and date of admission and/or release. Progress reports, infractions, problem areas, positive areas, like that. It's all coming off pretty clean and pretty blah."

"He's got personal stuff somewhere, and he was in a hurry to get gone. We'll find something."

Two hours later, Eve admitted defeat.

"Either he's a lot more devious than he comes off and McNab will find something back in the lab, or everything here's clean, aboveboard and as boring as ginger-flavored rice cakes."

"They're not so bad," Peabody commented. "Especially if you drizzle just a little chocolate-flavored syrup on them, which negates the purpose, but still. Rice cakes. I think I'm punchy."

"We're lucky our brains aren't leaking out of our ears when we spend half a day combing through this place and the most interesting thing we found was a single smashed joint of zoner inside an air vent that looked like it had been there for months. Maybe years."

She stayed out of the way while McNab and the uniforms hauled out what few electronics seemed worth a second pass.

Shivitz literally wrung her hands. "Our records."

"You were instructed to make copies of anything needed for daily operation."

"What if I forgot something?"

"You never do," Philadelphia assured her.

She'd gone pale again as the effects of the soother wore off. The strain tightened around her eyes, her mouth, but she had her voice under control.

Still, she bit her lip when Uniform Carmichael carried out boxes of archived discs, labeled by year.

"We keep careful records, Lieutenant. We have inspections. We have—"

"I don't expect to find any problem with your operation. Some of this is just procedure."

Eve turned so she faced Philadelphia, looked straight into her eyes.

"I have to impress on you again, if your brother contacts you, you need to persuade him to come in. You don't want him hauled in to Central in cuffs."

"No." She groped for Shivitz's hand. "Please."

"Then convince him to turn himself in. Failing that, find out where he is. Either way, you need to contact me immediately."

"I will. I gave you my word. No one I spoke with has seen or heard from him."

"You've got a sister in Australia."

"I contacted Selma. He hasn't contacted her, and now she's trying everything to find him. I hated to pull her in, and now she's as worried as I am. I even spoke with our father, though Nash wouldn't go to him."

"No?"

"Father would insist he come back right away. He'd never allow Nash the quiet, contemplative time I believe, absolutely believe, he's taking if he understood we had a problem. I'm sure he's just taking time to think, and he'll be in touch with me soon. He wouldn't want me to worry."

She looked around, over, back, as if she expected to see him coming down the steps, striding down a hallway any moment.

"Nash is very protective. He wouldn't want me to worry."

Maybe that was true, Eve thought. Maybe that was the core of it.

She walked out, ridiculously thrilled to be outside again even with the thin spit of sleet splatting on the sidewalk.

"Go with McNab," she told Peabody.

"Always my plan."

"Ha-ha. Do another round on the retreat list, in case he decides to try a late check-in. And let's have the locals have a talk with both the father and the other sister. Just tie that off. Otherwise . . . I'm going to work from home," she said as she started to her car. "If he digs out those contacts, or anything else, I know the second after he does."

"You got that. Hey, you never got your consult with Mira."

"Shit." She stopped, shoved at her dampening hair—and what the hell, dragged the snowflake cap out of her pocket and pulled it on. "Shit," she said again, and yanked out her 'link as she hoofed to the car.

Mira's office contact went straight to the off-hours recording. Cursing again, Eve gave in, pulled on the red gloves, and formulating apologies, tried Mira's personal 'link.

"Eve. I'm sorry we couldn't manage that five minutes between us today."

"I got hung up at HPCCY. Some things are breaking—I think. I've got new information, and a direction. But I could use corroboration on that direction. I'm just heading out now. I hate to ask again, but if I could stop by for just a few minutes . . ."

"I'm actually not quite home yet myself, as I got hung up a bit, too. Dennis and I are going out to see some friends later this evening."

"Oh well, fine." Damn actual life, Eve thought. "If we could set something up for tomorrow."

"We could stop by your home on our way."

"I don't want to mess up your night."

"It's practically on the way. We could be there in about . . . let's say ninety minutes if that works."

"If it does for you, that's great."

"About ninety minutes then. I'll tell Dennis you wore the cap. He'll be pleased."

"Oh, ha. These, too." She waved a red-gloved hand in front of the screen.

Mira laughed. "Very pleased. See you shortly."

She attacked traffic. She wanted home—home where she could take a few minutes to think, to organize her thoughts, put her theories in order before meeting with Mira.

Was she supposed to let Roarke know the Miras were coming? It wasn't a social visit; it was work. He didn't have to let her know if he had a business associate come by. Did he?

Oh hell, she'd never figure all the rules out, so better to err on the side of caution.

She'd just send him a quick text, and that hit somewhere in the middle, she decided.

She ordered his personal 'link, ordered text mode. And had barely begun to compose the text when the whole thing shifted. He came on screen.

"I'd rather hear your voice."

"I'm going to be home in . . . a couple of weeks if this traffic doesn't Get The Hell Moving! How did that asshole get a license to drive a maxibus? *How?* You have to take a test. Just hold it a minute. Fucker."

She skimmed in front of a shiny limo, muttered, "Bite me," at the dignified protest of horns, shimmied in beside the offending bus, then around.

"I swear I'd pull the asshole over and impound the goddamn bus and everyone in it if I had time."

"Yes, I'd rather hear your voice, anytime."

"Better now. I'm about ten minutes out, maybe less. I've had some movement on things, and a whole bunch of bullshit. I need a consult with Mira and couldn't get to her today, so they're going to stop by on their way to some deal."

"It'll be lovely to see them."

"Okay. I just . . . wanted to tell you."

"Because you decided it might fall into the rules. I'm probably a few minutes behind you. Where did you get that fetching cap?"

"Crap." Instinctively, she slapped a hand over the snowflake.

"And those . . . adorable gloves."

"Crap and crap." She dropped her hand. "Mr. Mira. I've got to go to war with these fucking cabs. Later."

She clicked off on his laughter, geared up for battle.

When she finally pulled up in front of the house, she decided the drive home had been more exciting than most of her workday. And that just showed how tedious a full building search could be when people lived like droids.

No sex toys, no porn, she thought as she got out, hunched against the sleet as she walked to the door. No cache of money or ill-gotten gains, no illegal weapons. Just one ancient joint.

Really, how did anyone live that way?

She stepped inside, to the cat, to Summerset, wondering just how many interesting things a full house search of her own would turn up, and that didn't even count Roarke's private office with the unregistered equipment.

"Well," Summerset said, "this is new."

"What? Don't start."

"You appear to be wearing a glittering snowflake, and fuzzy gloves."

"Crap, crap." She yanked it all off. "They were gifts, so knock it off. The Miras are coming by in about an hour. Not socially. It's a consult."

"I believe we can still be cordial and welcoming."

"I can. You'll still have all the cordiality of a corpse."

Since it was the best she could do with her mind so damn crowded, she bolted upstairs, and straight into her office.

She pulled off her coat, tossed it on the sleep chair, then immediately had to lift the cat off it. She should've known better.

She picked up the coat, put down the cat, tossed the coat elsewhere.

Coffee, she thought. Please God, some coffee. Programming some, she just stood, drank half the mug, then breathed out.

Setting it aside, she made some minor adjustments to her board. She sat at her desk, cobbled together some notes, made some additions, reordered them.

Then she picked up the coffee, put her boots up, and let her mind clear.

Because it was clear, the first thing that popped in when Roarke stepped inside was: He's so pretty.

"You couldn't have been more right or more succinct about the traffic. It was bloody vicious."

"We won. We're home."

"You're right. That calls for a drink."

"I guess maybe."

He came over to her first, put his hands on the arms of her chair, leaned down to kiss her.

She surprised him, undid him, by rising up, wrapping her arms tight around him, and making it much more than a welcome-home kiss.

"Well now, I might arrange for bloody vicious traffic daily."

"You don't have to. We live in New York."

"What's all this then?"

"I don't know." She'd surprised herself as much as him. "I guess . . . The Miras this morning, then this couple later. It . . ." Her mind, she realized, wasn't as clear as she'd thought. "I'll have that drink, and tell you."

"All right. Let's have it downstairs. You can come up with Mira if you feel you must," he added, anticipating her protest, "but we should go down, greet them first, as friends."

"You're right." She wrapped around him again, just to hold. "We'll go downstairs."

He tipped her head back, looked into her eyes. "You're not sad."

"No, I'm not sad."

Thoughtful then, he decided, taking her hand as they went back down.

Summerset had lit the fire, and the tree. The parlor looked, well, amazing, she thought. It looked like home—her home—despite its elegance, its exceptional taste and style, the gleam of antiques, the art, the color, the lovely blending of old and new.

"What is it, Eve?"

She shook her head, sat on the arm of a chair because you could do that at home.

"I was in the Miras' house this morning, and thinking how pretty it is there, how calm and pretty and easy to be in. This is, too. Isn't that funny that this is, too? They have a tree. We have a tree. Well, I don't know how many trees we have in here because who could count?"

"Twenty."

"Okay. We have twenty trees." It struck her suddenly. Twenty trees. "Seriously?"

"Yes." He smiled, as much at his own need to fill the house with Christmas as with her reaction. "We'll go around and have a look at all of them sometime."

"It'll take a while. Anyway, they had a fire, and we have one. But it's not that, do you know what I mean? It's the feeling. I used to envy that feeling. I could recognize it. You'd go into somebody's place to interview them, notify them, even arrest them, and you'd recognize the feeling of home when it was there."

"I know that envy, very well." Which, he understood, explained all the trees, among other things.

"I thought when I moved in here it would always be a house, and always be yours. I don't even know when that changed, not exactly, and it became mine. Ours. That's pretty amazing."

"It was a house, one I enjoyed very much. But it wasn't a home until you." He looked around the parlor as she had. Candles and firelight, tree glowing, colors rich, wood gleaming.

"What I put in it was for comfort, for show, or because I could. It mattered to have it, this place. My place. But I could never quite reach that feeling, until you."

"I get that," she realized. "It matters that you mean it, and that I get it." She took a breath while he opened a bottle of wine. "You know how they are, the Miras. So connected, so just right. I swear if I didn't love you, if it wasn't for her, I'd really go for him."

At Roarke's laugh, she shook her head again, took the wine he offered.

"I think I could take him," Roarke considered.

"I don't know. He might surprise you. Anyway, it's not like that really. There's just . . . he's just . . . There's something about him that hits all my soft spots. I didn't know I had some of them."

"I think that's lovely."

"He brought me those silly gloves and that stupid hat, and put them on me like I was a kid. I ended up wearing them because he can't button his sweater right half the time but he hunted up a cap and gloves for me because it's cold out. He's so kind, and they have this amazing connection between them."

She had to take a steadying breath, amazed at how sloppy she felt about . . . all of it.

"I want that. I mean when we've been together like them a couple decades, I want that with us."

"Darling Eve." This time he pressed his lips to the top of her head. "There's more every day."

"It feels like it. Sometimes I don't know how I got through not feeling it. And later, this couple. I need to talk to Mira about her. DeLonna."

"Ah." He sat now. "Sebastian came through. I thought he must have when you didn't ask me to dig him up."

"She goes by Lonna, Sebastian neglected to tell me he'd helped her change her name off the books. Lonna Moon. She and her guy own this swank little club. The Purple Moon."

"I know it."

"You don't own the building, do you?"

"I don't, but I've heard of the club. It has a good rep." His hand glided gently along her thigh. Affection. Connection. "We should go."

"We should. Yeah, we should. I'll get into the whole thing, but what I wanted to say to you was listening to her, seeing them together, it struck close to home. She's solid, no washout, but he worries about her because of what she went through. She has nightmares."

Those eyes, those wild blue eyes met hers. He didn't have to say a thing to say everything.

"Looking at them, *seeing* them, I could see some of us. And it was really good, what I saw. I don't know his story, but there's something there. Slick, he's slick, and looks like he can and has handled himself. But they were connected."

"So." She let out another breath. "I want to let you know if the day comes when you forget how to button-your sweater—when you start wearing those button-sweater deals—I'll fix it."

"Every day there's more," he murmured. Swamped with love, he drew her off the arm of the chair into his lap.

She curled there, utterly content.

"They still have sex. You can tell."

Now he let out a laughing sigh. "I'd as soon not think too deeply on that."

"Me either. I'm just saying that mixing up your socks or buttons doesn't mean you don't have sex." Lifting her head, she touched her lips to his.

"You might wait to indulge yourselves," Summerset said from the doorway, in the tone of a parent catching kids sneaking cookies before dinner. "Your guests are arriving. I've cleared them through the gate."

Eve rolled her eyes as he walked away. "Indulging? You know his problem is he doesn't have anyone bored or stupid enough to indulge with him."

"I wouldn't be quite so sure."

She frowned down at Roarke, saw the knowledgeable gleam in his eyes. "Eeuuww. Don't tell me. Seriously. Don't. Ever. Tell me."

She pulled herself up, and decided she really wanted that glass of wine now.

Roarke rose as well, greeting the Miras when Summerset brought them in.

"Charlotte, you look lovely." The exchange of cheek kisses was followed by a warm handshake for Dennis. "It's so good to see you."

"I appreciate you making the detour," Eve began.

"We're just having some wine." Roarke spoke smoothly before Eve could launch into her case notes. "What can I get you?"

"I'd love whatever you're having. Wouldn't you, Dennis?"

"That'd be nice." He smiled at the tree in his dreamy way. "That's a pretty one. It looks good in here. The whole place looks festive when you drive up. There's nothing like Christmas."

"Dennis loves Christmas." Mira gave him an indulgent look as Roarke led them to a sofa near the fire. "The lights, the music, the bustle. The cookies."

"I have a weak spot for Charlie's snickerdoodles."

"You bake cookies," Eve said with a kind of wonder.

"At Christmas I do, then hide half of them or Dennis wouldn't leave a crumb for company. Thank you," she added when Roarke served the wine. "We're looking forward to your party later this month. It's always memorable."

She turned to Eve. "So. I know you sent me a report this evening, but I didn't have time to read it. Can you fill me in?"

"Yeah, sure. Ah, should we go up to my office?"

"Dennis doesn't mind if we talk shop, do you, Dennis?"

"No."

He settled back comfortably, as someone might to watch an entertaining vid. He always looked comfortable to Eve's eye. In his own skin, in the moment.

"I like hearing about the work. Fascinating, isn't it?" he said to Roarke.

"I couldn't agree more."

"Okay then. Highlights. Nashville Jones is in the wind."

Mira arched her eyebrows. "I see."

"We interviewed Philadelphia Jones this afternoon. I pushed her on the premise the younger brother lured and killed the victims, starting with Shelby Stubacker and Linh Penbroke."

She laid out her theory on that, standing to pace it off, to think on her feet.

"You speculate the younger brother did the killings, and had the basic skills to conceal the bodies in the building he considered his home, his place. And the older brother was complicit."

"He knew something, maybe not until toward the end, but he knew. The sister, I don't think so. Big brother, head of the family, protects the female sib. It's ingrained behavior impressed on him by the parents, and I'd say especially the father. He's in charge."

"Yes, I agree with that."

"Between the time I saw you this morning and my interview with Philadelphia, I met with DeLonna."

"Friend of Shelby's," Mira said, refreshing her memory. "Liked to sing. Remained at HPCCY until she went into a work/study program."

"Yeah. I believe she was an intended victim, and a survivor. I believe she survived because Jones—the elder—found her, after she'd been tranq'd, before the younger had the chance to finish her. He stopped it."

"But she didn't report it before now?" Mira asked.

"She doesn't remember, not clearly. She remembers climbing out the window of her room, just barely fitting through the opening. I checked that and it jibes. Climbing down, running to the subway, riding it, running toward the old building because she wanted to find her friend. She wanted to find Shelby, who'd left, and never sent for her as planned. Couldn't, being dead. But she remembers everything up to that point, then it blurs on her."

"Blurs," Mira asked, "or blanks?"

"Blurs. She dreams about voices, and shouting. Someone talking about cleansing, washing the bad girl clean. She dreams of dark, being cold. Then she remembers, or dreams this feeling as if she was floating, and that's it. She woke up in her bed, back at HPCCY, and the window was shut, and she's wearing her uniform nightclothes. She felt sick and out of it. She has nightmares about it, has had them ever since."

"Voices and sensations only?"

"That's how it comes. Because it wants to come back, but she's suppressing it. I think she heard enough, saw enough to know, but she was a kid, and blocked it."

Mira watched Eve's face. Between them flowed the knowledge there'd been another child, another trauma, another block.

"Very possible, very likely," Mira said after a moment, "from what you say and what we know. The trauma combined with the drug could very well have resulted in a memory block."

"I gave her your card, and I'm hoping she'll contact you. She wants to help. She's got a new life now, a good one. She's got a good man. But she wants to help, wants to know who killed her friends. And who would have killed her if she hadn't gotten the break."

"If she contacts me, I'll make room for her right away."

"People do terrible things to children because they can," Dennis said.

Eve stopped, looked at him.

"The power isn't with the child, you see, but with the stronger, the cannier. There are people who, rather than defend and tend the child, do terrible things. There's little that's truly evil. But that is. You'll help her, Charlie. It's what you do. And you," he said to Eve.

Taking a moment, Eve sat again. "I think, maybe to protect the child, Nashville Jones killed his brother. He got the kid back, put her back in bed, then he disposed of the body. He didn't know there were already twelve girls concealed right there. But he still had to protect his brother, his sister. He still had to do his duty, right? So he arranged for this missionary position, and sent someone to pose as his brother. An opportunity, or a mission of faith. However he managed it."

"Why not send the brother?" Dennis wondered. "I'm sorry, I don't mean to step in."

"That's okay. The brother had emotional issues. He was shy, unskilled, inexperienced. If you study his background, his makeup, then you compare that to the reports on the missionary in Africa, they're two different people. The missionary's devout, friendly, outgoing, interested in photography, compassionate, and so on. None of those words are used when describing Montclair Jones."

"But by sending a substitute in his brother's name," Mira continued, "he could somehow honor his brother, even while concealing the crimes both had committed."

"Then fate stepped in," Eve added, "because sometimes shit happens. The missionary's killed, mauled by a rogue lion. Nobody does DNA or specific ID, because as far as they're concerned, he's Montclair Jones. He's cremated, his ashes sent back here, and that's that. Including a plaque in the new building to memorialize him.

"It's as somebody said to me today, bogus. Jones figured he'd done what he had to do, gave it up to the higher power or whatever worked for him. He'd saved the kid, who's too traumatized and drug-hazed to remember. He'd stopped his brother from, as far as I think he knew, committing murder, and he'd protected him in the end by the pretense that baby brother followed family tradition."

"He'd need to find someone willing to masquerade as the brother," Roarke pointed out.

"Yeah. Jones knows a lot of people in that line. They go to these retreats, plus he was raised in that world. Going to Africa? It's a big opportunity, right, for a missionary type? It's . . . a kind of bartering, maybe. And say the missionary wants to come back one day, that's fine. He comes back as himself, and Jones can say his brother was lost. He's vanished. It's a mystery, but he did his good work, and that's what matters."

"Fascinating," Dennis commented and gave Roarke his smile.

"To kill in defense of another. The innocent. The child," Mira said with a nod to her husband. "A child in his care. His responsibility. The brother, troubled, younger, also his responsibility. Yes, a man who had been raised, trained, indoctrinated to be responsible, to stand as the family head, could make that choice. If he killed his brother, it may have been an accident, a struggle between them with the child at stake."

"I don't think so."

"No, you think, and I largely agree, that while the elder brother was raised to be in charge, the younger was raised to obey him. He would have stopped, at least in that moment. He wouldn't have defied his brother, not face-to-face. But while again I largely agree, he might have been under the influence of drugs or alcohol, or simple fervor."

"Fervor?"

"The religious overtones. A fervor to complete the rite, if indeed it was a rite. If Nashville killed Montclair in that building where he had poured such hope and effort to fulfill what he saw as his duty and destiny, it adds to the complete withdrawal from it."

Once again, Eve sat on the arm of a chair. "I didn't think of that. That plays."

"The abandonment of it, which goes beyond the financial situation," Mira continued. "The Mark of Cain—fratricide. This would weigh on a man of faith and responsibility, even as he justified it. And rather than report to the authorities, he, too, concealed. Not for himself, but for his brother, his family, and the greater mission."

"So what, in the end he decides it was a selfless act?"

"How else could he live with it?" Mira asked.

"Why run now? That's not selfless. That's self-preservation."

"Are you sure he's running?"

"He's gone," Eve pointed out. "He took a suitcase and cash. He's not using credit cards, he hasn't contacted his sister."

"I believe he will, contact his sister. I believe his makeup will demand that he come back. It's his duty."

"Well, that would be easy," Eve replied. "Then all I have to do is prove all the other stuff."

"To continue the theme, I have faith you will. If the girl—woman now—DeLonna—"

"She's just Lonna now. Lonna Moon."

"Lovely name. If she reaches out to me, I'll help her remember. It'll unburden her, and give you what you need."

Two for one, Eve thought. Maybe Jones figured the same. He'd unburdened his brother of evil, and given his sister the illusion she needed.

21 LATER, BECAUSE THEY WERE ALREADY DOWN-
stairs, she had dinner with Roarke in the dining
room. Another fire simmering, another tree glittering. And some really excellent chunky soup of some kind along with
crusty bread slathered in herbed butter.

"Did you ever wish for a sibling?" she asked him.

"My mates were enough. I wouldn't have wished my father and
Meg on anyone else."

"Yeah, I never thought about a brother or sister either. It can be
complicated and full of drama, right? I mean somebody like Peabody, with all her sibs, she's good with it. Happy with it," Eve corrected. "It all adds something for her. I bet they had plenty of fights
growing up, but that's part of it, I think. Probably."

"Likely."

"There's that whole rivalry thing. Who gets what, who doesn't
think they got a fair shake, who wants more—or just wants yours."

"Do you think that plays into it, with the Joneses?"

"I don't know. Just spitballing. Families are minefields, even the good ones have little traps you can step into. You and me, it was what it was. It was overt and ugly and painful, and not much else. It was like that for some of the vics. Not all, but some. It's why you're doing what you're doing with what's still my crime scene."

"It was what it was," he agreed. "And when you're in it, it's just your life, however vicious."

"But when you're out of it and you look back, it's still hard. When you look at somebody else, somebody going through some of the same . . ."

"Who's powerless, particularly. What Dennis said about evil is absolute truth to my mind. We've both seen plenty of it, but when it's a child, it's magnified. If you have the power to stop it for some, if you have the means, it makes a difference."

"I think Jones stopped it, without knowing how far it had already gone. I don't think he could've lived with it if he'd known. Not even for his brother."

"You see him as a good man."

She shook her head. "I see him as a man, and one who's worked to try to make a difference. I'll give him that. But if this went down the way I see it, or along the lines? It's not right. All these years parents, siblings, they've had that hole in their lives. That not-knowing. And okay, maybe, probably, he didn't know. But I see it more as he didn't let himself know. How could he assume Lonna was the first, the only?"

"I'd think," Roarke considered as he tore a piece of bread to share with her, "it could be inconceivable. Your brother—and younger at that. Inconceivable to believe he'd killed, that what you found and stopped wasn't the first time."

"Maybe so." Eve bit into the bread. "Maybe, but that's just shutting your eyes. And more—even giving him that, how could he let the kid live with that nightmare, that not-knowing, or the not being able to face?"

"There we walk the same line." He touched her hand, just a graze. "Homeland did that, and worse, to you. Knowing what Troy did to you, even hearing it, and putting their *mission*, we'll say, above your welfare. Even your life."

He'd never forget, she thought, or forgive. That was fair, she decided. Neither would she.

"And Jones put his brother's welfare—maybe his mission—ahead of the needs and welfare of the child. The kid should've gotten help. She should've gotten justice fifteen years ago."

"I can't argue with you as I agree. But I can see the how and the why of what he did. So can you."

She shook her head again. "That doesn't make it right. He made a martyr out of a murderer, and left a lot of people hurting for a long time."

"Blood's thicker, they say."

"Yeah, I said the same to Peabody before. If that holds true, then he'll do what Mira thinks he will. He'll come back. I have to be ready for him."

In her home office she scraped at every detail she could find on Nashville Jones. Financials—and she sent an e-mail to her go-to ADA to see if she had enough for a warrant to freeze those financials—his medicals, his education, his travel.

Nearly all travel, right back to his childhood, was primarily what she thought of as work related. Retreats, conferences, missions. Spreading the word or gathering more words to spread and different methods of spreading them.

And they called her work-obsessed? As far as she could tell he had very little life outside the work.

She'd been there once, understood the territory.

She ran searches for anything written about him or either house he'd founded.

When she found them, she read carefully, looking for any direction he might have taken.

No favorite places she could see, no haunts, no little cabin in the woods.

Still she culled out anything she found remotely interesting, filed it, then did exactly the same on the brother she believed had died right here in New York, and not thousands of miles away in some lion-eating jungle.

"He never traveled alone," she said, jabbing a finger in the air when Roarke joined her. "Not one time I can find here. Not even to see big sis—and the locals checked her out. Jones didn't take his passport, so he's not hiding on a sheep ranch in Australia, but she let him—even insisted—they check all her communications, so we'd know he hasn't contacted her."

"Some are what they seem," he commented. "Law-abiding."

"Some. When little brother went anywhere, he was either with big brother, big sister, the parents. The father acted as chaperone or whatever they'd call it the single time he went on a mission—a youth group deal. Everything I find has one of them with corresponding travel. So I call a big pile of bullshit on him sailing off to Africa, for Christ's sake, to break his cherry."

"One way to put it. You'd already concluded the younger brother didn't go to Africa."

"Conclusions aren't proof, and neither is this. But it adds weight. I travel," she said. "Now. I travel now. We go places where there aren't dead bodies."

"We do, on occasion. And as you've mentioned it, I thought we might do just that for a few days after the holidays. Go somewhere without corpses."

"Oh."

He flicked a finger down the dent in her chin. "Your usual enthusiastic reaction. I'm thinking warm, blue skies, blue water, white beaches, and foolish drinks with umbrellas stuck in them."

"Oh," she said in an entirely different tone.

"I know your weakness, yes." Now he kissed her lightly. "I thought the island, unless you have some secret desire to see another tropical locale."

Not everybody had a husband with his own island, she thought. She'd even mostly stopped feeling weird about it. Because white sand, blue water hooked her like a fish.

"I could put in for the time, if I'm not in the middle of a hot one."

"We'll imagine us both in several hot ones—on the island. It's already, tentatively, on your calendar."

"That damn calendar has a life of its own."

"Which means so do you."

"Yeah. He doesn't." She gestured to Jones's photo. "His work's his life, and I get it. But he struck me as sort of balanced and content on that initial impression thing. Not like little brother. They surrounded him. No solo travel, like I said—at least none that shows. No particular job, and what he did have they ran. No hint of relationships unless we count Shelby and her famous bjs."

"Let's not."

"No one mentions any friends, none of the staff ever had anything but the lightest, vaguest things to say. He never left an impression. He was weightless. What time is it in Zimbabwe?"

"Too late. And here as well. Sleep on it." He pulled her to her feet. "If Mira's right, and she most often is, he'll come back. At the very least he'll contact his sister. Will she tell you?"

"I think she will. Blood may be thicker, but she's scared, and she's sick. People who are scared and sick call the cops."

"Then sleep on it."

She stopped on her way out with him, looked back at the board. "The last vic? We can't find her. No matches, not yet, and we've been running the search for hours. Feeney's doing a global, and no matches. She's no one."

"She's yours."

For now, Eve thought, that had to be enough.

S he had all the faces, and woke with a faint memory of dreaming of them again. But she couldn't remember what they'd said. She felt as though there was little left for the girls to tell her now.

She had it all in front of her, somehow. If she'd taken the right track, if her beliefs were valid, she would deliver justice, what she could of it, to the victims. She would give answers to those who'd loved and searched for them.

And if she'd gone wrong, if she'd turned the wrong way, she'd go back and start again.

She said as much to Roarke as she dressed for the day.

"You're not wrong, not about the core of it. I've slept on it as well," he added. "And a man doesn't leave his work, work he's devoted to, along with a sister he feels strongly he's bound to protect for no reason."

"A side skirt I haven't turned up, and a sudden need to nail her like a bagful of hammers. And no," she said, "I would've found her if he had an important woman, or if he had an important man for that matter. Plus, sex isn't nearly as important to him as his mission, and his sister. He wouldn't leave her to deal with me alone without some sort of solid purpose or desperation."

"So you're left with his involvement in some way, and a woman whose memory of her experience as a child, almost certainly in that building, is partially blocked."

She sat for a moment, an indulgence, and added to it with more coffee. "I've got the core of it, you're right about that. But I have a whole ream of unanswered questions that keep it from firming up. If it wasn't Montclair Jones in Africa, and I'm pretty damn sure it wasn't, who ended up in a lion's digestive system, and why did he agree to masquerade as Jones's brother? What did Jones do with his brother's body, because the only way a serial killer stops cold is death or incarceration."

"A spanner in the works."

"That's a wrench. I remember that one. Why don't you say *wrench*, because this is America."

"A wrench then. Is it plausible it went somewhat as you see it, but on that night when DeLonna was taken, Jones discovered them, but rather than play Cain, his brother was afraid of the discovery, of his brother's righteous wrath, of the thought of being exposed, going to prison, he agreed to go away, to go to Africa. Where he was able to control his urges for that short time, perhaps even believed that higher power he'd been raised on had given him a sign. Then fate or justice, or whatever you chose, intervened to punish him."

"I don't like it. I don't like it because it's just over the edge of plausible. And I don't like it because I can't believe, and neither can you, that after killing twelve—and the time line reads the count comes in at under three weeks. Twelve murders in what comes out to roughly eighteen days. Somebody does that, he doesn't just stop, and say, 'Hallelujah, I repent, and I'm going to Zimbabwe to spread the good word.'"

He gave her a friendly little poke. "You just like saying Zimbabwe."

"It's hard to give up. But regardless, my 'I don't like it' stands. But it's plausible."

She got up. "I'm going to contact Zimbabwe now, and review my notes one more time before I head in."

"I'll walk with you." He slid a hand around her waist and they started out, and the cat streaked by them. "That's a place we've never been. Africa."

"We haven't. Have you?"

"Not to spend any quality time, so to speak. There are, however, many exceptional channels for smuggling in Africa. But that was long ago." He danced his fingers up her ribs. "We could go, take a safari."

"You've got to be kidding. I'm not sure cows aren't going to try some payback and stage a mass revolution, why would I risk going where there are lions just walking around loose, and really big snakes who'll wrap around you and squeeze and swallow you whole? And, oh yeah, quicksand. I've seen the vids. Of course, now I know how to deal with quicksand if that ever happens."

"Do you now?"

"Yeah, long story. I'll give you some tips sometime. The river's probably the thing."

"Which river? I think Africa has several."

"Not in Africa. Here. Jones could have weighed his brother down, dumped him in the river. Or taken him out to New Jersey, up to Connecticut, somewhere where there's a lot of ground, woods, buried him. They've got a van now, which Jones didn't take on his getaway. Maybe they had one then, too. Something to check."

"While you do, I'm in my office."

She went to her desk first, saw the incoming light blinking, ordered the messages up.

"Damn it!"

Roarke stopped in his doorway, turned around. "Bad news?"

"No, no, Zimbabwe sent me an e-mail with attachment a few hours ago. Stupid Earth, axis, revolving crap. It's a picture. Two pictures."

Curious now, Roarke walked over to study them with her. One showed a man wearing a safari-style hat, amber sunshades, a khaki shirt, and pants. He smiled out, a camera strapped around his neck, a little white building at his back.

"Supposed to be Montclair Jones. It *could* be him. Same coloring, same basic body type. Hat and sunshades make it tough to be sure. Same with the group shot here."

In that one, the man, similarly dressed, stood with several others in front of the same building.

"I can enhance, sharpen it up. I can do that. I can run a match with his last ID shot. But . . . before I do."

She turned to her 'link, ordered Philadelphia's personal contact.

Philadelphia answered before the first beep had completed. "Lieutenant, you found Nash."

"No. I'm sending you a picture. I want you to tell me who this person is."

"Oh. I was so sure that . . . Whose picture? Sorry, you don't know, otherwise why would you ask."

"It's coming your way now."

"Yes, I see. Give me a moment. There it is. Oh, it's—" Then she shook her head, sighed. "My brothers are so much on my mind, for a moment I thought it was Monty. But it's . . . what was his name? He worked with us for a short time, though he rarely stayed in one place long as I recall. He's actually a cousin, distant, which we discovered as he and Monty looked more like brothers than Nash and Monty. It's on the tip of my tongue. Kyle! Yes, yes, Kyle Channing, a cousin on my mother's side. Third or fourth or fifth."

"You're sure of that?"

"Oh yes, that's Kyle. But this had to have been taken years ago. He'd be in his forties now. How did you get this picture?"

"I'm coming to you," Eve said, and broke connection, then slapped her hand on the desk.

"I knew it."

"Plausible alternatives or not, it seems your theory is on the mark."

"Jones sends the cousin in his brother's name, with his brother's ID, documentation. Maybe he paid him, blackmailed him, or just asked for a favor. But Montclair Jones didn't go to Africa. He didn't die in Africa. He killed twelve girls. His brother stopped him before he could make it thirteen. And he dealt with him. I've got to go."

"Contact me, will you, if Jones reappears? I'd like to hear the whole story."

"Me, too."

She grabbed up her 'link, tagging Peabody as she dashed downstairs. "Meet me at HPCCY, now."

"Okay, I'm just—"

"No. Zimbabwe sent pictures—and Philadelphia just identified a man named Kyle Channing, not her brother."

"You were right."

"Fucking A."

She yanked her coat off the newel post. "Get there." As she swung the coat on, she remembered taking it up to her office the evening before. So how did it . . . Summerset, she realized, and just decided not to think about it.

Philadelphia was pacing the halls when Eve came in.

"Lieutenant, I'm very confused, and I'm very worried. I'm worried something must have happened to Nash. I contacted hospitals, health centers, but . . . I think I should file a Missing Persons report."

"We've got a BOLO out on him. He's not missing. He's just not here."

"He could've become ill," she insisted. "The stress of these last few days—"

"This goes back a lot longer." She glanced around, watching kids come out of here, head to there, clomp out of there, slump their way elsewhere.

"What's going on?"

"If I *knew* I'd . . . You mean the residents. Breakfast shifts, early classes, or personal sessions." She wore her hair down today, and pulled nervously at the ends. "It's important to keep the children on routine."

"I don't think you want to discuss this out here." Eve signaled to Shivitz. "My partner's on her way. Send her into Ms. Jones's office when she gets here."

Eve went into the office, waited for Philadelphia to follow, shut the door. "The photo you identified as Kyle Channing was taken in Zimbabwe fourteen years ago. At that time, Channing was going under the name Montclair Jones, with all accompanying documentation."

"That's ridiculous. That's impossible."

"Contact your cousin." Eve gestured to the desk 'link. "I'd like to speak with him."

"I don't know how to contact him. I don't know where he is."

"When's the last time you saw or spoke to him?"

"I don't know. I'm not sure." She sat, hugged her elbows. "I barely knew him. He spent more time with Nash. Kyle's a nomad, he travels. He stayed with us, worked with us for a short time years ago when he was between missions. My brother Monty went to Africa, Lieutenant. He died there."

"No, he didn't. Your brother Monty fit in nowhere, was troubled, was shy of people, and could never compete with either you or Nash. He developed an attachment, an unhealthy one, for Shelby Stubacker, one she probably initiated, one she certainly exploited."

She didn't pause when Peabody slipped in.

"And when she'd gotten what she wanted from him—his assistance in getting her cleanly out of the system—she cut him off. Being a kid, being a tough kid, she probably did or said something that hurt him, that pissed him off, that made him feel worthless."

"No, no. No. He would have talked to me."

"Talked to his sister about the thirteen-year-old giving him blow jobs? I don't think so. Now he's ashamed. He knows he's done something bad, something against the code, against all of his upbringing. And it's her fault. It's Shelby's fault. One of the bad girls," she added, thinking of what Lonna remembered.

"She needs to be punished, or saved, or both. He needs to make it right, to . . . wash it away. And the night he plans to do this, she comes in—to *his* home, to The Sanctuary—because this place, this bright, clean, new place isn't *his*—he's waiting. She thinks it's hers, that she'll have her bad girl club there, but she won't. Even though she comes in with another girl, she won't make it hers."

"You can't know this, believe this. You can't."

"I can see it," Eve countered. "I can put together everything I know, and see it. She probably tells him to get lost, but he's ready for that. Probably put the sedative in some brews. He knows she'll barter for that, let him stay if he gives her something in return."

Yes, she could see it. The big, empty building, the young girls, the man with his offering. And with his mission.

"They'll take the beer. They've got snacks they bought at the market next store, so they eat, they drink, Shelby probably shows off the place, talks about her plans with this other girl, this pretty Asian girl. They start to feel off, and by the time they understand, if they ever did, it's too late. They pass out."

"Please stop." Tears rolled. "Please."

"Over the next couple weeks, other girls come, or he brings them in himself. He knows his avocation now, his mission now. He knows enough carpentry to build the walls. I imagine he took pride in it, made sure he did good work. He'd never be alone. They'd be with him, in the home he made. Something of his.

"But the night DeLonna sneaks out, and comes there looking for Shelby, it doesn't go the way it's supposed to. Nash comes, Nash sees. Nash doesn't understand."

"DeLonna. She never—"

"Yeah, she did." Eve placed the flats of her hands on the desk, leaned in. "She wanted to see Shelby, so she climbed out her bedroom window one September night and went to the old building. I found her, and she remembers most of it. She'll remember more. That night your older brother found your younger brother in the building. They shout, they fight, your brothers, when Nash finds DeLonna, drugged, naked, the tub filled and waiting for her. You tell me what Nash would have done if he found his brother about to drown a young girl, a young girl in your care."

"It couldn't—it would have broken his heart. I'd have known."

"Not if he didn't want you to know. He's supposed to protect you, he's in charge. This terrible thing was happening when he was in charge. His brother is the one who's broken. He brought DeLonna, still unconscious, back when he'd taken care of Monty, dressed her in her nightclothes, closed her window. And he said nothing to you."

"No, she has to be mistaken." But both doubt and horror crept into Philadelphia's voice.

"He never told you. How could he? You could never know the terrible thing your brother had done, the terrible thing he'd had to do to the youngest of you. So he told you he'd sent Monty to Africa."

"But no. No. Monty told me he was going to Africa." Hope rose in her voice, into her eyes. "You're wrong, you see? Monty came to me, said Nash was sending him. He was afraid, and he cried, asked me to let him stay. Nash and I argued about it."

Eve's eyes sharpened. "When was this?"

"Just days before. Just days before he left. Nash was absolutely un-yielding, so unlike himself, and pushed it all through so quickly. He said Monty had to go, for his own sake. Something about it being the only way, the only choice. He wouldn't even let me go with them when he took Monty to the transpo center."

"Was Kyle still here?"

"No. No . . . ah . . ." Little hitches of fear came back to bounce in her words. "I think he'd left a day or two before, but I don't really remember. It was an upsetting time. I felt we were sending Monty off to strangers, to a place he didn't know, to try to be something he couldn't be. But he did so well. Nash was right. He—"

"It was never him. It was Kyle. You didn't tell me any of this, the argument, the upset about leaving."

"I didn't see how our personal upset so long ago pertained. There has to be another explanation for all of this. Nash will explain everything."

"How long was he gone, supposedly taking Monty to the transpo center? Don't lie to me now," Eve said when Philadelphia hesitated. "It won't help your brother."

"He didn't come back for hours. He was gone all day. I was so angry. I accused him of staying away so he wouldn't have to face me, after what he'd done. It hurt him. I remember how he looked when I said it."

"What did he do when he got back from taking Monty away?"

"He . . . he went into the Quiet Room. It wasn't fully set up yet. We were still doing that, but I remember very clearly, as we were both so upset, barely speaking to each other, that he went in there, said he wasn't to be disturbed."

"In there," Eve considered, "where you put the plaque for Montclair."

"Yes, it's our meditative, restorative space. Nash stayed in for more than an hour, maybe nearer two. We avoided each other until the next day when we got an e-mail from Monty to let us know he'd arrived safe. And he said how beautiful it was, how it felt like the most spiritual place on Earth. It was such a happy, positive note, I apologized to Nash. I said I'd been wrong. Things went back to normal. We were so busy putting everything in place, getting a new routine."

"Peabody, the Quiet Room. Start going over it again. This time we're taking it apart."

"Yes, sir."

"Why?" Philadelphia demanded. "You already searched."

"We're looking again. Still setting it up, you said. What does that mean, exactly?"

"I just meant we hadn't finished the painting or having the benches installed. We didn't want it to look like a chapel as much as a peaceful, meditative space. We were still putting in the water feature, the wall fountain, the flowers and plants."

"Okay. You can go about your usual routine. I'll be with my partner. Nobody comes in there."

"Lieutenant." She stood there, the sister between two brothers, looking stricken. "Monty—Monty never went to Africa."

"No, he didn't."

"You think, you actually believe Nash . . . hurt him. He couldn't. He's incapable of harming someone. And he loved Monty, deeply. He would never hurt him. I swear it to you."

"Then where is he? Can you tell me where either of your brothers are?"

"No, I can't. I pray you find them."

Eve pulled out her 'link as she left the office and made her way to the Quiet Room.

"Electronics aren't allowed in there," Shivitz told her.

Ignoring her, Eve stepped in. Peabody already had the few pieces of art off the walls, running a miniscanner over them.

"Death or incarceration," Eve said.

"The two things that stop a serial killer."

"Exactly right. Roarke."

"Lieutenant," he said from his 'link to hers.

"I need a favor. Jones's financials come off balanced, nothing off."

"Would you like me to take a look at them?"

"No, his sister runs them, so there wouldn't be anything in there. It's possible he has another account, one she doesn't know about. One he's kept under the radar."

"Prying into someone else's money isn't a favor. It's fun."

"I figured you'd say that."

"I'll let you know if I find anything."

"I think he might use his brother's name in it. Maybe look for Montclair as a surname."

"You'll only annoy me if you tell me how to play my game."

"Okay. Have fun."

She clicked off. "Two ways this goes," she told Peabody. "Either Jones took baby brother off, ostensibly to transpo, killed him, disposed of the body, which makes it seriously premeditated murder. Or he took him somewhere and had him locked up."

"Death or incarceration."

"Yeah. Death, we find Jones and sweat the details out of him. Incarceration? We find out where, because locking someone up takes money and a place that locks people up, and isn't prison."

"An institution?"

"Which takes money. Roarke's looking for the money. Let's see if Jones left us anything to go by in here."

"You think he hid something in here?"

"I think he didn't just sit in here meditating for a couple hours when he could have gone to his quarters or to his office, or just stayed the hell away for a while longer. According to the all-knowing, all-seeing Quilla, he still spends a lot of time in here."

Eve rolled her shoulders. "Let's take it apart."

22 THEY TOOK PICTURES OUT OF FRAMES, PULLED covers off cushions, emptied pots of their plants and dirt.

"She said they were still setting up, still installing, still painting." Eve gave the walls a narrow look. "Maybe he had the same idea as his brother, hid something behind the walls."

"We'll need a bigger scanner."

Odds were low, Eve thought, but . . . "Let's get one down here. He's shocked, guilty, living a lie now. Comes in here to think, to pray, meditate, whatever. He's taken his brother away, put him away, can't look his sister in the eye. He's head of the family," she continued, wandering the room. "He's done what he believes, or convinced himself to believe, is the right thing. He's got to shoulder this alone. But that's not what they do, right?"

"Scanner and a couple of sweepers on the way," Peabody told her. "What?"

"The shouldering-it-alone thing. That's not it. It's the whole trusting the higher power, right?"

"Well . . ."

"There's no religious stuff in here though. No crosses, Buddhas, pentacles, stars."

"They're nondenominational. But they have symbols, the elements."

"What symbols, what elements?"

"The plants—growing things, earth. The candles for fire. The mural there of clouds, that says air to me. And the—"

"Fountain. The fountain's water. He found his brother about to drown Lonna. Water."

The thin, clear sheet of water slid down a two-foot section of the wall over what she assumed was a faux stone veneer. It fell soft and musical into a narrow trench designed to resemble copper gone green with verdigris where it pooled over little white pebbles.

"It's a pretty one," Peabody commented. "We always had fountains back home—solar ones—in the gardens. And my dad built this really gorgeous little stone fountain in the solarium. I guess that was our quiet room. It was full of plants and stone benches, floor cushions. Not so different than this, except for the glass walls. We used to—you don't care."

"How do you turn this thing off?"

"We were solar run, almost completely, but something like this probably has a master shutoff in their utility space. It probably has a safety switch somewhere though, in case it goes haywire and starts spewing water everywhere."

Peabody looked up, frowning at the top bar. "It's a nice design—see, that delivery up there looks like the ceiling molding, blends in, so it gives the illusion the water's just flowing right out of the wall. But you'd want the safety switch where you could reach it."

She hunkered down, then began to crawl on all fours around the trough. "I just don't see . . . wait, here we go. You can barely see this panel." She opened it, turned the little switch inside.

The run of water slowed, dripped, stopped.

"Huh. Good eye."

"Peabodys are handy." And the handy Peabody sat back on her heels. "What this does, is recycles. The water comes down into the pool, then it runs back up through the pipe system behind the wall."

"It doesn't drain?"

"You'd drain it if there's a problem."

"Twelve dead, missing suspects equals a problem."

"Right." Peabody returned to all fours, turned another switch, and with a gurgle, the water level began to drop.

"Peabodys are handy." Eve knelt down, shoved up her sleeve, and began to push through the layer of pebbles. "We need a bucket or something."

"I'll get a bucket or something."

Eve continued to dig through the draining water, the smooth white stones. Probably nothing here, she thought. He probably just sat in here feeling sorry for himself and asking the universe why his brother turned out to be a homicidal whack job.

But then her fingers hooked on something. When she tugged it free, she held up a dripping pendant on a silver chain.

Half a pendant, she corrected, like half a puzzle piece inscribed with NASH on one side, BROTHERS on the other.

"Look here, Peabody," she said when she heard the door open. "A clue."

"Wow, you made a big fucking mess in here."

"Quilla." Damn it. "You can't be in here."

"I just want to see. How come you made such a big fucking mess? Was that in the fountain? Why would somebody put their unity necklace in the fountain? It's all wet."

"Fountains will do that. Unity necklace?"

"Sure. Some of the kids get them with their BFFs. You know, we're two halves of the same whole, or we fit each other just right, some crap like that. It's total lametown."

But even as she said it, Quilla eyed the pendant as if she wanted one.

"Maybe. Do you wear your own name, or the BFF's?"

"Duh. The BFF's. It's the point, right?"

"Okay. Go away."

"Come on, everybody's creeping around out there like they're afraid to wake up some monster. It's boring."

"Go be bored. Peabody," Eve snapped when her partner came in with a big white bucket.

"Oh hey, you really shouldn't be in here right now."

"It's totally not the Quiet Room, not with you guys in here. Are you going to empty the fountain? I could help."

"No," Eve said firmly. "Go."

"Shit, talk about lametown."

She sulked her way out.

"This has a match. It'll have Monty on it."

"They had unity necklaces. That's mostly a girl or a couple thing, and kind of on the young side for men."

"He put Monty's in here, so he put his in here. That way he could keep them, hidden away, but together. Stanch some of the guilt maybe, symbolize cleansing; we'll let Mira chew on that one. Bag it."

Peabody took the pendant, set down the bucket. "Aren't you going to take the stones out?"

"Let me just . . . got it. And that's the set."

She held up the second half with MONTY inscribed on one side and FOREVER on the other.

"Names on the fronts, 'brothers forever' on the backs. United, coming and going. But he couldn't make himself wear his, not after what was done. He couldn't allow his brother to keep his. But Jones would always know they were here. He could sit in here, think of his brother, tell himself what he'd done had been for the best."

"It's sad, when you think about it."

"Maybe it's sad, but it's also stupid. Real responsibility means doing what's right, even when it's hard. Dealing with his brother himself, one way or the other? That's self-indulgence. It's stealing a dog."

"A dog? Oh, like DeWinter and Bones. Okay, but the dog's really happy."

"The dog could've been just as happy if the situation had been dealt with properly, by the rules of law. And something's missing."

"Missing?"

"Something to represent the sisters." She went back to digging through the stones. "And wouldn't he also feel responsible for the cousin? Wouldn't he think I sent him to his death, or something like that? He'd need to . . ."

As she dug, her eyes tracked to the plaque:

In Loving Memory of
Montclair Jones
Beloved Brother of
Selma, Nashville, and Philadelphia
He lives in our hearts.

"'He lives,'" Eve muttered. "Take that plaque off the wall."

"You want the plaque off the wall?" Scratching her nose, Peabody studied it. "It's screwed on. I need to get—"

"Quilla," Eve said, barely raising her voice.

The girl poked her head in. "I was just—"

"Never mind that. Get me a screwdriver thing."

"I'm on that!"

"This is just adding weight," Eve said as she gave up and started scooping out the wet stones into the bucket. "It's not telling us where Jones is, or confirming his brother's alive."

"I've got one!" Quilla raced in, a battery-operated screwdriver in her hand. "Can I do it?"

"No. Peabody."

"Why don't you hold the screws when I take them out?" With a humming whirl, Peabody set bit on screw.

"How come you want to take it off the wall? It's been up there forever. Matron's going to have six baskets of kittens when she sees what you've done in here. How come you—"

"Quiet. I might forget you're in here where you're not supposed to be if you're fricking quiet."

Quilla rolled her eyes at Eve's back, but closed her mouth firmly.

"Last screw. It's heavier than it looks. Hold that side, Quilla, so it doesn't— There."

Peabody lifted it from the wall. "They went for real bronze. It's got serious weight, and . . . It's double-sided."

"The cousin's on the back," Eve said.

"Nail, head, hit."

When Peabody turned it around, Eve read:

With deep regret and sorrow, in memory of Kyle.
A man of faith, loyalty, and pure spirit.

"Who's Kyle?" Quilla demanded. "How come he has to face the wall. That doesn't seem fair."

"Really doesn't. Bag it, Peabody. Got something else." She pulled out a little gold heart on a thin chain. "Oldest sister's. It's got Selma inscribed on the back."

Peabody walked over with an evidence bag. "It just feels sadder."

"Screw sad," Eve stated, and dug in again. "And here we are, the missing piece."

Eve held up a ring.

"Wow! That was in there, too? What else is in there?"

"Don't touch anything," Eve snapped at Quilla.

She examined the ring, its entwined hearts with a tiny white stone at their intersection.

"It's pretty," Quilla said, but kept her hands behind her back.

Peabody huffed as she sealed the heavy plaque. "The kind of ring you give a sweetheart."

"Is it?" With that in mind, Eve turned it, aimed toward the light. "Good call. It's inscribed inside. *P&P=1 heart*."

"Let's find out who the second P is. Clear out," Eve ordered Quilla. "And keep it zipped."

"Copy that." She grinned. "This is fucking frosty stuff. I'm going to write about it."

"Everybody's writing about something. Have the sweepers take the evidence in, log it, and seal the room."

"Copy that," Peabody said with a smile. "I'm just going to put the plants back in the pots so they don't die."

"Make it fast."

She walked out and up to Shivitz's station. "Where's Ms. Jones?"

"She's in session."

"Get her out, now, or I will."

"I think you're cold and cruel. I'm sorry for you."

"Think whatever you like, just get her."

With her nose pointed toward the ceiling, Shivitz stalked down a hallway. Moments later, Philadelphia walked quickly back the same route.

"What is it? What happened?"

"Who's the other P on this?"

"Oh my goodness!" For a moment, light bloomed in her eyes. "Oh, where did you find it?" The light still shining, she reached for it. "I thought I'd lost it. I had lost it, years ago. It broke my heart a little."

"Who's P?"

"Peter. Peter Gibbons. He was my first love. We were just teenagers, but we were so urgently in love. My parents didn't approve, of course. We were so young, and he was . . . he was a boy of logic and science, not faith. He gave me this on my eighteenth birthday, right before I left for college."

Eve said nothing as Philadelphia slipped it on her finger, studied it with a soft smile. "He went off to college, too, but we vowed we'd marry one day, have a family. Of course that wasn't to be. I married a man my father approved of. It didn't work out for either of us. He's a good man, my former husband, but we were never really happy. I wonder if you ever feel for someone the way you feel for your first love."

She looked up from the ring. "Thank you so much, but where did you find it?"

"Where your brother Nash put it, along with your sister Selma's gold heart pendant."

"Selma's little heart—but . . ."

"And the unity necklaces that belonged to him and your other brother. All of them were buried under the stones of the fountain."

"But that doesn't make any sense." The light went out of her eyes. "Why would he take my ring, why would he—"

"Where's Peter Gibbons?"

"I—we haven't kept in close touch. He's a doctor, a psychiatrist. He runs a small private institute upstate."

"Where?" Eve demanded just as her 'link signaled.

"It's in the Adirondacks, near Newton Falls. The Full Light Institute for Wellness." Pressing a hand to her heart, Philadelphia rubbed it there in shaky circles. "You think Monty's there. You think Nash took Monty to Peter."

"Hold on." She yanked out her 'link. "What?"

"Reporting as requested, Lieutenant. The secondary account, under the name Kyle Montclair, opened fifteen years ago, had an initial deposit of eight thousand even. There've been small but regular deposits thereafter, with all autopayments going to—"

"The Full Light Institute for Wellness."

"I don't know why I bother if you're going to step on my lines."

"It's upstate, near some place called Newton Falls."

"I'm aware," he said dryly. "I completed my assignment."

"I've got another. I need to get there, as fast as possible."

"All right. The West Side transpo center, private air station. Twenty minutes."

"Thanks. Big thanks."

"I need to go with you," Philadelphia said when Eve clicked off.

"If what you believe is true, all true, I have to see my brothers. I have to speak with my brothers."

"That's probably a good idea." She glanced around as two sweepers came in with a portable scanner, gestured toward the room.

"I just need to tell Matron."

"You've got two minutes. Peabody," she called as she stepped back toward the room. "With me. Quilla, for Christ's sake, stay out of here."

"What's going on?"

"Lots of official stuff. Look," she said, relenting a little, "you helped, so I'll fill you in later. Peabody, we're moving."

S he'd expected an air shuttle, which was bad enough. But found herself, churning stomach and all, loading onto a jet-copter with Roarke at the helm.

"In the back," she ordered Philadelphia, and shoved ear protectors at her. "Put these on, keep them on."

"This is the ult," Peabody declared, and harnessed herself in. "I've never been to the Adirondacks. I should've worn snow boots. I bet there's snow."

"We'll survive. Recap." She brought Roarke up to speed, filled in the Peter Gibbons connection for both him and Peabody. It helped keep her mind off the fact she was flying, at great speed, in a toy with blades. It didn't help when they flew, at great speed, over snow-covered mountains.

That looked entirely too big, entirely too close.

"Just some crosswinds," Roarke told her when the copter shuddered.

"He couldn't just stay in the city, there are lots of places in the city, but oh no, he's got to do this in some mountain cabin where there's nothing but rocks and trees. Fucking, fucking big rocks and trees."

"It's gorgeous!" Peabody, her nose plastered to the window, bounced in her seat. "There's a lake! It's all frozen."

"When we crash into it, we'll bounce instead of drown."

Roarke laughed, began to circle.

She gripped the sides of her seat like lifelines. "What are you doing!"

"Descending, darling. There's the institute."

Teeth gritted, she forced herself to look down. It wasn't a cabin in the woods, but a large, sprawling complex in the valley of the really big, snowy mountains. From her reluctant bird's-eye view, it resembled a very large mansion, more, she corrected, an important school.

Then because it made her dizzy, she stopped looking below, just held on until she felt the copter touch smoothly down.

She climbed down to the pad immediately, waiting for her legs to get solid again. She wasn't quite there when several people ran toward the pad from the main building. Even slightly queasy, she recognized security when it charged toward her.

"This is a private institution. I need to ask you to—"

Eve just held up her badge. "Peter Gibbons."

"I'll need your business with Dr. Gibbons."

"No, you don't. He does. He sees me now, or I'll have this place surrounded by cops, and shut down. Gibbons," she repeated.

"We'll take this inside."

"Nobody leaves the premises." She fell in line with him. Peabody had been right about the snow, but the pathways were pristine, cutting neat stone paths through the blankets of white. "How long has Montclair Jones been here?"

"I can't discuss patients with you."

Didn't have to, Eve thought. He'd just confirmed her suspicions.

Inside, the building was church-quiet. Not hospital-like so much as cushy rehab center for the really rich. Plants thriving, floors sparkling, even a gas fire simmering.

"Wait here," security told her. His two companions stood on guard as he walked up a short sweep of stairs.

"Will you let me see Monty?" Philadelphia asked.

"We'll get to that."

"You're going to arrest him. Both my brothers. You're going to put them both in prison."

Eve said nothing, but watched a man hurry down the stairs. Average height, average looks until you took a second study. Sharp eyes of winter blue, a strong jaw added something.

"I'm Dr. Gibbons," he began. Those winter blue eyes widened, then went warm as summer. "Philly." He moved right past Eve, hands extended, gripped both of Philadelphia's. "You look the same."

"No. Of course I don't."

"To me you do. Nash contacted you. I'm so glad. I'm terribly sorry, but he couldn't keep this from you. I couldn't keep it from you."

"You've been keeping it from everyone for fifteen years."

He turned, eyes cooling again when they met Eve's. "No, not what you're thinking. We should go up to the conference room. My office is a bit small to fit everyone."

"Where is Montclair Jones?"

"His room's on the third floor, east wing." At Philadelphia's gasp, he looked at her again. "I'm so sorry. Nash is with him. If I could explain things to you—it's Lieutenant Dallas, correct?"

"That's right. Explaining's a good start. Peabody, I want you on the door of Jones's room."

"Neither of them would leave, but I understand. Security will escort you," he told Peabody.

As Peabody peeled off with security, Eve went with Gibbons up the stairs.

"Just this way. Nash came to my home yesterday evening. He was in a state of deep anxiety, even panic."

"I bet."

Gibbons opened a door, gestured.

It struck her more like a lounge than a conference room, though there was the requisite long table. Gibbons led Philadelphia to a sofa. "Can I get you anything? Your hands are cold. Some tea?"

"No, nothing."

"You're still wearing it," he said quietly.

"No." She looked down at the ring, then up at him. "I . . . oh, Peter."

"This is difficult for you. For us all." He sat beside her, took her hand in his, then met Eve's eyes again.

"I should start fifteen years ago. We were fairly new at that time. I'd come on board the year before, at the inception. I'd kept in touch with Nash over the years."

"I didn't know that."

"We'd both married, both divorced. You had your life, and I was making mine. Nash contacted me all those years ago, shaken, desperate. He told me Monty was in trouble, that he'd tried to hurt one of the girls in your care, and didn't seem to understand the scope of his actions. The girl was safe, but he couldn't allow Monty to be around the children, couldn't allow him to go on without serious psychiatric help. Of course I agreed to take him as a patient, though we disagreed when he insisted you weren't to know, Philly."

"At the very least, Montclair Jones had committed assault," Eve pointed out.

"Should the police have been notified? Perhaps. But a friend asked me to help his brother. I did. When Monty came here he was like a child. He remembered me, and that helped. He was happy to see me, and assumed you'd be coming any day, Philly, as I was here."

"He always liked you, so much," Philadelphia said.

"And that helped," Peter replied. "He'd been afraid he was being sent away, to Africa of all places. His mental and emotional states were very fragile."

"Like my mother," Philadelphia added.

"He's not suicidal," Gibbons assured her. "Has never been, though we took precautions initially. I took it slowly with him at first. He was passive, obedient. He believed if he behaved, he could go home again, or you and Nash would come here. When we talked of what happened, he said the girl was bad, and he wanted to cleanse her in the waters of home, and once clean she could stay home. They would be home."

"He would have drowned her," Eve said.

"In his mind, he was helping her. Washing her clean of sin, giving her life—not taking it. His mother died in sin. That's what your father believed, Philly."

"I know. I don't. I can't. But our father does."

"And impressed that on Monty, and Monty believed he might end the same way and be cast out from home."

"Oh God. We tried so hard to make him feel safe."

"His illness prevented that. I've told Nash how I feel about the treatment both he and your mother received. We'll talk about that later. But with Monty, whenever I tried to go deeper into the root of that illness, he'd become agitated, often to the point we'd need to se-date him. Instead of progressing, he regressed. Nothing I've done, tried to do, nothing has reached him."

"He killed twelve girls," Eve interrupted. "He never mentioned it?"

Frustration ran over Gibbons's face as he shook his head. "He talked of cleansing rites, of home, and never having to leave it. He no longer talks of going home as he believes this is his home. Through the sessions it became clear that if he were allowed to leave, he would attempt this cleansing again. He sees this as his mission. He sees himself as finally having a purpose, as he sees you and Nash have. To save the girls, to cleanse them, and bring them home."

"Twelve of them," Eve said.

"I suspected there might have been another attempt, but I could never reach him, never bring out what he'd done. I wasn't able to get him to speak about why he had this mission, and the sexual elements of it. I can only tell you now that neither Nash nor I knew, rather than Nash finding him with the first before he could finish, he'd found Monty with the last.

"I could spend hours discussing his psyche with you, explaining my opinion on the whys, the hows, and how he's concealed and sup-pressed what he's done. But I can tell you he believes he did what was right and necessary, that his brother didn't understand, didn't trust him, didn't believe in him so he was unable to do his work. It's only been in the last few years that he's been able to rebond with Nash to some extent."

"His psyche is something for you and other shrinks to argue over. He killed twelve girls, attempted to kill another. Instead of being brought to justice, he's lived here, in comfort, without consequences."

"I wouldn't agree about the consequences. We didn't know about the murders. When he understood Monty was responsible, Nash came here, and told me everything."

"You still didn't contact the police."

"We were about to when you arrived. Nash wanted to spend a little time with his brother before he, with me accompanying them, brought Monty back to New York and turned him over to you."

Gibbons took Philadelphia's hand again. "Nash was shattered when he came to me last night, Philly. Because he knew he'd have to give his brother to the police. The brother you both love, the brother he feels responsible for. And you'd have to know what Monty's done."

"I need to see them both."

"I know. Monty's nervous about going on a trip, about going back to New York. I've given him something for the anxiety. He won't go to prison, Lieutenant. No doctor, no court will judge him legally sane. He'll never be free, and he'll never know what it is to have a life, to fall in love, have a family, a job, a real home. It's not true justice, perhaps, but it's consequences."

"I need to see him." Eve rose. "I need to speak to him."

"Yes, you do."

"Can't I—"

"No, not now," Eve said before Philadelphia could finish.

"It's best to wait," Gibbons assured her. "He's already having difficultly adjusting to the idea of leaving here. But when the police are ready to take him, it will help if you're there with him."

"We'll have that tea now, shall we?" Roarke suggested with a glance at Gibbons.

"Yes, good idea. I'll arrange it. Lieutenant, I'll take you to him."

She waited until they were out of the room, going up another set of stairs. "In all these years, you never got him to admit to the murders."

"It never occurred to me there had been murders. Lieutenant, he's nonviolent, and as I said, passive. He spoke of girls, plural, but we assumed—and actually assumed correctly—that he saw them as a whole. The bad girls, the lost girls. He would save them. He's delusional, and his upbringing—well, as I said, it would take hours to explain. You're going to find he doesn't see them as dead, but saved. He doesn't understand he killed them. His mind is childlike. There is anger, but it's diffused now. He has duties here, a routine, those who tend to him. He isn't asked to do what he feels unable to do."

He stopped in front of the door where Peabody stood.

"Will you permit me to remain, and Nash? He'd be less anxious."

"We'll try it that way. If you interfere, you're out."

With a nod, Gibbons opened the door.

Nash Jones rose immediately, all but launching out of the chair where he sat watching his brother slowly fold clothes into a small suitcase.

"Lieutenant, I—"

Gibbons shook his head. "Monty, you have some company."

"I'm going on a trip."

He looked like a child in a man's body. His face, soft, going doughy, sat pale under a messy crop of sandy hair. His eyes had a dull, disengaged look to them.

"I'm packing. I can do it myself."

"I need to ask you some questions."

"Dr. Gibbons asks the questions."

"So do I."

"Are you a doctor?"

"No, I'm the police."

"Uh-oh, somebody's in trouble!" He grinned at his brother as if they shared a joke.

"I'm going to read you your rights. Do you understand about rights?"

"It's all right if I have dessert first sometimes, as long as I eat the rest."

Oh boy, Eve thought, but read off the Revised Miranda. "Do you understand any of that?"

"I don't have to talk to you unless I want to."

"That's right. And you can have a lawyer here."

"I have Monty and Dr. Gibbons. They're smart." Carefully, he folded a navy blue sweater into the suitcase. "I can be smart if I think about it."

"Okay. I want to talk to you about when you lived in New York. About The Sanctuary."

"I can't go there anymore. It's not home anymore. This is home."

"But when it was home, you knew Shelby. You remember Shelby."

"She's bad. She said she was my friend, but she was mean to me. She's bad," Monty said under his breath. "I want to pack for my trip."

"You can talk to Lieutenant Dallas while you pack," Gibbons said gently.

"Dallas is a city in Texas. Everybody knows that. I'm a city, too."

"How was Shelby mean to you?"

"How come I have to tell you? Nash made me tell him. He said I *had* to tell him because he's my brother. You're not my brother."

"You should tell her what you told me." His voice thick with tears, Nash laid a hand on his brother's shoulder.

"You got mad. I don't like it when you get mad."

"I got mad in New York, a long time ago. I was upset, and I

shouldn't have talked to you that way. But I didn't get mad today, when you talked to me, when you told me about Shelby, and—and the others."

"Because we're Nash and Monty. Brothers forever."

"Why didn't you tell Monty about Shelby, and the other girls, before?" Eve asked him.

"He was mad, so I didn't tell. Then I had to come here, but Peter's here, so that's good. Then I forgot. They don't have bad girls here, and I forgot about it. I don't even dream about it anymore."

"Why don't you tell me about it, about Shelby?" Eve prompted.

"It's all right to tell her, Monty," Peter urged him. "She won't get mad."

"Shelby said she'd make me feel good a special way, a secret way. She did, but it's bad. She'll get in trouble if I tell you. I don't tattle."

He mimed zipping his lip.

"That's okay. What happened to Shelby?"

"*Nothing.*" He lifted his hands in the air, shook them. "Nothing, nothing. She wanted to stay in The Sanctuary. Me, too, but Monty and Philly said no. But the other place wasn't *home*, so me and Shelby wanted to stay. Shelby said I could, then she said I couldn't because I was stupid. And it hurt my feelings. She was bad. We're supposed to help the bad girls be good. I helped her be good. And her friend, too. And I helped the girls so they could be good and stay home. Now I'm going on a trip."

"How did you help them?"

"I don't remember." Slyly, just a little slyly, he tracked his eyes right and left. "I don't think about it."

"I think you do. You put a sedative in some drinks. You needed them to be quiet and still."

"I had to." Monty puffed out his cheeks, then released all the air.

"They wouldn't understand when they were bad. After, then they'd understand. Once we'd washed the bad out. I filled the tub, nice and warm. Cold water's not fun. I didn't want them to be cold because I had to take their clothes off. I didn't touch. I promise!"

He crossed his heart.

"But they couldn't have clothes in the water, they wouldn't really get clean. I put Shelby in the warm water, and I prayed like you're supposed to. Then she was clean, and sleeping so quiet. I wrapped her up, nice and snug, before I helped her friend. Then I took them downstairs. People would come and tell them they couldn't stay, but I fixed it so nobody would see them, and they could stay home."

"How?"

"I can build, so I made a new wall, so they had a secret place. Like a club."

"Okay." She strolled over, picked up a ratty stuffed dog from a shelf. "Where'd you get this?"

"That's my dog. He was lost. I found him. He's mine. His name is Baby."

"Baby used to belong to somebody else."

"Maybe, but she didn't take care of him. I do."

"You found Baby. You found other bad girls."

"When you're a missionary, you have to go to the people with sin, and help them. But not in Africa. It's scary there. I don't want to go to Africa, Nash."

"No, you don't have to."

"But I'm going on a trip. I have to pack," he told Eve.

"Yeah, go ahead. Pack for your trip."

EPILOGUE

AT THE END OF THE LONG AND MISERABLE DAY, EVE dragged herself into the house. She wanted a shower, blistering hot, and oblivion.

Instead of Summerset and the cat looming in the foyer, Roarke walked to her, with the cat on his heels.

"This is different."

"I wanted to be here when you got home. You look exhausted."

"That's how I feel. Thanks for the assist—the financial hacking wizardry, the transpo."

"Those are easy, and fun. This?" He put an arm around her, leading her up the stairs. "This is necessary. It's certainly in the marriage rules."

"What is?"

"Holding on at the end of a hard day. You don't have to talk about it."

"Actually, maybe it would help to get it out. He doesn't know what the hell's going on. Monty Jones."

"What is going on?"

She sat on the side of the bed, managed a smile when he crouched and pulled off her boots. "He'll be spending some time in the mentally defective ward of Rikers for now. He'll be examined, interviewed, tested, prodded, and poked. When I start to feel sorry for him, I think about the girls on my board."

She flopped on her back a moment, stared at the ceiling. "He knew what he was doing when he killed Shelby. I'd bet my badge on it. He was pissed and hurt, and he tangled that up making her pay with making her good. But he knew. And I think that's what broke him. Realizing what he'd done when it was too late to change it. So he had to kill Linh, then he had to believe it was a mission. But he knew with Shelby. He would've been judged legally sane if we'd caught him then."

"And now?"

"Now he's pathetic." She shoved up again, blinked at the wine he held out to her. "Oh yeah, that's a really good idea. Gibbons is right. He won't go into a cage, but he's going to spend the rest of his life in that ward. He'll never get out, and that has to be enough. I guess it is enough, because that's what there is."

"It'd be easier if he was vicious and violent and sane."

"God, yes. Like some of the vics' parents were, like mine were, like your father. You can put that clearly and cleanly on one side of the line, and know. And when I see the faces of the victims, I can say, okay, I did my job, I did my best to stand for you."

"You did just that." He sat beside her. "Just exactly that."

"Nobody saw it. Not his family, not trained staff, not even the shrink—not really. Here's this walking, talking time bomb, but they don't see. It's just shy, slow Monty. There was a caginess in there at one time, Roarke. It's gone now, but it had to be there. He was cagey enough to know how to incapacitate the victims, how to get them where he wanted, how to conceal them, how to conceal himself from those closest to him. That person wasn't in the room today, but he existed once."

"Maybe that's justice as well. That person's gone, locked up somewhere else. If he ever gets out, he'll be dealt with."

"He took a lot with him. Twelve young lives."

"What about his brother?"

"I worked him. I have to buy he didn't know about the murders. He just couldn't conceive of it. He's going to have to answer for how he handled what he did, but I can already figure the PA's not going to charge him, not with what equals cage time. What's the point? He's going to go through his life feeling he failed his brother, his sister, knowing his brother killed. And Gibbons, he'll get a slap, too. He may lose his position, maybe even his license. I don't know. But he'll bounce back. Probably bounce on Philly, too."

With a laugh, Roarke hugged her to his side. "There you are."

"She's out of it. She didn't do a damn thing but believe in her brothers and her work. You can't blame her for that. And the doc? Mostly he tried to help a friend, tried to help the friend's brother. I can't begrudge them a little bouncing if it comes to that."

"You shouldn't begrudge yourself a feeling of not quite full satisfaction."

"It's closed, questions are answered. Except . . . The last victim. She doesn't have a name. She's not on any record anyway. If she was, Feeney would have found her. Whoever she came from didn't bother to name her. It—"

"Makes you think of yourself."

"They didn't name me, because I was a thing to them. I guess I see her as something of the same. To whoever brought her into the world, she was just a thing. She didn't matter to anyone, except, for a short time, to the man who killed her. He didn't even know her name."

"Give her one."

"What? She's Jane Doe."

"Give her better than that. Give her a name."

"What do I know about names?"

"You named the cat."

She frowned at Galahad, currently sleeping on the bed with all four legs in the air. "Yeah, I did. But a person, that's two names."

"She was found on the West Side. West for her surname. There, I've done mine. What's her first name?"

"I don't . . . Angel." Since that flashed into her mind, Eve went with it. "Might as well do the higher power thing. She deserves something."

"Angel West she is then. And she matters."

"Okay." She let out a long breath. "Why don't we just sit here awhile, drink this wine, and look at the tree."

"A fine idea."

"I like it." She tipped her head to his shoulder. "Christmas. I guess I have to buy stuff."

"Horrors."

She laughed, sipped her wine.

She'd put it aside, she told herself. Take down her board, close her murder book. She'd done her job, she'd done her best. Now she was home with the fire warm, the tree shining, the cat snoring, and the man who loved her sitting beside her.

It was a lot more than enough.